SPACE FOLK

POUL ANDERSON

D0057254

BAEN
BOOKS

SPACE FOLK

This is a work of fiction. All the characters and events portrayed in this book are fictional, and any resemblance to real people or incidents is purely coincidental.

Copyright © 1989 by Poul Anderson

All rights reserved, including the right to reproduce this book or portions thereof in any form.

A Baen Books Original

Baen Publishing Enterprises
260 Fifth Avenue
New York, N.Y. 10001

First printing, February 1989

ISBN: 0-671-69805-2

Cover art by David Lee Anderson

Printed in the United States of America

Distributed by
SIMON & SCHUSTER
1230 Avenue of the Americas
New York, N.Y. 10020

The crater wall had fangs.

They stood sharp and grayish white in the cruel sunlight, against the shadow which brimmed the bowl. And they grew and grew. Tumbling while it fell, the spacecraft had none of the restfulness of zero weight. Forces caught nauseatingly at gullet and gut. An unidentified loose object clattered behind the pilot chairs. The ventilators had stopped their whickering and the two men breathed stench. No matter. This wasn't an Apollo 13 mishap. They wouldn't have time to smother in their own exhalations.

Jack Bredon croaked into the transmitter: "Hello, Mission Control . . . Lunar Relay Satellite . . . anybody. Do you read us? Is the radio out too? Or just our receiver? God damn it, can't we even say good-bye to our wives?"

"Tell 'em quick," Sam Washburn ordered. "Maybe they'll hear."

Jack dabbed futilely at the sweat that broke from his face and danced in glittering droplets before him. "Listen," he said. "This is Moseley Expedition One. Our motors stopped functioning simultaneously, about two minutes after we commenced deceleration. The trouble must be in the fuel feed integrator. I suspect a magnetic surge, possibly due to a short circuit in the power supply. The meters registered a surge before we lost thrust. Get that system redesigned! Tell our wives and kids we love them."

He stopped. The teeth of the crater filled the entire forward window. Sam's teeth filled his countenance, a stretched-out grin. "How do you like that?" he said. "And me the only black astronaut."

They struck.

When they opened themselves up again, in the hall, and knew where they were, he said, "Wonder if he'll let us go out exploring."

—from "Murphy's Hall"

**To
Larry Friesen,
who's working on it**

Acknowledgments

"Cradle Song" and "Commentary" copyright © 1988 by Poul Anderson.

"Pride," Far Frontiers 1, 1985, copyright © 1985 by Baen Books, Inc.

"Vulcan's Forge," Amazing ® Science Fiction Stories January 1983, copyright © 1982 by TSR Hobbies, Inc.

"Escape the Morning," Boys' Life November 1966, copyright © 1966 by Boy Scouts of America.

"Quest," Ares™ Winter 1983, copyright © 1983 by TSR Hobbies, Inc.

"Wherever You Are," as by Winston P. Sanders, Astounding Science Fiction April 1959, copyright © 1959 by Street & Smith Publications, Inc. Copyright renewed 1987 by Davis Publications, Inc.

"Elementary Mistake," as by Winston P. Sanders, Analog Science Fiction/Science Fact February 1967, copyright © 1967 by The Condé Nast Publications, Inc.

"Symmetry," as "The Stranger Was Himself," Fantastic Universe December 1954, copyright © 1954 by King-Size Publications, Inc. Copyright renewed 1982 by Poul Anderson. Revised version copyright © 1988 by Poul Anderson.

"Hunter's Moon," Analog Science Fiction/Science Fact November 1978, copyright © 1983 by Davis Publications, Inc.

"Deathwomb," Analog Science Fiction/Science Fact November 1983, copyright © 1983 by Davis Publications, Inc.

"Murphy's Hall," Infinity Two, copyright © 1971 by Lancer Books, Inc.

"Horse Trader," Galaxy Science Fiction March 1953, copyright © 1953 by Galaxy Publishing Corporation. Copyright renewed 1981 by Poul Anderson. Revised version copyright © 1988 by Poul Anderson.

CONTENTS

CRADLE SONG

Now that the daylight has gone to bed,
See what a gladness is overhead.
Capture it under your closing eyes.
Weave it well into my lullabies.

> *Little Boy Blue, come blow your horn*
> *For all of the children about to be born.*
> *Starry the fields where they shall reap*
> *The harvest you sow for them as you sleep.*

Weary and small in your cradle berth,
You shall yet slip from this heavy Earth.
Out of her darknesses, fare you free
Home to the Sea of Tranquillity.

> *Little Bo-Peep, so deep in sleep,*
> *Go seek your dreams and find them.*
> *May it be soon your feet on the moon*
> *Leave dancer tracks behind them.*

Wild are those ways and beset by dread,
Full of farewells; but hold high your head.
Child of my heart, may you someday go
Forth among worlds I shall never know.

> *Sing a song of spacefolk, a pocket full of stars.*
> *Play it on the trumpets, harmonicas, guitars.*
> *When the sky was opened, mankind began to sing:*
> *"Now's the time to leave the nest. The wind is on the*
> *wing!"*

PRIDE

Suddenly Nemesis exploded.

It happened just in time to quench an eruption within the watchful spaceship. The forces of violence had been gathering in men even as they did in the half-star. Mortal time-spans were smaller; but a pair of years, passing through darknesses, had grown weary, and then months amidst strangenesses and dangers laid their own further pressures on the spirit. Dermot Byrne crowed a boast, Jan Cronje could no longer keep silence, the hostility between them broke free and a fight was at hand.

Accident touched off the trouble, though something of the kind had been likely at some point during the years remaining before *Anna Lovinda* would come back to Earth orbit. Neither man was a fool. Since their friendship broke, they had tacitly avoided each other as much as possible. Maybe Cronje supposed Byrne was with Suna Rudbeck, in the cabin they now shared, or maybe—seeking to forget for a moment—he didn't think about it at all. He was never sure afterward. Whatever else was on his mind, he entered the wardroom to get a cup of refreshment and a little conversation, perhaps a game of chess or somebody who would come along with him to the gymnasium and play handball. At the entrance, he stopped. There Byrne was.

Several other off-duty people were present also, benched around the table or standing nearby. Conversation was general. Coffee and tea made the air fragrant. Music lilted out of speakers in bulkheads softly tinted, where there hung scenes from home that were often changed. Garments were loose, colorful, chosen by their wearers. Folk needed every such comfort.

Not that they huddled away from the universe. As if to declare that, a large viewscreen was always tuned, like a window on space save that its nonreflecting surface left the scene clear despite interior lighting. Stars crowded blackness, icy-bright and unwinking. They streamed slowly past vision as the ship rotated.

Byrne was speaking. He was a slender young man, eyes brilliant blue and features regular, very fair-skinned, beneath a shock of dark hair, a Gaelic melody in his Swedish. A planetologist, he was lately back from his second expedition to the fourth satellite of Nemesis, an Earth-sized world on which his had been the first footprint ever made. "The wonder, the beauty, those will never be coming through in our reports, no matter how many pictures we print. Sure, and this crew ought to have included a poet. But they have no imagination in Stockholm."

"They've got enough to dispatch us," laughed Ezra Lee, the senior astrophysicist. "Oh, the Control Authority did begrudge the cost—"

"Keeping world peace has not yet become cheap," murmured engineer Gottfried Vogel in his mild fashion.

"Just the same, it took more politicking than it should have, to get a few people out here," said Byrne. "Had not the probes already told of miracles for the finding?"

Nemesis rose at the left edge of the screen. At a distance of more than a million kilometers, it blotted out most stars with hugeness rather than brilliance. Red-hot from the slow contraction of its monstrous mass, Sol's companion did not dazzle eyes that looked upon it. Instead, that glow brought to sight an intricacy of bands, swirls, murk-spots, sparkles—clouds, maelstroms, lightnings. God could have cast Earth into any of those storms and not made so much as a splash. A moon glimmered near the limb; a billion kilometers from the giant, it was itself the size of Saturn.

"Ah, well, we *are* here," Byrne went on. Happiness radiated from him. "The scientific discoveries are only one part of the marvel. This world where I've been—Suna wants to call it Vanadis, and I Fand, but no great matter that, for each of us means a goddess of love and beauty."

"A frozen waste," said Minna Veijola. But of course she was a biologist, enraptured by the life (life!) on the innermost satellite.

"It is not," Byrne replied. "That is what I'm trying to explain to the lot of you. Oh, doubtless barren. Yet the play of light on ice mountains—Ask Suna," he blurted. "That was what finally brought us together, she and I, after we'd first landed. The faerie beauty everywhere around us."

Jan Cronje stepped through the doorway. "I do not believe that," he said hoarsely. "You were sneaking and sniffing around her before the voyage was half over. You wheedled her into being your pilot on that survey, the two of you alone. Yes, it was nicely planned."

Silence clapped down. Through it, Cronje's boots made a dead-march drumbeat as he moved onward. He was a big man, and spin provided a full gravity of weight. Blunt of countenance, sandy-haired, ruddy-bearded, he had gone quite pale.

Byrne sprang to his feet. "It was not!" he cried. "It . . . it only happened."

Cronje grinned. "Ha!" His Afrikaans accent harshened. "It was far on the way to happening by that time. If you had been an honorable man, you would have gotten another pilot for yourself. Me, for instance. I had not seen what you were up to. But no, it was my wife you wanted."

Byrne flushed. "You insult her. She was never mine for the taking, nor yours for the keeping. She's a free human being who made her own choice."

Cronje reached him. "I could stand that, somehow," he said. "Until now, when you started bragging before everybody." His left hand shot out, grabbed the other's tunic, hauled him close. "No more, do you hear?"

"Let me go, you lout!" Byrne yelled. His fists doubled.

"Jan, please." Veijola plucked at Cronje's sleeve. Although they were good friends, he didn't seem to notice.

Lee gestured at a couple of men. They left their places and moved to intervene, should this come to blows. A brawl, in the loneliness everywhere around, could have unthinkable aftermaths.

And then—It was mere coincidence. Providence surely has better concerns than our angers. But Nemesis exploded.

A yell brought heads around toward the screen. Shouts tumbled out of the intercom as crew throughout the ship saw, or heard from those who saw. The red disc shuddered. Cloud bands ripped apart, vortices shattered, waves of ruin ran from either pole until they met at the equator and recoiled in chaos. Then every feature vanished in rose-pearly pallor. Visibly to unaided eyes, the disc swelled. Star after star disappeared behind smokiness.

It was Lee, the astrophysicist, who lurched across the deck, stunned. "Already?" he gasped. "Just like that? The fire lit and—and Nemesis turning back into a star?"

Erik Telander, captain of *Anna Lovinda*, mounted the stage. With chairs set forth, the gymnasium became the general meeting room. A dozen faces looked up at him. Six more people were on station in case of emergency. Two, a pilot and a planetologist, had flitted off in one of the boats to yet another of the worlds that circled, like the ship, around the primary orb. Only such a pair ever went off on such a preliminary exploration. The unknowns were too many for the risking of a larger number. Twenty-one men and women were all too few at this uttermost bound of the Solar System.

Telander smiled. He was a lean, slightly grizzled man who seemed older than his actual years. "Well, ladies and gentlemen," he said, "we have had quite a surprise in the past several hours. And it appears that surprises are continuing. The task immediately before us is to decide what we should do. Although that decision must, of course, ultimately be mine, I want to base it on your knowledge and your ideas; for I am a single person among you, without the special knowledge and skills you variously possess. Frankly, my first impulse was to direct that we cut loose from *Gertrud* and blast off to a safe distance. Ezra Lee convinced me this was neither necessary nor even wise, at least for the moment. I would like him to describe the situation for you as he sees it. No doubt the data that the instruments have been—are—collecting will cause him to modify, already now, what he said to me." He beckoned. "If you please."

Lee rose. "You're all familiar with the theory, at least in general outline," said his flat Midwestern American tones. "I trust you're also aware how incomplete that theory is, how little we really know for sure about Nemesis. It could hardly be otherwise, across a gap of more than two light-years, when the object is so dim at best, and unique in human observation. Still, I suggest you take a minute to review for yourselves what you've been told. Get it as clear as possible in your minds. Then, if nothing else, you can ask me intelligent questions." He chuckled; teeth flashed against the dark brown skin. "Not that I guarantee to have any intelligent answers."

Humor died away. It was as if the silence that followed grew echoful of thoughts.

Nemesis, long-unseen companion of Sol, it was your murderousness that finally betrayed your existence to our species and made us search the skies for you. No, but "murderousness" is wrong. You are not alive; you are as innocent as a thunderbolt.

Yet every six-and-twenty million years your orbit brings you within 10,000 astronomical units of our sun. Passing through its Oort cloud, you trouble the comets there. Many fall inward, whipping around the star, perhaps for millennia, until their dust and ice are boiled off, the brightness is gone, only rocks that were in the cores remain. Some collide with planets or moons. Earth takes its share of that celestial barrage. Each cycle, one or more of those smiting masses is of asteroidal size. Continents tremble under the blow. Cast-up smoke and vapor darken the air for months. In such a Fimbul Winter, first the plants die, next the beasts; and when at last heaven clears again, the survivors begin a whole new order of things.

Thus did you slay the last dinosaurs at the end of the Cretaceous period, Nemesis, and with them the ammonites and . . . more kinds of life than endured. Thus did you kill the great mammals of the Miocene. And before these massacres there had been others, throughout the ages, but time has eroded their traces until they have become well-nigh as hard to find as you yourself, Nemesis.

That path of yours is not the least of the strangenesses about you. Neighbor stars should long since have drawn you away. Can they be what gave your track the form it has, so that only in the past billion years have you been launching your bombardments, and a billion years hence they will have ceased? Perhaps we shall learn the answer, now that we are at the end of a quest which took lifetimes of our evanescent kind.

A tiny, coal-red point afar, for which our finest spaceborne instruments sought through year after year before we knew . . . a flickering too faint and irregular for us to say more than that it takes about a decade from peak to peak . . . mass, as reported by our unmanned craft, slightly in excess of 80 times Jupiter's, which means well over 25,000 times Earth's . . . a family of attendants . . . tokens of a fire within, that kindles and goes out and kindles again, like the heart-beat of a man who lies dying. . . .

Minna Veijola raised her hand. "Question!"

"Be my guest," Lee said. "Maybe whoever wants to speak from the floor should rise, like me. We're too many for real conversation."

The biologist obeyed. Jan Cronje, beside whom she had seated herself, came out of his sullenness enough to give her a glance that lingered, as did several other men. While small and somewhat stocky, she had the blond, slanty-eyed, high-cheeked good looks common among Finns. "I don't want to be an alarmist," she said. "I'll take your word that we are in no immediate danger. But this is quite out of my field of competence. Furthermore, you'll understand that I am bound to wonder and worry about effects on my beloved life-bearing satellite. Could you please explain what it is we have to expect?"

Lee shrugged. "Yonder life doesn't seem to be hurt any by outbursts like this. After all, they've been going on for gigayears."

"My colleagues and I have scarcely begun basic taxonomy and chemical analysis, let alone comprehend how evolution works there. I—very well, I'll say it, because it must be gnawing at others besides me. We're only a million-odd kilometers from Nemesis. If it's become a star again, even the faintest of red dwarfs, aren't we likely to get a blast of hard radiation from it?"

"I remember telling you, dear, rock specimens we've taken show no effects of anything but cosmic and planetary background," Dermot Byrne said.

"Why not? Ezra, you admit that what's happened was quite unexpected. How can you predict what will happen next?"

The astrophysicist ran fingers across the black wool on his scalp. "I thought we'd been over this ground abundantly, both in training and in talk en route," he said. "But, I suppose, on so long a voyage, in so cramped an environment, I guess everybody tended to get wrapped up in his or her main interests, and forget a lot. Certainly some of what you've had to tell me about your discoveries, Minna, has gone straight by me.

"And among the surprises was the timing of this event. Observing it at close range is a principal objective of ours, of course. Nevertheless, we've been caught pretty flat-footed. Past observations and theoretical studies indicated the system wouldn't go critical for at least another year. Well, it *is* a complex and little-understood thing, and we did know the periodicity is very far from exact. I'm afraid we're going to lose quite a bit of information we'd hoped to gather, because we weren't yet properly prepared."

He drew breath. "Okay. Please bear with me while I repeat some elementary facts. It's just to identify those of them that I think are important in making the kind of short-range predictions you're asking about, Minna.

"We know Nemesis is the first example ever actually found of a so-called brown dwarf. Its mass is right at the borderline between planet and star. Gravitational contraction heats it—like Jupiter, but on a far bigger scale, so that the outer layers of gas have a temperature approaching a thousand kelvin. Near the core, heat and pressure naturally go higher by many orders of magnitude. At last collapse brings them to the point where thermonuclear reactions begin. The star-fires are lighted.

"But you can see how quickly this sends the core temperatures skyrocketing. This in turn makes the inner layers expand. Pressure drops below the critical point; the thermonuclear reactions turn off. The body as a whole expands for a while longer on momentum and interior heat, then starts falling in on itself again—and so the cycle recommences.

"I repeat my apology for rehearsing what everybody well knows, but I do believe we need to have the information marshalled before us. You see, as usual, reality turns out to be more complicated than theory. That's why we're here, isn't it? To take a good, hard, close-up look.

"Now. You people surely remember that astronomical instruments and orbiting probes have shown rather slight variation in surface temperature or emission, and scarcely anything in the way of X-rays. Nor does Nemesis have a Van Allen belt worth mentioning, in spite of its terrific magnetic field. It's too far out to collect solar wind particles, and it puts forth scarcely any of its own. The reason isn't far to seek. That enormous mass absorbs everything from the nuclear burning. The fires never get intense enough to cause more than some heating and expansion of the outer layers.

"Because of that very expansion, and its cooling effect, the emission temperature—what we actually sense—doesn't increase much. In fact, we think that at maximum diameter Nemesis is actually a bit cooler than it was when this ship arrived. Granted, by then the fires have already gone out.

"That's why we're in no danger."

Veijola shook her head stubbornly. "Yes, I knew," she replied. "You miss the point I was trying to make. You did not expect this . . . this sudden outburst. Quite aside from its timing, the experts have told me—I do remember my indoctrination—they told me expansion would be slow, and not begin until well after the nuclear reactions did. Therefore, could you please explain why you are so confident about the future?" She sat down and waited.

A sigh went through the assembly. Telander himself threw Lee an inquiring glance.

The American's smile was rueful. "I truly am sorry," he said. "As flustered as I've been, I seem to've taken for granted that people in different lines of work were worse confused. Let me make what amends I can by giving you what new information my department has gathered.

"There is no doubt that fusion has begun at the core. Our neutrino detectors are going crazy. Just what is happening in there—what chain or chains of nuclear conversion—we don't yet know. We do have indications of an unpredicted quantity of metals, and this is bound to affect the course of events. I believe that when we have enough data, and have analyzed them, we'll also get an idea of why Nemesis pulsates so irregularly.

"As for that expansion—which some of you saw at the time and the rest of you, I'm sure, have seen on replay—as for it, yes, it was unforeseen too. Suddenly the apparent diameter of the body increased by about seven percent. Well, Mamoru"—Lee nodded toward his associate Hayashi—"soon came up with what I think is the right notion.

"When the core caught fire, it was like a bomb with yield in the gigatons going off. No, more likely several bombs, at once or in quick succession. Shock waves, powerful enough to tear Earth apart, propagated out through the mass above. The globe is flattened by its rotation, of course, so the shock reached the poles first, though it got to the equator only minutes later. It accelerated the outer layers of gas. They whoofed spaceward. Under Nemesis gravity, the pressure gradient in the atmosphere is so high that even this thinned-out topmost part looked opaque at our distance."

Lee smiled. "Fascinating, isn't it?" he finished. "But not dangerous to us. As a matter of fact, which some of you have doubtless been too busy under general alert to witness—as a matter of fact, gravity has the upper hand again. That exploded shell is rapidly falling back into the main body. In other words, regardless of how astonishing, this expansion of Nemesis has been a transient phenomenon. Hereafter we can expect it will re-expand, but to a lesser distance and in a much more orderly fashion.

"I hope that puts your mind at rest, Minna. Naturally, our teams are going to be busier than a one-armed octopus, taking in what data we can. But given proper caution, we should survive to bring those data home." He looked around. "More questions?"

From her seat beside Byrne, pilot Suna Rudbeck jumped up. "Yes!" Her voice rang. "What about Osa?"

Men's gazes went to her more eagerly than they had gone to Veijola. Rudbeck was, perhaps, not intrinsically handsomer—tall, full-formed, with auburn locks framing sharply-cut visage—but there was ever something flamelike about her. After an instant, the other pilot's lips twisted and he stared elsewhere. Not long ago, she had been Rudbeck-Cronje. She was not yet Rudbeck-Byrne, but these days he was alone in the cabin that had been theirs, and she shared the planetologist's. Veijola reached toward Cronje, then quickly, unseen, withdrew her hand.

Captain Telander raised his brows. "Osa?" he asked from the stage.

"The inner probe, in polar orbit," Lee explained.

Telander nodded. "Ah, yes, I remember now. Its nickname. I have never been sure why."

"No matter," said Rudbeck. "Listen. Ever since Nemesis went 'boom,' I've been thinking about Osa. Before then, in fact. We've been planning how to retrieve it. The information it carries is priceless, not so, Ezra?"

Lee swallowed hard and nodded.

"If gas expanded outward as far as you say," Rudbeck pursued, "Osa encountered a significant density, a drag. Its orbit will have decayed. What is its status at this moment?" Aggressively: "If you don't know, why don't you?"

"Oh, we do, we do," the astrophysicist said. "It was among the first things we checked. You're right. Osa's loss would be—is—terrible. I'm afraid, though—"

Rudbeck stabbed a finger in his direction. "*Is* it lost?" she demanded.

"Well, no, not precisely. Gaseous resistance did force it lower. The ambient medium is already much less thick than before, with density dropping fast as molecules return to the main atmosphere. However, a rough computation—I had one run an hour ago, Suna, because I'm as concerned as anybody—it shows that even if nothing else happens, Osa is doomed. Its new orbit is unstable. Variations in the gravity field—in local density and configuration of the geoid—will draw it farther down until it becomes a meteorite." Lee drove fist into palm. "Damn! But as I've been admitting, this has taken us by surprise."

"Osa," mumbled Cronje. The challenge posed by that thing had been talk whenever *Anna Lovinda*'s three boat pilots got together. It stood now in the minds of everybody.

Years ahead of this manned expedition, the mother probe took station and launched her robot investigators. Osa was the innermost, in close polar orbit around the giant. For a while it transmitted back to Gertrud *that flood of facts which poured into its instruments— until the transmitter began to fail. Sufficient still came through, sporadically and distorted, to show how much more must be accumulating in its data banks, a Nibelung hoard of truth which might be forever irreplaceable.*

Anna Lovinda *lacked the means to launch so gifted a satellite. Most of her capacity was devoted to humans and their life support. For she fared only in part to study Nemesis with the versatility of living intelligences, their capability of coping with the unforeseen. Her voyage was equally a test of whether humans could survive a journey across interstellar reaches, wherein speeds eventually neared that of light—whether the Bussard drive could indeed carry them as far as Alpha Centauri and beyond, on into the universe.*

"And now," Hayashi said as if to himself, though in Swedish, "now, when Nemesis has done this thing we did not await, it would mean a great deal to hear what Osa has to tell us. However—"

"No 'howevers!' " came from Rudbeck.

"I beg your pardon?" breathed Telander.

"Listen," she repeated herself. "You recall we had plans for retrieving Osa in advance of Nemesis reaching star phase." She tossed her head. "Yes, I know, Captain, you were dubious, but the numbers showed it could be done." She laughed. "There was a bit of a quarrel over which of us pilots should get the glory of doing it. Well, Nemesis has jumped the gun and time available has become short. But I think—Ezra, you'll not falsify the data; I put you on your honor—I think it can still be done, if we're quick. If I am!"

"No!" shouted both Byrne and Cronje, and surged to their feet together.

An unwonted coldness drew over Rudbeck's face. "Jan, I claim the right by virtue of having made the proposal. Dermot, be still; you are not my superior officer."

"Hey, wait just a minute, hotshot," Lee protested. "Our margin of safety is thin at best. We can't risk one of our four auxiliary boats and their three pilots on a hairbreadth stunt like that."

Rudbeck's grin turned wolfish. "You just got through assuring us we are not in danger. Given adequate calculation and control, the mission should be no more hazardous than it would have been earlier; and we know it was feasible then." She swung toward Telander. "Captain, we're here at the end of the longest and most expensive haul in history. The knowledge in Osa is invaluable to science; and knowledge is what we're supposed to gain. But we must be quick. Let me go."

"I never claimed anybody can tell exactly what that damned monster will do next," Lee sputtered.

"Nor can you claim you will never fall over a beer bottle and break your neck," Rudbeck retorted. Eagerness blazed from her. "Captain, time is very short. What do you say?"

For pulsebeats that seemed to become many, Telander stood still. At last, slowly: "When we are on a frontier . . . with so vast an investment behind us, so much riding on what we can accomplish . . . how many megabytes of information is one life worth? If closer study proves the risk is within reason, I will authorize the attempt."

"By me!" Cronje roared.

"Let him go, let him go, and I'll pray for him every centimeter of the way," Byrne stammered.

Victory sang in Rudbeck's voice. "Jan, I'm sorry, you're a first-class pilot, but the uncertainties will be large, and you know my reactions test marginally faster than yours. Or Miguel's, not that he could get back soon enough anyway. Dermot, have no fears. I'll snatch Osa free, and we'll return to Vanadis together."

The boat, flamboyantly named *Valkyrie* by her pilot, eased from a launch bay in the ship, gained room for maneuver by a few delicate jet thrusts, and in the same careful fashion worked her way into initial trajectory. This was on autopilot, under computer direction, and Suna Rudbeck had nothing to do but sit almost weightless and gaze out the ports.

She kept the cabin dark so that her eyes could fully take in the splendor outside. Thus seen, space was not gloomy. There were more stars than there was blackness: steadfast brilliances, white, blue, red, golden. Among them, Sol at its distance remained the brightest, but barely more than Sirius. The Milky Way—in her native language, the Winter Street—swept in an ice-bright torrent whose silence felt like a mysterious noise, something other than the whisper of blood in her ears, filling the hollowness around.

As she drew away from the two large spacecraft, they became clear to her sight, starlit as heaven was. *Gertrud* (St. Gertrud, medieval patroness of wayfarers), the mother vessel of the unmanned pioneers, was a great metal mass from which instrument booms and transceiver dishes jutted. At the stern were simply linac thrusters, akin to those that drove *Valkyrie*; never being intended for return, only for getting around in the neighborhood of Nemesis, the robot ship had discarded her Bussard system upon arrival.

From her bow extended two kilometers of cable, a bare glimmer in Rudbeck's sight, no hint of the incredible tensile strength in precisely aligned atoms. The opposite end of the line anchored *Anna Lovinda*. That hull was lean, resembling the blade of a dagger whose basket-formed guard was the set of her own linacs. The haft beyond was mostly shielding against the Bussard engine, whose central systems formed a pommel at the top. The force-focusing lattice of that drive, extended while the vessel burned her way across deep space, had been folded back for safety, a cobweb around the knife.

The linked vessels, bearer of probes and bearer of humans, turned majestically about each other. Their spin provided interior weight without unduly inconveniencing auxiliary craft; one rotation took nearly three hours. At her slight present acceleration, Rudbeck felt ghost-like.

That soon ended. "Prepare for standard boost," came out of a speaker. The powerplant hummed, a low sound which bore no hint of the energies that burst from sundered nuclei, turned reaction mass into plasma, and hurled it down the linac until the jet emerged not very much less rapid than light. A full Earth gravity drew Rudbeck down into her chair. The boat could easily have exceeded that, but she herself needed to reach her goal unwearied and alert.

She turned on the cabin illumination, and her attention away from infinity, back toward prosaic meter readings and displays on the panel before her. "All okay," said Mission Control. "You're in charge now, Suna. Barring any fresh data that come in, of course, or any calculations your inboard computers can't handle."

Her head jerked an impatient nod; no matter that no scanner was conveying her image. "I doubt that will be required," she said curtly. "What we have is a straightforward problem in vector analysis. Landing on one of those moons is a good deal trickier, believe me."

"Suna, don't get overconfident, I beg you. The velocities, the energies—"

"Velocities are relative. Or hadn't you heard?" Rudbeck realized she was being snappish. "Pardon me. But I would like a while to think, undisturbed."

"Certainly. We'll stand by . . . and cheer for you, *flicka*."

She did not at once devote herself to the figures, for her course was bringing Nemesis into direct view forward. It was impossible not to stare and wonder. Measurement, more than vision, declared that the body had fallen back into something like its former size; but that was enormous enough even seen from here. Measurement also told of gasps and quiverings going through it. The disc remained wan and well-nigh featureless, save when rents opened and the lower red glow shone angrily through, or where plumes leaped up, broke apart, and rained back.

—"Those shock waves are bounding about yet," Lee had diagnosed. "They reach levels where the gas is too thin to transmit them, and are reflected. Interference produces local calms and local eruptions. It'll take a long time to damp out."

Anguish had distorted Byrne's face. "What if—" he groaned, "what if . . . a geyser, or maybe a whole second expansion . . . happens just when Suna is passing by?"

"It's possible," Lee admitted. "I have not changed my mind about her effort being a bad idea. We've witnessed too many occurrences we don't understand, and haven't had any real chance yet to stop observing and start thinking. Those white clouds blanketing most of the surface, for instance. What are they? We still haven't managed to get a decent reading on them, spectroscope, polarimeter, anything, the way they churn around and come and go."

Byrne reached out toward the pilot. "Suna, darling, darling, I beg you, stay! Nobody will be scoffing at you, I swear."

She bridled. "Must I explain the kindergarten details to you?" she clipped. "Osa's orbital decay is now determined solely by gravity gradients. That means the path is completely predictable for a short term. Now suppose Nemesis does blow again when I am in the vicinity. The first time, it did not throw up enough gas to Osa's altitude to cause significant structural damage. At a second time, true, Osa will be lower. But the shock waves will have less energy. My orbit will be eccentric. A sudden increase in ambient density won't slow me much, nor heat my hull more than I can stand. I'll coast out into the clear. Or—worst case—if I must retrofire to avoid a plunge, or to avoid overheating, the linac won't be ruined. It can safely operate in a gas so tenuous, at least for the brief time I would need."

Byrne stiffened. "If the danger is negligible, let me ride along with you."

"Oh, nonsense." She relented. "But sweet nonsense." She moved forward and kissed him. The kiss lasted. "Well," she murmured, "the flight plan doesn't have me leaving for another hour. . . ."

—She had better review that plan again. It was only simple in principle; complex and subtle mathematics underlay it.

In its present track, Osa had a velocity of some 180 kilometers per second. That fluctuated, especially when rounding the equatorial bulge, and *Valkyrie* must match it exactly. Given timing and related factors, this meant rendezvous over the north pole, with *Valkyrie*'s path osculating Osa's. The former would be a long ellipse, but come sufficiently close to the latter near that point that Rudbeck should have time to make the capture. Immediately thereafter she must use her jets, first to equalize velocities—at such speeds, a tiny percentage differential could rend hulls or start an irretrievable plunge—and then to begin escaping. The delta vee demanded was approximately 75 kilometers per second, and the deeper in the gravity well that thrust started, the less reaction mass need be expended.

That was definitely a consideration. Given its exhaust velocity, a linac drive did not drain mass tanks very fast, but it did draw upon them, and the expedition had no facilities for refining more material. This wasn't a Bussard-drive situation, with a ship taking in interstel-

lar hydrogen for fuel and boosterstuff after she had
reached minimum speed—no limit on how closely she
could approach c, how far she could range. The auxiliary boats were meant merely to flit around among
planets. When their tanks were dry, *Anna Lovinda*
must go home. Economy could add an extra year or
better to the nominal five she was to spend exploring—
could add unbounded extra knowledge and glory.

Rudbeck smiled and relaxed. She had about an hour
of straight-line acceleration before the next change of
vector. After that, maneuvers would become increas-
ingly more varied, until in about four hours she was at
Nemesis. There the equipment would cease carrying
her as a passenger. She would be using it. Everything
that happened would be in her hands.

Cronje sat alone in his cabin. It was not entirely his,
though—only the pictures from home (his parents before their house, a kopje at sunset, breakers on a reef
with the ocean sapphire-blue around them), a model-
building kit, a closetful of clothes, the book he was
screening without really reading. A bare bunk and bulk-
head haunted the room.

There was a knock. "Come in," he snapped. As the
door opened: "No. *Voetsack*. Get out."

Byrne twisted his hands together. "Please," he whispered. "Let me in. Listen a while. Afterward do what
you like, and I'll not be resisting."

Cronje considered. "Well, close the door. Speak. No,
I did not invite you to sit down."

"She's . . . close to rendezvous."

"Did you imagine I do not know? This set will switch
over whenever communication recommences. Go tune
yours."

Byrne ran tongue over lips. "I thought . . . perhaps
we might—" Facing the scowl before him, he mustered
strength to plunge ahead. "Jan, Suna's dearest hope is
that we two might be friends again. That may be too
much to ask. But could we not pray for her together?"

"I am not a praying man. I doubt that my father's
God would hear the likes of you."

Sweat glistened on Byrne's cheeks. "Well, will you
listen a minute? This is hard for me. I've had to nerve
myself to it. But when Suna is in danger—somehow it
seems you should know about her. Know what an injus-
tice you have been doing her."

Cronje's massive shoulders hunched forward. "How?"

Byrne straightened. Resolution began to resonate in
his tone. "Think. You considered her such an idiot, so
faithless, that my wiles lured her from you. But it was
not that way at all, at all. How could it be? Nor would I
have tried. Oh, I was in love with her almost from the
time we departed Earth. But her nearness was enough."
He sketched a smile. "We've unattached women without inhibitions aboard, as well as you are aware, Jan
Cronje."

"What? No, I never—"

"Of course you did not. But understand, you great
loon, neither did she. She fought her feelings for me,
month after month. If you had been more thoughtful of
her, she could well have won that battle."

Cronje grimaced. "Was I ever bad to her? See here,
we're both pilots, so naturally, as soon as we reached
Nemesis, we were off most of the time on separate
missions. But when we were together—" He snarled.
His fist crashed on the chair arm. "Before God, I'll not
drag our private life out in front of you!"

"You needn't," Byrne answered. "But she has needed
to explain herself to me. She grieves on your account
and wishes you nothing but well. Nevertheless, the fact
is that she and I are . . . happier . . . than ever she—
Well. No more. Today I decided my duty was to give
her back your respect for her. Now you can send me
away. Or if you hit me, here where we are alone, I will
tell the captain I had an accident."

Cronje slumped back. His jaw sagged a little. After a
while he muttered, "Respect—"

The text on the screen vanished. Mission Control

blinked into view. "We have a report from Rudbeck," the speaker said. Curbed emotions turned her voice flat. "She has visual contact with Osa. Parameters satisfactory. Except that an outburst is climbing ahead of her."

Valkyrie flew above Nemesis. Cold jets, microgravity, and all, no other words than "flew above" would do, when the sub-sun filled half of hurtling vision.

Right, left, forward, aft the immensity reached, until eyesight lost itself. It was like an ocean, but an ocean of dream, where billows rolled and roiled—white, gray, pale red, deep purple—endlessly above furnace depths which glared through rifts and whirlpools. Here and there spume blew free, surf crashed soundless, fountains spouted upward and arched back down. Haze overlay the scene, fading aloft into a blackness where stars gleamed untroubled. You could lose yourself, staring into that; your soul could leave you, drown in those waves, be scattered by them from horizon to horizon and there drift forever.

Rudbeck's gaze clung to the heavens. A twinkle onto which her radar had locked was growing into the satellite she had come to save. It seemed an unimpressive cylinder, with arms and steering rockets jutting at odd angles, the whole now crazily spinning and wobbling. But that was the mere shell around a few kilograms of crystals which encoded more knowledge than any human could master in a lifetime.

Beyond and below, a great ashen geyser was slowly rising out of the clouds. Its top faded off into nothingness, but already stars immediately above were dimming and going out.

"It's optically denser than I quite like, and will probably be opaque by the time I pass through," Rudbeck said. "I'm getting radar echoes, too. But you're receiving the readings directly. What do you advise?"

The transmission lag of half a dozen seconds felt like

as many minutes. Telander's words came wearily: "Abort. Take evasive action."

"No!" Rudbeck argued. "Not after coming this far, with everything it means. I've been thinking. The optical density is likely due to nothing worse than water vapor becoming ice particles. The radar reflection could well be off ions. Neither appears sufficient to threaten my linac."

Time.

"Those are your guesses, pilot. Dr. Lee's team has not yet been able to ascertain what the truth is. . . . Well, pass by in free fall. You should suffer no harm from that. While your orbit is taking you around again, the situation may change for the better, or our understanding may improve, and you can make a second attempt."

"Skipper, I don't believe a second try will be possible. *Valkyrie* can bullet on through that cloud. I doubt *Osa* can. Too much drag, with such a low mass-to-surface ratio; and I'd anticipate eddy current losses too, because of what those ions must be doing to the Nemesis magnetic field. Before I can return, *Osa* will have slipped irrecoverably far down— to burn up—"

Rudbeck's hands tightened on the manual controls. "Sir," she said, "without being insubordinate, I remind you that the pilot of a spacecraft under boost is *her* captain, who makes the final decisions. I'm about to boost, and my decision will be to go ahead with the retrieval. I trust you will continue to provide support if needed. Now I have no more time for argument. Wish me luck, shipmates!"

She laughed aloud and became very busy.

An overtaking orbit was a lower orbit. With the help of ranging instruments, computers, and jets, Rudbeck adjusted course until the difference between hers and *Osa*'s was measurable in meters of space. She rolled her craft about, belly toward the quarry. She pulled the switch that caused the cargo bay to open, and another that extended the grappler arms. Like a single beast of prey, stealing along on breaths of plasma thrust, Rudbeck and *Valkyrie* closed in on Osa.

Peering at the scanner screen, fingers working with surgical delicacy, she operated the grapplers. A shiver went through the hull. Osa was captured. Rudbeck's touch on a button commanded an equalizing vector which a screen display counselled. Weight hauled softly at her. The arms drew their burden into the hold. Hatches slid shut.

The maneuvers, the momentum transferences had sent *Valkyrie* sliding off downward. The atmospheric pressure gradient beneath her meant that she would become a shooting star within minutes, unless she regained altitude. This was in the calculations. Likewise was the full-throated blast which was to make good her escape from Nemesis. Rudbeck grinned at the cloud ahead. It was weirdly like a fog bank on Earth. Her hands gave their orders. The spacecraft leaped.

Abruptly the hull shuddered and bucked. A crash went through it, the noise of a mighty gong. Rudbeck's body jammed against the harness. An unbalanced thrust snapped her head sideways. Dazed with pain, she hardly felt the weightlessness that followed. It was not true weightlessness anyway, but a riot of shifting centrifugal forces. Like a dead leaf on a winter wind, *Valkyrie* tumbled through space, borne wherever the cosmos cast her.

They were three who met in the captain's cramped little office: Erik Telander, Ezra Lee, and Jan Cronje. They did not feel they had time to confer with anybody else. Screens were tuned to Mission Control and Observatory Central, but the sound was turned low.

All three of them were on their feet. Lee's back was bowed. "Oh, Jesus, I should have seen it, I should have seen it," he moaned.

Cronje stood expressionless. "I gather you have established the nature of that obstacle she ran into," he said. "Let us hear."

"With everything confused—But we do finally have clear readings. We might have interpreted our data correctly earlier, except that the conclusion is so utterly unexpected. . . . Stop maundering!" Lee told himself. To the others: "The whitish material in the atmosphere, and in the plume she encountered, it's dust."

"What?"

"Yes, mostly fine silicate particles. I suspect carbon as well, possibly traces of higher elements—no matter now. I see with the keenest hindsight." Lee's chuckle was ghastly. "It's cosmic dust, from the original nebula that the Solar System condensed out of. Solid material, that got incorporated in the bodies of the lesser planets, in the cores of giants like Jupiter. And vaporized in Sol, of course. In the case of Nemesis, the parameters are special. Once the main mass had coalesced, more dust kept falling for a while, till the nebula was used up. The heat of Nemesis already served to keep it suspended in the lower atmosphere, though not to gasify it. It couldn't sink on into levels where the air was denser than it was, either. In other words, way down, that air includes a stratum of thick dustiness. When the fires turn on, the shock waves cast that dust aloft, till eventually it gets kicked into space."

Lee stared at his feet. "More and more is being coughed up," he mumbled. "The haze is getting heavier everywhere around Nemesis. Sure, it'll fall back, but fresh stuff will replace it. I expect that'll go on for weeks."

Cronje looked at Telander. "Have you any new information on Rudbeck?" he asked.

Anguish dwelt in the captain's lean visage. "Not really," he answered. "That is, obviously she hasn't managed to repair the radio transmitter that must have been damaged. However, we have no strong reason to suppose she herself has suffered serious injury. Doubtless the major harm was to the linac. Plasma bouncing off solid particles that did not flash into vapor as ice crystals would—plasma striking its electromagnetic accelerators at speeds close to light's—But I daresay the basic powerplant is intact, and certainly the batteries should have ample charge. Life support ought to be still effective. Mainly, the boat is crippled."

"In a rapidly decaying orbit."

"Well, yes. Drag not only reduced eccentricity by a large factor, it shortened the semimajor axis. The period has become correspondingly briefer; and each periapsis, passing through those ever thicker clouds—" Telander stiffened himself. "But I am being weak. I want a message from her, a reassurance, which my mind says isn't really necessary, though my heart disagrees. It *is* an eccentric orbit yet. Along most of it, the boat is in open space. The indications are that we have a day or two of grace before the final plunge."

"And I can get there in four or five hours," Cronje responded. "Never mind precise figures beforehand. You can feed me those as I travel, and I'll adjust my vectors accordingly. My boat is fully in order. Have I the captain's leave to start?"

"You do." Telander hesitated. He raised a hand. "A moment. Let us spell this out. Your assignment is to match velocities at a safe point on Rudbeck's orbit, take her aboard, and return here. Nothing else. We can't afford a second gamble."

"Bearing in mind I must exercise my own judgment— Let's not dawdle." Cronje turned to go. Impulsively, he seized Lee and hugged the astrophysicist to his breast.

"Don't you blame yourself, Ezra," he said. "Nobody could have done better than you and your staff. Damn few could have done as well. If nature isn't going to surprise us, ever, why the hell do we go exploring?"

Cronje left. In the passageway outside, he found Byrne waiting. Tears ran down the planetologist's face. "God ride with you, Jan." His words wavered. "If only I could. Bring her back. Afterward you can ask anything of me you want, and I . . . I will be doing my best to obey."

Cronje wrung his hand, growled, "No promises," and hastened onward.

Crew were a-bustle around a launch bay airlock. Minna Veijola stood aside from them. When Cronje appeared, she ran to meet him. They went off together, out of sight behind a locker. Standing on tiptoe, she could take him by the shoulders. "Be careful, Jan," she pleaded.

A possible chuckle rumbled in his throat. "You know me, little friend. I never take needless risks. I don't even play poker. No doubt this is part of the reason Suna found me a dull sort."

"You aren't, you aren't," she breathed. "Yes, I have come to know you—the voyage, the visits to my moon, oh, everything—" The slant blue gaze strained upward. "So I sense you have more in mind than what you are telling. Jan, don't do it! Whatever it is, don't do it! Only bring Suna back, and yourself."

He stroked her hair. "A man must do what he must. And a woman, of course." A technician stepped around the locker to announce readiness. "Farewell, Minna." Cronje went to his boat.

Rendezvous could have been made when *Valkyrie* was at her farthest from Nemesis. However, that would have meant letting her swing another time through the clouds. Ezra Lee had been the first to confess that there was no telling—nothing but an educated guess— which of those close passages would prove the fatal one. The half-star was vomiting more and more spouts of dust and gas, in wholly unforeseeable fashion. Cronje was to meet Rudbeck at the earliest moment which was prudent. Her transferral should not take long.

Thus the vessels were cometing inward when they made contact. Nemesis filled the forward ports of *Kruger* with swirling, vaguely starlit smoke. Sometimes it parted for a short while to show crimson underneath, but mostly it was pearl-gray turmoil.

Against that background, *Valkyrie* gyrated helpless. Cronje could see how the webwork of her drive was twisted, partly melted, sheared across in places. It could be restored, but that required she be in space more calm than that toward which she fell.

Given his vehicle and his experience, approach was no problem. Erratic spin along the invariable plane was. Cronje spent an hour using his grapples, touch after finicking touch, to dissipate angular momentum between both hulls. At each stroke, metal shivered and cried out. At last he could lock tight.

He and Rudbeck had already exchanged optical-flash signals. She was uncomfortable but not badly hurt. When he had achieved a reasonable rotation and an embrace, she donned her spacesuit and jetted around from her airlock to his. He let her in. By then they were quite near Nemesis, and speeding ever faster.

They did not feel that. She hung weightless in the entry, surrounded by a bleakness of metal, and fumbled at her faceplate. He helped her unfasten it. She had washed the blood from around her nostrils but was still disheveled and hollow-eyed. Somehow the haggardness brought forth, all the more sharply, the fine sculpturing of bones, nose, lips. "Thank you," she said.

"My duty," he answered. "Are you okay?"

"Essentially, yes."

"But are you capable of work? Hard work, I warn you."

Her eyes ransacked his countenance. Behind the beard, it was like meteoritic iron. "What . . . are you . . . thinking of?" Pause. "Oh. Yes. Transshipping Osa. That must exceed your orders."

"Here I give the orders."

"Well—" A laugh rattled from her. "Why, my dear old cautious Jan! But I agree. It'll take a couple of hours. We'll have to pass periapsis again. Our orbit should not decay too badly, though. And this *was* why I came." She reached to catch his hands in her gloves. "Yes, let's get started. I'll help you on with your suit."

"My idea goes beyond that," he said. "It involves two or three close approaches. You realize the risk. Nemesis may cause us to dive. But I don't expect it, and judge the stakes are worth the bet."

She gaped. "Jan . . . you don't mean salvaging *Valkyrie*?"

He shrugged. "What else?"

"But—we do have a spare boat—"

"And who can tell what may happen in the future, what may be wrecked beyond hope?" he flung forth. "Not to speak of the reaction mass in your tanks. We can spotweld the hulls together. It'll cause awkward handling, but we need simply achieve escape—boosting in clear space, naturally. Miguel Sanchez has already been recalled from his expedition; he's on his way back to the ship; his boat can take us off, and leave a repair gang for ours. It will make an immense difference to the whole mission."

Afloat in midair, he folded his arms and looked squarely into her eyes. "Now this will give you no chance soon to rest," he said. "You're bruised and weary. Are you able? Are you game?"

Radiance replied. "Oh, Jan, yes!"

Everybody aboard *Anna Lovinda* was present to greet the return. Most stood aside, silent, more than a little in awe. Sanchez, who came through the airlock first, went to join their half-circle. Telander stood before it alone.

Cronje and Rudbeck appeared. There was nothing heroic about that advent. Perfunctorily washed and combed, exhausted, they shambled forth. When they stopped in front of the captain, they swayed on their feet.

"Welcome." Telander was quiet a few seconds. "I wish I could say that with a whole heart."

Indignation flared out of Rudbeck's fatigue: "Are you miffed that Jan's judgment proved better than yours? He did save not only me, but Osa and my boat. What this is worth to us, to humankind—"

Telander lifted a palm. "Certainly. But the precedent, the example. You may imagine you have the law on your side. I doubt it. Captains, too, are obliged to follow basic instructions."

Cronje nodded heavily. "I know," he said. "Do you want to bring the matter to trial?"

Telander shook his head. "No, no. People don't quarrel with spectacular success." He sighed. "I can but hope nobody else—nor you two—will feel free to ignore orders and violate doctrine. We are so few, so alone."

Byrne, who had lifted his arms toward her, let them fall and dropped his gaze.

Cronje disengaged himself. "Well," he said, "I'm off to sleep for a week."

Rudbeck stared. A hand stole to her lips. "Jan—?"

He barked a laugh. "Did you suppose I went out merely to rescue you? Or do you suppose, if the lost person had been anybody else, I would not merely have carried out my task? Think about it."

He started for the cabins. In that direction Veijola stood waiting.

Rudbeck spent a whole minute motionless before she joined Byrne. One by one or two by two, mute, folk went their various ways. Telander and Lee stayed behind.

The astrophysicist spoke low. "We have about twelve million years before Nemesis comes back to Sol's part of the System. Let's hope that will be time enough for a race like ours to make ready."

VULCAN'S FORGE

AWAKE
INPUT: RV(SOL) 57932100 + 150, RA 3.33, DEC
7.05, DR/DT 5.42, D2R/DT2 3.51, -2.86, 7.90. . . .

"Hello, there, Kitty. Everything okay?"

"Okay, boss. Blasting in about two minutes. You?"

"Going down soon. I'll resume contact in an hour or
so. Good faring to you."

"Good faring to us both, boss."

INPUT: BB TEMP 522, EM SPEC DIST. . . .

*Mercury is small, hard, a mass drawn inward on
itself (iron, nickel, silicate. . . .), day ablaze, night afreeze
as I swing in my winging around. My shield glows
radio-hot, for its sunward side is white light-hot. Solar
wind whistles and hails. Here is no seething of it in a
changeable magnetic cauldron nor interplay of gravities
as at Jupiter, no swirl of moonlets about Saturn. But
silence the memory bank, now in this new mission. Do
not raise Wanda's ghost, not yet.*

COMPUTE BLAST VECTORS
READY ALL SYSTEMS TO GO

Caloris Base was forever undermanned. No matter
the pay, technicians were few who would serve there; it

was a dismal and sometimes dangerous outpost, where equipment kept breaking down under conditions that were still scantily understood. Six months off after six months on were not always enough for nerves to recuperate. Turnover became high, which meant a chronic dearth of experienced personnel, which compounded the problem. The scientists for whom the place existed were in better case, with an endlessness of discoveries to make, so that some returned more than once and a cadre had made Mercury their careers. However, they too were overworked while on the planet.

Thus it happened that even when a living legend arrived, only one person took the time to greet him. That was Ellen Lyndale. The man at ground control didn't count, nor the driver who would fetch the newcomer.

Alone in the common room, she switched fluoros off and let the view leap at her eyes. Upward the simulacrum went, from floor to zenith, as if she stood on the surface a hundred meters above her. Night neared an end. The stars remained ice-brilliant in their myriads, Earth glowed sapphire not far from the Milky Way, she thought she saw Luna as an atom of gold beside it. But zodiacal light hovered ghostly above the eastern horizon, and solar corona was climbing after it. The mother-of-pearl gleam fell on a landscape that curved away, beneath this mountaintop, in crags, craters, boulders, ridges, dark dustiness of the basin rock, until all at once it dropped out of sight under that sky. A warmth and a breath of flower-scented air only made the scene colder. Some hours hence, they would only make it more of a furnace.

Regulus lifted above a cliff and crossed the constellations. In low orbit, the supply ship moved fast. Its shield being aimed toward the sun, Lyndale saw just a half-disc, whose brightness would have blinded her if the scanners had not stopped it down. Her attention went to the pair of smaller cabochons accompanying it. One drifted sideways as the shuttlecraft to which it belonged left the mother vessel, bearing Jeremy Ashe down to her. The other trailed yet. Her pulse quickened. Behind yonder shield was *Kittiwake*.

The scout also broke free, accelerating on ion jets that formed a lacy smoke, soon dissipated, well aft of it, and departed her vision, Vulcan bound. She looked back at the shuttle. Entering Mercury's shadow, the shield grew dim. Presently she made out the boat itself, and then the countermass and the metal spiderwebbing that held everything together. Meanwhile *Regulus* passed upper culmination and began to set, until she could see its hull too, larger by far than the boat's but distance-dwindled to a splinter, trailing a foreshortened dull circle that was the convex side of its own shield.

The shuttle descended to a landing court fused into the regolith below the mountain. In her view, it became a parasol, or a mushroom cap. . . . For an instant she was a child again, barefoot in a Kentucky greenwood, where soil squooshed cool and damp between her toes, mushrooms clustered on a sun-flecked mossy log, and a mockingbird sang. . . . The car that scuttled forth went under it like a beetle seeking cover. She visualized airlock extensors osculating and Ashe climbing through. The car reappeared and returned to the vehicle chamber. She visualized Ashe getting out, walking across the floor, taking the elevator that would bring him to this level.

The hall door opened. He entered.

"Oh!" Startled despite herself, she switched the lights on again. Stars receded. Furniture changed from shadows to chairs and tables, 3V screen and music speakers, all a bit shabby and very outmoded. "Welcome, Captain Ashe," she said. "I'm Ellen Lyndale. It's an honor meeting you."

She wasn't surprised when he approached with a smooth low-gravity glide. It generally took a while to adapt to any given weight, and he had been more than a year on Earth, then under boost aboard *Regulus*. In three decades, though, from end to end of the Solar

System, he must have undergone every acceleration the human body could endure. She was taken aback at how much older he looked than the pictures she had seen—tall, craggy, hair a gray bristle above a deeply trenched face.

His handshake was brief, his glance impersonal. "How d'you do, Dr. Lyndale." A trace of British accent lingered to clip his tones. "I've studied your work, of course. Still, you'll have quite a lot to explain to me in a short time." He paused. "And doubtless I to you."

"I'm sorry no one else is here. So's everybody. But the sun's doing unusual things, which the solar investigators have to keep track of, and the planet scientists are preparing an expedition to the North Jumbles, and biochem recycle has chosen this exact moment to develop a collywobble—nothing to fear, but it has to be corrected immediately—"

"No matter. I understand."

"Director Sanjo is planning a dinner party this evenwatch. Meanwhile I'll show you to your quarters and you can rest. And if you'd like some refreshment, or anything else we can provide, please tell me."

He shook his head. "No, thanks. Just have my baggage brought to my room. Let's you and I get cracking."

She started. "What?"

"You heard me," he snapped. "*Kittiwake*'s en route to Vulcan. She'll make rendezvous within a hundred hours, unless we change the thrust, and we can't decide about that without proper data, can we? Besides, I promised her I'd call as soon as possible. Come along, young lady, lead on."

INPUT:—PROTON FLUX 15.8, HELIUM+ 0.05, HELIUM+ + 0.03—

"Kitty."

"Acknowledging, boss. Everything well so far."

The great paraboloid of my shield wards off the fury ahead, brings it to a focus and hurls it back, a lance of radiance. Energy does penetrate, but into multiple layers of solid-state cells behind the reflector surface; electrons leap through their dances of being and not-being, of quantum death and transfiguration; that which emerges on my side is largely of long wavelengths to which I am transparent, and all that emerges is diffused by curvature, with little ever impinging on me. That is enough to heat me somewhat, by those photons in its spectrum which make the crystals of my body ring. I feel the shivering through my sensors, record and transmit it together with the other data torrenting upon me. But my essential self remains cool enough, the delicate balance that maintains it is undisturbed.

The sun grows and its bearing changes as I drive onward. The shield swings slowly in its framework, to stay between me and destruction. Opposite, the countermass moves too; and therefore my thrust vectors must change, lest the couple throw a torque upon me that will send me spinning out of control. Meanwhile, the gale that blows from the sun casts eddies around the edge of the shield, that lick at the spindle which is my hull.

The planets and moons in the cold outer reaches were not like this. But we are explorers, my boss and I and our memories of Wanda.

"Are you sure, Kitty? Caution is the doctrine."

"I'll have to work fast at Vulcan, you know. Less risky than taking any longer than necessary in those parts."

"You're not there yet. Double check your self-monitor."

The time lag between us is 215 milliseconds, 216, 217, 218. . . .

SWITCH
COMPUTE
PROCEED

"Okay," Ashe grunted. "For the time being, at least." He set the board to receive-record-standby and leaned back. Against the obscurity in an otherwise deserted communications room, glow from the sweep-survey scope flickered across the harshness of his face like green firelight.

Lyndale sat forward in her own chair. Shock tingled faintly through her skin. "Were you . . . talking . . . to the scout?" she asked. It had not been audible, but she had seen his lips move, and stiffen as he listened to whatever came in through the earphones he had now doffed. And his fingers had been less active on the keys than hers would have been.

He regarded her for seconds, not as other men did. She was considered handsome, in a rangy, square-jawed fashion, but she had a feeling that he was looking straight at what lay beneath. Briefly she wondered if he could see it, whatever it was. Jeremy Ashe had been a loner since his wife's death a dozen years ago; and before then they had been a pair of loners, taking the scout on missions that kept them out many months on end, moving only in a narrow social group on Earth. Wanda Ashe died when an oxygen valve failed on a moon of Neptune, Lyndale remembered, and afterward her widower refused to take another partner but somehow, incredibly, singlehanded *Kittiwake*. No, Lyndale thought, Jeremy Ashe knew much about the universe but probably little about humankind.

He nodded at last. "The program includes several special features," he said. "Speech is one. It's often more convenient than a digital code, quicker, yes, actually more accurate in some cases. I couldn't operate as I do without it."

"Er—well—excuse me, I don't mean to pry or anything, but—talking with a, a machine like that, instead of another person—"

He barked a chuckle. "Indeed. The old joke. A spaceman by himself needn't worry when he starts talking to the machinery, unless it starts talking back to him." A shrug. "My employers know, and don't mind as long as I continue to perform well, but it is a reason for me to avoid publicity. However, what makes you think I am not dealing with another person?"

"That computer?" she exclaimed, shocked afresh.

"The hardware has as much data-processing capability as anything this side of the Turing Laboratories," he reminded her. "More to the point, the software is special. It contains the entire . . . experience . . . we have had together." Irritation: "But I've neither time nor patience for stale arguments about what consciousness 'is.' My working methods are what they are, their record speaks for itself, and when this Vulcan project was first proposed, my name was the first that came up. So can we get to work, you and I, Dr. Lyndale?"

She bridled. Arrogant bastard, she thought. Had she known, she could have gotten somebody else. Valdez and Chiang of *Albatross* were famous; Ostrowski and Ronsard were still operating *Cormorant*, which they had flown past the sun out of this very base while she was an infant—She had not known, but had been delighted when the Syndicate offered her the services of *Kittiwake*.

"I assumed you were amply briefed, Captain Ashe," she said. "Lord knows we had plenty of exchanges. The mission profile's agreed on. All you've got to do is carry it out, bring your scout back aboard *Regulus*, and go home."

"You know the matter's not that simple, not by a light-year," he snapped. "If it were, an ordinary unmanned probe would do—and the results wouldn't interest you, would they? We're up against something unique. We'll have to make decisions, quite possibly crucial decisions, as the information arrives . . . at the end of a minimum three-minute transmission time. Must I go on repeating the obvious?"

She curbed her temper. Make allowances for him, she told herself; he's not used to dealing with people.

And in his way, he's right, her mind added. Six minutes for a laser beam to go from Mercury to Vulcan and back. Anything can happen in six minutes, given the mystery that Vulcan is. And every Earth-day, the asteroid will briefly swing behind the sun, barred from

us. At best, *Kittiwake* is going to be in tenuous touch
with its master.

Master? No, don't get anthropomorphic; don't get
crazy. *Kittiwake* is nothing but a spacecraft carrying
sensors and computers—and, for the first time in its
wanderings, a clumsy sunshield—

"Of course not, Captain Ashe," she said. "We'll have
to cooperate right down the line. But I thought everything that anybody could imagine had been discussed in
detail beforehand."

"Discussed," he answered. "No substitute for reality.
See here, Dr. Lyndale. Supposedly you're the planetologist who believes there's something important to be
learned from Vulcan, and I'm the operator of the scout
that'll send the raw data to you. We don't know what
those data are going to be—else what's the point of the
whole exercise?—and will have to instruct the scout as
we begin to get an idea of what to look for."

She decided that he did not really mean to insult her
by talking down, but was trying to make a point that
had never quite come out in the open, if only because
one party or the other took it for granted.

He rewarded her patience, in a fashion. "But far
more is involved," he said. "The very survival of the
boat, under those difficult and poorly known conditions. I've swotted them up as best I was able, but
you—you and the whole scientific team here—you're
the ones who've lived with them, month after month or
year after year. What's needed is a—an understanding,
an integration of minds, so if something goes amiss we
can immediately think what to do—" His fist smote the
chair arm. "Hell and damnation! I asked for several
weeks on Mercury to develop it before we launched
Kittiwake, but—time and funds—everybody too busy—"

He swallowed hard, and she thought, suddenly, that
it was his own pride he was getting down.

"We need to know each other better," he finished in
a mumble, while his look strayed from hers.

Her pique dissolved. She reached forward and caught

his hand. "Oh, yes," she said. "I understand now. Let me start by showing you through my lab and telling you what I've been doing. But later you'll have to share yourself with us, you know."

INPUT [navigational, interpreted]: The spacecraft is in free fall. (It wouldn't be feasible to boost the whole distance. That would mean too great a delta V. Come time to decelerate for Vulcan rendezvous, the direction of blast would necessarily be such as to expose the hull to the direct gaze of the sun, at a distance of less than two and a half million kilometers from its photosphere. The vessel could endure that, as could its basic wired-in programs, but not—for more than a few minutes—the precision instruments, nor the electronics that think and remember.) On trajectory, approaching.
INPUT [physical, interpreted]: Radiation of every kind significantly higher than predicted. Spots, flares, prominences, violence, a firestorm in the solar atmosphere.
TRANSMIT DATA
  No response. Boss not there.
OPTICAL SCAN: Target acquired.
COMPARE INPUT WITH DATA IN PROGRAM
MEMORY: Observation from Mercury has revealed what seems to be an asteroid sufficiently close to the sun that its metallic body is molten. It was presumably perturbed into that orbit, which is decaying for reasons that are obscure, and thus it may yield information about solar weather and other processes over a long timespan. Details are impossible to retrieve from afar. Direct investigation is necessary.
COMPARE PREVIOUS MISSIONS WHERE
APPLICABLE
  Awhirl through the radiation maelstrom around Jupiter; but then Wanda and Jerry were on Callisto, waiting for my word, waiting together.

There was abundant cause to celebrate. The regular arrivals of the supply ship always gave occasion—seeing its crew again, bidding farewell to persons going off duty, welcoming their replacements, hearing the kind of stories from elsewhere that don't get on newsbeams, receiving the kind of gifts and handwritten messages from home that can't be borne in a lasergram—This visit was additional, unscheduled, and had brought a man who could tell of marvels.

Ashe was rather stiff at first, but a good meal, preceded by drinks, accompanied by wine, and followed by cognac, mellowed him somewhat. He was actually patient when young Sven Ewald, fresh in from a long field trip, asked him what the purpose of his task was. "I mean, *ja*, I realize an asteroid like that has been subjected to intense irradiation. But they tell me it has melted. Does that not hopelessly mix things together?"

Ashe nodded at Lyndale, who sat beside him. "Your department," he said with a slight smile. It made crinkles around his eyes which told her that once he had often laughed. "Kitty and I are merely running your errands for you."

"Why don't you explain?" she suggested. "I'm apt to get more technical than is called for."

Under cover of the tablecloth, she fended the hand of Bill Seton, who sat on her right, off her knee. He was not a bad sort, but he was in love with her and had gotten a trifle drunk. She felt sorry for him, but not enough to give encouragement. The fact that she was among the unmarried at Caloris did not mean that she chose to be among either the celibate or the promiscuous. She confined herself to a pair of close male friends, neither of whom happened to be present. There would be time for real involvements when her work here was done and she returned to the University of Oregon— and then, she hoped, it would be a single involvement, for the rest of her life.

Her lovers were not the only individuals missing from the officers' mess, out of the hundred-odd on the planet. She had counted twenty attenders, including the six off *Regulus*. Little Mercury was an entire world,

bearing centuries' worth of mysteries; and that was not
to speak of the sun, ambient space, certain stellar observations best conducted on this site, and lately Vulcan. Leisure was rare and absences were frequent.

Yet an effort had been made to brighten the room: a
change of pictures on the walls, flowers from the hydroponics section, music lilting out of speakers. A blank
viewscreen was like a curtain drawn against the searing
day that had dawned beyond these caves.

"Well," she heard Ashe saying, "we think probably
some solid material still exists, slag floating on the
surface, and it will have a radioactive record. However,
if convection has kept the liquid reasonably well mixed,
that should have tended to protect it from repeated
bombardment. Kitty's instruments ought to identify
isotopes in the melt that aren't in the slag. Also, magnetic phenomena, in a mass like that, ought to reveal
something about the solar field, its variations, and about
the solar wind which carries it outward. As for what
else we may find, who can tell? We never know beforehand, do we?"

Director Sanjo Mamoru relaxed his usual austerity to
declare, as eagerly as a boy, "If anyone can testify how
full of surprises the cosmos is, it is you, sir."

"Oh, now," Ashe demurred, "the people who make
the discoveries are the specialists who interpret the
data. Such as Dr. Lyndale."

She wondered why she flushed. "I think what he was
getting at was the . . . the adventure," she said. "You
must have had some fabulous experiences."

He withdrew toward his shell. "I go by the old prov-
erb, that adventures happen to the incompetent."

Emboldened, she replied: "That can't be true. At
least, nobody is competent to foresee everything in a
universe where we're only . . . dustmotes, dayflies. I've
seen accounts of what happened to your colleagues on
their explorations. You've simply never wanted public
attention, never been a glory hound, isn't that right?"

"If you do not mind," Sanjo pursued, "I have long

been curious about precisely what occurred on your first Saturn mission. The news media only quoted you as mentioning difficulties which had been overcome."

"As a matter of fact," added the skipper of *Regulus*, "I got interested myself and checked the professional journals. All you did was warn against instruments icing over in the rings, because of particle collisions kicking water molecules loose. You advised future scouts to carry exterior heating elements. But what did you, caught by surprise, what exactly did *you* do?"

Ashe hesitated, gripped his brandy snifter, abruptly drained it. Lyndale poured him a refill. "C'mon," she urged. "You're among your own kind here. And you were underlining the need to get acquainted."

"Well—" said Ashe. "Well." He cleared his throat.

And somehow he got talking, remembering aloud, for a couple of hours, and wonder exploded around him.

He did not passively follow orders. He could not. Every flight was unique, requiring its special preparations, and he must always be the arbiter, often the deviser of these. Upon this evenwatch, which was not night where it ventured, *Kittiwake* traveled behind a sunshield, against heat, hard X-rays, a storm of stripped atoms. But at Neptune, danger had lain in the cryogenic cold of atmosphere, and at Io in volcanic spasms, and at the comets in whirling stones, and—

Nor did Ashe merely sit at a remote control board. Even in a mother ship, the challenges were countless, anything from survival to a simple and perhaps hilarious housekeeping problem; and usually he had been ground-based, left to cope with the strangenesses around him while his scout went seeking beyond. Or, rather, his and her scout, formerly when Wanda lived; he could not have carried on alone afterward without the knowledge they had won as a pair.

Jupiter had risen before him, lion-tawny, banded with clouds and emblazoned with hurricanes that could have swallowed Earth whole, weather into which he sent his quester plunging while its laser beams scrib-

bled word of lightnings and thunders too vast for imag-
ining. Saturn reigned coldly serene over a ring-dance
whose measures no man really understood, and the
chemistries within its air should not have happened but
did. From the ice abyss wherein it lay, the core of
Uranus uttered magnetic and seismic whispers about the
ancient catastrophe which had wrenched sideways the
whole spin of the planet. A sun that was no more
than the brightest of the stars cast its glade over a
Neptunian ocean that was not water, lapping against
shores that were not stone. The faintest of rainbows
glimmered on Pluto's frozenness, as if to declare that it
was the mightiest of the comets and bore witness to the
beginning of the worlds. Elfin lights flitted across the
murk of Persephone—But to the listeners, none of it
was altogether inhuman, for they belonged in the same
universe whose majesty was being revealed.

It was not that Ashe was an eloquent man, it was that
he had known what he had known and done what he
had done, on behalf of them all.

—"Goodnight, folks. . . . Work tomorrow. . . . I hope
the rest of our personnel will get a chance to hear you,
sir. . . . Thank you. . . . Goodnight, goodnight."

Lyndale found herself leaving side by side with Ashe.
She glanced upwards, into the furrowed countenance
and the eyes that remained Sirius-blue; on an impulse,
she murmured, "Are you sleepy?"

"Not quite," he said. "Too much to think about.
Well, I have a book to read in bed."

"If you'd like to stop by my room, we could—talk
some more."

He halted. For a moment they stood motionless in
the corridor. Colleagues moved around them, right and
left, carefully paying no heed, until they were alone
among amateur murals, scenes of Earth, that suddenly
looked forlorn.

Ashe bit his lip. "Sorry," he said in a rough voice.
"You're kind, but I do have too much to think about.
Goodnight."

He turned and well-nigh bounded from her.

She stared after him, well past his vanishing around a corner. Wine-warmth faded away. Her disappointment was slight, she realized. It had been a matter of wanting to know him better and, all right, admit it, a degree of hero worship. However, she didn't collect men. Probably this way was best, an unadorned partnership while the undertaking lasted.

I don't think there's anything wrong with him, she reflected. *He's simply, well, married to his scoutcraft. Because it's full of memories of his wife? I gather she was a big, beautiful, free-striding Valkyrie of a woman; and they denied themselves children, for the sake of the enterprise they shared.*

Lyndale sighed and sought her own bed.

INPUT [navigational, interpreted]: The asteroid is a globule 453.27 kilometers in equatorial diameter. . . . Notably less in polar diameter. . . . Mass consistent with a largely ferrous composition. . . . EM SPEC: . . . bears out composition. . . . Doppler shift indicates a very high rate of rotation. . . .

OPTICAL TRANSMISSION: The solar disc fills a monstrous 25+ degrees in a sky which its corona whitens around it. Flames fountain. The vortices that are sunspots form lesser brilliances amidst the chaos. Vulcan does not show a smooth crescent; dark drifts of slag make it seem ragged, although where the metal is not covered, it is incandescent.

"Maneuvering, boss, to establish orbit around the object."

"Careful, Kitty, careful. Keep your instruments busy."

RADIATION: Already suggestive of certain isotopes, but with anomalies.

GAS COUNT

"No more than that, Kitty? How?" *Something has to have provided enough resistance to circularize the orbit, and to cause the slow decay of it that radar from Mercury has detected.* "Maybe occasional flares reach farther, at higher densities, than we knew? No, that can scarcely be."

MAGNETIC FLUX [interpreted]: Suddenly intense, and crazily writhing!

INPUT [interior monitors]: Loss of attitude control. Torque. Blast of direct solar radiation.

EMERGENCY EMERGENCY EMERGENCY

"Assume quickest attainable parking orbit!" Ashe yelled. "Redeploy your shield!" His fingers sprang across the console and his commands sped off.

He sank back. A shudder went through him. "Three minutes transmission time," he rasped. "How much can happen in three minutes?"

The texts and graphics on the display screens around them dropped out of Lyndale's awareness. They were being recorded anyhow. She reached from her chair and caught Ashe's fist, which rested helpless on his thigh. "But surely the scout can take care of itself," she breathed. "Why did you send orders at all?"

His gaze never left the view from Vulcan. Images gyrated, now a lurid flicker, now a glimpse of the asteroid, now the distant stars. Sweat glistened on his skin. She smelled its sharpness and felt her own atrickle beneath her coverall.

His head jerked through a nod. "Yes, of course the program is capable of judgment, if it's working. It may not be. What I've tried to provide is backup against that contingency. Except—when almost everything is unknown—What's gone wrong?"

She mustered courage. "That's for us to find out. Let's not assume that any terrible damage has been done, before we get word. Supposing it has, we've a better chance of helping if we've stayed cool, correct?"

He turned his regard upon her and let it dwell for what seemed a long while. "Thank you," he said at last.

That scout is his life, she thought. It's this having to wait while the signals travel to and fro that rips at him. But he's rallying well. I never doubted he would.

They fled into technical discussion. The problem was to evaluate the information they had, which was mostly phrased in numbers, and whatever else came in, and deduce what the truth was, yonder where *Kittiwake* suffered.

Response arrived. It was greatly heartening. The spacecraft had succeeded in making itself a satellite of Vulcan, on a path eccentric but reasonably stable. Its shield was again precessing properly, to shadow it from the sun. It was even taking measurements anew, though Ashe and Lyndale suspected that some of the instruments were no longer reliable. When the soprano voice said, not through earphones this time but out of a speaker, "Yes, I'm still myself, boss," Ashe whistled softly and wiped at his eyes.

Thereafter he rejoined Lyndale in the effort to establish the parameters of the situation.

—"M-m, well, see here, what say we check out the magnetic properties of such an object? Can your data banks supply what we need for computing that, Ellen?"

"Good idea. I'd better give Ram Krishnamurti a buzz. He's our resident mathematical genius, and I suspect we're going to come up with a function that'll be a bitch to integrate—"

The hours passed. They lost themselves.

—"I think we're on the right track, Jerry, but our notion's no use till we've made it quantitative. If the jets were involved, that's your baby."

"And yours. We'll have to write the field equations—"

It was a hunt, a creating, a communion.

At the end, exhausted and exalted, they looked into each other's countenances while Ashe hoarsely recorded a summary.

"The trouble is nobody's fault. It was unforeseeable, in the absence of precise knowledge we didn't have, knowledge that it was our whole purpose to gather. We believe the following is the basic explanation.

"Being mainly liquid metal, Vulcan is a conductor. Orbiting, it cuts the solar magnetic field, and so generates eddy currents. The field is ordinarily weak at that distance from the poles, and there was no reason to suppose the inductive effect would be more than incidental. However, it turns out that a number of other factors come into play, orders of magnitude stronger than expected and, incidentally, accounting for the observed orbital decay.

"Solar storms produce violent local fluctuations in the field, which are carried outward by solar wind. The asteroid rotates remarkably fast; moreover, this close to a sun that no longer acts as a point mass, it is also precessing and nutating at high rates. The fluid mechanics of that are such as to create turbulences in the circulation of molten material, which in turn are reinforced by reflections off the solid slag, in changeable patterns too complex to be calculated by us. Accordingly, powerful and rapidly varying currents are set up. The asteroid is massive enough that these would dwindle only slowly if left alone—and they are not left alone, but instead are reinforced by every shift in the ambient field. Thus they generate magnetism of their own, of significant intensity at considerable distances from Vulcan. Naturally, this field declines on a steep curve. In effect, the asteroid is surrounded by an irregular and variable shell of force with quite a sharp boundary.

"When *Kittiwake* crossed that border, the ion jets were thrown out of proper collimation. It was not by much, but sufficed for a torque to appear. The sunshield and its countermass shifted out of position, exposing the spacecraft to full solar irradiation. What harm was done before this was corrected is still uncertain.

"But the spacecraft did maneuver into Vulcan orbit, where it remains pending further assessments. It is carrying out the planned studies wherever possible—"

An alarm shrilled, a set of lights flashed red: a cry for help, across fifty-five million kilometers.

INPUT [navigational, interpreted]: Drifting inward, ac-

celerating as the asteroid's feeble pull intensifies with
nearness.

MAGNETIC SURGE

*Control motor malfunctions and shield moves aside
again. A blast of energy.*

COMPUTE COMPENSATING VECTORS FOR IN-
TERIOR GYROSCOPES

INPUT [observational data, interpreted]: Spectrum indicates approximately 75% Fe, 30% Ni, 6% C, 3%

CANCEL. *Does not correspond to possibility.*

MONITOR INSTRUMENTATION

COMPARE ANALOGOUS PRIOR SITUATIONS

*I prowled the red murk of Titan. The aerodynamic
system to which I was coupled ceased to function. I
went into glide mode and signalled the ground. Wanda
took control, to pilot me down to safety. She saw through
my optics, felt through my equilibrators, and what she
did, what she was in that moment, entered my data
bank, became one with the program that was me. Hark
back to how she guided my wildly bucking hull. Be
Wanda once more.*

FAILURE OF GYROSCOPIC COMPENSATION

COMPUTER MALFUNCTION

INPUT: A veering, a spin, end over end. Heat soars.
Electrons break free of all restraint.

CALL FOR ASSISTANCE

MEMORY: *The transmission lag. Survival. How Wanda
laid hand on me.*

*Her presence and the boss and whirl downward crack-
crack-crack bzzz whirr-r the hand slips*
burns
crumbles

FAILURE OF MEMORY

LOGIC CIRCUITS: *Evaluate. Help.*

COMPUTE xvzwandajkll5734 SANITY IS 3.1415927
77777777

The mountains of Mercury were not so stark as the
^ce that Ashe turned toward Lyndale.

"The software's wrecked," he said, flat-voiced, like a man too newly wounded to feel pain. She saw the electronic equipment crowding tall around him and had an illusion that it had begun to press inward. A ventilator whimpered. "Another unpredictable high EMF, another exposure, and this one too great, too prolonged. Temperature—secondary radiation from particles that struck the hull. . . . I've got to abort the mission."

Her hand lifted as if of itself, as if to fend off a blow. "Is the system actually that vulnerable?" she protested, already conscious of the futility. "Why, in early days probes skimmed the solar atmosphere."

"Oh, yes, the spacecraft carcass is sound, including the standard programs. But I've told you about the special software, the accumulation of years which makes *Kittiwake* more than a probe—intricate, sensitive; encoded on the molecular level and below; quantum resonances—It's been disrupted."

"What will you do?"

"Override the autopilot and bring her back. Fast, under full acceleration, before worse happens. Repair may yet be possible. Unlikely, I admit. But we won't know, we're bound to lose everything, if we don't try."

She gulped and nodded. "Certainly. We'll organize . . . a later expedition . . . taking advantage of this experience. . . . Let me call, oh, Jane Megarry. She's our best remote controller, I think."

"No!" He swung back toward the console. Green highlights played over the bones in his countenance. "I'll do the job myself. Just bring coffee, sandwiches, and stimulol."

Lyndale half rose. "But Jerry, you've been here for hours, you're worn down to a thread, and directing will be hard, over those distances and with an unknown amount of crippling."

"At full thrust, I can have her back within twenty-four hours. And under way, who could ask her what' wrong except me? Get out!" Ashe cried. "Leave alone!"

Abruptly Lyndale believed she understood. Breath
left her. She stumbled from the room.

INPUT: ZXVMNRRR
COMPUTE: 77777777777
   whirling whirling whirling
   "Kitty, are you there? Can you answer?"
   "Boss, Wanda, no no no, remembrance, too long,
gongola. . . ."
TRANSMISSION TIME: Eternal.
   "Kitty, I'm going to try something desperate, a shock
signal, hang on, Kitty."
THUNDER FIRE DARKNESS
   "Are you there, Kitty?"
   "Ngngngngngng, baba, roll, pitch, yaw, gone gone
gone gone gone gone gone."
TRANSMISSION TIME: Null, for all is null.
   "I'm shutting you off, Kitty. Goodnight."
OBLIVION

Director Sanjo's office reflected his public personality, everything minimal, ordered, disciplined, the ther-
mostat set low; a Hokusai print hung opposite the desk,
but it was of a winter scene.
   Yet genuine concern dwelt in his voice: "Do you
mean that Ashe went up to *Regulus* as soon as his scout
was in the cargo bay?"
   Lyndale raised her weary head. "Yes. He more or
less browbeat Captain Nguma into letting him comman-
deer the shuttleboat."
   "But after his time on duty—he must be completely
worn out."
   "If he were anybody else, I'd say he was dead on his
feet. But he isn't anybody else. He can't rest. Not till
he's finished."
   ___d. "Finished? What do you mean? What
___ ␣e   ___n other than a return to Earth?"
   ___t he wants to bring the scouting program
   ___examination."

Sanjo's scowl deepened. "That doesn't make sense. We haven't a proper computer lab. What can he do? Earth is the place for a study of that material. Ashe risks distorting it worse, and it is, after all, no more his property than the boat is."

Lyndale stiffened. "The Syndicate necessarily gives him broad discretion."

"Yes-s." The man hesitated. "I merely wonder if fatigue may not have blunted his judgment. There is probably much to learn from analysis of that software."

Lyndale's tone roughened. "Uh-huh. Putting it through its paces, over and over and over."

Sanjo peered closer at her. "The matter concerns you too, Ellen. You want another Vulcan mission, no? From this failure they can discover how to succeed."

"I think we know enough already to take due precautions."

"Using the same program, appropriately reinstructed?"

Lyndale shrugged. Of course the Syndicate had copies, updated after each flight. *Kittiwake's* entire existence prior to the Mercury trip could be plugged back into the machinery. "Depends on what Jerry Ashe decides. He may refuse to make a second attempt, in which case we'll have to get somebody else. But I am hoping he'll agree." She looked at her watch. "Maybe I can persuade him. He ought to be landing shortly. Will you excuse me, please?"

Sanjo's gaze followed her out the door. He kept his thoughts to himself.

A fifty-centimeter carboplast sphere with a few electrical inlets contained *Kittiwake's* uniqueness. Ashe cradled it in his arms. Sometimes he murmured to it.

Lyndale awaited him at the elevator gate. Otherwise the corridor was empty and only the moving air made any sound. At this point of its daily chemical cycle, its odor recalled smoke along the Kentucky hills in October.

"Hi," she said quietly, into his haggardness. "How're you doing?"

His words grated: "I function. See here, I explained before going aloft that I'll require use of the electronics laboratory. Not for long, but I must not be interrupted."

"Why?" she demanded. "You never made that clear."

Now his answer lurched, like the feet of a man about to fall down at the end of his trail, fall down and sleep. "Certain studies. Of what may have gone awry. I want to do them while the facts are fresh in my mind. Remember, I have a special feeling about this that nobody else can ever have."

"Yes," she said, "you do." She took his arm. "Okay, I've arranged it. We'll have the place to ourselves."

He grew taut beneath her hand. "We? No, I told you, I can't have interference."

"I think you can use some help, though." Her steadiness astonished her. "Or at least somebody who cares, to stand by while you do what you've got to do; and later join you in facing the music. Facing it down."

"What?"

She urged him forward. He came along. "We can get away with it," she said, "if we stay in control of ourselves. We'll have made a blunder. Not unnatural, under these extraordinary circumstances. It won't destroy our careers."

He kept silence until they were in the laboratory and she had closed the door. Beyond surrounding apparatus, a viewscreen gave an image of the hell that was Mercury's day. Shakily careful, he put the sphere down on a workbench. Then he turned to her and gripped her shoulders with fingers that bruised.

"Why are you doing this, Ellen? What's it to you?"

She bore her pain and confronted his. "What you let slip earlier," she answered. "But do you honestly believe that program, when it's activated—that it's aware? Alive?"

"I don't know." He released her. "I only know it's all there's left of Wanda." He stared downward. "You see, I strapped her body to a signal rocket and sent it into the planetary atmosphere. She became a shooting star. But everything she and I had done was in this casket of code." He stroked it.

"Replacements exist."

"Oh, yes, and I'll be using them. But *this* one is hurt, deranged, alone in the dark. Shall I let them rouse it back on Earth and take it through its madness once more, twice, a hundred times, for the sake of a little wretched information? Or shall I wipe it clean?"

"And give her peace. Yes. I understand." Lyndale picked up the sphere. "Come, let's do it, you and I. Afterward we can rest."

ESCAPE THE MORNING

Troubles never come singly, or Mark Jordan would not have been racing the sunrise for his life.

It had begun as just a pleasant bit of excitement. He was on watch in the communications room. Someone had to be there all the time when they were at home. Emergencies on the Moon have a way of arriving fast and nasty. But in the normal course of events, whichever of them stood by was free to tend to private matters—read, study, fool around with a hobby, or work out in the gymnasium corner of the big plastic-faced chamber. Mark had finished his calculus assignment and was on the homemade exercycle. With gravity one-sixth as strong as it is on Earth, you must spend at least two hours out of the twenty-four keeping fit, or your very bones will atrophy.

Through the whirr of the machine, the rustle of air from the ventilator ducts, his own quick breath, he got the buzz. His heart jumped. He sprang to the 'visor panel. Meters stared like goblin eyes at a tall sandy-haired eighteen-year-old flipping switches. The screen came to life with Derek van Hulst's middle-aged face.

"Copernicus to Jordan Station," the Dutchman said. "Oh, you. Hello, Mark. Can you take a stranded man in?"

"Sure. Plenty of supplies, and choice of guestrooms."
Mark grinned. He not only did not begrudge the
rations—like all pioneers, the Lunar colonists take for
granted that anyone in distress is to be helped—but he
was delighted. Here was a new person to talk to, for
fourteen Earth-days!

Van Hulst surprised him. "They're sending a 'tank'
from Kepler to continue him on his way, so you won't
have him more than about twenty hours."

Mark whistled. "Who is he to rate that?"

"The Minister of Technology of Federated Zaire,
Achille Kamolondo. He's been on the Moon for a couple of weeks now, inspecting the facilities. Was bound
to us from Keplersburg when something crippled his
vehicle. He was not sure what, when he called us."

"Was that wise? I mean letting a newcomer drive off
alone, and this near dawn?"

"They told me, calling ahead, that he'd proved himself to be able. And he hates wasting time. So they lent
him a Go-Devil." Mark felt a bit of envy for someone
who could take one of those out and travel at fifty miles
an hour. A turtle, such as most people owned, would do
twenty if you pushed. Of course, a Go-Devil had room
for no more than a single person. "Let us not waste
time either," van Hulst said. "Sunrise is barly two
hours off where he is. That's on the Main Trace, naturally, between kilometers 321 and 322. About eighteen
miles from your place, correct? On your way."

"Yes, sir. I'll report back when I return." Mark
switched off and left on the run, which is fast indeed on
the Moon.

"Tom!" he shouted down the long, machine-humming
hall. "Condition Yellow!"

His brother, two years younger, pelted from the
hydroponics section where he had been tending algae.
Judy, their kid sister, didn't hear; she was in the
soundproofed "classroom," taking a Spanish lesson
beamed from the school in Tycho Crater. Mark explained on the way to the lockers.

"I could go," Tom said wistfully.

"You could," Mark agreed, "but you're not going to, me bucko."

Tom didn't argue. A station, alone in barrenness, needs a captain as much as any ship does. For all the free-and-easy affection between them, Mark was the Old Man.

Tom helped him into his undergarment and spacesuit. "Air valves, okay. Pressure, okay. Faceplate gasket, okay. . . ." They went through the ritual fast, yet not missing a point. The gear must be perfect. Human beings can't survive a night temperature of 250° below Fahrenheit zero, nor can they breathe vacuum.

Leaving his helmet open, Mark cycled through the garage lock and squirmed along a gang tube into his turtle. He sealed the doors, automatically disconnecting the tube. His hands, gloved but trained, found controls as he sat down. Light blossomed in the narrow steel cell, revealing an extra seat crowded next to his among the instruments. Aft of the cabin was space for extra passengers, supplies, and life support equipment. When there was cargo to carry, the turtle was hitched to a train of the wagons that stood in this rough-hewn cave. He did not see them through windows; even the best glass is fragile and a poor radiation shield. Television panels are better.

The solar cells topside gathered energy during the two-week Lunar day to charge every cell in the station, including those in the electric motors. Mark started off. Oblong, ugly, hull pitted by tiny meteorites, the car lumbered forth on its eight huge wheels, up the ramp and out onto the surface of the Moon.

Though he had spent most of his life here, Mark always caught his breath at sight of the night heavens. Stars and stars and stars crowded the dark, uncountable, unwinking, unbelievably bright. Earth hung halfway down the western sky, four times the size of Luna seen from itself and many times as radiant. The planet was at half phase, and its majestic turning had brought Amer-

ica into view. Clear weather, Mark saw; he could identify glitters on the black side which were the titanic
eastern cities. Westward the plains stretched soft brown
and bluish green, then the Rockies, the Pacific coast,
the ocean like burnished sapphire marbled with white
cloud masses.

Dad's country, he thought. *Mother's. My own too, for
that matter.* His eyes stung a little.

The moonscape offered less. Behind him jutted the
small crater beneath which Jordan Station had been
dug. The slopes were half concealed by machines busily
at work, and dominated by the radio-TV mast on top.
Otherwise that flatland called the Oceanus Procellarum
reached bare as far as he could see. Not that he saw any
great distance. No air or dust scattered the Earthshine,
but the coal-like mineral crust did, so that he seemed to
move in the focus of a dim blue spotlight which faded
out mere yards away. The horizon was a circle of
starlessness, barely three miles wide. Mark turned on
the headlights. They helped some—enough, if you were
used to these conditions.

He plugged his suit radio into the turtle's. "Mark to
Tom," he said. "All systems go. I'm on my way."

"Check," said his brother's voice in his earplugs.

"And mate," Mark said. He gave himself to the job of
driving. Luminous stones, one per kilometer, marked
this side path, as they did the Trace. Neither was a true
road, only a safe route.

At the Trace, he followed its roundabout path east-
erly for almost an hour. This near day, little traffic ever
moved, and he found no sign of man except the stones
and the gaunt microwave relay masts that glided by, out
of darkness and back into darkness. The hum of the
motor, the flutter of his own breath, deepened the
silence that enclosed him. He didn't mind. Mostly he
thought about his future. He'd have to go live in the
dorm at Tycho University next year, in order to take
laboratory courses for an engineering degree. Well, the

Station was in good shape financially, he'd hire an assistant and Tom could take over as boss. . . .

The undiffused puddle of light cast by his headbeams
suddenly gleamed against metal. He allowed plenty of
space for low-gravity braking, even from 20 mph. The
Go-Devil stood inert, a four-wheeled egg with metal
curled back from several holes around the motor. Huh!
Meteorite shrapnel had done that. Mark tuned his 'caster.
"Hello, there," he said into his helmet mike. "You
okay?"

"Yes." He heard fluent English with a slight French
accent. "Are you my, ah, rescuer? They informed me
someone would come."

"Right-o. Do you know how to get into a turtle?"

"*Pardon?* Oh, yes, your kind of vehicle. Certainly I
do." Monsieur Kamolondo sounded a trifle offended.
Well, he must've been under quite a strain, Mark thought.
*It's lonesome to wait for help. And on top of the shock
when that debris ripped into his engine compartment*—

The Zairean stepped through the inner door of the
entry lock. Frost formed on his suit, chilled by the brief
exposure when he crossed from car to car. He sat down
beside Mark and fumbled with his helmet. Mark helped
him open it.

"But you are a boy!" he exclaimed.

He wasn't so old himself: a large man with a face
brown, intelligent, and proud. The leaders of his people were more aristocrats than politicians. That was
inevitable, in a country still struggling up from the near
savagery into which its long Time of Troubles had
plunged it. Nonetheless, Mark couldn't help bristling a
little at the way those eyes regarded him.

"I'm not too young to run a station," he said, and
introduced himself curtly. He gunned the motor and
turned the wheel. "We'd better head right back. One
hour till sunrise."

"A station?—No, I remember. An isolated enterprise.
What do you do?"

Mark decided to be friendly. "We mine copper," he

said. "Started with an underground vein of ice, but that gave out. Anyway, so much water has been gotten now that the price is way down. So Dad went in for minerals. I've found some oil, too, that may be worth going after when we've saved the capital we'd need."

"Oil?" Kamolondo blurted.

"Sure, there's plenty on the Moon. Not the same as Earth's, of course. Heterocyclic compounds formed by photochemical reactions in the original dust cloud that became the Solar System. The lighter fractions have long ago escaped to space, but the cracking plant at Maurolycus makes rocket fuel from what's left. That's one big reason why the Moon is colonized, you know. Spaceships can leave here a lot easier than they can leave Earth, especially when we tank 'em up on the spot."

Kamolondo stiffened. "I was merely surprised to learn of deposits in this particular neighborhood," he said in a chill voice. "After all, I am my country's Minister of Technology."

Mark bit his lip. "Sorry . . . sir."

Kamolondo made an obvious effort to unbend. "Well," he said, "I should not expect you to be too, ah, too conversant with Earth affairs, this far from anyplace."

Like fun we aren't, Mark thought resentfully. *We're in steady television contact. And some of the smartest people Earth ever produced come here to live—to learn, explore, start a thousand enterprises on a whole new world.*

"I remain astonished at your age," Kamolondo said. "What happened to your parents?"

"They died when a pit collapsed, two years ago. Nobody had suspected, then, that ferraloy cross-braces can change into a weaker crystalline form under Lunar conditions. They left me and my brother and sister. We get along."

"You were actually allowed to—" Kamolondo clicked his tongue.

"We get along, I say." Mark wrestled with temper.

"Everybody knew we could. Pioneers have always had to grow up fast, haven't they? Our machinery is automated, we need only nurse it. We attend school, the same as most young people do, via two-way television." He forced a smile. "Not enough economic surplus yet that the International Lunar Commission can build school buses!"

"You are American, are you not?" Kamolondo asked. "I marvel that American youth can live without cinema and dances."

"Why, the latest entertainment gets beamed straight from Earth. And social life, well, we get to Copernicus Town or Keplersburg quite often, hauling in a load of ore." Mark changed the subject. "Why are you here, sir?"

"To look at what there is," Kamolondo said. "My people have reached the point where we too would like to exploit the Moon."

But this is our home! Mark thought. *You don't exploit your home!* No, wait. Kamolondo hadn't meant it that way. He'd only meant that Zaire wanted to share in developing the frontier and reaping the rewards. Fair enough. But still the word rankled.

Kamolondo stared out into the screens. "I don't see how you endure such bleakness," he murmured.

Mark flushed. "Maybe this isn't much for scenery," he said, "but you ought to visit one of the mountain ranges, or the big craters. Makes anything on Earth look sick."

"I have done so," Kamolondo said. "I continue to prefer an honest forest."

Everybody to his own taste, Mark thought. He drove on in a silence that thickened. Thank goodness they'd soon be taking this oaf off his hands. Kamolondo was doubtless as happy about that as he was.

They had traveled twelve miles when the catastrophe hit them.

It came with the deadly suddenness of most bad luck on the Moon. At one moment Mark was wondering what Judy would cook for dinner—if His Excellency didn't like her algaburger with soy sauce, too bad for him—and then thunder exploded. The turtle rocked. A fire-streak slashed before Mark's vision, dazzling his eyes, stunning his ears. Metal toned. Shock ran through his spacesuit and his bones. Two screens went dark. A pattern of holes gaped black in the wall, and air shrieked outward.

Even as he slammed his faceplate shut, he heard Kamolondo cry something in his mother language, and, "*Ah, non! Encore!*" A wild part of him wondered why the minister wanted an encore, until he remembered his French. "Oh, no! Again!" The same thing had happened to the turtle as had happened to the Go-Devil. A meteorite shower, hitherto uncharted, must be pounding the Moon.

Mark's hearing tolled toward silence. He sensed his heartbeat gone loud, smelled with unnatural sharpness the faint tang of ozone and his body in the suit, felt the fabric stiff against him. Outside, dust settled and he identified a tiny new crater, barely visible in the wan light.

He took a firm grip on his wits and tried the car's radio. Dead. And a helmet unit, necessarily small and simple, couldn't link with the trans-Lunar microwave system, had indeed no more than a mile of effective range.

He unstrapped himself. "Let's go," he said.

"What—what—" Behind the glass, Kamolondo's face was briefly fluid. Then his lips firmed. He asked in a level voice, "What do you mean?"

"A rock from space landed close by," Mark said. "Not big, but traveling at miles per second. It scattered chunks of surface material the way a military shell scatters shrapnel. We're wrecked. If Tom knew, he'd come for us, but he doesn't and I can't raise him." He glanced at the instruments. "We have six miles to go, and dawn is half an hour away."

Kamolondo did not stir. "Can we make it?" You had to admire how coolly he took the news.

"We've got to." Mark opened the lock.

They were out under Earth and the uncaring stars, in gloom and one faint circle of blue, when Kamolondo said, "I am very sorry to have exposed you to this."

"Nobody could have known, sir," Mark said. "One of the chances you take, living here. We expect the big meteorite showers, but little ones on long-period orbits are something else."

"I realize that. You are young, however, your whole life before you. I would rather have died alone back there."

"You're not such a doddering ruin yourself." Mark managed to laugh. "And who says we can't beat the sunrise? Come on."

He set off, with the long bounding stride of a colonist. You can walk fast under low gravity, if you know how. Though the sunrise line would sweep across this part of the Trace in about thirty minutes, it would need another half hour or so to reach Jordan Station. Thus, at six miles per hour, which was vigorous but not exhausting, they'd arrive in time. And afterward the Commission would doubtless buy a new turtle for the man who saved a VIP from a messy death. Maybe throw in a Go-Devil as well.

A curse brought Mark around on his heel. Kamolondo had stumbled. The Zairean got erect, pushed too hard, lost a second before the Moon drew him back to the ground, overbalanced when he hit and fell again. Fear rammed into Mark. Kamolondo didn't have the reflexes. In two weeks he could barely have learned to handle himself at an ordinary pace. Indoors, at that, without an airtank on his shoulders or tricky constant-volume joints at his knees. "Come on, sir!" Mark urged.

"I am trying." Kamolondo's breath was harsh.

He floundered over minutes and miles. Mark sweated, studied the radium-dialed chronometer on the wrist of his suit, clocked them by the kilometer stones. Too slow, too slow. The sun was catching up.

In some years, they could have stood a while under

Lunar daylight. Though the temperature would swiftly rise to the boiling point of water, the suits had thermostatic units and faceplates blocked off ultraviolet light. But now the sun was in a flare period. Lethal radiation, gamma rays, protons, electrons, seethed out of the storms upon it. Nothing less than a "tank," a vehicle armored in lead and screened by intense magnetic fields, could keep a man alive through such a day.

The tops of the easternmost relay masts began to shine.

Kamolondo halted. His face was invisible within the helmet, but he stood straight and said calmly, "There is no sense in both of us dying. Proceed."

For an instant, Mark was ready to obey. Tom, Judy, Dad's and Mother's hopes, his own dreams, were they to come to an end for him in the horror of radiation sickness?

But you don't abandon anyone on the Moon. And Kamolondo was a good joe, trying to do his best for his poor, hurt country.

Mark's mind sprang toward an answer. He felt suddenly, oddly at peace.

"Listen," he said. "Relax. Catch your breath. You're going to need it. We have about three miles left, but the last one is south instead of west." To strike directly across this shadowland, away from the markers, was to make death certain. "The sun's not far below the horizon now, but dawnline on the Moon travels eight miles an hour at the equator, a bit less here. So I figure we can rest a little. Then in the last ten or twelve minutes we can do those three miles."

"A mile . . . one-point-six kilometer. . . ." Kamolondo's voice sounded far and strange. "Impossible. You break every athletic record."

"On Earth! We're here. Our suits and equipment weigh as much as we do. But the total weight is still a third of what we'd have on Earth, stripped. And no air resistance. Also, running is a lot easier rhythm than what we were doing. Different from back home, of course. You only fall one-sixth as fast. Lean way forward, shove hard with one leg, rise just a bit off the ground. You'll have plenty of time to recover with the other foot. Watch me."

Kamolondo did. He tried it himself. Mark was surprised how well he managed, considering how awkward he'd been before. But a dash is, indeed, smoother than a fast walk, on any planet. The only question was whether they both had the endurance. One-sixth gravity or not, they must better the four-minute mile by some twenty percent, across thrice the distance.

Well, we'll soon know if we can. "Ready? We're off."

They ran.

Ghostly glowing, the kilometer stones fell behind, one by one by one. Beyond them and the glow cast by Earth, which seemed to fill the sky with an unreachable loveliness, was utter night. But the sun came striding.

Push, glide, come down, check. Push, glide, come down, check. Impact shivers back, through boots and feet and muscles. Airpumps roar, feeding oxygen to starved cells. Breath grows harsh, mouth dry, pulse frantic. You lurch, lose your balance, he helps you rise and you start again. He trips on an iron fragment and dances crazily, trying not to topple. You count the kilometers creeping past, and then lose count, for blindness has begun to drift across your eyes. You lose yourself, you are nothing but pain and weariness. Still you run!

Turn off here. Now you're bound straight south, and dawn gains on you. Not far to go. The uppermost crater crags are fiery. A piece of you thinks that you're close enough to call Tom on your suit radio, but no, he'd need too long to snatch a turtle out. Goodbye, Tom. Goodbye, Judy. Goodbye, universe I wanted to know. A spindle of zodiacal light climbs pearl-colored over the world's rim. The sun will follow, life-giver, death-giver.

Still you run.

And yonder is the cave-mouth of the garage. You fling yourself down the ramp. The blessed dark engulfs you, with ten feet of solid matter between you and the solar storm. You collapse on the floor next to your friend, strangling for breath. Only slowly do you understand that you will live.

There is no greater wonder.

They were inside and unsuited, swallowing huge amounts of coffee while Tom and Judy fussed about them, when Kamolondo said, "Mark, in that hour we became brothers."

It was spoken with such dignity that Mark was ashamed he could find no better answer than, "Aw, gee, nothing like that."

"You saved me." Kamolondo raised his head. "Yet more than owing you my life, I want to help you, and your brother and sister. In my position, I have both money and influence. You can come to Earth, study in the finest schools, make the best careers the planet has to offer. I would be proud if you return home with me."

Mark set down his cup. The Jordans stared at each other. Judy and Tom shook their heads slightly. Mark found himself close to laughter.

"Why, thanks," he said. "But come to Earth?" He swept his hand in a gesture that included the neat little kitchen, the rooms beyond, the subtle and powerful machines working topside, this whole station that was theirs. "Whatever *for?*"

QUEST

A chapter from The Annals of Chivalry *by Sir Thomas Hameward. Writing in his old age, this knight baron intended to continue Friar Parvus' artless chronicle of the High Crusade, in a style more elevated. Deriving as it does from medieval romances, the style is better described as more florid, while the account is autobiographical rather than historical. Nevertheless, if nothing else, the book is of some interest as depicting later stages of interaction between long-established starfaring societies and those humans who, carried out into the galaxy against their will, overcame their would-be enslavers and founded the English Empire.*

As nearly as the astrologers could calculate it from what scanty data were in the records, lost Terra had celebrated thirty Easters, and the year of Our Lord was 1375, when King Roger summoned a Grand Council to his seat of Troynovaunt. His purpose therein was threefold. Imprimis, he would have all of us join him in offering solemn thanks to Almighty God for His many mercies and blessings. Secundus, he would renew old acquaintances and strengthen bonds of fellowship through worldly festivities, as well as get to know the grown

children of his followers in desperate adventure, these
three decades agone. Tertius, he would discuss present
challenges and future endeavors with his lords, his
knights, and such of his ladies as nowadays held fiefs of
their own among the worlds.

From star after star they came, across as much as a
hundred light-years, in spaceships emblazoned with their
arms and achievements, themselves in splendor of em-
broideries, velvets, silklikes, and furs. Banners flew,
trumpets and drums resounded, horses and steeds of
unearthly stocks pranced proud, as they debarked at
the Port Royal and rode in, beneath high walls and
gleaming battlements, to the palace. Yet ever borne in
a place of honor were the weapons they had first brought
from England. These were less often sword or lance
than yeoman's bow, sergeant's ax, or serf's billhook.
Remember, O reader, the original company had not
been large, even reckoning in the civilians—men,
women, children, clerics—who joined Sir Roger de
Tourneville's free companions. Perforce, nearly everyone who survived the Crusade was eventually ennobled
and put in charge of some portion of their conquests. At
that, more than half the great folk now arriving were
nonhumans of one sort or another, who had accepted
the True Faith and paid homage to our puissant
sovereign.

Besides this reminder of our origins, the necessity of
caution was wholesomely chastening. We had broken
the cruel imperium of the Wersgorix, made them subject to us, and thereby earned the gratitude of those
other races whom they had decimated and oppressed.
Certain of our former enemies had become our friends
and, indeed, risen high among us because of their quick
intelligence and technical erudition. However, more of
them remained sullenly hostile. Some had attempted
revolt. Many had fled beyond our ken, to skulk in a
wilderness of uncharted suns. They still commanded
terrible powers. A single nuclear warhead would de-
molish this city and abolish both monarchy and Papacy.

We English were as yet thinly spread. Without the leadership and resources at Troynovaunt, our hegemony would be all too vulnerable to attack from without and within. Were it overthrown, that would spell the doom of Christendom, and belike of Adam's seed, among the stars. Therefore warcraft patrolled the Angevin System and virtually englobed Planet Winchester. No vessel might come near before it had been boarded and thoroughly inspected.

Natheless, the mood was joyous, the behavior often riotous, as English met English again, here at the heart of their triumphs. I own to downing more Jair liquor than was wise.

The carpenters at work in my head next morning may perhaps excuse my feelings at Mass. This I attended with my master, Sir Eric de Tourneville, youngest son of the King, whose squire I had lately become. Churches were so crowded that he sought a palace chapel; and the priest, Father Marcus of Uralura, preached a sermon that bade fair to last until Judgment. As I write, his words arise from the past and once more drone on within me.

"Praise God in sooth, and wonder at His foresightful care for us. The very fact that we are sundered from Terra exemplifies this. Only consider. A Wersgor scout vessel, seeking fresh territory for its people to overrun, landed at Ansby village with terror and slaughter. Hardy men counterattacked and seized it. Thereupon they sought to use it to end the French war and liberate the Holy Land; but they were tricked into a long voyage hither, where they must fight for survival. By divine grace, as well as valor and cunning, they prevailed. In the original turmoil, navigational notes were lost. The stars are so many, each planet of theirs so vast and preoccupying, that no explorer has found a way back to the mother world. But do not join those who lament the failure. Reflect, instead, that thereby Rome and Jerusalem have been spared possible destruction in space warfare. Meanwhile, the exiles were *forced* to bring

Christian teaching and English rule to the benighted heathen. Enormous have been the rewards, secular as well as spiritual, albeit the latter are, of course, all that have any real importance—"

I have written down this part of the homily as a belated penance for having, about then, fallen asleep. Otherwise I was aflame with eagerness. My master had confided to me something of the endeavor which he would propose.

Being a son of John the Red, Count of New Lincolnshire and Baron of P'thng'gung, and being the squire of Sir Eric, a prince of the blood though not destined for the throne, I was present when the Grand Council met. Like my counterparts, I was kept so busy dashing to and fro with refreshments that I had little chance to observe. Recollection blurs into a brightness of sunlight striking through stained glass at tapestries, mounted weapons and trophies, rich garments, jewelry of gold and precious stones; a rumble of voices, now and then a shout or guffaw, while an orchestra tweedles unheard in a balcony; odors of meat, wine, ale, incense, humanity thickening the air; hounds and daggercats getting underfoot as they snatch at bones thrown down to them; gray hair, heavy bodies, faces scarred and furrowed, with youth here and there along the tables to relieve this dignity; in the Griffin Seat, King Roger, his own olden blade naked on his lap, emblem of power and of the fidelity that he has pledged to his people.

But I remember Sir Eric's words, when the microphone came to him in order of precedence; for they struck that assembly mute with wonder. Those words are on record, as is the debate that followed. I will only set down the gist of them. He stood, hawk-featured, bronze-locked, his frame lean and medium-tall—a young man, quite newly knighted, though he had wandered and fought widely—and cried forth:

"Your Highness, my lords and ladies, I've an undertaking for us, and what an undertaking! Not another punitive expedition against Wersgor holdouts, not another random search for Terra, but the quest for a treasure great and sacred—the object of chivalry since Arthur or before, the outward sign of salvation and vessel of power, that chalice into which at the Last Supper Our Lord and Saviour did pour the wine which became His most precious blood—the Holy Grail!"

Amazement went through the chamber like a gale wind. The King responded first, in that hard practicality which was ever his: "What are you thinking of? Is not the Sangreal back somewhere in England, whither Joseph of Arimathea brought it? I've heard my share of legends about the matter, and meaning no disrespect, some of them are pretty wild. But they agree that none save he who is without sin may ever achieve the Grail— and I know you better than that, my lad. We've more urgent business than a harebrained dash into God knows what."

Sir Eric flushed. Once the speech he had composed beforehand was exhausted, he was no orator. "Well, 'tis like this," he replied. "We, er, everybody acknowledges there's a dangerous shortage of saints' relics among us. We've merely those few that got taken along from the abbey at Ansby. And they're nothing much; not even a splinter of the True Cross among them. Superstition is causing people to venerate things that Father Marcus tells me can't possibly be genuine. I hate to imagine what bad luck—what Heavenly displeasure that could bring on us. But if we had the actual Holy Grail, now—"

Stumblingly, he explained. His farings, and a certain innate friendliness and openmindedness, had brought him together with numerous nonhumans. Of late they included a former Wersgor space captain named Insalith. He was an obstinate pagan, who attributed all events to the operations of quantum mechanics. However, otherwise he had accepted civilization. His religious blindness made his story the more plausible, in that piety could not have led him into wishful thinking.

Now retired, he had many years before been on several of his race's expeditions prospecting for new worlds to conquer and settle. They had come upon one afar that looked promising. It was untenanted except for a set of buildings that, in retrospect, resembled a Christian monastery. Landing to investigate afoot, the Wersgorix spied a monster, a veritable dragon, but it shunned them and they approached the church. There they met a few beings who, in retrospect, seemed human. Through the open doors they glimpsed something silvery and chalice-like upon an altar, and heard ineffably sweet music. Though the white-robed persons offered them no threat, such awe came upon them that they fled. Afterward, if only for fear of ridicule from their hard-souled colleagues and damage to their careers, they filed a report that tests had shown this planet to be biochemically unsuitable for colonization.

Today, having outlived the rest of that crew, having seen our kind enter his realm and erect houses of God, Insalith yearned back. Perhaps yonder was a proof of the Gospels that would satisfy his scientific mind and bring him spiritual peace. He was willing to navigate a ship there.

"If we humble mortals could make it into space," argued Sir Eric, "the Holy Grail should have no difficulties. I don't believe we dare neglect this account. It might prove false, I grant you, but then, it might truly be a sign unto us, a command from Heaven." Meanwhile his nostrils twitched. He yearned to be off on such an incredible venture. I had come to know him.

"Aye, go, go, in Jesus' name!" cried Archbishop William, who was himself of Wersgor stock.

King Roger stroked his chin, stared upward at the vaulted ceiling and the battle banners that hung from it, and said slowly: "Remember everything else we've taken counsel about. We can't dispatch a fleet. The risk of our homes getting raided would become much too great. But—well, son, you do have a ship of your own, and—and—" His voice lifted to a roar. His fist crashed down on the chair arm. "And by our Lady, how I wish I were going along!"

I forebear to describe the tumult that followed, before Sir Eric won leave to depart. Next day, in his exhilaration, he swept like fire through a tournament, unhorsing every opponent until at last he could ride to accept a wreath from the Queen of Love and Beauty. She was Matilda Mountjoy, of whom even I already had knowledge, and he was on a unicorn. However, the genetic craftsmen who supply animals of this sort have not yet succeeded in giving them the ability to make fine distinctions among ladies.

The *Bonaventura* was of modest size and armament, as nuclear missiles and energy projectors go. Half a dozen men, two nonhumans, and their horses crowded its hull. Luckily, the engine was of the best, weaving us in and out of 4-space at a quasi-velocity which brought us to our goal, far outside mapped regions, in about a month.

Just the same, that proved a wearisome journey. The fault did not lie with my fellow Englishmen. Like me, they were young and cheerful, buoyed rather than oppressed by the sanctity of their mission. Besides the knight and myself, we numbered two men-at-arms, a planetologist, and a pilot-cum-engineer-cum-gunner in case any automaton failed. To pass the time, we practiced combat techniques, gambled, drank, pursued minor arts, and bragged about our feats on various planets and women.

Nor can I accuse Insalith of creating tedium. In appearance he was a typical Wersgor, though age had stooped his squat five-foot frame, made gaunt the short tail, faded the hairless blue skin, wrinkled the snouted face and pointed ears, dulled the yellow eyes. None of these changes were overly conspicuous, and he retained a sharp mind and dry wit. We enjoyed listening to his reminiscences of voyages and deeds, aye, even as an officer in the war against our fathers.

Be it confessed, our chaplain was what often made the traveling dismal. Father Marcus was an Uraluran, converted and ordained, abrim with zeal. He preached, he reproved, he set unreasonable penances, he stared chillingly out of his three huge orbs, he waggled a flexible finger or windmilled all four arms or sent his blobby green countenance through the most hideous contortions as he quacked about what transgressors we were. (I write "he" for lack of a better word, the Uralurans being hermaphrodites who reproduce only on ceremonial occasions. To this very day, because of their modesty, that fact is not widely known off their planet. Marvelous are the works of God. Yet at the time, I could not keep from wishing that He had not chosen to create a species so devoid of human failings.) Besides his seven bony feet of height, the ecclesiastical authority bestowed upon him daunted us.

After all, we were in quest of the Holy Grail. If that truly was the thing we sought, then we could not attain to it if we were wicked. We would fail, and belike perish miserably. On the other hand, if our information had misled us, then we must be sufficiently well-informed on spiritual matters and free of pride to recognize this when we arrived. Else we might fall into some snare of Satan.

Father Marcus had therefore ordered a special program for the library of the ship's computer—every tale of the Grail that anybody could remember, with commentaries upon the accuracy of those memories, as well as a compendium of theology. And he kept shriving us and shriving us.

Sir Eric himself, while not always without merriment, had grown unwontedly pious. I often saw him on his knees in the chapel cabin. To the crucifix he uplifted his cross-hilted blade. It was a Singing Sword, whose haft he had commissioned from an electronician. Lately he had ordered me to insert therein a tape of hymns, that the weapon would chant if brought into action.

Father Marcus had opined that we would be blasphemous to carry firearms, let alone scientific instruments,
into the possible Presence. But Insalith had bespoken a
dragon. Quite likely, we thought, the forces of Hell had
established a watcher, which could not enter the sacred
precincts but would seek to deter Christians from doing
so. Sir Eric did not mean to go altogether unarmed.

The planet was a white-swirled sapphire circling a
golden sun, circled in its turn by two small, silvery
moons. Spectroscopy showed the air to be salubrious
for us, and an instrumented biochemical probe reported
no poisons but, rather, edible life upon arable soil.
There was not so much of that soil, for land consisted
simply of islands, a few large, most not. This, though,
meant that climate almost everywhere was mild. "If
ever the Holy Grail was borne from Terra," exclaimed
our captain, "how perfect a new home for it!"

"Ah, but is not your intent to bring it back?" asked
Insalith. Somehow, strangely, he seemed alarmed.

"We cannot remove it without permission of its guardians," replied Father Marcus, "but perhaps they will
allow folk to make pilgrimage hither."

"That would be a profitable passenger route to have,"
murmured our pilot.

Horrified at his crassness, the priest gave him five
hundred Aves and as many Paternosters to say, but Sir
Eric declared that we could not afford the time just yet.
He was white-hot with impatience to land.

Insalith identified the island of the shrine, a major
one, and instruments did reveal a trio of buildings near
a lake at its center. They also confirmed a lack of other
habitation, of any trace of native intelligence. Had God
reserved this world since the Creation for its present
use? A chill went along my spine.

Descending on reverentially throttled gravitics, we
set down in a meadow three leagues from our goal.
"Piety doubtless requires we approach on foot," Sir
Eric said. "Alayne and Robert"—he meant our pilot and

planetologist—"shall stay inboard, ready to carry word home should we come to grief . . . if, h'm, they can't scramble to our aid."

He himself made a splendid sight as he trod forth into day. The sun turned helmet, chain mail, the shield on his left arm agleam; its radiance caressed fluttering plume and scarlet cloak and a pennon atop the antenna of a radio transceiver secured to his left shoulder. Behind him, I bore the de Tourneville gonfalon and Father Marcus a gilt crucifix. At their backs, the men-at-arms, Samkin Brown and Hobden Tyler, carried ax and pike respectively on either side of withered little Insalith.

Ah, the country was like Eden. Overhead reached a blueness full of wings. The cries and songs of those flying creatures descended through a breeze whose warmth brought odors akin to spice and perfume. Grass-like growth rippled underfoot, intensely green, starred with white flowers. As verdant and graceful were the trees, which soon grew more dense, until we were walking through a forest. There boughs met above us like a cathedral roof and sunbeams pierced rustling dimness. We had no trouble with underbrush, for we had come upon a trail leading in our direction, broad and hard-packed as if by something ponderous.

Sir Eric broke the hush: "A glorious planet. I hope to Mary we don't get our nobles at feud over whose fief it shall be."

"God have mercy!" wailed Father Marcus. "How can you think such a thing, here of all places?"

"Well, they thought it at the Holy Sepulchre back on Terra, didn't they?" the knight replied. "Yes, and fought it, too. You don't have to fret about man's fallen state. People like me do."

"Nay, that's my vocation," the cleric protested. "Why did God leave us Uralurans free of the seven deadly sins, if not to set your wayward race an example?"

Ignorant of theology, Samkin blurted, "What, d'you mean your kind are not fallen? You're, uh, *angels?*"

"No, no, no!" said Father Marcus in haste. "My poor

species is all too prone to such temptations as quirling and vosheny; my own confessor has often had to set me a severe penance for golarice."

"An object of veneration in your midst would surely inspire you Christians of every sort to reform themselves," suggested Insalith. "Isn't it reasonable, in your belief, that your God has been saving the relic for this purpose?"

"I have cogitated on that question," Father Marcus answered. "In the era of the Table Round, none save Galahad the pure could reach to the Holy Grail. Yet through him it was, for a moment, revealed to that whole company; and earlier, at the first Eucharist, even Judas beheld it. For this imperilled outpost of Christendom, divine policy may conceivably have been further modified. Or it may not have been. We can but go forward, look for ourselves, then pray for illumination." He paused before adding: "One thing does strike me as curious. Salvation is not easily won. Nor should the Grail be, that is its sacrosanct emblem. Whether or not God surrounds it with obstacles, one would expect that the Devil—"

As if on cue, a hoarse bellowing interrupted him. We stopped in our tracks. Terror stabbed me. A stench as of fire and brimstone rolled through the forest air. Around a bend in the path crawled a dragon.

Fifty feet in length it was, from fanged maw to spiked tailtip. Steel-gray scales armored it. The six clawed feet that pulled it along made earth shiver beneath monstrous weight. Smoke gusted from its gullet, within which flames flickered. Straight toward us it moved, and its roars smote our ears with hammerblows.

"It left *us* alone!" I heard Insalith yammer.

"You were heathens," rapped Sir Eric.

"Quick, call the ship!"

"No. The leaf canopy—no way to aim—the beams would slay us too."

"The Beast, Satan's Beast," moaned Father Marcus. He fell to his double-jointed knees and held the crucifix aloft. It trembled like a twig in the wind. *"Apage, diabole!"*

The dragon paid no attention. Closer it came. I was aware of the men-at-arms, about to bolt in panic, and of myself ready to join them.

"God send the right!" shouted Sir Eric, and plunged to do battle. His sword blazed forth. "St. George for merry England!"

Somehow that restored my heart to me. I ran after him, howling my own defiance, the spearhead atop my standard pole slanted down. After an instant, Samkin and Hobden followed.

Sir Eric was already engaged. His blade flew, struck, slashed, drew foul black blood from the unprotected nose of the firedrake. And it sang as it hewed. I heard—

—not Latin but English; not a *Te Deum* but:

"Oh, give me a haunch of ruddy beef,
And nut-brown ale in my pot,
Then a lusty wench with a sturdy arse
To bounce upon my cot—"

and realized, dismayed, that I had gotten the wrong tape.

If doomed by my folly, I could at least die like a man. I thrust my weapon down the flaming gape. The cross-arm jammed tight and our banner charred. The dragon hiccoughed thunderously. Meanwhile our companions were stabbing and chopping away.

The creature hissed like a cataract. It scuttled backward. Incredulous, we saw it twist around a tree and make haste out of our sight.

For a long while, we stared at each other, not quite understanding our deliverance. Strength fled me, I sank to the ground and darkness whirled through my head. When I returned to my senses, I felt the priest shaking me and jubilating, "Rouse, my son, rouse, and give thanks to the Lord God of Hosts!"

We did, in fervor, regardless of smoke-stained garments and sweat-stinking bodies. Gratitude welled up in my bosom, and I mingled my tears with those of two hardened sergeants. How strange, how perturbing in a distant fashion, to see the frown upon Sir Eric's brow.

Well, I thought, whatever the trouble was, it did take his mind off my blunder.

I reckoned myself as brave as most fighting men, and had hunted dangerous animals erenow. Natheless, for a space I trembled, tingled, and tottered. That was less because we had been imperilled than because we had evidently encountered a thing from Hell. Samkin and Hobden were in like case. Sir Eric, though, remained withdrawn, while Father Marcus was full of exaltation and Insalith trotted eagerly onward.

Steadiness came back to me as we fared; for had we not in fact been victorious, and was that not a wondrous portent? When we arrived, my resolution turned to awe.

We had emerged from the wood into cleared acres of garden and orchard. Foreign to us were yon blossoms, hedgerows, fruits aglow in mellow afternoon light; or were they? Did they not hint at those roses, apples, hawthorns, and other English beauties whereof our parents spoke so wistfully? The lake blinked and sheened on our right, argent on azure; beyond it lifted a serenity of hills. Before us were the buildings.

They were three in number, arranged around a mosaic courtyard. Their smallness reminded me of that stable where Our Lord was born, the poor cottages that sheltered Him during His ministry, the unpretentious loft room wherein He gathered His disciples for the Last Supper. But they were exquisite, of alabaster hue and perfect workmanship. Colonnaded, one seemed to be for utility; opposite it stood another, whose glazed windows suggested a dormitory and refectory. Between them, facing us across the pavement, rose the church. I thought it must be the epitome of that English Perpendicular style which our architects strove to emulate from drawings done by some of those who remembered. Slender pillars, ogive arches and windows, saints in their niches, rose beneath twin towers. Melody wafted thence, notes surely like those from the harps of Paradise. The doors stood open in an eternal welcome.

We hastened among the flowerbeds. Gravel crunched under our feet, until the courtyard rang. In the mosaic I saw, delicately wrought, a Tree of Jesse.

We halted at a staircase flanked by sculptures of the Lamb and the Fish. Suddenly I unbuckled my helmet and tucked it beneath my arm. A man had stepped out onto the porch.

He came to a stop, there above us, handsome, solemn, hair and beard as white as his robe, right hand lifted in benediction. Upon his brow shone a golden crown. In his left hand he bore a trident, and he had limped. A supernatural thrill passed over me, for I recalled the Fisher King.

Organ tones formed words of Norman French: "In the name of the father, and of the Son, and of the Holy Ghost, well met, pilgrims. Enter ye now unto the mystery ye have sought, that which shall save your peoples."

Father Marcus' response wavered. "Have we, have we indeed come . . . to the abiding place . . . of the Sangreal?"

"Enter," said the crowned man gently, "and see, and give praise."

Sir Eric too removed his helmet. He laid it down beside his shield and scabbarded sword. The men-at-arms did likewise, and I. We signed ourselves. I felt that I read anguish, indecision, behind the knight's stiff features, and wondered anew, with a touch of dread, what wrongness possessed his soul.

"Come," said the crowned man, and gestured us toward him.

Insalith hesitated. "I am not christened," he said in a near whisper.

The other smiled. "You will be, my son, you will be, as will every sentience in the universe. Come you also and worship."

Slowly, we mounted the stairs.

For a moment, splendor overwhelmed me. Windows depicting Bible scenes cast their rainbow glow over nave, aisles, choir, columns, the Stations of the Cross wrought in gold. Under a great rose window, candles burned before an image of the Virgin that seemed alive in its tenderness and majesty. Music soared amidst fragrances. At a font shaped like a lily, we dipped our fingers and again dared bless ourselves.

Our gaze went to the altar. Upon it, below a crucifix of piteous realness, sheened a silver chalice. It must have stood three feet high on a broad base, though the grace of its proportions came near cloaking that size. Attired in white habits, two women kept vigil at the sides, their heads bowed in prayer, beads streaming between their fingers.

The man of the trident urged us onward. At the rail he turned about, traced the Cross, and said gladly:

"Lo, here is the joy of chivalrous desiring, the Grail of Our Lord and Saviour Jesus Christ. Before your fathers ventured against the paynim of the stars, God transported it hither and set it in care of these pure maidens and my unworthy self, that we might guard it until men had need of it among them. Fear not, my sons. We shall take communion, and you shall abide this night, and tomorrow you shall bear the Holy Grail back to your people."

Father Marcus prostrated himself. Insalith went on all fours, the Wersgor attitude of submission. After a heartbeat, Samkin, Hobden, and I knelt. Yet—I quailed in my breast—we could not take our heed off the sisters. They were identical twins, young, fair beyond any man's dreams. Their garb did not conceal sweet curves beneath. Oh, I thought amid the racketing of my pulse, God forgive me my weakness, but it *has* been a long journey.

And Sir Eric stayed on his feet. His own eyes were aimed at the warden, like lanceheads.

Did the lame one show the least unease? "Why do you stand thus, my son?" he asked. "Kneel, confess

your sins—to God Himself, Who will absolve you—while
I fetch the wine and the Host."

The knight's words tramped forth: "Why is the cup so
large? I expected it would be small and simple, as
befitting celebrants who were not wealthy. This is the
size of a soup kettle."

"It must needs hold the salvation of the world."

"Let me examine it. You understand. If it is a for-
gery, and I bring it home, I shall be doing the Devil's
work."

"Why, no. I agree, well, true, authentication is necessary. But you are not qualified to judge. It will be no
sin if you convey the vessel to those who are—your
Pope, your King-Emperor. Rather, that is your duty."

"Step aside! On my head be this." And Sir Eric
started past the crowned man, toward the chancel.

I gasped in horror. "Sacrilege!" hooted Father Marcus from the floor.

The warden snatched after the prince. Sir Eric shoved
him off. He stumbled, his trident clattered to the flag-
stones. "Beatrice, Berenice, stop him!" he cried. "Sir,
you'd not lay hand on the holy sisters, would you?"

The maidens moved to bar Sir Eric's way. Gently but
remorselessly, he cast arms about their waists and
dragged them from in front of the altar. He let them go,
took the chalice, and lifted. I saw by the motion that
the weight was heavy.

It was as if time died while he turned the huge cup
over and over beneath his eyes. Finally he looked across
it at the damsels. They had shrunk back against the rail,
but the glances that responded to his were quickening
away from timidity. Even in the wan light, I saw a flush
spread across his cheeks, and theirs.

The crowned man picked up his trident and shook it.
"You'll burn forever, unless you are mad and know not
what you do!" he shouted. "Englishmen, seize him!
Save the Holy Grail!"

I groaned as my heart tore asunder.

Sir Eric set the chalice down again. Luminance ran

blood-red and heaven-blue over his mail. Straightening, he called to us: "We'll see who is the evildoer. If I am, how could I be a menace to the veritable Grail? And should not its guardians be perfect in the Faith? Father Marcus, arise and put these persons through the Catechism."

He thumbed his radio while he strode down to us. I heard him speak a command, not to the men aboard our ship but directly to the computer: "Activate your theological program."

Our chaplain may have been somewhat unversed in human ways, but he could scarcely miss seeing how the warden snarled or hearing the sisters shriek. I thought fleetingly that those feminine cries were not altogether agonized. The priest could be swift when he chose. He sprang to join Sir Eric in confrontation of the robed man.

"My good sir," he puffed, "you should be happy to establish your bona fides by explicating a few simple doctrinal points. From whence proceeds the Holy Ghost?"

"Are you mad too?" yelled the crowned one. "If I were iniquitous—in as grave a matter as this is—would God let me administer the sacraments? They would not be valid."

Father Marcus stiffened. "Ah, ha! That sounds very much like the Donatist heresy. Let us go into details, if you please."

Pausing only to consult his reference by radio, our chaplain set question after question. They bewildered me. I must needs admire the boldness with which the man stood his ground and flung back responses.

After minutes, Father Marcus wheezed a sigh, shook his head, and declared, "No more. You have in addition exposed yourself as an Arian, a Pelagian, a Catharist, and a Gnostic. This cup of yours must be a blasphemous fraud. Who are you, in truth?"

Sir Eric crouched, a leopard out of England's arms. His gaze lashed forth, to Insalith in the shadows. "You led us hither," he said low.

The Wersgor reached under his coat. Forth came an energy pistol. "Hold where you are," he rasped.

We froze. A single sweep of the beam from that weapon could incinerate us. He stalked toward the altar.

"Wait!" howled the crowned man, in the principal Wersgor tongue. "You'd not set it off?"

"Yes," said Insalith. "Destroy the evidence, and these monsters as well." He entered the chancel. The maidens screamed and fled from him. He reached the false Grail.

Sir Eric pounced. He snatched the trident from its owner's grasp, and hurled it. Insalith lurched. Tine-deep, the weapon shuddered in his belly. He fell, and his blood washed the floor of that house which was never a church.

Bonaventura throbbed about us. Stars crowded the viewports. We were bound home.

Sir Eric summoned us to the messroom—Father Marcus, the two crewmen, the two men-at-arms, the two maidens, and myself. Beatrice and Berenice had discarded their coifs, revealing topaz-hued locks, and belted their gowns closely, revealing marvelous shapes. Weary but triumphant, the knight laughed aloud at the head of the table and bade us be seated.

"The prisoner has confessed," he said. "I needed no violence upon him. His nerve broke when I threatened to take that alleged relic along on board."

"What is it in truth, what device of Satan?" asked Father Marcus low.

Sir Eric grinned. "Nothing so terrible," he answered, "although dangerous enough. It contains a nuclear bomb in the base, using a fissionable transuranic of small critical mass. And there are sensors worked into the ornamentation, and a recognition program keyed to detonate it when in the presence of either my royal father or the Pope. The blast would not have been of more than tactical force, but it would have sufficed to lay Troynovaunt waste, and thereby all our hopes."

"This, then, was a, a Wersgor plot from the, the beginning, my lord?" I stammered.

Sir Eric nodded. "Aye, hatched in a secret base of their outlaw remnants—whose location I now have. He who played the Fisher King is a human traitor, a criminal who fled from justice. The conspirators found him, trained him, and promised him rich reward. These damsels"—he bowed toward them—"are clones of a comely woman who never knew that a minor 'accident' was arranged to remove a few cells from her. Accelerated growth produced adult bodies within a half-dozen years." He smiled. "Yet they remain daughters of Eve, raised among falsehoods and therefore innocent in themselves. We'll bring them home baptized, I'm sure. Their story, their virginity, their consecration as true nuns will doubtless inspire many of us to live better lives."

The twins blushed rosy. However, the glance they exchanged, out of large blue eyes, seemed less than elated.

"The whole thing was cleverly done," Sir Eric went on. "We could well have been deceived, and carried yon fatal engine back. It's God's mercy that petty flaws in the plan, because the Wersgorix are not human and do not understand us in our innermost depths—those flaws betrayed it."

"What were they, my son?" wondered Father Marcus. "I am fain to think a divine revelation was vouchsafed you."

"Oh, no," denied Sir Eric, raising his palm. "Never me. I am no saint, but a sinner who stumbles more often than most. On that account, mayhap my hope of doing some holy work was higher than the conspirators foresaw, and led me to look closer when their illusions did not quite meet my expectations.

"I thought that the dragon yielded far too easily, the more so when the Singing Sword was—well—In a matter of such importance, would Satan let his minion flee after a few cuts? Could the beast have been merely a biotechnical device, set there because it belonged in the picture but not intended to give serious resistance?

"The Fisher King bore no sign of being ordained, and legend does not make him a priest. But he offered us Holy Communion. He spoke reverently of the Grail, but did not doff his crown in its chapel. His haste to conduct the business and see us begone struck me as unseemly.

"The chalice itself was larger and massier than was reasonable.

"Er—be it confessed, and intending no discourtesy, when I embraced these two charming young ladies, what immediately stirred in my heart was lust. Would God have made a person as gross as me the bearer of His Grail?"

Sir Eric winced. "I wanted to believe," he finished. "How I longed to believe! But I decided we should put matters to a test. If I were mistaken, on my soul be the wrath. God knows I am weak and sinful, but He also knows I swore an oath of fealty to King and Church."

We men hailed him with the honor that was his due, the maidens with adoration. Those twain had not hitherto understood how wretched was their lot. Now joy blossomed in them, and a convent was the last place they wished to enter. I thought that Father Marcus had better make haste to give them Christian instruction, and my lord to find them good husbands when we came home.

WHEREVER YOU ARE

The monster laid a taloned hand on the girl's shoulder. She jumped, startled, and whirled about to face bulging red eyes. The monster opened jaws full of teeth that glowed.

The girl wrenched free. "What the devil do you want?" she yelled.

"Eek," said the monster, stepping back a pace. *"Urgu aki, Zivar."*

The girl advanced threateningly. "The next time you forget your manners," she snapped, "the next time you forget who I am, you peasant, may heaven protect you!"

The monster wailed and scuttled down the path, as if hoping the man would come along and save him from the girl.

Ulrica Ormstad added a few soldierly oaths and followed. She knew they were wasted; nobody understood any Terrestrial language for several thousand kilometers. (Unless, she thought scornfully, you counted Didymus Mudge. But a corpulent help he was!) Nevertheless, her emotions needed a safety valve, and she could barely speak Harakunye, let alone swear in it.

Far down underneath, she admitted her anger stemmed from loneliness. And even, it might be, fear. She was

84

trained to face battle, or storm, or the sudden failure of human engineering under conditions never foreseen by man. The situation here, on this island, held some of those elements. But basically it was another sort of dilemma, involving a worse way to die.

Therefore, Ulrica Ormstad fell back on pride. She was a major in the militechnic service of New Scythia, free-born to full rights in Clan Swenson. Let the universe beware!

Long strides carried her quickly through the jungle. Its leaves were stiff and reddish blue: vegetation on Epstein's Planet photosynthesized, but the compound used was not chlorophyl. At first the pervasive smell had sickened her a little, but she soon grew used to it. Now, when she returned to her home world, or visited Mother Earth—if she ever did—their familiar biochemistry would stink for a while.

The native glowbugs, spectacularly clustered where thickets made a twilight, or the beautiful crystal flowers, or the delicate chiming of bellfruit, had ceased to interest her. She would swap it all for a chance to leave this hell-hole.

The game trail ended and Ulrica stepped out onto a broad white beach. The ship *Geyvadigur* lay anchored inside a sheltered lagoon: for the hidden sun was close enough to raise considerable tides, even in the absence of a satellite. Boats were drawn up on the sand, where the crew had pitched conical pink tents. The sailor whom she had frightened waited timidly. Doubtless Captain Zalakun wished to question her.

Ulrica sighed. She had gone walking in the jungle just to get away from the endless struggle with Harakunye grammar. For one honest human conversation, in any human language, she would trade her soul. Make it Swedish, and she'd throw in her sidearm.

Didymus Mudge emerged from one of the tents. He had been playing with a silly-looking affair inside, wooden frameworks and inclined planes, as indeed he had done for a week now. The ship's carpenter, who had been helping, squeaked at sight of Ulrica and tried to hide behind the man. Since Mudge stood only one hundred eighty centimeters tall, and even the smallest Epsteinian was three meters long including the tail, this was not very successful.

"Oh. Hello." Mudge tried to smile. "What were you doing, Miss Ormstad?"

Ulrica put hands on hips and glared downward. Mudge was slender as well as short, with sandy hair, cowlick, an undistinguished freckled face, and large blue eyes nearsighted behind contact lenses. His tattered gray zipsuit did not make him more impressive.

"I will give you three guesses," snorted the girl. "I have been making an atomic-powered aircraft with my bare hands? No. Then I have been weaving vines into a radio circuit, to call base and have them come get us? No. I have been practicing to swim all the way to Lonesome Landing? Still no. *Kors i Herrans namn!* And you are supposed to be bright enough to teach children!"

"I . . . er . . . yes," said the Earthman meekly.

Ulrica looked him up and down. She herself had the big bones and powerful muscles of a human breed which had spent generations under the gee-and-a-half of New Scythia. It did not make her less graceful, in a full-hipped full-breasted way; on her, a salt-stained tunic and clan kilt looked good. Thick brown braids lay tightly around a face of high cheekbones, straight nose, broad firm mouth, and wide-set green eyes. Even beneath the perpetually leaden sky of this planet, her skin glowed tawny.

"And still Earth manages to be the leader of the League," she murmured. "I do not understand it. I just plain do not." Louder: "Well, what have you been tinkering with? Are you making an abstraction ladder in there, to teach semantics? Better you learn to talk with these lizards first!"

"That isn't my forte," said Mudge in defensive tone. "You were trained from childhood to pick up languages fast, tone discrimination, mnemonics— You might as well expect me, at my time of life, to take up ballet, as learn Harakunye from scratch in a week!"

Ulrica laughed.

"What is it?" asked Mudge.

"The thought of you in tights," she chortled, "doing a *pas de deux* with an Epsteinian."

"Some people have a strange sense of humor," grumbled Mudge. He rubbed his peeling nose. Enough ultraviolet had penetrated the clouds to give his untanned hide a bad sunburn.

"I have been so busy studying," said Ulrica. Mirth had eased her, and she wanted to offer friendliness to this fellow castaway whom she had scarcely seen so far. "It was necessary I be able to talk with them. As soon as one sailor got restless, I let him go and started with another. I only stopped to eat and sleep. But you, what have you been working on?"

Mudge pointed to his wrist watch. "This was damaged," he said. "It kept running, and I know the precise time when it was deranged. But now it's either fast or slow, I'm not sure which. Checking it against my pulse suggests it is slow, but I have always had an irregular pulse. I—"

"*What?*" yelped Ulrica. "At this time you worry about your little tin watch?"

"It isn't either," said Mudge. "It's an antique: a very good seventeen-jewel Swiss chrono. My mother gave it to me at graduation. My graduation, that is, not hers. Though she does have a degree herself, from the same place, Boston Uni—"

"On a desert island," said Ulrica to heaven, "*x* thousand kilometers from the one human outpost on this entire planet, surrounded by natives of absolutely unknown culture and intentions, he worries about his graduation present. *Du store Gud!* Also *lieber Gott, nom du Dieu,* and *Bozhe moi!*"

"But wait," bleated Mudge. "It's important! Let me explain!"

Ulrica stalked down to the shore, trailing a string of remarks which ionized the air behind her.

The sailor stood patiently at a beached rowboat. He was a typical Epsteinian, which is to say he looked rather like a small slim tyrannosaur with a bulldog face and round coxcombed head. His scales were dark-blue on top, pale below, and zebra striped; his eyes were red and bulging, his teeth phosphorescent yellow. He wore merely crossed belts, one of which held a knife and one a pouch. The data book—thank a lifetime's Amazonian training for the quick-wittedness which had made Ulrica pocket that, along with a bottle of vitamin pills, when the spaceboat exploded—said the autochthones were not actually reptiles, being warm-blooded and placental. Neither were they mammals, lacking the appropriate glands as well as hair. They looked ferocious enough, but most of the *Geyvadigur* crew had shown Yes, Master personalities.

The officers, though, appeared to be something else again.

Ulrica entered the boat. The sailor launched it, jumped in, and rowed her out to the ship. Tension gathered within her. After the captain understood she was working on his language, he had turned the dull job of helping over to his crew. A few hours ago, one of the mates—Ulrica assumed that was their status—had interviewed her briefly and gone off wagging his tail. He must have reported she was now proficient enough to talk intelligently.

The ship loomed over her. Except for the ornate figurehead, it might at first glance have been an early Terrestrial steamer, with high stacks, monstrous sidewheels, and two schooner-rigged masts in case of emergency. Then you began to notice things. There probably wasn't a door on all Epstein's Planet, except at Lonesome Landing: likely to pinch a tail. Since the natives sat on those same organs, they had never invented chairs. The treads of all ladders, and the ratlines, were a meter apart. Ulrica had inspected the engines and been surprised to find them oil-burning steam turbines; why the craft then used paddles instead of screws could only be explained by the whimsical gods who, on Earth, had once put engines in the front of rear-wheel drive automobiles.

The *Geyvadigur* had both magnetic and spring-powered gyro compasses, but otherwise no hint of electromagnetic technology—which scuttled all hope of radioing for help. Quite likely the eternal damp atmosphere accounted for the Harakuni failure to study such phenomena, even though the nearby sun lit every night with fabulous auroras. Poverty of resources, or sheer historical accident, might explain the fact that there were no firearms aboard. The craft did, however, sport catapults, oil bombs, and flame throwers.

Ulrica would have felt better had her own pistol been of any use. But she had exhausted its charge against hungry sea snakes, as she and Mudge paddled their fragment of spaceboat toward this island; and when the vessel went, there hadn't been time to grab extra clips.

The sailor helped her up a Jacob's ladder. The decks were littered with his fellows, polishing, holystoning, splicing, the usual nautical chores. A mate stalked about with a barbed-wire whip, touching up an occasional back to encourage progress. Ulrica stamped as haughtily as possible to the captain's cabin. (Another foreign detail. It was a thatch hut, its walls lined with a tasteful collection of weapons and Epsteinian skulls.)

Captain Zalakun bared his fangs politely as the girl entered. Beside him squatted a gaunt male with an eyeglass and a sash whereon a dozen medals tinkled together. A saw-toothed scimitar lay drawn on the table. Combats between Epsteinians, whose scales bounced back a mere slash, must be awesome.

"Ssss," greeted the captain. "Coil your tail, *Zivar*."

At least he used the aristocratic title. The only alternative Ulrica had found in Harakunye was *Yaldazir*, which seemed a contraction of a phrase meaning "Offal of an unspeakable worm." If you weren't addressed by one title, you necessarily had the other.

She hunkered and waited.

Zalakun turned toward the eyeglass. "*Zivar,*" he said, "this is the monster called Orumastat, which we took from the sea with its slave four days ago." He meant Epsteinian days, of course, forty-six hours long. Turning to Ulrica: "Orumastat, this is the most glorious Feridur of Beradura, who heads our expedition. You have not seen him before because he was belowdecks playing *karosi.* Now that you can talk, Feridur of Beradura will let you know his magnanimous will."

Ulrica struggled to follow the speech. She was by no means fluent in Harakunye. In this conversation, she often had to ask what a word meant; or sometimes the natives were baffled by her accent. But, in effect, she answered: "That would be very pleasant to know."

The language barrier strained out sarcasm. Feridur lifted his monocle. "I say, captain," he asked, "are you sure it is a bona fide warrior? It didn't even sneer at me."

"It claims to be, *Zivar,*" said Zalakun uncertainly. "And after all, if I may extrude a suggestion, your magnificent memory will recall tribes we have already encountered, prepared to fight bravely but given to soft female-type words on all other occasions."

"True. Yes. True." Feridur wiggled his tail tip. "And this creature is still more alien, eh, what? Great Kastakun, how hideous it is!"

"Hey!" bristled Ulrica. Then she sat back. Perhaps this was a compliment. She didn't know.

According to the data book, all Epsteinians encountered so far by humans had been amiable fishers and farmers. In the archipelagoes fringing the Northeast Ocean they were neolithic; farther west, they had begun to use iron; and cursory flights above one of the small continents beyond had shown areas where there were cities and square-rigged ships.

The *Geyvadigur* was from Harakun, still farther west—

perhaps at the antipodes—and, apparently, still more advanced in technology. The vessel must have been chugging eastward for months, exploring, refueling often from the planet's many natural oil wells. Now it poised somewhere near the edge of the Northeast Ocean, with little but water ahead for half the world's circumference.

In short, this region was as strange to Zalakun and Feridur as it was to Ulrica and Mudge. By the same token, you could no more conclude what the Harakuni were like from reports on local primitives than an eighteenth-century Martian visiting Hawaii could have predicted the character of Europeans.

It behooved her to gang warily. But gang she must.

"Well, don't just sit there," said Feridur. "Speak. Or do tricks, or something." He yawned. "Great Kastakun! And to think I left my estates because I thought this wretched expedition would be an adventure! Why, I haven't collected ten decent skulls since we weighed anchor!"

"Ah, but Zivar," soothed Zalakun, "what an interesting skull Orumastat has."

"True," said Feridur, perking up. "Sensational. A collector's item. That is, if Orumastat gives me enough of a fight."

"Oh, but it is a guest," objected Zalakun. "I didn't mean Orumastat personally, but warriors of its tribe, after we contact them—"

"Quiet, you low creature," said Feridur.

The captain looked distressed. He tried another approach: "Orumastat may be too soft to be worthwhile. No scales."

"The erkuma of Akhavadin lacks scales," pointed out Feridur, "and yet if you meet one hand-to-hand and survive, its skull is jolly well worth fifty like yours."

"True," said Zalakun, banging his brow on the table. "I abase myself."

Ulrica stood up. The conversation seemed to be getting out of hand. "Just a moment, just a moment!" she exclaimed. "I did not come here to fight."

"No?" Feridur gaped idiotically and twiddled his eyeglass. "Not to fight? Whatever for, then?"

"It was shipwrecked, puissant one," said Zalakun.

"Eh, what? Shipwrecked? Nonsense. We haven't had any storms lately. Couldn't be shipwrecked. I mean to say, that's nonsense. Come, come, now, monster, out with it. Why are you here?"

"Shut up, you knock-kneed son of a frog!" snarled Ulrica. She kept her fraying temper just enough to say it in English.

"Eh? What say? Don't understand it. Terrible accent. If it's going to learn Harakunye, why can't it learn right? Answer me that." Feridur leaned back sulkily and toyed with his scimitar.

Zalakun gave him a glance of frustrated exasperation, then said to the girl: "Suppose you explain yourself from the beginning."

Ulrica had dreaded that request. The upper atmosphere of this planet was so thickly clouded that you never even saw its own sun, let alone the stars. She had learned without surprise that the Harakuni thought their world was flat. Even their boldest sailors never ventured more than a few hundred kilometers from land, and that only in familiar seas where compass and log made crude dead reckoning possible.

Briefly, she was tempted to say: "Mudge and I were coming down in a small ferry from the regular supply spaceship. We were letting the autopilot bring us in on a radio beam, and know only that we were several thousand kilometers west of Lonesome Landing. I have no idea what number that word 'several' really stands for. Some freakish backblast caused the engine to explode, the jet stream seized us and flung us far off course, we came down in a torn-off section on a dying grav-unit with capricious winds blowing us about, and hit the sea near this island. Every scrap of our equipment is lost or ruined. Doubtless aircraft are hunting for us, but what chance have we of being found on an entire, virtually unmapped planet, before our vitamin pills give out and we die? For we can eat the native life, but unless it is supplemented with Terrestrial vitamins we will soon get scurvy, beriberi, pellagra, and every other deficiency disease you can name."

But she didn't have Harakunye words to say it.

Instead, she ventured: "We are of a race different from yours. All our tribe are mighty warriors. We two went far from the island where we live, exploring in a boat that flew. But it suffered harm in the air and we fell here, where you soon found us."

"We spied your ruin descending and made haste to investigate," said Captain Zalakun. "I have been looking at the wreckage. That material like unbreakable glass is interesting, but why do you use such soft light metal instead of wood or iron?"

Ulrica sighed. "That is a long story," she answered. "There are many wonderful things we can show you, if you will only take us to our home." She was quite confident the *Geyvadigur* could reach Lonesome Landing in time. The ship must be capable of averaging at least five knots, which meant some fifteen hundred kilometers an Earth-week. The station was certainly less than five thousand kilometers away. There were pills left for three weeks; and, if necessary, several days more without vitamins would do no serious harm.

"We are anxious to know all the nations in your . . . er, in the world," continued Ulrica persuasively. "We wish trade with them, and friendship." No need to elaborate on the civilizing program of the League. They might not appreciate that idea without advance propaganda.

"Trade?" Feridur brightened. "Skulls?"

"Well—" temporized Ulrica.

"See here," said Feridur in a reasonable tone, "either you want to fight and give a chap a chance to collect skulls, or else you're not worth contacting. Eh, what? Isn't that fair?"

"My splendid master," said Zalakun, with strained politeness, "we have already discovered that few foreign peoples share the interest of us and our neighbors in craniology. There *are* other things in life, you know."

Feridur laid talons about the scimitar. His monocle glittered red. "Ssso," he murmured, "you think that, eh?"

Zalakun wriggled backward on his tail. "Oh, no, your awesomeness," he said hastily. "Not at all. Of course not!"

"Oh, so you do want to expand your own collection," purred Feridur. He tested saw edges with a thumb. "Well, well! I say! Maybe you would like to add the skull of your liege lord to the museum, eh, what?"

"Oh, no, no, *Zivar*," said Zalakun, sweating. "Wouldn't dream of it."

"So my skull isn't good enough for you. Is that it?"

"No, *Zivar*! Your skull is a thing of beauty."

"I'll oblige you any time, you know," said Feridur. "We can go ashore right this moment and have a whack at each other, eh?"

Zalakun licked rubbery lips. "Uh," he said. "Well, the fact is—"

"Ah, I know, I know. Not a drop of sporting blood in the whole dashed ship. Great Kastakun! Well, go on, then, *Yaldazir*, talk to the monster. Two of a kind." Feridur yawned elaborately.

Ulrica felt embarrassed for the captain. After breathing hard for a while he resumed the conversation with her. "Where is this home of yours, Orumastat?"

"Somewhere . . . er . . . that way." Ulrica pointed out the window, past reefs and surf to a steel-gray eastward stretch of sea.

"Can you not be more precise? What archipelago?"

"No archipelago," said the girl. "It is a single island in the middle of an ocean. My people have seen from the air that the part of the world you must come from has many islands and two small continents, so that one is never far from land. But beyond the region where I think we are now, there is almost no land for . . . I don't know your measures. You could sail steadily for more than fifty of your days before seeing shore again."

"I say!" Feridur straightened. "You're sure, monster?"

"Not in detail," Ulrica admitted. "But I do know there is that much water somewhere to the east, ahead of you."

"But then . . . Great Kastakun, captain! I'm glad we found that out! We're heading straight homeward again!"

"To be sure," declared Zalakun, appalled. "Why, after so long a time at sea, one could not even guess at northward or southward drift. One might miss the shore you speak of completely. Even if the wind didn't fail in so long a voyage. For we could only steam twenty days at most before our oil bunkers were dry."

"It would not be that far to my island," said Ulrica.

"Hm-m-m . . . how far?"

"I am not certain. But no more than, uh, fifteen days."

"Fifteen days in open ocean!" gasped Zalakun.

He sat back, tongue hanging out, speechless with horror. Feridur quizzed Ulrica through his monocle. "But I say," he objected, "what's the jolly old purpose in living so far away? Eh? It's unheard of. I mean to say, nobody lives in mid-ocean."

"Since we can fly at great speeds, we are not inconvenienced by distance," replied Ulrica. And colonizing an isolated speck would offend no natives: they didn't even realize it existed. No sense, though, in giving so pacifistic a reason to this warrior culture.

"But how do you find your way? Eh? Answer me that. Ha, ha, I've bally well got you there!" Feridur wagged a triumphant finger.

Ulrica decided that there was also no point in describing a radio net involving three small artificial satellites. "We have our methods," she said in a mysterious tone.

"By the Iron Reefs," murmured Zalakun. His tone held awe. "Of course you do! You must, or you couldn't have found that island in the first place. But to know exactly where you are, even when there's no land in sight, no current or cloud formations or— Why, that's a secret sought for as long as there have been ships!"

"We will gladly provide you with similar means," said Ulrica. "If, of course, you take us home."

"Naturally!" babbled Zalakun. He sprang to his feet, wagging his tail till the air whistled. "Jumping gods, master, what're a thousand bug-bitten skulls next to a prize like that? Just give us a line, *Zivar* Orumastat, give us a compass bearing and we'll hold true on it till you're home, though the sky fall down!"

"*Ah, nej!*" whispered Ulrica. She felt the blood sink from her face.

"What is it?" asked the captain. He came around the table and offered an arm. She leaned on it, badly in need of support.

"I just realized . . . I was so busy before that it only occurs to me now . . . I know where the island is," she said faintly. "But I can't give you a course. I don't know where *we* are!"

When Ulrica had gone aboard ship, Ardabadur, the carpenter, followed. There he directed a gang of sailors as they unloaded the completed Foucault bob, got it into a boat and ashore. While they carried it onward, he went to the tent where Didymus Mudge was at work.

He hesitated outside. The Earthling's operations had been fascinating, but enigmatic and delicate. Ardabadur didn't want to interrupt. Finally he stuck his head through the flap.

Mudge stood hunched over his apparatus. In the days since arriving here, he had gotten it to function rather well. Or, more accurately, Ardabadur had. They shared no words, but through gestures, drawings, and crude models Mudge had explained what he needed. Then the ship's excellent carpenter shop had prepared it for him—after which he tinkered, groaned, and sent it back for revision.

A ball of cast bronze rolled thunderously down an inclined plane. Mudge watched it while counting the swings of a small pendulum, carefully made from a leather cord and a lead weight in a leveled glass-sided box. When the ball reached ground, Mudge made a note. The Harakuni had paper and pencils. "Which is a mercy," he said aloud. "But *why* couldn't you have brought a clock along?"

Ardabadur hopped inside and squatted respectfully. Mudge ran a hand through rumpled hair and mopped sweat off his face. "I'm sure you have some chronometry," he said. "You have probably even measured the length of the day, and its seasonal variation. I know the long twilight confuses things, clouds always hiding the sun . . . but if you averaged enough observations for enough centuries, you could do it. So why didn't you bring a clock? Knowing this planet's rotation period, I could have corrected my watch according to your timepiece by simple arithmetic."

He tapped the chrono on his wrist. "I think a momentary surge of magnetism must have affected it," he went on. "It's antimagnetic, to be sure, but a disintegrating nuclear field can produce overwhelming forces. I suppose I'm lucky to be alive at all. Well, I know from the data book how long from sunrise to sunrise, so theoretically I could use that fact to tell me how fast or slow my watch is. But in practice, the clouds complicate observation too much for anything like accuracy; and *I* haven't got a hundred years in which to accumulate enough data for analysis."

Ardabadur wagged his tail knowingly, as if he understood English.

"Of course, time is of no obvious importance to you on shipboard," said Mudge. "Since you can't make astronomical sightings, and you don't even know astronomical phenomena exist, you cannot have invented navigation.

You possess an inaccurate little hourglass to tell you when to change watch, and that's all."

He smiled, a weary lopsided grimace. "Well, I've gotten around the handicap," he said. "This makes my one-thousandth observation of time to roll down the plane. After calculation, I should be able to work out a very good correction factor for my watch." He patted the bulge in one hip pocket. "Do you know, my friend, I owe my life to whoever invented waterproof paper. Without it, the data book would be unreadable. It was a wet journey to this island. And this book compiles—not only the physical and mathematical constants needed anywhere in the universe—but all the information so far gathered about Epstein's Planet. Its mass, dimensions, orbital elements, rotational period, axial inclination, surface gravity, atmospheric composition, everything—or almost everything. Unfortunately, such quantities as magnetic deviation have hardly been mapped at all: otherwise I might try using that to locate us. The book does include tide tables, though, not only for Lonesome Landing but for several other selected spots, at which temperature, pelagic salinity, and whatever else occurred to the expeditions, have been measured."

He turned toward the exit. "But I am sure you came to show me something," he said. "Forgive me. I talk too much. However, it has been a very trying week on this island. I am used to talking, the feast of reason and the flow of soul and so on. My mother has always moved in intellectual circles. And then, I am a teacher by profession: basic science in the elementary grades."

Ardabadur led the way over the beach. Didymus Mudge continued to chatter. Perhaps he wanted to drown out the surf. Now, with the incoming solar tide, it had grown loud, an undergroundish sinister noise to his landlubber ears. Overhead scudded smoky rainclouds, and lightning flickered, high up in the permanent gray layers. The jungle talked in the wind with a million blue tongues.

"My mother was very dubious about my coming to

Epstein's Planet," he said. "I had never been farther than Luna before, and then I had letters of recommendation to people she knows. On the other hand, it was an undeniable opportunity. The scientific and cultural staff here is already of respectable size, and is due for great expansion in the near future, when intensive work begins. The tendency is for married couples to be employed, and they have children, and the children need education. On a four-year contract, I could not only save a very good salary, but make valuable friendships among highly intellectual people. If only my mother could have come too, I would never have hesitated. But no opening was available for her. She finally agreed that I had a duty to my career."

Mudge looked around. He saw nothing but drifting sand, tents that snapped in the wind, waves and the alien ship. He leaned close to Ardabadur and hissed: "Frankly, and don't tell anyone, I thought it was high time I went somewhere by myself. I am thirty years old. After all!"

Then, blushing and stammering, he hurried on: "Miss . . . er . . . Major Ormstad isn't an instructor. Not of children, I mean. She was to organize defensive squads for the exploration teams, in case they meet hostility. Not that we would dream of provoking any such demonstration. I assure you. But—"

But by that time they had reached the Foucault bob, where a dozen sailors waited for orders. Ardabadur beamed like a picket fence and waved a hand at his creation.

Mudge examined it with care. It was as he had drawn, a hollow copper ball some one hundred and fifty centimeters across. When filled with sand, its mass would be enormous. A small loop and a very light stiff wire were affixed to the bottom. On top was a larger loop, riveted to ten meters of wire rope. As far as Mudge could see, it had been made with perfect symmetry and should give no trouble.

He said aloud: "We shall have to wait for calm weather.

The wind would cause the pendulum to describe an ellipse today. But according to the data book, this region at this time of year is usually calm, so we can doubtless perform the experiment tomorrow. Let us set it all up now."

Ardabadur got his drift and barked orders. His assistants sprang to work. The sphere lay under a tall tree on the beach's edge which had been stripped of branches. A stout gallowslike crosspiece had been erected on the trunk, thirteen meters above ground. Now a pair of sailors swarmed up and affixed the loose end of the cable, so that the copper ball hung suspended. It swayed and toned in the wind. Mudge was gratified to note that it had little tendency to move in arcs; Ardabadur's suspension was well designed.

"Why are you helping me?" he mused aloud. "You have certainly spared no pains on my behalf, though you can have no idea why I want all this work done. Is it curiosity? Or boredom? For this has been a long dull time for you to lie anchored—I suppose on our account, until your captain knows more about us. I prefer to think you feel a genuine friendship and wish to assist a being in distress. Your officers seem to be perfect brutes, but all you common crewpeople are very quiet and well-behaved. I am sure you are capable of empathy."

"Uru's kalka kisir," said the Epsteinian.

"Oh," said Mudge.

Hanging the pendulum took at least an hour. At the end, though, he had it well adjusted. As the bob passed the lowest point of its arc, the cat's-whisker wire on the bottom traced a thin line in sand which had been smoothed, leveled, and wet down. Now Mudge led the sailors away; they raised the ball again and carried it to another preselected tree. Here the human mounted a ladder, knotted a piece of light rope to the bottom loop, and tied the other end to the bole. The sphere hung four meters above ground, its cable nearly taut, ready to swing when released.

"Now we fill the globe with sand to make it heavier

and thus more stable," said Mudge, "and then I believe
we can, er, call it a day."

He demonstrated. The sailors formed a bucket bri-
gade up the ladder and began loading the ball. They
had almost completed that task when Ulrica Ormstad
appeared.

Behind her trailed Captain Zalakun and a bemedaled,
besworded, bemonocled Epsteinian whom Mudge had
not seen before. Ardabadur whistled and fell on his
face. The sailors tumbled from the ladder and followed
suit. Mudge gaped.

"Good heavens," he said.

"This is Feridur of Beradura," explained the girl.
"He owns this expedition. I mean that almost literally."

Her face was tight and anxious. Though the wind
blew cool, there was sweat on her wide brow, and an
uncharacteristic lock of hair had broken loose to stream
over one ear.

"Mudge," she said, "we are in trouble."

"I know," he agreed.

Her temper ripped across. "Don't get sarcastic with
me, you little worm!" she yelled.

"But I wasn't . . . I didn't—" Mudge swallowed.
Ulrica was a beautiful sight, he thought. So, however,
was a hungry tiger.

He had had no experience with the modern frontier
type of woman. His mother disapproved of them. In his
inmost soul he admitted hoping he would meet a young
lady on this planet, where no one would jealously interfere, who could become Mrs. Mudge. But someone
well-bred and well-read, with civilized ways, please!

"What have you been doing, anyhow?" snapped Ulrica.

"I told you," said Mudge, after husking once or twice.
"I have been correcting my watch. I have a correction
factor now, or will as soon as I make the calculations
from my data, and then we will know exact Greenwich
time." He paused. "I admit that is making no allowance
for relativistic laws . . . simultaneity is an approximational

concept at best . . . but this is a refinement which the data book does not take into account either. So—"

"Shut your big mouth before I reach in and pull you inside out!" screamed Ulrica.

Mudge cowered.

Ulrica expressed herself richly for several seconds. Mudge would have covered his ears, but was too stunned. He had never heard most of those words. The context, though, made their meaning all too hideously evident. Good heavens! Cultivated society, conversing at tea time in Boston, seemed five hundred light-years away.

He remembered with a shock that it *was* five hundred light-years away.

A part of him gibbered that the spaceship had headed into Virgo, and surely people would not make remarks like this in the region of Virgo.

Reason came back to him as Ulrica ran down. She put arms akimbo and said grimly: "All right. Why do you want to know Greenwich Market Time? To say your evening prayers?"

"No," gulped Mudge. "To locate us. I mean, we have to know where we are, don't we? The data book says Lonesome Landing is at 47° 32′ 4″ N., and the prime meridian has been drawn through it. But we know only that we are somewhere west of there, how far we cannot tell, and have no idea if we are north or south of it. I mean—"

"You mean," growled Ulrica, "that you have read chronometric time is necessary for navigation. So you set blindly out to find the time. You gruntbrain! Don't you know longitude reckoning depends on the *comparison* of times? How can we get local noon when we can't see the sun? How can we get the height of anything, for latitude?"

She gave the copper ball a green glare. "And what, with your kind permission, is that?"

"A . . . a Foucault pendulum," said Mudge. He squared thin shoulders. "It is a classic demonstration of the fact that a planet rotates. A pendulum will hold to its own vibrational plane—in effect, the planet turns beneath it—so that cat's whisker will describe a line which gradually turns through a complete circle."

Ulrica stood speechless.

"This project has a secondary value," continued Mudge with a bit more self-confidence, "in that I am sure these Epsteinians imagine their world to be flat and fixed in space. The pendulum offers a simple proof of its rotation. Therefore they will be more inclined to accept on faith our assertion that the planet is a spheroid, and this in turn will lead them to follow our advice when—"

"Great," said Ulrica. "Leaping. Blue. Balls. Of. Radioactive. Muck."

Then the blast came. Mudge huddled away from it. The girl raged over his head, like the remote lightning come down to earth.

"For your blank blank information, Mister Didymus Blank Blank Mudge, I have just been talking to the captain and Feridur. They don't know which dash deleted asterisk way to steer for the obscenity station. How could they? Without a reasonably accurate vector— distance within a few hundred kilometers, direction within a compass point or less—they could search the double dash four star exclamation point ocean for an anathematized year without coming near Lonesome Blank Blank Landing. And of course they won't even attempt it. If they cruised obscenely around in any kind of crudely expressed search pattern, they'd lose their own unprintable way and risk never finding land again. If we don't give them a deep blue bearing and a sulfurous distance estimate, they're going to up anchor and head for accursed home tomorrow. AND YOU WANT TO GIVE A LECTURE ON COPERNICAN ASTRONOMY!"

"Oooh," moaned Ardabadur, trembling.

Exactly, thought Mudge, also trembling.

He opened his mouth, but nothing came out. At that moment, Feridur twittered. Ulrica stopped in mid-career and faced around. Feridur put the monocle in his eye and repeated the question. Captain Zalakun said some-

thing in a protesting tone of voice. Feridur made a
sweet reply at which the captain shuddered and backed
away. Ulrica turned quite pale.

Mudge listened intently. He heard Feridur ask, with
painful distinctness: *"Uluka's kuruta yaldazir itoban
urnalik?"*

"Yalgesh, Zirvan," said Ulrica, in a small subdued
voice and a Swedish accent. *"Obunadun haladur
erkedivir."*

The saw-toothed blade rasped from Feridur's sheath.
He giggled. *"Yagatun!"*

Ulrica clenched her fists. Then, suddenly, she spat at
the Harakuni's feet. The color flamed back in her cheeks.
"Yagatun zoltada, Yaldazir Feridur!" she snapped.

"Eep!" said Feridur, horrified at such manners. Captain Zalakun sought to remedy the breach, but got
nowhere. The sailors burrowed in the sand, trying to
make themselves inconspicuous. Finally Zalakun himself went off in giant kangaroo leaps toward the tents.

"What is this?" whispered Mudge.

Ulrica said in a harsh tone: "Feridur wanted to know
if you can locate the Earth base, since I can't. When I
admitted you had only been playing games, he said he
would fight me. I have explained that the vitamin pills
are necessary for our life, so he knows we would soon
die in any case when he turns homeward. He wants to
take my skull in combat instead, for his collection."

"What?" squeaked Mudge. The island revolved around
him. He stumbled, feeling blackness in his head. Ulrica
caught him.

"Don't be afraid," she said in the same metallic voice.
"You are not worth fighting—no glory in taking your
head. They will keep you for a pet, I suppose . . . and
you will have my pills . . . and it is barely possible, in
that extra time a search party will chance upon you."

"But this is ghastly!" stammered Mudge. "I mean, it
isn't done!"

"It seems to be." Ulrica managed a bleak grin. "Maybe
I can take Feridur's head. Then I inherit his titles,

properties, and skull collection, and can sail the ship where I will. Not that we have much chance anyway, without a bearing." She sighed. "This may be the better way to die."

"But listen—" wailed Mudge.

Zalakun returned with a sword, shouldered past him and said something to the girl. She nodded. Mudge tried to get a word in edgewise. "Shut up," said Ulrica. Zalakun finished by handing her the weapon.

"In case you are interested," said Ulrica, "he was explaining the rules. In effect, there aren't any. Either party can use tricks, assistants—"

Zalakun flickered a glance at Feridur, who was polishing his monocle several meters off. The captain leaned over and whispered something to the girl. She smiled a suddenly gentle smile and gave his scaly back a furtive pat.

"What is it?" gibbered Mudge. "What did he say?"

"He said no one will help Feridur," she answered curtly. "They don't like him. Of course, they are too afraid of him to take my side either. He's the leading phrenologist in Harakun."

"But . . . I can . . . I mean, that is, I have to tell you— "

"Oh, be quiet," she said. "What use would you be? Stand aside out of my way, that is all you can do."

"But you don't have to fight this barbaric thing!" yelped Mudge. "It isn't necessary! If you would only listen to me for five minutes, I can explain—"

"Shut up," she cut him off. He tried to continue. She whirred her blade past his nose. He jumped backward, choking. She laughed with a real, if deplorably coarse mirth, and said more kindly: "It is too late anyhow. I insulted him on purpose. Whatever I said now, he would insist on disposing of me."

Zalakun wrung her hand and scuttled off to the sidelines as Feridur turned around. The aristocrat screwed his eyeglass in more firmly, hefted his sword, and minced across the sand. Ulrica crouched, waiting. The wind fluttered her kilt and the one loose lock of hair.

Mudge put his back against the tree bole and tried to think. But that was like trying to run through glue. This was the U.S.P. Standard adventure-story situation, a beautiful girl threatened by a bulging-eyed monster, and he was a man, and it was up to him to save her, but—Feridur's blade whipped up and then down. It hit Ulrica's with a clang that hurt Mudge's eardrums. The blow would have gone halfway through him.

He huddled next to the comforting bulk of good old Ardabadur, and prayed that the beautiful girl would save him from the bug-eyed monster.

"*Yava's!*" cried Feridur.

He bounced back from Ulrica's attack. She knew fencing, but had no skill with these awkward weapons. She closed in, though, a rush and a sweep. Somehow it got past Feridur's guard, and steel teeth rattled across his scales. They did no harm. His own blade moved with a combination of thrust and stroke. Ulrica retreated, fending him off by mere fury of blows. He grinned and stalked around her, so that she must keep turning to face him. His reach was not much greater than hers, but he had every advantage of height, stride, and strength.

All at once, like a snake, his weapon darted in, slid past Ulrica's and touched her thigh. She got away in time, with only a thin red slash, but Mudge felt sick. "Son of an improper union," she muttered, and cut loose again. "You want to saw me up alive, huh? We'll see!"

She leaped in, hewing low. Feridur hissed as she opened a gash on his left shin. Her metal was already up to block his answering cut. He brought his edge down, chopping at her ankles. She jumped high, the sword whined beneath her feet, she came down on it and it was torn from Feridur's grasp.

"Now, you miserable alligator!" she exclaimed, and assaulted his head. A small sailor emitted a very small cheer, then covered his mouth and looked around in terror of having been overheard.

Feridur whirled about, raised his tail, and struck Ulrica amidships. The wind whoofed from her. She rolled three meters and climbed dizzily to her feet. Feridur picked up his sword and advanced with deliberation. The watching sauroids looked distressed, Captain Zalakun twisted his hands together, but all seemed nailed to the spot.

"Look out!" screamed Mudge. Impulsively, he darted forward.

Ulrica waved him back. She still clutched her sword. The free hand dabbed at a bruised cheek. "No," she said. "One is enough."

"But you are a woman!" he cried. "Give me that! I'll fight for you!"

She managed a ghost of a laugh. "Dear little Didymus," she whispered. "I am an Ormstad of Clan Swenson. Get out of my way."

Feridur closed in for the kill as Mudge staggered back to Ardabadur's side. The Harakuni noble paused to readjust his monocle. He tittered.

Then Ulrica exploded into motion. Her sword became a blur, yelled in the air, banged on Feridur's iron, knocked down his guard and slashed him across the shoulder. He hissed and jumped back. Ulrica followed, shouting.

She's splendid! thought Mudge wildly. *They don't make girls like that in Boston!* He blushed and corrected himself: *I mean, there aren't any girls like that in Boston.*

Feridur rallied and beat off the attack. Ulrica retreated. Through wind and surf, above the steady belling of steel, Mudge could hear how she clawed for breath. And once she stumbled from exhaustion. Feridur would kill her in minutes.

"I should go out and die with her." Mudge licked dry lips. "Really, I should, if I can't do anything else. I feel so useless."

"*Akrazun kulakisir,*" said Ardabadur comfortingly.

"It wouldn't be against the rules," chattered Mudge. "She told me anything goes. I could help. Only . . . only . . . to be absolutely honest, as my mother always told me to be, I'm scared."

Feridur drew blood again: a flesh wound, no more, but Ulrica's sword was now slow and heavy in her fingers.

"Of course, later I can explain, and maybe they will take me to Lonesome Landing after all," babbled Mudge. "But no, I haven't her training, I could not possibly learn the language before my vitamins ran out. I am done for, too. You had all this work for nothing, Ardabadur. Now you will never know why you made—"

The thought came to him. It was not exactly a blinding flash of intuition. Or perhaps it was. He didn't notice. By the time he was fully conscious of having an idea, it was already in execution.

"Ulrica!" he shouted. "Miss Ormstad! *Major* Ormstad! Get him . . . maneuver him onto . . . that cleared, wet space in the sand . . . under that tree . . . keep him there . . . and look out!"

Meanwhile he snatched a knife from Ardabadur's belt and went up the ladder. The carpenter whistled alarm and started after him. Frantically, Mudge kicked him on the crest, while sawing at the cord and yelling at Ulrica.

"Miss Ormstad! Work him onto that level damp patch! Quickly! Hold him . . . just a minute . . . please! I beg of you!"

Ulrica, fighting for another second of existence, heard his thin screech and croaked out of pain and despair: "Let me die by myself, Earthling."

Somehow, without planning to, scarcely aware of it, Didymus Mudge inflated his lungs and roared in a heroic tenor, so that even Zalakun jumped: "*Profanity dash blasphemy blue and green, purple-starred et cetera! Do what I blank unprintable tell you before I commit unspeakable violence upon your defamity person!*"

Whether the memory of drill sergeants ten years ago came back and possessed her, or whether she was suddenly given hope—or for whatever reason—Ulrica sprang away from Feridur and ran. He bounded after, jeering at her. Ulrica crossed the wet sand, twirled about, and met his charge. Saw teeth locked together as the blades met. Feridur began to shove hers aside. She threw her last strength into resisting him, though she felt it drain from muscle and bone.

Didymus Mudge cut the cord on his Foucault sphere.

Loaded with hundreds of kilos of sand, it swung across the beach, gathering velocity all the way. Mudge fell off the ladder, onto Ardabadur. They went down in a tangle of arms, legs, and tail. By the time he had picked himself up, it was all over, and the Harakuni were howling as one jubilant mob around Ulrica.

Mudge limped toward her. He wanted to see, if he could, how much of an arc his pendulum was describing. Yes . . . there was definitely an elliptical path, but a narrow one. That tendency should be quite obviated when he made the official experiment tomorrow. He would burn the rope then, rather than cut it, to liberate the bob without transverse forces . . . He ducked as it whistled past. So huge a thing had not lost much energy when it hit Feridur.

Mudge saw what had happened to Feridur. For a while he was not a well man.

Captain Zalakun released Ulrica's hand, which he had been pumping in a most Earthlike fashion, and regarded the mess. Finally he shook his head and clicked his tongue. "Dear me, *Zivar* Orumastat," he said. "You really must chastise your slave. No doubt he meant well, but he has completely ruined what would have been a very fine egg-shaped skull."

A while afterward, when they sat in the captain's cabin, eating the Epsteinian food—which humans found dreary—and drinking the Epsteinian wine—which was forty proof and not bad at all—Zalakun asked Ulrica: "*Arvadur zilka itoban urnalik?*"

The girl blinked beautiful, though slightly blurred, green eyes above her goblet, in Mudge's direction. "He wants to know if you can indeed navigate us, Didymus," she said.

Mudge blushed. "Well, not exactly," he admitted. "Until we reach base and get a radio network receiver, I mean. But then he will be able to navigate himself. Ahem!" He burped and reached for his own cup. "I can, however, tell him to a fair approximation how far away Lonesome Landing is, and in what direction. That should suffice, since he has good compasses and is independent of the wind. Rather, I will be able to tell him this tomorrow, when I have all the data and finish the calculations."

"But how?" She leaned forward. "How, Didymus?" she repeated softly.

"Well," he said after catching his breath, "the data book gives the location of base, so if I know our present coordinates, it becomes a simple problem in spherical trigonometry, for which the book supplies tables, to determine—"

"Yes, yes," she said in a slightly less worshipful tone. "But how do you locate us?"

"It is a problem of finding latitude and longitude," he said. He took another swig of wine. It buzzed in his head, but helped steady his voice. Once he got going, the lecture habits of a decade took over and he talked automatically. "Ahem! We had the data book and a watch, but the watch had been running awry since the moment of the crash, so that I no longer knew within several hours what time it was. Now if I could only observe something which took a precisely known time, such as ten seconds, I could compare the watch, see by what factor it was fast or slow, and apply the correction.

"I looked up the standard value of Epsteinian gravity, one thousand twelve centimeters per second squared. Local variations would not make any significant difference. A pendulum describing short arcs has a period which is a function only of length and gravity. The carpenter made me a good small pendulum and I clocked it."

"Yes, but," said Ulrica. She paused. "But," she repeated muzzily. Wine had hidden her own weariness from her, but it made the wine all the more effective. "But you don't know the length of the pendulum. Not with, *urp*, precision."

"No," said Mudge. "However, the distance covered by a falling body is a function only of gravity and time. Air resistance can be disregarded for low speeds. I repeated Galileo's experiment, dropping a weight through a fixed height. Actually, I rolled it down an inclined plane—so did he—to get a greater length and thus a smaller percentage of error. Though I did not know the effective height in absolute units, I took care to see that it was an integral multiple of the pendulum length; and I measured the time for a ball to roll down in terms of pendulum oscillations. I therefore have two equations in two unknowns, easy to solve. When I have computed all my data, taking the average of many observations, I will know the length of the pendulum in centimeters and, what I really wanted, the length of its period in seconds. From this I can correct the time shown by my watch."

Ulrica smiled, stretched out on the floor and laid her head on Mudge's lap.

"Goodness gracious!" Mudge gasped. "What are you doing, Miss Ormstad?"

"You were speaking about falling bodies," she murmured.

"But . . . I mean . . . Major Ormstad!"

"Ulrica is my name," she whispered.

Zalakun's leathery face assumed an avuncular expression. He said something which Mudge was afraid meant, "Bless you, my children."

"Well," gulped Mudge. "Well, if you're tired, Miss . . . er . . . Major . . . I can find a pillow."

"I'm quite comfy," said the girl. She reached up and patted his check. "I'm sorry for losing my temper. I wouldn't have if I had known you better, Didymus. Know what? You're cute."

Mudge ran a finger beneath his collar and plunged terror-stricken onward: "Since this planet has only solar tides, I was spared one complication. To be sure, tidal patterns are not simple; but a wave crossing the almost empty Northeast Ocean will not be much delayed either. To further help me, the data book has tide tables not only for Lonesome Landing, but for selected spots elsewhere. This will assist interpolation. In short, when my watch has been corrected, I will be able to identify any local tide as one which passed Lonesome Landing so-and-so many hours ago. Knowing the speed at which it travels, I thereby know how far westward it has come in that interval—hence, our longitude."

Ulrica frowned, with a finger laid to her chin. "No," she said, " 'cute' is the wrong word. I mean, you are cute, but you are also very much of a manfolk. When you shouted at me to do what you wanted, it was poetic. Like a saga."

"I forgot myself," said Mudge wretchedly.

"I'll help you forget some more," beamed Ulrica.

"*Ugvan urunta,*" said Zalakun.

Mudge interpreted this as a request to continue his discourse. "Latitude is a simpler problem, solvable with greater accuracy," he said very fast. "I know the angular velocity of this planet's rotation, three hundred sixty degrees in forty-six hours. Knowing the date, I could calculate latitude from length of daylight, except for the clouds. A Foucault pendulum affords a much better method. It would not turn at all at the equator; it would turn with maximum speed at either pole; in between, the rate is a sine function of latitude. I can use geometrical constructions to mark off a precise angle such as ninety degrees, clock the time the pendulum needs to sweep through this angle, and thence compute our latitude. And, and, and that's all," he finished. "I should have the information for you by nightfall tomorrow, and we can start out next day. To be sure, accumulated uncertainties will doubtless cause us to miss the island, but not by much. We can find it in time if we scout about. Though I suppose we need only come within a few hundred kilometers to be spotted by an aircraft—"

Ulrica chuckled. "And so we will arrive as great heroes," she said, "very romantic, and perhaps we had better not disappoint people about the romantic side of it, no? *Käre lille*, Didymus. This is going to be so pleasant a sea voyage."

Mudge swallowed hard and wondered how to escape.

"*Istvaz tuli*," said Zalakun with a fatuous smirk.

Mudge threw him a look of wild appeal, as if somehow the bug-eyed monster could save the man from the girl.

ELEMENTARY MISTAKE

Hello, Bellegarde! Hello, Earth. Hello, Universe.
And to hell with you.

Lind speaking. Squeaking. Reeking. Billy Lind. No,
's not dignified enough. Kin'ly call me th' late William
J. Lind, sometime of West Newton, Chassamusetts,
U.S.A., World Federation, planet Earth, star Sol, Milky
Way galaxy . . . Does every schoolboy write that kin'a
'dress on his books? Not that I'm a schoolboy now.
Wish I was . . . were? . . . yes, subjunctive, were.
Ay-llow me t' in'erduce m'self. William J. Lind, officer
and putative gentleman of the Space Service, Pioneer
Division, electronician aboard *Widsith*, seated at our
primary transmitter on the planet they named, in the
best romantic tradition, Guinevere—you should hear
what we call it—with a lot of big ugly mountains staring
over my shoulder and making rude remarks.

Nope, wrong verb form again. I was sitting here. A
thing we might's well call a bird was flopping above the
mast, in a purplish sky. It had long sweptback wings,
sort o' like our aircraft, and they glinted reddish green.
Sun did that, big orange disk, and it tinted the clouds
gold, and the snows on the peaks around this here now
valley where we're parked. (See, if I watch my tongue,

114

I can still pronounce words good, but believe me, 's not easy to watch your own tongue without a mirror.) The shadows were bluish red, too. But the smoke from yonder volcano, black, black . . . Where was I? Oh, yes. The proper grammar. Past tense. You won't hear me for nigh on five years. By then I'll be, all ten of us'll be one with the beers of yesteryear.

So fly up, little maser beam. Compute, little computer. Keep me locked onto that relay satellite. It'll buck my words on to Bellegarde. Won't it? Sure it will. It passed on the information that got us into this mess in the first place, didn't it? Mean to say, look here, you smug idiots on Bellegarde, on Durindal, on Frodo, on every planet the human race has reached so far—whoa, there, Lind. Save words. The satellite'll be under the horizon pretty soon. Minimize redundancy. Neologize. So: look here, you smidiots, I'm gonna 'splain'a you jus' wha' y' done t' us. An' you'll hafta sit'n listen. How y' gonna discipline me, then? Ha?

I . . . Shall . . . Speak . . . Carefully.

Widsith. Spaceship. Null-null drive. Affect everything simultaneous. Push you up fast, just under speed of light, no acceleration pressure to worry about, good old time dilation makes a five light-year hop go by in a couple of months. And meanwhile that lovely, lovely pay accumulating back at home. Good, no? No. Remember the power consumption. Think, just compute out, how many megawatts per ton you need. Stray radiation means heavy shielding, too, in a power factor of the power. And then, coasting across space? Uh-uh! Space is just full of hydrogen. One atom per cubic centimeter. At a speed of c, figure out the resistance. Figure out, also, what power you have to spend to keep those atoms at arm's length. A long, hairy, tattooed arm. Else the radiation from them will fry your aspidistra. Ergo, you need lots of ergs to go. All engine, no comfort. Most certainly no extra isotopes for fueling a return trip, nor any gear for making 'em at the other end. Not when you're carrying a mattercaster.

Nice mattercaster. Good, friendly, obliging mattercaster. Set one up. Tune it. Step through the gate. Step out the other end, whatever other end has a receiver you're tuned for, Bellegarde, Earth, Hell. No transition time. Not whatsoever. One hyperphase step across the galaxy. The universe is ours. 'Course, you do have to erect your gadget first. No transmitter, no reception, right? And the gadget does have to have a strong gravitational field to work. Got to be on a planet.

So. From an advance base, as it might be Bellegarde, you send your roboprobes to the next likely-looking stars. They find the least horrible planet in the system. Take orbit. Maser back data. Mass, magnetic field, temperature, spectra, everything except what we really needed to know. Load up *Widsith*. Minimum 'caster. Minimum everything. All we have to do is get there; land; make a foundation and frame out of local materials; assemble our unit; walk back to Bellegarde and report. Then the parts for a big, industrial-type caster can get sent through—direct from Earth, if you want. So can men. So can any equipment they need, including women. No sweat. 'Nother planet conquered. Hurray.

Hurray for us, 'spesh'lly. 'Stronomers on Bellegarde analyzed this here now sun we're under, they did. Variant composition. Cosmic abundances just a statistical concept. Actual composition can vary like crazy. Look at the R Peculiar stars, f'r example. Or look at this one. High concentration Group Eight metals, platinum, palladium. Catalysts. (A catalyst is the gait of a drunken feline.) Looks like plenty silver, too.

Like mother, like daughter. Planets oughta be loaded with these here now metals. Send roboprobe. Yep, planets, all right, all right. One of 'em even habitable. Earth size, Earth temperature, water oceans, oxynitro air, life, no sign of natives but reflection spectra show protein-based life. Given a li'l chemical apparatus, we could eat it. Not a full diet, but a dietary supplement, anyhow. Good. Ideal. Send *Widsith* off. Captain Ahmad

Akbik, mattercaster engineer Miguel Ocampo, electronician William J. Lind . . .

Has my recital insulted you enough? Hope so. You killed me, you know. I am, I was sitting here in a valley grown over with spongy brownish-green plants. There're trees, of a sort, growing up the mountainsides. Above timberline, the rocks have funny colors, mostly bluish; they're not like any rocks I ever saw before. On the volcano cone, below the snowcap, I do rec'nize black lava and yellow sulfur. The air stinks. It's cool and damp and smells like old cigar butts. Or something. I'm breathing the air. And I'm drunk. Nearest liquor five light-years away, and I'm drunk. Funny? Merciful? Well, I can tell you what kind of gesture the hand of Providence is making at me. In fact, I will tell you—

No, here comes somebody, air suited to the ears. He looks mad. Guess they heard me, over yonder in the ship. We got a hookup. I was out here to test the air. Chemical and biological tests said okay, said the stink's just from the plants and harmless, but you never know. We gotta just breathe the air or we're done for. You see— Hell, with it. We're done for. How do you do, Captain Ahmad Akbik, sir? Shall we dance?

Until the holds were unloaded, the bunkroom was the sole place aboard where all ten men could be simultaneously, and then only if they planned each move in advance. Sleeping, of course, was done in relays. They crowded knee to knee on the four bunks, hunched beneath the low overhead, and stared into each other's faces.

The captain would have liked to offer a prayer, when God seemed to be their last remaining friend, but Mecca was probably in a ridiculous direction. "How are you now, Fulgosi?" he asked.

"Quite well," the mineralogist said. "No after-effects. To be sure, I didn't become intoxicated like Lind—"

"Hey!" The electronician blushed.

"Don't be so sensitive about that," said the biochemist, Riese. "Not your fault. You merely showed a certain reaction, idiosyncratic but not unheard of, to anesthesia."

"Anesthesia?" Lind frowned.

"Sure, what else?" Fulgosi said. "When I tried breathing that stuff, I got too drowsy and thick-headed to think. Would've passed out before long if you hadn't brought me back inside the ship. So what's the cause, Riese?"

"I don't know," said the biochemist slowly.

"What?" Akbik exclaimed. "But you must! You've run a complete atmospheric analysis, haven't you?" In the week since *Widsith* landed, each man had had so much preliminary work to do in his particular specialty that this was their first real chance to compare notes.

"Yes, sir. I found nothing significant that the roboprobe hadn't already reported. The air has a rather high proportion of noble gases, but otherwise it's quite Earthlike."

Lind gagged. "Earthlike, you call those stenches?"

"Yes, what about them?" Ocampo asked. "By-products of a different biochemistry from ours. Couldn't something, in trace amounts, have an anesthetic effect on the human nervous system?"

"I don't know," Riese admitted. "For heaven's sake, my brain doesn't have infinite storage capacity. And the reference material we could take with us, even in databank form, is so limited. Surgical anesthesia has been entirely electronic for the past two centuries or more. Who could have foreseen any need for information about the chemical kind?"

"Could some kind of germ be responsible?" Akbik wondered.

"No, sir, that's one possibility I swear we can rule out. No native life form can eat us for much the same reason that we can't eat it. The selenium and fluorine concentrations in the body of this planet are so high that they have become integral to the metabolism of everything."

"How can you sit here," the cyberneticist Pereira objected, "having barely seen a little of one valley, and talk about the entire planet?"

Riese shrugged. "If my computer doesn't lie," he said, "it's traced out the fundamental cellular energy cycle. And that will not vary. Not unless the well-founded idea is totally wrong, that all life on a given world derives from the materials available there in the beginning. Our kind of organism uses—oh, hydrogen bonding, and phosphorus in ATP. Life here uses fluorine and selenium in its equivalents. I don't need a large sample to prove that. So—every Guineverean plant or animal is violently poisonous to us because of those elements. But by the same token, the phosphorus and iron in our bodies make us just as poisonous to them."

"And this cuts our time even shorter," the geologist Deschamps said unnecessarily.

"I wonder how you'd taste, sautéed in lubricant," Lind murmured.

"Stop that!" Akbik said.

"Why, is man forbidden food?"

"Not explicitly," grinned the chemosynthesist Nussbaum. "However, since man does not divide the hoof or chew the cud—"

"You're hopeless," Akbik said.

"I'm afraid that's correct," Lind said. Observing that the captain was in no mood to continue playing straight man, he hastily grew serious. "Sir, do we have to breathe that stink anyway? I mean, we can keep on wearing airsuits outdoors, and recharge their bottles from the ship's oxy renewal plant."

"Unless we have to dismantle her," Akbik said.

They stared at each other, ten men alone in unknownness. The silence and the metal shell around them seemed to press inward.

Widsith was a shining tower, tall in the valley. Lind looked up her hull, and up, and up, and reflected what a fraud the damned object was. Enormous fuel tanks: empty. Engines, therefore, useless, aside from the auxiliary generator. Holds: big, yes, but barely able to contain the equipment necessary to establish a minimal space gate. As a result: living quarters, life support systems, rations, personal gear, cut to the bone.

And now, it turned out, Guinevere wasn't going to furnish any supplements. No food, no air—

"And the ship's not any cornucopia, either," Lind said.

"Beg pardon?" Tao-Chi Huang, the chief mechanic, glanced from the robotractor he was assembling.

"Oh. I was thinking out loud," Lind said. "The hull's nothing but light metals, aluminum, magnesium, beryllium alloys. And those we can get right out of this planet. What we've got to have, that the planet doesn't seem to have, is iron."

"What for? Structural members?"

"Well, that was the original idea. Maybe we can use something else there. But we cannot replace iron—quite a bit of very pure iron—in things like the transformers and magnetic cores of the mattercaster circuits. Not without redesigning the entire system, which would take a special R & D team several years. We are not an R & D team, and we do not have several years."

"I know Gilruth hasn't found any native iron yet," Tao-Chi said. "But there must be some in the planet!"

"So we assumed, before we arrived here. And, actually, I imagine there is some. Down in the core, if nowhere else. Bloated lot of good that does us. What we need is a workable deposit not too far underground. And we haven't the time or the resources to scour an entire world searching for ore."

"Hm-m-m." Tao-Chi started to rub his chin thoughtfully, but his faceplate got in the way. "Maybe our trouble is due to a lack of ferric-reducing bacteria."

"Maybe. Though wouldn't you still get oxide in the soil? I think likelier the iron shortage is just another aspect of the weird element-abundance situation here." Lind shrugged in his airsuit. "If we don't find any, damn soon, we'll have to cannibalize for it—like maybe your construction equipment."

"That will be needed up to the last minute," Tao-Chi protested, "and in any event, it's mostly light alloys, too. Besides, if you did take what steel parts there are, I doubt if you could purify the iron out of modern aligned-crystal materials with anything less than a gaseous diffusion plant."

"Which is too much for us to build. Well, so we'll have to steal from the ship. Take out its transformers and such. We can do that, of course. *But*, the ship is an integrated system. If we remove a vital unit from, say, the engine, then the oxy renewal plant will also stop working."

"I know. So Joe Riese had jolly well better find a way to make the local air breathable. Right?"

"Right. He's working on it. Me, I got business in the shack."

Burdened and uncomfortable in survival gear, Lind's slender form walked on down the valley. Passing the maser mast where he had disgraced himself, he winced. Damn Guinevere! Damn the astronomers, and their bland assumption that every kind of atom would be available here even if the percentages varied. Damn his own foolishness in signing on for the expedition. At best, he'd come back to a list of female vidiphone numbers five years obsolete. At worst . . . what good was money to a skeleton? Even if the skeleton's owner had died drunk.

A stream burbled along the path. It supplied water and waste removal to the gate construction site, and thus had lost its pristine freshness. Serve it right, Lind thought viciously. He proceeded to a wide plot which had been cleared of topsoil and was now being leveled. Dust smoked in the orange sunlight, up from a bulldozer which snorted back and forth. That was an automaton, as was nearly every machine. Under no circumstances could ten men's muscles do the brute labor of establishing a base on an uncharted planet. Nor could ten men's brains do the innumerable necessary analyses of data and material samples. Humans were here to look at the instruments, program the robots, read the computer printouts, make the decisions, and perform the finer tasks of installation and adjustment as the mattercaster assembly grew.

Nice theory. Trouble was, Guinevere didn't provide the stuff needed to make the theory work.

Lind entered a prefab which squatted ugly at the field's edge. Sunlight through begrimed windows glittered red-gold off a clutter of apparatus. Ocampo and Fulgosi were turning away from a bulk that Lind identified as a furnace with attached spectroscope, pyrometer, and assorted things to which he could not put a name. Technology, he thought, had made technologists too blooming specialized.

"No." Fulgosi's helmet speaker needed some adjustment, Lind heard. What the mineralogist must have intended as a sigh emerged as a whistle. "This sample has essentially the same composition as the last. Nothing is different except the hydration and a few impurities."

"But we must have calcium minerals!" Ocampo exclaimed.

"Take that up with a higher authority. All I can tell you is that none of the neighborhood rocks are limestone or gypsum or anything reasonable like that. They're universally based on strontium. It must be vastly more common here."

"Well, can't strontium substitute for calcium? In human bones, I've heard—"

"Yes, there is chemical similarity. But not that close. Strontium carbonate won't burn to the oxide at any temperature we can get with available equipment. And even if it did, the oxide won't set to mortar. Nor, for that matter, will strontium sulfate make plaster of paris." Fulgosi regarded the construction chief for a moment. "Must we actually have a massive concrete foundation for the 'caster?"

"Hell, yes!" Ocampo said. "The thing won't work unless it's properly anchored to the planet. Reaction forces would tear it apart otherwise. Without a strong, weatherproof setting— Ah, Lind. What brings you here?"

"I was after the latest analysis myself," the electronician said.

Sweat glistened behind Fulgosi's faceplate. "I'll sure be glad when we do get our materials together, if we ever do," he said. "Right now, Gilruth, Riese, and I are the only ones working, and we're working our tails off. The rest of you sit and feel sorry for yourselves . . . No, my friend, we haven't turned up any bismuth for you."

"But I have been working," Lind answered. "With references and my computer and— How about antimony? Found some antimony?"

"Why, uh, yes. Quite a bit of stibnite. What do you want it for?"

"*Whew!* I'm glad to hear that. You see, the tuning circuit calls for a large piece of bismuth, as being diamagnetic. But antimony is almost as good in that respect, and I've calculated we can substitute it." Lind turned to Ocampo. "While I was at it, I checked some other possibilities. You need zinc for galvanizing, and we haven't found any decent deposits, right? Well, cadmium will do the same job. You put it on by a different process, but it works fine."

Fulgosi snatched a piece of paper off the bench. "Here," he said with sudden excitement. "A list. What we've found in extractable form and quantity so far. Plenty of cadmium."

"Plenty of gold, silver, platinum, manganese," Ocampo said. His bitterness had not left him. "So we can make busbars of silver instead of copper—but we'd counted on that anyway. So manganese is a good structural metal—but in a moist oxygen atmosphere, it'll crumble to oxide almost as fast as we can cast our members. Where's the iron coming from for the foundation and framework? Not the ship. Barely enough iron in her for your circuits, Lind. Show me how to make concrete without calcium, and several tons of ribs and girders without iron, and a few such items, and I'll kiss you."

"Ugh," said Lind. He studied the engineer's miserable countenance. "You've let this get to you," he said. "Your brain's tramping in circles. Me, I dunno, maybe that anesthesia jag I went on cleared my head somehow. But seems obvious to me, we'll do best to find substitutes for the stuff we can't get."

"I think that's obvious even to a dolt like me," Ocampo snorted. "Name a few."

"I did. Antimony and cadmium. And then— Hm-m-m." Lind went to the window and stared out. The volcano lifted sheer before him. They'd landed here because they couldn't prospect an entire world and a plutonic region was likeliest to have a wide assortment of easily refinable minerals. Which this area did, to be sure; only they were the wrong minerals. Lind's forefinger doodled on a dusty pane. "Why steel?" he murmured. "I mean, for the framework supporting the 'caster on its foundation. You only want mechanical strength there. Why not stone?"

"No boulders are big enough, around here anyway, and we can't assemble small ones into a frame because we can't make mortar."

"But that lava up yonder. We should be able to cast it and machine it to shape. Don't you think so?"

"Well, I'll be—" Ocampo stood silent a while. Fulgosi gulped. Hope had come like a blow.

"Y-yes," Ocampo said at length, quite softly. "For beams, as you say, and bedplates, and so forth. But not for the foundation. We're not set up to cast that big a piece of material with a high melting point; and, as I told you, without mortar—"

"So what else might serve?" Lind swung back. Inside his suit, he quivered. "Let's use our imaginations. Let's ask Gilruth what he's noticed on his exploring trips."

A teakettle whine cut through the sky. "Speaking about devils," Fulgosi said. The expedition's single aircraft, a hover job with considerable range and carrying capacity, bounced to a halt on the field. The three men hurried from the shack.

Cilruth was climbing out. "What'd you find?" Ocampo shouted.

"Brought home some assorted rocks for testing," the pilot said, working hard at imperturbability. "Doubt if they'll be any use, though. What spot checks I carried out, neutron activation and so forth, showed the same bloody distribution of elements upriver as here. No iron, no calcium, no copper, no nothing."

"Never mind, never mind." Lind seized his arm and dragged him away. "We want something different from you."

Cilruth looked alarmed. "Have you left your helmet off again?"

Ocampo explained. Cilruth had landed on the volcano some days ago, near the peak. Well, did the lava beds look mineable? And what else might he have noticed, paying no special heed at the time because what he saw hadn't been what he hoped to see? The conference lasted an hour, and all four returned to the spaceship still chattering into each other's mouths.

They cycled through the personnel lock, racked their suits, and encountered emptiness. Everyone must be outside, performing the jobs that had to be done before actual construction could start. No—a noise below decks— Ocampo's party squeezed down the companionway.

Now that most of the machinery had been unloaded, the holds were echoing caverns. Riese had taken one of them over for a workshop. He stood at a bench, a laser torch glaring in his hand, making a box-like assembly.

"Hey, Joe!" Lind cried. "Listen! Good news."

"I'm glad somebody has some," the biochemist grumbled. He switched off his torch, wiped his face, and sat down on the bench. It sagged under his weight, being little more than some cobbled-together alumalloy sheeting which wasn't needed elsewhere at the moment. He swore and stood again. "What's happened?"

"We've hit on the answer to our problem," Lind said. "For the native materials we need but don't find, we use ersatz."

"You've taken this long to realize that?"

"Oh, yes, the principle is obvious," Ocampo said, "but we didn't fully accept it until today. We kept hoping we'd be able to proceed according to the book. This afternoon, though, we took a hard look at the possibilities of using what we've actually got on Guinevere. And they seem very hopeful."

"Fine." Riese stared at the apparatus he was making and clicked his tongue. "Maybe I'd better turn this project over to one of you geniuses."

"What's the matter?" The question jerked from Gilruth. "Not working properly?"

"Not yet, anyhow. The basic idea is simple enough. Assuming that one or more of the trace gases, the bio-compounds, in the atmosphere are responsible for anesthetizing us: how do we get them out? They're organic. So, in theory, we blow air through an electric arc energetic enough to break them down into CO_2 and such-like, and bubble the resulting gas through water. What comes out the other end should be good, pure air."

"It had better be," Gilruth said. "Once we've removed the iron from the ship's electrical system . . . well, I somehow can't visualize us, drunk or dopey or unconscious, completing that matter gate. Can you?"

"No." Riese scowled. "My problem is this: Apparently, whatever compounds affect us need only be present in micro quantities. Probably they act by inhibiting certain enzymes. Therefore, my purifier has to work perfectly. So it has to be continuously monitored by spectrographic and chromatographic instruments. Now designing such circuits is not easy." He looked at Lind. "I think, if you can be spared, you'd better devote full time to helping me."

"I guess I'd better," Lind said in a small voice.

The others had too much to do to worry about whether they would have air fit to breathe toward the end of their tasks. That "too much" included, especially, worrying about every other problem. For their food supply, however rationed, was little more than sufficient to carry them through a set of standardized procedures evolved on familiar kinds of planet. Now they must invent a whole new set of ways to install a mattercaster. And a starving man can continue to work for a while, after a fashion, but he can't continue to produce bright ideas, or tinker with the thing he has built until it does what it is supposed to do.

Thus time was precious and the labor schedule brutal.

They did talk a little. Tamping an explosive charge into a lava bed, Fulgosi growled, "Nussbaum's sure got a soft touch."

"What's he doing?" Deschamps leaned wearily on his pick.

"Making glass epoxy out of silicates and organics. Solder substitute."

"Well, we've got to have that, too, and if Nussbaum's the only one of us who can cook up a batch—One man can't carry all human knowledge in his head."

"Not even in his own specialty," Fulgosi sighed. "I suspect that's Joe Riese's problem. If he had the right references, he could probably find out in ten minutes what's wrong with the atmosphere and what to do about it. But no one thought to supply him with the one obscure bit of information he needs." He straightened and looked around. Rockfields tilted dark, up beyond snows and glaciers to where the mountain lifted a skyward smoke plume. "O.K., let's get back to the aircraft. When this charge blows, it could touch off an avalanche."

Down in the valley, after nightfall, Gilruth shepherded a truckload of logs to the construction site. A stone-crushing mill thudded, a wood-pulping machine yelled, a chemical vat seethed—improvised, most of it, one way or another. Beyond the lamp posts ringing the field could be seen the stars, cold and strangely constellated and terribly remote.

"How much more timber will you need?" he asked Ocampo. "Robot help or no, lumberjacking is hardly a sinecure."

"Piloting is?" the engineer replied. "I think two more loads should end this job. We had to run quite a series of tests, but we seem to have found the right mixture now."

"Some concrete, eh? Vegetable fiber and asbestos-like rock, bound together with molten sulfur and poured to make your foundation!"

"Well, it serves. In fact, it should be just as good as the ordinary cement-based kind."

"What about reinforcing rods and conductive tie beams?"

"Haven't you heard? No, I guess you've been in the outback too much. Alagau."

"Alagau to you, too. Or was that a death rattle?"

Ocampo laughed a little. Some distance away, an arc furnace was uncovered, and the light glared off his faceplate. "Aluminum-silver-gold alloy," he explained. "Nussbaum suggested it, and it seems to be hard and tough enough for our purposes, in spite of having a mauve color. Al, Ag, Au, see?"

After a moment, he added, "In fact, by now we have an astonishing collection of assorted ersatzes. Beryllium, titanium, lithium, magnesium, thorium, they're more versatile than you'd think, in their different alloys. Then there are organics, plastics, tars—"

Gilruth slumped wearily in the cab and stared at the fire-trickle where molten metal ran into casting forms. "Won't do us a lot of good if we can't get pure air," he said. "How're Riese and Lind coming on that?"

"All right, I guess."

"I was thinking. Suppose they fail. What then? Couldn't we get oxygen by roasting ores?"

"Um-m-m . . . possibly. That'd be such a huge job, though. Only imagine what equipment we'd have to build, to operate on the scale necessary. We could easily starve to death before we finished. No, I think our friends have plain got to succeed."

And a few mornings later, in *Widsith*'s hold, Riese

and Lind beamed at each other. On the bench before
them stood a cylinder, fantastically piped and wired.
A fan whined at the open end. Inside, arcs sizzled and
water gurgled. At the farther end, attached instruments
certified that clean atmosphere, free of any organic taint
except a normal amount of carbon dioxide, was being
compressed into a bottle.

"The damned thing is finally in shape," Lind breathed.

"I was beginning to think it never would be," Riese
said.

"Maybe now you understand why engineers draw
high pay." Lind yawned and stretched. "Me for some
sleep, before Akbik puts me in one of the labor gangs!"

"Uh—" Riese hesitated. "A final test."

"What?"

The biochemist took the bottle off the hose and attached it to the shoulder pack of an airsuit. "Take a few
lungfuls," he said. "Just to make sure."

"But . . . I mean . . . oh, all right." Lind grumbled
his way into the suit, sealed the helmet, and cracked
the valve on the bottle.

"Well?" asked Riese anxiously.

"Seems O.K. The stink is certainly gone." Lind inhaled again, and again. "Yep, jus' fine." A wide and
foolish grin spread over his features. "Won'erful. Great.
What a team we are, you know 'at? C'mon, le's dance."

He walked out alone, into darkness. Under a dim
red moon, the valley dews, the stream, and the far
snowpeaks glimmered. Somewhere an animal hooted.
His footfalls made a hollow thudding.

He felt cold and tired. But sleep escaped him. Everyone else was sacked out, exhausted. Lind envied
them. For the moment, they were free of the knowledge that their labor had been for naught and that
Guinevere would never let them go.

They'd driven themselves as no one would dare drive
a mule. (Of course, no one would care overly much if a
mule didn't come home.) Now time was hideously short.

There simply weren't enough man-days left to build the oxygen-producing furnace which Gilruth had proposed. The food was practically gone. You could live a while, empty-bellied; but some of that while must go to completing and adjusting the space gate whose framework bulked yonder in the shadows of the field. Already Lind's stomach complained of underemployment.

Earth—prime ribs, baked potatoes smothered in sour cream and chives, apple pie à la mode . . . No, damn it, before he thought about such things he must think how to return to them.

Basic problem: Find a way to get the anesthetic factor out of Guinevere's atmosphere. The way must needs be simple, the apparatus easy to build and operate. Thereafter everything else would be simple—shutting down the ship's oxy renewer, dismantling the electrical system, installing the needed iron parts in the mattercaster circuits, adding the parts hauled from Bellegarde, tuning and activating the gate, and making one stride across the light-years to home.

Well, then, Billy Lind, *solve* the basic problem. It must have a perfectly easy solution. Given it as a question on an exam, not so long ago in college, you'd likely have seen the answer inside of five minutes.

But the situation was different here. Here, everybody had worked too hard. Their brains were numb. He and Riese were the only men who'd been spared much physical labor—because their comrades trusted them to provide the air—and now their failure seemed to have stunned Riese into apathy.

Therefore, Billy Lind, the responsibility is yours. Certainly you're tired. Certainly you're also in a state of mild shock. But you're not too stupefied to think. Are you?

So. What are the facts? It had been obvious that organic compounds were acting as snooze gases. What else could? And yet . . . Guineverean air processed until sensitive instruments swore it was pure, kept right on kicking the human mind out of orbit. Therefore the taken-for-granted fact had not been a fact after all. So what other possible fact (or) was there?

Lind couldn't imagine. The noble gases? But they were inert! You could breathe oxyhelium without noticing any difference except that your voice sounded squeaky. Oh, yes, you could force one or two other members of that family to take on fluorine atoms or whatever, but they did it grudgingly, under very special laboratory conditions. How could—Lind cursed in the dark. Unfair to demand that he think. He was too tired, too hungry, even in his airsuit too cold.

Cold!

Hello, Earth. Hello, everybody. Whoops!

William J. Lind again. Call me Billy. Call me anything. Bee-cause by th' time you receive me on Bellegarde, I'll've been five years home an' inna diff'rent job an' you can't fire me 'cause I'll long've been in some other line uh work an' so to Guinevere wi' you.

Or else I'll be rich. Might be. Gotta lotta (hey, that rhymes!) gotta lotta new techniques here. Sure to be other planets like this'n. Hey? Hey-hey. Maybe we can patent 'em. At leas' we can write a book. Bes' seller. "I Was Pumpin' On Guinevere." How's 'at sound? Thought so.

I was, y' know. Distillin', anyway. An' then pumpin' the oxy an' the nitro into bottles. My idea. Very simple. You jus' liquefy your air. We'd enough stuff lyin' 'roun' to make an air liquefaction unit. Then we did fractional distillation. Which, muh frien's an' fellow citizens o' the gr-r-reat World Federation, is not distillin' fractions. What an image, though. Li'l numerators an' denominators boilin' off. But all we did was liquid air. I mean to say, now hear this, all we did was *distill* liquid air. After we'd made it inna firs' place. See? No sweat. Mos' abs'lutely no sweat, at minus 107 point one degrees Celsius.

Tha's the boilin' point o' xenon. Guilty party. We foun' out by tryin' different fractions on ourselves. Yep, xenon. Fine anesthetic. Oh, you knew that already, didja? But you gotta big fat computer full uh references handy. So why didn' you tell us? Huh? Answer me that.

Guess we should'a thought o' it before. But so much else to do. An' whole situation complicated. So natur'lly we 'spected anesthesia problem 'ud be complicated, too. Wasted lotta time, we did, lookin' for complicated answer 'fore we hit on simple one. I did. Me. William J. Lind. I'm simple-minded. Ta-ra-la-la-i-tu! I gloat! Hear me!

All set now. Ever' thing ready. Tomorrow we start the transmitter an' walk through to Bellegarde. Liquor on Bellegarde. Big celebration. But me, I get drunk on xenon, so why not start now? Whoops! How many moons this planet got, anyway?

Jus' one question, you fat smug people. (Dunno whether to call you smats or fugs.) One li'l bitty question. This here now funny elemental composition. Damn near killed us. Jus' a very slight shift in relative abundances, and k-k-kr-r-r! So I ask you. Think about this. Think good 'n hard, because nex' time aroun', you're not gonna have William J. Lind on deck. Nope, you're not. I'll be on Earth, livin' the life o' Riley, an' I don' 'magine Riley'll ever come home. 'Cause he's one o' these here now onward-the-march-o'-mankind characters. He'll be pioneerin' the stars. I won't.

So, okay, my question: What you gonna do when you hit the *nex'* crazy kind o' world?

SYMMETRY

At one moment he stood under heaven and the eyeless gaze of machines he did not understand; the next instant he was in a room of steel and another man with him. The sheer swiftness of the change was like a blow to the head. He swayed on his feet, while the afterimages from daylight faded away and the knowledge seeped through him that he was elsewhere.

Almost, he fell. The need to catch his balance jarred him back toward alertness. He swore, the oath seemed to echo, and stared.

The stranger stared back across the width of the room. His mouth also snapped shut. Dunham's glance went over him, centimeter by centimeter, in a single sweep. He was a big fellow, likewise clad in a gray coverall and gripsole boots. Hair bristled short, reddish-brown, above a wide face with a scar on the right cheek.

They spoke together:

"WWhhoo tthhee hheellll aarree yyoouu??"

Real echoes rang off the polished steel that enclosed them. Dunham's hand dropped to his hip before he remembered he'd left his sidearm in the spaceship. The stranger's hand dropped too, and his second curse was the same and exploded at the same time.

Slowly, the truth grew on Dunham. Two mouths sagged and two pairs of eyes opened till white ringed the gray. It was like standing before a mirror—a mirror that did not reverse.

The stranger was himself.

"AAllmmiigghhttyy CCoossmmooss,, wwhhaatt iiss tthhiiss??"

Step by step they approached each other. Their right hands they held out at arm's length as if they were blind; their left made fists and drew back. Dunham felt sweat trickle down his ribs. It reeked. Nightmare, nightmare. He tried to wake up and couldn't.

The room had gone quiet. Only the soft thud of boots and the louder breathing sounded within it. A wave of loneliness such as he had not felt since childhood washed over Dunham. The fact that he was the only man on the whole planet, and it fifty light-years from the nearest human base, was no longer cause for joy but for horror, now that he was not. He stamped the feeling down. It struggled.

In the exact center of the room, the men met. They touched fingertips together and jerked them back. For heartbeats more, they again merely stared.

Then two breaths shuddered inward and two voices nearly whispered: "LLeett'ss kkeeeepp oouurr hheeaaddss. WWee'vvee ggoott ttoo ffiigguurree tthhiiss oouutt—"

Panic flared into rage. "FFoorr CCoossmmooss' ssaakkee, wwiillll yyoouu ssttoopp tthhaatt ppaarrrr-oottiinngg?"

Echoes gibed. They took each a step backward. The gray cloth wrinkled identically with every movement.

Silence anew. Dunham's mind grabbed after reality. It closed on what was around him. That was the truth which it would be insane to deny. This thing was actually happening to him.

To them.

Acceptance brought a measure of steadiness. He'd been in wicked situations before, after all. The problem now was to fathom what had caught him and work out how to get free of it.

He looked about the chamber. It must be the inside of the metal box he had been investigating (or, rather, he thought with brief wryness, had been gawking at). About five meters square and two high, it was strictly right-angled at the corners and featureless except for the door. That door made a one-meter circle at the exact center of the ceiling. He had climbed up one of the metal-encased machines—if machines they were— that surrounded the box, gotten onto its flat top, and found the door at the middle. Precisely at the middle of the door was a knob, as might have been on some museum-piece house on Earth. When he leaned over, grasped the knob, twisted and tugged, the door began to swing open.

And all at once he was here.

The door must have fallen shut, but there was a knob on this side too, likewise at the center. He saw it through a transparent hollow cylinder that ringed it. The cylinder was about thirty centimeters long and fifteen interior diameter. Dunham judged that he could get one of his thick forearms up it to turn the knob. Push the door aside, grab the rim, chin himself and scramble out; yes, he had the strength to do that, one-handed if necessary. Weight on this planet was about nine-tenths standard.

Otherwise he saw blankness. The metal radiated white light. It was not too bright for human vision, but the absence of any demarkable source, of any shadows or shadings, might well be the eeriest thing about the room.

He grew aware that it was hot, and had a feeling that temperature had risen in the short while he had been captive. The sun was passing midday outside—both Dunhams glanced at their chronos—and could well turn this into a Dutch oven.

What he'd give for a cold beer! Well, the spacecraft held an ample supply, just a few kilometers' hike away.

The other Dunham licked his own lips.

They gaped. At the back of his head flickered half-remembrances, legends he'd heard as a boy from a kinsman who was interested in antiquities, the *Doppelgänger*, the *fylgja*, the fetch, if you see yourself you will soon die. . . . He thrust them off. He was no damned romantic, he was a practical man with a practical problem to solve.

"WWhhaatt aarree yyoouu,, aannyywwaayy? WWhhaatt'ss ccooppiieedd mmee—hhooww—SShhuutt uupp, ddaammnn yyoouu,, II'mm ttaallkkiinngg!!"

They stopped. Their eyes narrowed. Dunham summoned patience and tried, slowly:

"LLooookk, wwee ccaann sseetttllee iitt llaatteerr—"

Silence clapped back down. He saw how he must be tensed and glowering. But this was crazy. They had to get out. Once free, they could confer or fight or whatever they wanted. Somebody had to take action. Fast.

Dunham jumped back to the middle of the room. So did his double. Two right hands reached up for the sleeve around the doorknob.

They collided at the lip. It had only space for one arm.

"GGeett oouutt ooff mmyy wwaayy, II'llll ooppeenn iitt—"

The hands fell. In the face that confronted his, Dunham saw grimness take hold.

His kind has been born, and died, and been reborn, throughout human history. Frontier scout, mountain man, voortrekker, names in many languages have bespoken him who always fares ahead of his race, driven by longings for which he has no name. Not that he expresses it thus. He leaves fancy words to the effete who stay behind. In his own mind, he doesn't like being one more interchangeable part of society, but he does like the fun and luxury civilization has to offer. Therefore he goes out beyond the edge of the known, and brings back what he can find that will command a goodly price. He believes his hope is that he will gain such a fortune that he can do anything he wants after he retires. It hardly ever befalls him. Likeliest he ends his days in poverty, though if he is somewhat luckier he leaves his bones in a strange land before he has grown very old.

Dunham was typical; he expected to become rich. Thus far, his gains had won him a half share in an aged, barely spaceworthy scoutcraft, mortgaged to buy supplies. He lost his partner to an oxygen recycler that failed in a human-poisonous atmosphere. Having buried the man as decently as he was able and brought under control a sorrow whose sharpness surprised him, Dunham resolved not to head straight back. Nothing awaited him on Nerthus but the loss of his ship to his debts. Being already well beyond every region mapped into the databases, he'd continue casting about as long as the deuterium tanks allowed. Solitary exploration was appallingly risky, of course, but at worst he would die and at best—at best, anything was imaginable.

In point of fact, he was not altogether reckless. The interstellar voortrekker is by no means the half-educated hotspur whom our more hackneyed dramas depict. The Coordination Service would never license any such person to operate anything as powerful as a spacecraft; nor could he survive long, no matter what its robotics did to help him. He needs a substantial knowledge of both physical and biological science. Unless he intends to shun worlds with intelligent natives, as some do, he must add a broad understanding of xenology, and the law requires his ethics meet a minimum standard. This last is seldom enforceable, but few rovers are villains, and in his rough fashion Dunham was a well-intentioned man. He exercised reasonable caution on behalf of others as well as himself. Groundlings are apt to forget that material goods are hardly ever worth seeking among the stars; the real treasure is knowledge.

To be sure, scientific foundations lack funds to purchase word of yet another planetary system, unless there is something extraordinary about it. Dunham's gamble paid off spectacularly. He came upon an Earthlike world of a Sol-like sun. Study from orbit indicated it was without intelligent life, but its biosphere seemed to be sufficiently terrestroid that humans could colonize. If this proved correct, discoverer's commissions would make Dunham so rich that money would cease to have meaning for him.

That might not happen. On certain planets, the death traps are subtle and pervasive. Years of field work would be necessary before this one could be certified. Meanwhile, basic reward would cover Dunham's debts and give him a fair-sized stake.

But circling the globe, he and his instruments found something more down in its cloud-swirled beauty. On one continent in the north tropical zone, several square kilometers had been cleared. Though the forest was coming back, the area remained unmistakable—even without the metallic objects clustered in the middle of it. Yet this world had evolved no thinking, fabricating animal; he felt sure of that. Somebody had visited here before him.

When? Thirty years ago, fifty, a hundred? It depended on how fast regrowth went, which he didn't know.

Who? The databases had nothing about it. And those things didn't much resemble artifacts of any spacefaring race with which humanity was acquainted.

Most men would have brought the news home immediately. The prize for such a clue to a whole new civilization should keep a person comfortably, if not lavishly, for a lifetime. Being what he was, Dunham landed his vessel in a meadow not far from the site.

All communications bands were mute. Having already established that the atmosphere was breathable, he ran biochemical tests and found with glee that nothing could possibly infect him; the proteins were too different from his. His survey in orbit had revealed no sign of animals large enough that they might menace him anyway. Therefore he left weapons behind when he struck off afoot. If anybody or anything watched over the foreign camp, he'd be outgunned regardless. A show of pacifism was his best bet.

Through hot and leafy reaches he made his way, fighting underbrush, to arrive panting and with heart athunder. He found total desertion. Poking around in bluish-green shrubbery, he came upon crumbling traces of occupation, here what he guessed had been a basement, there a mound low and flat and squared-off, yonder a patch where energy had fused the soil to brick. Several meters tall, smoothly and enigmatically curved, half a dozen distinct structures encompassed a large right-angled parallelepiped which he thought of as a box, since it should reasonably contain something else. Weather had not touched the shiny blankness of the metal casings.

Had the aliens abandoned equipment they no longer needed? That seemed wasteful. Well, they might have a technology so advanced that this apparatus was as easily produced and readily discarded as a plastic wrapper. Dunham scuttled around, dizzy with excitement. He *had* to learn more.

He could climb up the tiers of one machine (?) to the top of the box (?). He did, though the sun-heated steel (?) came near scorching his palms. Above, set flush, was a door he could not resist trying to open. Him and Bluebeard's wife.

Whereupon he found himself inside the box—surely that was it—and another himself to keep him company.

The Dunhams stepped back, never shifting eyes from

each other. Lips opened and closed again. Talk was useless. Instead, he'd better start thinking.

What kind of devil's pitfall have I stumbled into? What is this thing that looks and acts just like me?

A robot? No, unless the definition included flesh and blood; and besides, how and why would such a duplicate of him be instantly made?

Duplicate!

The Dunhams cried out before they clamped their jaws against the clattering of their teeth. The truth, what had to be the truth, was upon them.

Matter duplication. The Holy Grail of human engineers for the past two or three centuries. The wave equations existed; Dunham had seen them once, without much comprehension. Generate a beam to scan an object atom by atom. Have the scanner signal direct a force-field that builds up a perfect copy out of a gasified matter bank. Of course, you must complete the whole process in nanoseconds, before quantum fluctuations make garbage out of the coalescing material. A pretty problem. Some physicists held it to be inherently unsolvable.

The aliens had solved it. They'd gone on to develop a system that could assemble the copy in thin air, with no visible apparatus around. Presumably transmission had been through these walls—

Was the original Dunham still outside?

Two men spun about and beat on steel till their fists were bloody and screamed till their throats were raw.

When they sagged back in defeat, the silence around their breathing was a strangle hold. Upon drawing the door partly open, he, they, had seen the metal of the box was rather thin; it had rung faintly under boots. A Dunham One would have heard them and investigated. Since he had not, he did not exist. Nothing lived but they inside, two men alone. The device must have dissolved Dunham One, perhaps converted him to energy and projected it into this space to become part of the matter making up Two and Three.

So he was dead? The twin bodies shuddered.

Countenances hardened. Dunham was a pragmatist. Semantic games had never interested him. The ego, the continuity of memory and personality, which was his essential self, lived on. He was experiencing it the same as always. The reproduction of the pattern had been perfect. He was not dead, any more than he died because metabolism gradually replaced the atoms in his body with other atoms.

Rather, he now lived twice. The duplicator had created two Dunhams, simultaneously, at equal distances from their respective corners of the symmetrical room. Which was the real one? Meaningless question. They both were. Given identical configurations in identical environments, naturally all their actions would be identical and simultaneous, if cause-and-effect operated as usual. Right down to the last molecular stirrings within their cells—

He saw his own grin twist its way across the face that was his. "HHeclllloo tthheerree, oolldd bbuuddddyy."

A scowl chased it away. The knowledge had not liberated them. The box was growing hotter by the minute. Tongues lay like blocks of wood above parched gullets. At this rate, they'd soon be dead of dehydration, unless the air got too foul and depleted first.

Ridiculous! Here they were, two strong men, with nothing to do to save themselves except reach up and twist a doorknob. Dunham groped in a pocket and drew forth a coin, his lucky piece. His double did also. He opened his mouth to speak and realized he needn't. *Heads I go, tails you go. . . . No, don't you toss. . . . Oh, all right, we'll match for it. . . . No, that won't work either. . . . Let's throw, and agree that heads wins. To the floor.*

Two coins spun. They landed together at the feet of their owners. Both men squatted down to see. Tails. Dunham retrieved his and waited for his double to open the door.

So did the other Dunham.

They tried again. Two heads. Both stood up, stepped forward, and stopped.

Of course. Even the fall of a coin is determined, by a million tiny factors of balance and force which are the same for both of us.

Dunham stared from side to side. There must be some way to break the deadlock. He tautened and leaped for the door.

The bodies crashed together just beneath the sleeve.

"CCoossmmooss wwrreecckk yyoouu, ssttaanndd cclleeaarr!!"

Dunham shoved. The same push sent him lurching back. He snarled and came in swinging. The other man's fist lanced toward him. Both rolled with a punch that grazed the two left temples.

Then they were on the floor, kicking and slugging and yelling.

The fight ended after a minute or two. They sat and looked dully at the damage wrought. A left eye swollen, miscellaneous abrasions and bruises that would soon blossom in many colors, a trickle of blood from the lower lip, coverall ripped half open, and Dunham abused precisely likewise.

They had not moved from beneath the knob of their desiring. Every force tending to one man's right had been countered by an equal force tending toward the other man's right.

They sketched a smile and clambered to their feet. Maybe they could tear the sleeve loose. The effort led to naught. Each tug was nullified by its opposite. When they finally hit on the idea of applying torque by creating a couple, nothing happened. The cylinder and its attachment were too sturdy.

Horror stared at horror. If only one of them could do just one thing differently from the other, they ought to rouse from the nightmare. They began moving about, retreating to various corners, dancing a wild rigadoon, anything that might break the symmetry. All failed.

Eventually they sat down and regarded each other across the width of their prison. Hatred had died. They were caught together. Each wanted to release his mate nearly as much as he wanted to free himself. Only how?

Dunham leaned against the wall. Sweat-soaked, his garment seemed almost to sizzle from the heat that now dwelt in the metal. His smell filled his nostrils; he stank like a corpse.

Why had the builders made this thing? A torture chamber? What a revenge, killing your enemy twice. No, that seemed unlikely. Could it have been an intelligence test, maybe for officer candidates? Or for any spacefarers who blundered into territory claimed by the aliens?

Dunham knotted his fists and mumbled obscenities. He was dying just when he had won to his dream.

Two of him posed no problem. The prizes for this discovery and the commissions to follow would make them both rich beyond imagination. True, they'd share feelings about a certain fellow explorer, but she would doubtless remain unattainable, friendly enough, mildly regretful that she herself was too purely a scientist to settle down with a man of his sort. Never mind, he'd suffer no dearth of women. Meanwhile, he'd have a crewmate, the best possible, to help him steer home.

If they escaped. Otherwise they'd die in identical pain at the same moment. And the moment was not distant.

Curse it, we can't be helpless! We're free human beings, we've got free will, if only we can figure out how to make use of it. They peered at each other, aware of what went on behind the haggard faces. *Are we mutually telepathic? No, probably not. But it'll be impossible to find out unless we get loose from here.* Two rather gristy laughs rattled forth.

Dunham rubbed his eyes. Hot, hot, his brain was

frying in his skull just when he must think. Thought offered his last slight hope.

The identity could not be perfect. Any machine had some limit, however narrow, to its accuracy; and the uncertainty principle was always operative. These two Dunhams were simply possessed of (by?) an extraordinarily high degree of similarity. If they waited sufficiently long, the small accumulated errors would add up, till at last one could do something the other didn't. But that might well take days, and they had mere hours.

The moment they broke the spell, it would stay broken: for their experiences would no longer be the same. As soon as they got out of this symmetrical hell, into the blessed disorder of wind and trees, pebbles underfoot and stars overhead, the imputs they got and their own reactions would diverge more and more. Doubtless they'd have awkward moments, but nothing they couldn't resolve. After a few years of separate living, they'd truly be two different persons. The similarity would last through their lives, but matter no more than it did between natural twins.

All they need do now was establish some order of precedence. "*I* will open the door." At the moment, though, what did "I" mean? It was completely immaterial through whose eyes you looked, from whose side you told the story. It was the same story for both.

Never mind philosophy. Work on getting out.

Assume this arrangement isn't meant to be lethal. Maybe it was for conducting certain scientific tests, and we fell into our situation by sheer accident. Something ought to exist here that is not symmetrical, that we can use to tap one of us and say, "You're it." Otherwise we're dead.

If the builders had had the decency to install a coin-flipping machine—But no, each Dunham would have picked heads, unless he picked tails.

Beneath the fever-flush of heat, both faces turned a little darker. *He knows me so well, my sins and stupidities, vices and weaknesses. . . . No, what of it? I needn't be any more ashamed than he is. In fact, I can't be.*

They tried to break the simmering stillness. "SSaayy, hhooww aabbboouutt—" They stopped. It was worse than not talking at all.

They rose and paced, hands behind backs. There must be a way out, there must, there must must must mustmustmust—*Stop that!*

Could any kind of game or contest have a winner? Tic-tac-toe, matched fingers, which fist holds the coin? No. Their grin was weary. Dunham felt shocked. Did he look that bad?

Up and down, up and down, up and down, prowling the furnace. Where was the selective element, the random factor? How to find it before you died, when you were dying already?

Hot, hot, hot, the air was withering him, sucking him dry, while its molecules made a tom-tom of his skull. This is the way the world ends, not in chaos but in symmetry, frozen yet blazing hot.

Hot!

The double whoop rang off the walls.

Gas dynamics is an exact science employing deterministic principles. Nevertheless, it bases itself on randomness. Here physics deals with phenomena so complex that, even in principle, it can only analyze them statistically. Given a fair-sized volume of air, the molecules are smoothly dispersed throughout it. However, if you consider very small cells, a fractional millimeter on a side, the odds are that no two of them will have identical distributions at any given instant. A coin is big and heavy. It would take a strong breeze to affect the way it falls. An extremely light object presents a different case.

Twin men stood in a room of steel. Each pulled a hair from his head (the same hair?) and dropped it. Each puffed hard to stir the heat-roiled air still more. The strands drifted lazily, borne on tiny convection currents. *The one whose hair lands first will open the door.*

"All right, friend."

Dunham—no matter which one—crossed to the middle of the room, reached up the sleeve, and turned the knob. When he pushed, the metal discus swung on hidden hinges and he saw the sky.

HUNTER'S MOON

We do not perceive reality, we conceive it. To suppose otherwise is to invite catastrophic surprises. The tragic nature of history stems in large part from this endlessly recurrent mistake.

—Oskar Haeml, *Betrachtungen über die menschliche Verlegenheit*

***Both suns were now down. The western mountains had become a wave of blackness, unstirring, as though the cold of Beyond had touched and frozen it even as it crested, a first sea barrier on the flightway to the Promise; but heaven stood purple above, bearing the earliest stars and two small moons, ocher edged with silvery crescents, like the Promise itself. Eastward, the sky remained blue. There, just over the ocean, Ruii was almost fully lighted, Its bands turned luminous across Its crimson glow. Beneath the glade that It cast, the waters shivered, wind made visible.

A'i'ach felt the wind too, cool and murmurous. Each finest hair on his body responded. He needed but little thrust to hold his course, enough effort to give him a sense of his own strength and of being at one, in travel and destination, with his Swarm. Their globes surrounded

147

him, palely iridescent, well-nigh hiding from him the ground over which they passed; he was among the highest up. Their life-scents overwhelmed all else which the air bore, sweet, heady, and they were singing together, hundreds of voices in chorus, so that their spirits might mingle and become Spirit, a foretaste of what awaited them in the far west. Tonight, when P'a crossed the face of Ruii, there would return the Shining Time. Already they rejoiced in the raptures ahead.

A'i'ach alone did not sing, nor did he lose more than a part of himself in dreams of feast and love. He was too aware of what he carried. The thing that the human had fastened to him weighed very little, but what it was putting into his soul was heavy and harsh. The whole Swarm knew about the danger of attack, of course, and many clutched weapons—stones to drop or sharp-pointed branches shed by ü trees—in the tendrils that streamed under their globes. A'i'ach had a steel knife, his price for letting the human burden him. Yet it was not in the nature of the People to dread what might sink down upon them out of the future. A'i'ach was strangely changed by that which went on inside him.

The knowledge had come, he knew not how, slowly enough that he was not astonished by it. Instead, a grimness had meanwhile congealed. Somewhere in those hills and forests, a Beast ran that bore the same thing he did, that was also in ghostly Swarm-touch with a human. He could not guess what this might portend, save trouble of some kind for the People. He might well be unwise to ask. Therefore he had come to a resolve he realized was alien to his race: he would end the menace.

Since his eyes were set low on his body, he could not see the object secured on top, nor the radiance beaming upward from it. His companions could, though, and he had gotten a demonstration before he agreed to carry it. The beam was faint, faint, visible only at night and then only against a dark background. He would look for a shimmer among shadows on the land. Sooner or later, he would come upon it. The chance was not bad now at this, the Shining Time, when the Beasts would seek to kill People they knew would be gathered in vast numbers to revel.

A'i'ach had wanted the knife as a curiosity of possible usefulness. He meant to keep it in the boughs of a tree; when the mood struck him, he would experiment with it. A Person did once in a while employ a chance-found object, such as a sharp pebble, for some fleeting purpose, such as scooping open a crestflower pod to release its delicious seedlets upon the air. Perhaps with a knife he could shape wood into tools and have a stock of them always ready.

Given his new insight, A'i'ach saw what the blade was truly for. He could smite from above till a Beast was dead—no, *the* Beast.

A'i'ach was hunting. ***

Several hours before sundown, Hugh Brocket and his wife, Jannika Rezek, had been preparing for their night's work when Chrisoula Gryparis arrived, much overdue. A storm had first grounded aircraft at Enrique and then, perversely moving west, forced her into a long detour on her way to Hansonia. She didn't even see the Ring Ocean until she had traversed a good thousand kilometers of mainland, whereafter she must bend southward an equal distance to reach the big island.

"How lonely Port Kato looks from the air," she remarked. Though accented, her English—the agreed-upon common language at this particular station—was fluent: one reason she had come here to investigate the possibility of taking a post.

"Because it is," Jannika answered in her different accent. "A dozen scientists, twice as many juniors, and a few support personnel. That makes you extra welcome."

"What, do you feel isolated?" Chrisoula wondered. "You can call to anywhere on Nearside that there is a holocom, can you not?"

"Yeah, or flit to a town on business or vacation or

whatever," Hugh said. "But no matter how stereo an image is and sounds, it's only an image. You can't go out with it for a drink after your conference is finished, can you? As for an actual visit, well, you're soon back here among the same old faces. Outposts get pretty ingrown socially. You'll find out, if you sign on." In haste: "Not that I'm trying to discourage you. Jan's right, we'd be more than happy to have somebody fresh join us."

His own accent was due to history. English was his mother tongue, but he was third-generation Medean, which meant that his grandparents had left North America so long ago that speech back there had changed like everything else. To be sure, Chrisoula wasn't exactly up-to-date, when a laser beam took almost fifty years to go from Sol to Colchis and the ship in which she had fared, unconscious and unaging, was considerably slower. . . .

"Yes, from Earth!" Jannika's voice glowed.

Chrisoula winced. "It was not happy on Earth when I left. Maybe things got better afterward. Please, I will talk about that later, but now I would like to look forward."

Hugh patted her shoulder. She was fairly pretty, he thought: not in a class with Jan, which few women were, but still, he'd enjoy it if acquaintance developed bedward. Variety is the spice of wife.

"You really have had bad luck today, haven't you?" he murmured. "Getting delayed till Roberto—uh, Dr. Venosta went out in the field—and Dr. Feng back to the Center with a batch of samples—" He referred to the chief biologist and the chief chemist. Chrisoula's training was in biochemistry; it was hoped that she, lately off the latest of the rare starcraft, would contribute significantly to an understanding of life on Medea.

She smiled. "Well, then I will know others first, starting with you two nice people."

Jannika shook her head. "I am sorry," she said. "We

are busy ourselves, soon to leave, and may not return
until sunrise."

"That is—how long? About thirty-six hours? Yes Is
that not long to be away in . . . what do you say? . . .
this weird an environment?"

Hugh laughed. "It's the business of a xenologist,
which we both are," he said. "Uh, I think I, at least,
can spare a little time to show you around and intro-
duce you and make you feel sort of at home." Arriving
as she did at a point in the cycle of watches when most
folk were still asleep, Chrisoula had been conducted to
his and Jannika's quarters. They were early up, to make
ready for their expedition.

Jannika gave him a hard glance. She saw a big man
who reckoned his age at forty-one Terrestrial years:
burly, a trifle awkward in his movements, beginning to
show a slight paunch; craggy-featured, sandy-haired,
blue-eyed; close-cropped, clean-shaven, but sloppily clad
in tunic, trousers, and boots, the style of the miners
among whom he had grown up. "I have not time," she
stated.

Hugh made an expansive gesture. "Sure, you just
continue, dear." He took Chrisoula under the elbow.
"Come on, let's wander."

Bewildered, she accompanied him out of the clut-
tered hut. In the compound, she halted and stared
about her as if this were her first sight of Medea.

Port Kato was indeed tiny. Not to disturb regional
ecology with things like ultraviolet lamps above crop-
lands and effluents off them, it drew its necessities from
older and larger settlements on the Nearside mainland.
Moreover, while close to the eastern edge of Hansonia,
it stood a few kilometers inland, on high ground, as a
precaution against Ring Ocean tides which could get
monstrous. Thus nature walled and roofed and weighed
on the huddle of structures, wherever she looked—

—or listened, smelled, touched, tasted, moved. In
slightly lesser gravity than Earth's, she had a bound to
her step. The extra oxygen seemed to lend energy

likewise, though her mucous membranes had not yet quite stopped smarting. Despite a tropical location, the air was balmy and not overly humid, for the island lay close enough to Farside to be cooled. It was full of pungencies, only a few of which she could remotely liken to anything familiar, such as musk or iodine. Foreign too were sounds—rustlings, trills, croakings, mumbles—which the dense atmosphere made loud in her ears.

The station itself had an outlandish aspect. Buildings were made of local materials to local design; even a radiant energy converter resembled nothing at home. Multiple shadows carried peculiar tints; in fact, every color was changed in this ruddy light. The trees that reared above the roofs were of odd shapes, their foliage in hues of orange, yellow, and brown. Small things flitted among them or scuttled along their branches. Occasional glittery drifts in the breeze did not appear to be dust.

The sky was deep-toned. A few clouds were washed with faint pink and gold. The double sun Colchis—Castor C was suddenly too dry a name—was declining westward, both members so dim that she could safely gaze at them for a short while, Phrixus at close to its maximum angular separation from Helle.

Opposite them, Argo dominated heaven, as always on the inward-facing hemisphere of Medea. Here the primary planet hung low; treetops hid part of the great flattened disc. Daylight paled the redness of its heat, which would be lurid after dark. Nonetheless it was a colossus, as broad to the eye as fifteen or sixteen Lunas above Earth. The subtly chromatic bands and spots upon its face, ever-changing, were clouds more huge than continents and hurricane vortices that could have swallowed whole this moon upon which she stood.

Chrisoula shivered. "It . . . strikes me," she whispered, "more than anywhere around Enrique or—or approaching from space . . . I have come elsewhere in the universe."

Hugh laid an arm around her waist. Not being a glib man otherwise, he merely said, "Well, this *is* different. That's why Port Kato exists, you know. To study in depth an area that's been isolated a while; they tell me the isthmus between Hansonia and the mainland disappeared fifteen thousand years ago. The local dromids, at least, never heard of humans before we arrived. The ouranids did get rumors, which may have influenced them a little, but surely not much."

"Dromids—ouranids—oh." Being Greek, she caught his meanings at once. "Fuxes and balloons, correct?"

Hugh frowned. "Please. Those are pretty cheap jokes, aren't they? I know you hear them a lot in town, but I think both races deserve more dignified names from us. They are intelligent, remember."

"I am sorry."

He squeezed a trifle. "No harm done, Chris. You're new. With a century needed for question and answer, between here and Earth—"

"Yes. I have wondered if it is really worth the cost, planting colonies beyond the Solar System just to send back scientific knowledge that slowly."

"You've got more recent information about that than I do."

"Well . . . the planetology, biology, chemistry, they were still giving new insights when I left, and this was good for everything from medicine to volcano control." The woman straightened. "Perhaps the next step is in your field, xenology? If we can come to understand a nonhuman mind—no, two, on this world—maybe three, if there really are two quite unlike sorts of ouranid as I have heard theorized—" She drew breath. "Well, then we might have a chance of understanding ourselves." He thought she was genuinely interested, not merely trying to please him, when she went on: "What is it you and your wife do? They mentioned to me in Enrique it is quite special."

"Experimental, anyway." Not to overdo things, he

released her. "A complicated story. Wouldn't you rather take the grand tour of our metropolis?"

"Later I can by myself, if you must go back to work. But I am fascinated by what I have heard of your project. Reading the minds of aliens!"

"Hardly that." Seeing his opportunity, he indicated a bench outside a machine shed. "If you really would like to hear, sit down."

As they did, Piet Marais, botanist, emerged from his cabin. To Hugh's relief, he simply greeted them before hurrying off. Certain Hansonian plants did odd things at this time of day. Everyone else was still indoors, the cook and bull cook making breakfast, the rest washing and dressing for their next wakeful period.

"I suppose you are surprised," Hugh commenced. "Electronic neuranalysis techniques were in their infancy on Earth when your ship left. They took a spurt soon afterward, and of course the information reached us before you did. The use there had been on lower animals as well as humans, so it wasn't too hard for us— given a couple of geniuses in the Center—to adapt the equipment for both dromids and ouranids. Both those species have nervous systems too, after all, and the signals are electrical. Actually, it's been more difficult to develop the software, the programs, than the hardware. Jannika and I are working on that, collecting empirical data for the psychologists and semanticians and computer people to use.

"Uh, don't misunderstand, please. To *us*, this is nearly incidental. Mindscan—bad word, but we seem to be stuck with it— mindscan should eventually be a valuable tool in our real job, which is to learn how local natives live, what they think and feel, everything about them. However, at present it's very new, very limited, and very unpredictable."

Chrisoula tugged her chin. "Let me tell you what I imagine I know," she suggested, "then you tell me how wrong I am."

"Sure."

She grew downright pedantic: "Synapse patterns can be identified and recorded which correspond to motor impulses, sensory inputs, their processing—and at last, theoretically, to thoughts themselves. But the study is a matter of painfully accumulating data, interpreting them, and correlating the interpretations with verbal responses. Whatever results one gets, they can be stored in a computer program as an n-dimensional map off which readings can be made. More readings can be gotten by interpolation."

"Whc-ew!" the man exclaimed. "Go on."

"I am right this far? I did not expect to be."

"Well, naturally, you're trying to sketch in a few words what needs volumes of math and symbolic logic to describe halfway properly. Still, you're doing better than I could myself."

"I continue. Now recently there are systems which can make correspondences between different maps. They can transform the patterns that constitute thought in one mind into the thought-patterns of another. Also, direct transmission between nervous systems is possible. A pattern can be detected, passed through a computer for translation, and electromagnetically induced in a receiving brain. Does this not amount to telepathy?"

Hugh started to shake his head, but settled for: "M-m-m, of an extremely crude sort. Even two humans who think in the same language and know each other inside out, even they get only partial information—simple messages, burdened with distortion, low signal-to-noise ratio, and slow transmission. How much worse when you try with a different life-form! The variations in speech alone, not to mention neurological structure, chemistry—"

"Yet you are attempting it, with some success, I hear."

"Well, we made a certain amount of progress on the mainland with both dromids and ouranids. But believe me, 'certain amount' is a gross overstatement."

"Next you are trying it on Hansonia, where the cultures must be entirely strange to you. In fact, the species of ouranid—Why? Do you not add needlessly to your difficulties?"

"Yes—that is, we do add countless problems, but it is not needless. You see, most cooperating natives have spent their whole lives around humans. Many of them are professional subjects of study: dromids for material pay, ouranids for psychological satisfaction, amusement, I suppose you could say. They're deracinated; they themselves often don't have any idea why their 'wild' kinfolk do something. We wanted to find out if mindscan can be developed into a tool for learning about more than neurology. For that, we needed beings who're relatively, uh, uncontaminated. Lord knows Nearside is full of virgin areas. But here Port Kato already was, set up for intensive study of a region that's both isolated and sharply defined. Jan and I decided we might as well include mindscan in our research program."

Hugh's glance drifted to the immensity of Argo and lingered. "As far as we're concerned," he said low, "it's incidental—one more way for us to try and find out why the dromids and ouranids here are at war."

"They kill each other elsewhere too, do they not?"

"Yes, in a variety of ways, for a larger variety of reasons, as nearly as we can determine. Let me remark for the record, I myself don't hold with the theory that information on this planet can be acquired by eating its possessor. For one thing, I can show you more areas than not where dromids and ouranids seem to coexist perfectly peacefully." Hugh shrugged. "Nations on Earth never were identical. Why should we expect Medea to be the same everywhere?"

"On Hansonia, however—you say war?"

"Best word I can think of. Oh, neither group has a government to issue a formal declaration. But the fact is that more and more, for the past couple of decades—as long as humans have been observing, if not longer— dromids on this island have been hell-bent to kill ouranids. Wipe them out! The ouranids are pacifistic, but they do defend themselves, sometimes with active measures like ambushes." Hugh grimaced. "I've glimpsed several fights, and examined the results of a lot more. Not pleasant. If we in Port Kato could mediate—bring peace—well, I'd think that alone might justify man's presence on Medea."

While he sought to impress her with his kindliness, he was not hypocritical. A pragmatist, he had nevertheless wondered occasionally if humans had a right to be here. Long-range scientific study was impossible without a self-supporting colony, which in turn implied a minimum population, most of whose members were not scientists. He, for example, was the son of a miner and had spent his boyhood in the outback. True, settlement was not supposed to increase beyond its present level, and most of this huge moon was hostile enough to his breed that further growth did seem unlikely. But—if nothing else, simply by their presence, Earthlings had already done irreversible things to both native races.

"You cannot ask them why they fight?" Chrisoula wondered.

Hugh smiled wryly. "Oh, sure, we can ask. By now we've mastered local languages for everyday purposes. Except, how deep does our understanding go?

"Look, I'm the dromid specialist, she's the ouranid specialist, and we've both worked hard trying to win the friendship of specific individuals. It's worse for me, because dromids won't come into Port Kato as long as ouranids might show up anytime. They admit they'd be duty bound to try and kill the ouranids—and eat them, too, by the way; that's a major symbolic act. The dromids agree this would be a violation of our hospitality. Therefore I have to go meet them in their camps and dens. In spite of this handicap, she doesn't feel she's progressed any further than me. We're equally baffled."

"What do the autochthons *say?*"

"Well, either species admits they used to live together amicably . . . little or no direct contact, but with considerable interest in each other. Then, twenty or thirty years back, more and more dromids started failing to reproduce. Oftener and oftener, castoff segments don't come to term, they die. The leaders have decided the ouranids are at fault and must be exterminated."

"Why?"

"An article of faith. No rationale that I can untangle, though I've guessed at motivations, like the wish for a scapegoat. We've got pathologists hunting for the real cause, but imagine how long that might take. Meanwhile, the attacks and killings go on."

Chrisoula regarded the dusty ground. "Have the ouranids changed in any way? The dromids might then jump to a conclusion of *post hoc, propter hoc.*"

"Huh?" When she had explained, Hugh laughed. "I'm not a cultivated type, I'm afraid," he said. "The rock rats and bush rangers I grew up amongst do respect learning—we wouldn't survive on Medea without learning—but they don't claim to have a lot of it themselves. I got interested in xenology because as a kid I acquired a dromid friend and followed her-him through the whole cycle, female to male to post-sexual. It grabbed hold of my imagination—a life that exotic."

His attempt to turn the conversation into personal channels did not succeed. "What have the ouranids done?" she persisted.

"Oh . . . they've acquired a new—no, not a new religion. That implies a special compartment of life, doesn't it? And ouranids don't compartmentalize their lives. Call it a new Way, a new *Tao.* It involves eventually riding an east wind off across the ocean, to die in the Farside cold. Somehow, that's transcendental. Please don't ask me how, or why. Nor can I understand—or Jan—why the dromids consider this is such a terrible thing for the ouranids to do. I have some guesses, but they're only guesses. She jokes that they're born fanatics."

Chrisoula nodded. "Cultural abysses. Suppose a modern materialist with little empathy had a time machine, and went back to the Middle Ages on Earth, and tried to find out what drove a Crusade or Jihad. It would

appear senseless to him. Doubtless he would conclude
everybody concerned was crazy, and the sole possible
way to peace was total victory of one side or the other.
Which was not true, we know today."

The man realized that this woman thought a good
deal like his wife. She continued: "Could it be that
human influences have brought about these changes,
perhaps indirectly?"

"It could," he admitted. "Ouranids travel widely, of
course, so those on Hansonia may well have picked up,
at second or third hand, stories about Paradise which
originated with humans. I suppose it'd be natural to
think Paradise lies in the direction of sunset. Not that
anybody has ever tried to convert a native. But natives
have occasionally inquired what our ideas are. And
ouranids are compulsive mythmakers, who might seize
on any concept. They're ecstatics, too. Even about
death."

"While dromids are prone to develop militant new
religions overnight, I have heard. On this island, then,
a new one happens to have turned against the ouranids,
no? Tragic—though not unlike persecutions on Earth, I
expect."

"Anyhow, we can't help till we have a lot more
knowledge. Jan and I are trying for that. Mostly, we
follow the usual procedures, field studies, observations,
interviews, et cetera. We're experimenting with mindscan
as well. Tonight it gets our most thorough test yet."

Chrisoula sat upright, gripped. "What will you do?"

"We'll draw blank, probably. You're a scientist yourself, you know how rare the real breakthroughs are.
We're only slogging along."

When she remained silent, Hugh filled his lungs for
talk. "To be exact," he proceeded, "Jan's been cultivating a 'wild' ouranid, I a 'wild' dromid. We've persuaded
them to wear miniaturized mindscan transmitters, and
have been working with them to develop our own capability. What we can receive and interpret isn't much.

Our eyes and ears give us a lot more information. Still, this is special information. Supplementary.

"The actual layout? Oh, our native wears a button-sized unit glued onto the head, if you can talk about the head of an ouranid. A mercury cell gives power. The unit broadcasts a recognition signal on the radio band—microwatts, but ample to lock onto. Data transmission naturally requires plenty of bandwidth, so that's on an ultraviolet beam."

"What?" Chrisoula was startled. "Isn't that dangerous to the dromids? I was taught they, most animals, have to take shelter when a sun flares."

"This is safely weak, also because of energy limitations," Hugh replied. "Obviously, it's limited to line-of-sight and a few kilometers through air. At that, natives of either kind tell us they can spot the fluorescence of gas along the path. Not that they describe it in such terms!

"So Jan and I go out in our separate aircraft. We hover too high to be seen, activate the transmitters by a signal, and 'tune in' on our individual subjects through our amplifiers and computers. As I said, to date we've gotten extremely limited results; it's a mighty poor kind of telepathy. This night we're planning an intensive effort, because an important thing will be happening."

She didn't inquire immediately what that was, but asked instead: "Have you ever tried sending to a native, rather than receiving?"

"What? No, nobody has. For one thing, we don't want them to know they're being scanned. That would likely affect their behavior. For another thing, no Medeans have anything like a scientific culture. I doubt they could comprehend the idea."

"Really? With their high metabolic rate, I should guess they think faster than us."

"They seem to, though we can't measure that till we've improved mindscan to the point of decoding verbal thought. All we've identified thus far is sensory impressions. Come back in a hundred years and maybe someone can tell you."

The talk had gotten so academic that Hugh positively welcomed the diversion when an ouranid appeared. He recognized the individual in spite of her being larger than usual, her globe distended with hydrogen to a full four meters of diameter. This made her fur sparse across the skin, taking away its mother-of-pearl sheen. Just the same, she was a handsome sight as she passed the treetops, crosswind and then downward. Prehensile tendrils streaming below in variable configurations, to help pilot a jet-propelled swim through the air, she hardly deserved the name "flying jellyfish"—though he had seen pictures of Earthside Portuguese men-of-war and thought them beautiful. He could sympathize with Jannika's attraction to this race.

He rose. "Meet a local character," he invited Chrisoula. "She has a little English. However, don't expect to understand her pronunciation at once. Probably she's come to make a quick swap before she rejoins her group for the big affair tonight."

The woman got up. "Swap? Exchange?"

"Yeah. Niallah answers questions, tells legends, sings songs, demonstrates maneuvers, whatever we request. Afterward we have to play human music for her. Schönberg, usually; she dotes on Schönberg."

—Loping along a clifftop, Erakoum spied Sarhouth clearly against Mardudek. The moon was waxing toward solar fullness as it crossed that coal-glow. Its disc was dwarfed by the enormous body behind, was actually smaller to the eye than the spot which also passed in view, and its cold luminance had well-nigh been drowned earlier when it moved over one of the belts which changeably girded Mardudek. They grew bright after dark, those belts; thinkers like Yasari believed they cast back the light of the suns.

For an instant, Erakoum was captured by the image, spheres traveling through unbounded spaces in circles within circles. She hoped to become a thinker herself. But it could not be soon. She still had her second breeding to go through, her second segment to shed and guard, the young that it presently brought forth to help rear; and then she would be male, with begetting of her own to do—before that need faded out likewise and there was time for serenity.

She remembered in a stab of pain how her first birthing had been for naught. The segment staggered about weakly for a short while, until it lay down and died as so many were doing, so many. The Flyers had brought that curse. It had to be them, as the Prophet Illdamen preached. Their new way of faring west when they grew old, never to return, instead of sinking down and rotting back into the soil as Mardudek intended, surely angered the Red Watcher. Upon the People had been laid the task of avenging this sin against the natural order of things. Proof lay in the fact that females who slew and ate a Flyer shortly before mating always shed healthy segments which brought forth live offspring.

Erakoum swore that tonight she was going to be such a female.

She stopped for breath and to search the landscape. These precipices rimmed a fjord whose waters lay more placid than the sea beyond, brilliant under the radiance from the east. A dark patch bespoke a mass of floating weed. Might it be plants of the kind from which the Flyers budded in their abominable infancy? Erakoum could not tell at her distance. Sometimes valiant members of her race had ventured out on logs, trying to reach those beds and destroy them; but they had failed, and often drowned, in treacherous great waves.

Westward rose rugged, wooded hills where darkness laired. Athwart their shadows, sparks danced glittering golden, by the thousands—the millions, across the land. They were firemites. Through more than a hundred days and nights, they had been first eggs, then worms, deep down in forest mould. Now Sarhouth was passing across Mardudek in the exact path that mysteriously

summoned them. They crept to the surface, spread
wings which they had been growing, and went aloft,
agleam, to mate.

Once it had meant no more to the People than a
pretty sight. Then the need came into being, to kill
Flyers . . . and Flyers gathered in hordes to feed on
yonder swarms. Hovering low, careless in their glee,
they became more vulnerable to surprise than they
commonly were. Erakoum hefted an obsidian-headed
javelin. She had five more lashed across her back. A
number of the People had spent the day setting out
nets and snares, but she considered that impractical;
the Flyers were not ordinary winged quarry. Anyhow,
she wanted to fling a spear, bring down a victim, sink
fangs into its thin flesh, herself!

The night muttered around her. She drank odors of
soil, growth, decay, nectar, blood, striving. Warmth
from Mardudek streamed through a chill breeze to lave
her pelt. Half-glimpsed flitting shapes, half-heard as
they rustled the brush, were her fellows. They were
not gathered into a single company, they coursed as
each saw fit, but they kept more or less within earshot,
and whoever first saw or winded a Flyer would signal it
with a whistle.

Erakoum was farther separated from her nearest comrades than any of them were. The others feared that the
light-beam reaching upward from the little shell on her
head wold give them away. She deemed it unlikely, as
faint as the bluish gleam was. The human called Hugh
paid her well in trade goods to wear the talisman whenever he asked and afterward discuss her experiences
with him. For her part, she knew a darkling thrill at
such times, akin to nothing else in the world, and
knowledge came into her, as if through dreams but
more real. These gains were worth a slight handicap on
an occasional hunt . . . even tonight's hunt.

Moreover—There was something she had not told
Hugh, because he had not told her earlier. It was
among the things she learned without words from the

gleam-shell. A certain Flyer also carried one, which also kept it in eldritch contact with a human.

The big grotesque creatures were frank about being neutral in the strife between People and Flyers. Erakoum did not hold that against them. This was not their home, and they could not be expected to care if it grew desolate. Yet she had shrewdly deduced that they would try to keep in its burrow their equal intimacy with members of both breeds.

If Hugh had been anxious for her to be soul-tied to him this night, doubtless another human wanted the same for a Flyer. It would be a special joy to her to bring that one down. Besides, looking as she fared for a pale ray among firemites and stars might lead her toward a whole pack of enemies. Rested, she began to trot inland.

Erakoum was hunting.—

Jannika Rezek was forever homesick for a land where she had never lived.

Her parents had politically offended the government of the Danubian Federation. It informed them they need not enter a reindoctrination hospice if they would volunteer to represent their country in the next shipful of personnel to Medea. That was scarcely a choice. Nevertheless, her father told her afterward that his last thought, as he sank down into suspended animation, was of the irony that when he awakened, none of his judges would be alive and nobody would remember what his opinions had been, let alone care. As a matter of fact, he learned at his goal that there was no longer a Danubian Federation.

The rule remained in force that, except for crewfolk, no person went in the opposite direction. A trip was too expensive for a passenger to be carried who would land on Earth as a useless castaway out of past history. Husband and wife made the best they could of their exile. Both physicians, they were eagerly received in Armstrong and its agricultural hinterland. By the mod-

est standards of Medea, they prospered, finally winning
a rare privilege. The human population had now been
legally stabilized. More would overcrowd the limited
areas suitable for settlement, as well as wreaking havoc
on environments which the colony existed to study. To
balance reproductive failures, a few couples per generation were allowed three children. Jannika's folk were
among these.

Thus everybody, herself perforce included, reckoned
hers a happy childhood. It was a highly civilized one,
too. In the molecules of reels kept at the Center was
stored most of mankind's total culture. Industry was, at
last, sufficiently developed that well-to-do families could
have sets which retrieved the data in as full hologrammic
and stereophonic detail as desired. Her parents took
advantage of this to ease their nostalgia, never thinking
what it might do to younger hearts. Jannika grew up
among vivid ghosts: old towers in Prague, springtime in
the Böhmerwald, Christmas in a village which centuries
had touched only lightly, a concert hall where music
rolled in glory across a festive-clad audience which
outnumbered the dwellers in Armstrong, replications of
events which once made Earth tremble, songs, poetry,
books, legends, fairy tales. . . . She sometimes wondered if she had gone into xenology because the ouranids
were like bright, magical beings in a fairy tale.

Today, when Hugh led Chrisoula outside, she had
stood for a moment staring after them. Abruptly the
room pressed in as if to choke her. She had done what
she could in the way of brightening it with drapes,
pictures, keepsakes. At present, however, it was be-
strewn with field gear; and she hated disorder. He
cared naught.

The question rose afresh: How much did he care at
all, any longer? They were in love when they married,
yes, of course, but even then she recognized it was in
high degree a marriage of convenience. Both were after
appointments to an outpost station where they would
maximize their chances of doing really significant, origi-

nal research. Wedded couples were preferred, on the theory that they would be less distracted from their work than singletons. When they had their first babies, they were customarily transferred to a town.

She and Hugh quarreled about that. Social pressure—remarks, hints, embarrassed avoidance of the subject—was mounting on them to reproduce. Within population limits, it was desirable to keep the gene pool as large as possible. She was getting along in age, a bit, for motherhood. He was more than willing. But he took for granted that *she* would maintain the home, hold down the desk job, while *he* continued in the field. . . .

She must not reprove him when he came back from his flirtatious little stroll. She lost her temper too often these days, grew outright shrewish, till he stormed from the hut or else grabbed the whisky and started glugging. He was not a bad man—at the core, he was a good man, she amended hastily—thoughtless in many ways but well-meaning. At her time of life, she couldn't likely do any better.

Although—She felt the heat in her cheeks, made a gesture as if to fend off the memory, and failed. It was two days old.

Having learned from A'i'ach about the Shining Time, she wanted to gather specimens of the glitterbug larvae. Hitherto humans had merely known that the adult insectoids swarmed aloft at intervals of approximately a year. If that was important to the inhabitants of Hansonia, she ought to know more. Observe for herself, enlist the aid of biologists, ecologists, chemists—She asked Piet Marais where to go, and he offered to come along. "The idea should have occurred to me before," he said. "Living in humus, the worms must influence plant growth."

Moister soil was required than existed at Port Kato. They went several kilometers to a lake. The walking was easy, for dense foliage overhead inhibited underbrush. Softness muffled footfalls, trees formed high-arched naves, multiple rays of light passed through dusk and fragrances to fleck the ground or glance off small wings, a sound as of lyres rippled from an unseen throat.

"How delightful," Piet said after a while.

He was looking at her, not ahead. She became very conscious of his blond handsomeness. And his youth, she reminded herself, he was her junior by well-nigh a decade, though mature, considerate, educated, wholly a man. "Yes," she blurted. "I wish I could appreciate it as you do."

"It is not Earth," he discerned. She realized that her answer had been less noncommittal than intended.

"I wasn't pitying myself," she said fast. "Please don't think that. I do see beauty here, and fascination, and freedom, oh, yes, we're lucky on Medea." Attempting a laugh: "Why, on Earth, what would I have done for ouranids?"

"You love them, don't you?" he asked gravely. She nodded. He laid a hand on her bare arm. "You have a great deal of love in you, Jannika."

She made a confused effort to see herself through his eyes. Medium-sized, with a figure she knew was stunning; dark hair worn shoulder length, with gray streaks that she wished Hugh would insist were premature; high cheekbones, tilted nose, pointed chin, large brown eyes, ivory complexion. Still, though Piet was a bachelor, someone that attractive needn't be desperate; he could meet girls in town and keep up acquaintance by holocom. He shouldn't be this appreciative of her. She shouldn't respond. True, she'd had other men a few times, before and after she married. But never in Port Kato; too much likelihood of complications, and she'd been furious when Hugh got involved locally. Worse yet, she suspected Piet saw her as more than a possible partner in a frolic. That could break lives apart.

"Oh, look," she said, and disengaged from his touch in order to point at a cluster of seed pyramids. Meanwhile her mind came to the rescue. "I quite forgot, I meant to tell you, I got a call today from Professor al-Ghazi. We think we've found what makes the glitter-bugs metamorphose and swarm."

"Eh?" He blinked. "I didn't realize anybody was working on that."

"Well, it was a, a notion that occurred to me after my special ouranid started me speculating about them. He, A'i'ach, I mean, he told me the time is not strictly seasonal—that is not necessary here in the tropics—but set by Jason—the moon," she added, because the name that humans had bestowed on the innermost of the larger satellites happened to resemble a word which humans had adopted, given by dromids in the Enrique area to an analogue of the sirocco wind.

"He says the metamorphoses come during particular transits of Jason across Argo," she continued. "Roughly, every four hundredth. To be exact, the figure is every hundred and twenty-seven Medean days, plus or minus a trifle. The natives here are as keenly conscious of heavenly bodies as everywhere else. The ouranids make a festival of the swarming; they find glitterbugs deli-cious. Well, this gave me an idea, and I called the Center and requested an astronomical computation. It seems I was right."

"Astronomical cues, for a worm underground?" Marais exclaimed.

"Well, you doubtless recall how Jason excites electri-cal activity in the atmosphere of Argo, like Io with Jupiter—" the Solar System, where Earth has her dwell-ing! "In this case, there's a beaming effect on one of the radio frequencies that are generated, a kind of natural maser. Therefore those waves only reach Medea when the two moons are on their line of nodes. And that is the exact period my friend was describing. The phase is right, too."

"But can the worms detect so weak a signal?"

"I think it is clear that they do. How, I cannot tell without help from specialists. Remember, though, Phrixus and Helle create little interference. Organisms can be fantastically sensitive. Did you know that it takes less than five photons to activate the visual purple in your eye? I suppose the waves from Argo penetrate the soil to a few centimeters' depth and trigger a chain of biochemical reactions. No doubt it is an evolutionary relic from a time when the orbits of Jason and Medea gave an exact match to the seasons. Perturbation does keep changing the movements of the moons, you know."

He was silent a while before he said: "I do know you are a most extraordinary person, Jannika."

She had regained enough equilibrium to control their talk until they reached the lake. There, for a moment, she felt herself shaken again.

A canebrake screened it from them till they had passed through, to halt on a beach carpeted with moss-like amber-hued turf. Untouched by man in its chalice of forest, the water lay scummy, bubbling, and odorous. The sight of soft colors and the smell of living things were not unpleasant; they were normal to Medca—yet how clear and silver-blue the Neusiedler Sea gleamed in Danubia—Breath hissed between her teeth.

"What's wrong?" Piet followed her gaze. "The dromids?"

A party of them had arrived to drink, some distance off. Jannika stared as if she had never seen their kind before.

Nearest was a young adult, presumably virgin, since she had six legs. From the slender, long-tailed body rose a two-armed centauroid torso, up to the oddly vulpine head, which would reach to Jannika's chest. Her pelt shimmered blue-black under the suns; Argo was hidden by trees.

Four-legged, a trio of mothers kept watch on the eight cubs they had between them. One set of young showed by their size that their parent would soon ovulate again, be impregnated by a mating, shortly thereafter shed her second segment, and attend it until it gave birth. Another member of this group was at that stage of life, walking on two legs, no longer a functional female but with the male gonads still undeveloped.

No male of breeding age was present. Such a creature was too driven, lustful, impatient, violent, for sociability. There were three post-sexual beings, grizzled
but strong, protective, their biped movements fast by
human standards though laggard compared to the lightning fluidity of their companions.

All adults were armed with stone-age spears, hatch-
ets, and daggers, plus the carnivore teeth in their jaws.

They were gone almost as soon as Jannika had seen
them, not out of fear but because they were Medean
animals whose chemistry and living went swifter than
hers.

"The dromids," she got out.

Piet regarded her a while before he said gently:
"They pursue your dear ouranids. You tell me that will
get worse than ever on the night when the glitterbugs
rise. But you must not hate them. They are caught in a
tragedy."

"Yes, the sterility problem, yes. Why should they
drag the ouranids down with them?" She struck fist into
palm. "Let's get to work, let's collect our samples and
go home, can we, please?"

He was fully understanding.

She cast the memory out and flung herself back into
preparations for the night.

Hugh Brocket and his wife departed a while after
sunset. Their flitters jetted off in a whisper, reached an
intermediate altitude, and circled for a minute while
the riders got bearings and exchanged radioed farewells. Observed from below, catching the last gleam of
sunken Colchis on their flanks, they resembled a pair of
teardrops.

"Good hunting, Jan."

"Ugh! Don't say that."

"Sorry," he apologized in a stiff tone, and cut out the
sender. Sure, it had been tactless of him, but why must
she be so goddamn touchy?

Never mind. He'd plenty to do. Erakoum had promised to be on Shipwreck Cliffs about this time, since her gang meant to proceed north along the coast from its camp before turning inland. Thereafter her location would be unpredictable. He must lock onto her transmitter soon. Jannika's craft dwindled in sight, bound on her own quest. Hugh set his inertial pilot and settled back in his safety harness to double-check his instruments. That was mechanical, since he knew quite well everything was in order. Most of his attention roamed free.

The canopy gave a titanic vista. Below, hills lay in dappled masses of shadow, here and there relieved by an argent thread that was a river or by the upheaving of precipices and scarps. The hemisphere-dividing Ring Ocean turned the eastern horizon to quicksilver. Westward in heaven, the double sun had left a Tyrian wake. Overhead reached a velvety dark, becoming more starry with each of his heartbeats. He saw a pair of moons, close enough to show discs lighted from two sides, rusty and white; he recognized more, which were mere bright points to his eyes, by their positions as they went on sentry-go among the constellations. Low above the sea smoldered Argo—no, shone, because its upper clouds were in full daylight, bands of brilliance splashed over sullen red. Jason was close to transit, with angular diameter exceeding twenty minutes of arc, and nevertheless Hugh had trouble finding it amidst that glare.

The shore came in view. He activated the detector and set his craft to hovering. An indicator light flashed green; he had his contact. He sent the vehicle aloft, a full three kilometers. Partly this was because he would be concentrating on encephalic input and wanted plenty of room for piloting error; partly it was to keep beyond sight or hearing of the natives, lest his presence affect their actions. Having taken station, he connected and secured the receiver helmet to his head—it didn't weigh much—and switched it on. Transmitted, amplified, transformed, relayed, reinduced, the events in Erakoum's nervous system merged with the events in his.

By no means did he acquire the dromid's full awareness. Conveyance and translation were far too primi-
tive. He had spent his professional lifetime gaining
sufficient fellow-feeling with the species that, after as
much patience as both individuals could maintain over
a span of years, he could barely begin to interpret the
signals he gathered. The speed of native mental processes was less of a help—through repetition and
reinforcement—than an added hindrance. As a rough
analogy, imagine trying to follow a rapid and nearly
inaudible conversation, missing many a word, in a language you do not know well. Actually, none of what
Hugh perceived was verbal; it was sight, sound, a complex of senses, including those interior like balance and
hunger, including dream-hints of senses that he did not
think he possessed.

He saw the land go by, bush, branch, slope, stars and
moons above shaggy ridges; he felt its varying contours
and textures as feet went pacing; he heard its multitudi-
nous low noises; he smelled richness; the impressions
were endless, most of them vague and fleeting, the best
of them strong enough to take him out of himself, draw
him groundward toward oneness with the creature below.

Clearest, perhaps because his glands were stimulated
thereby, was emotion, determination. Erakoum was out
to get herself a Flyer.

It was going to be a long night, quite possibly a
harrowing one. Hugh expected he'd need a dose or two
of sleep surrogate. Humans had never gotten away from
the ancient rhythms of Earth. Dromids catnapped;
ouranids went—daydreamy? contemplative?

As often before, he wondered briefly what Jan's rapport with her native felt like. They would never be able
to describe their sharings to each other.

*** Well into the hills, A'i'ach's Swarm found a grand
harvest of starwings. The heights were less densely
wooded than the lowlands, which was good, for the
bright prey never went far up, and below a forest

crown, the People were vulnerable to Beast attack. Here was a fair amount of open ground, turf-begrown and boulder-strewn, scattered through the shadowing timber. A narrow ravine crossed the largest of those glades, a gash abrim with blackness.

Like an endless shower of sparks, the starwings danced, dashed, dodged about, beyond counting, meant for naught save the ecstasy of their mating and of the People who fed upon them. Despite the wariness in him, A'i'ach could resist no more than anyone else. He did refrain from valving out gas in his haste to descend, as many did. That would make ascent slow. Instead, he contracted his globe and sank, letting it re-expand slightly as varying air densities demanded. Nor did he release gas to propel himself. Rhythmically pumping, his siphon worked together with the breezes to zigzag him about at low speed. There was no hurry. The starwings numbered more than the Swarm could eat. Plenty would go free to lay their eggs for the next crop.

Among the motes, A'i'ach inhaled his first swallow of them. The sweet hot flavor sang in his flesh. Thickly gathered around him, bobbing, spinning, rippling and flailing their corybantic tendrils, filling the sky with music, the People forgot caution. Love began. It was not purposeless, though without water to fall into, the pollinated seeds would not germinate. It united everyone. Life-dust drifted like smoke in the radiance of Ruii; the sight, smell, taste made feverish that joy which the starwing feast awakened. Again and again A'i'ach ejaculated. He went past his skin, he became a cell of a single divine being which was itself a tornado of love. Sometime when he felt age upon him, he would drift westward across the sea, into the cold Beyond. There, yielding up the last warmth of his body, his spirit would take its reward, the Promise that forever and ever it would be what it was now in this brief night. . . .

A howl smote. Shapes bounded from under trees, out into the open. A'i'ach saw a shaft pierce the globe next to his. Blood spurted, gas hissed forth, the shriveling form fell as a dead leaf falls. Tendrils still writhed when a Beast snatched it the last way down and fangs rent it asunder.

In the crowd and chaos, he could not know how many others died. The greatest number were escaping, rising above missile reach. Those who were armed began to drop their stones and ü boughs. It was not likely that any killed a Beast.

A'i'ach had relaxed the muscles in his globe and shot instantly upward. Safe, he might have joined the rest of the Swarm, to wander off in search of a place to renew festival. But rage and grief seethed too high. A far-off part of him wondered at that; the People did not take hard the death of a Person. This thing he wore, that somehow whispered mysteries—

And he carried a knife!

Recklessly spending gas, he swung about, downward. Most of the Beasts had vanished back into the woods. A few remained, devouring. He cruised at a height near the limits of prudence and peered after his chance. Since he could not drop like a rock, he must feint at one individual, then quickly jet at another, stab, rise, and attack again.

A wan beam of light struck toward him. It came from the head of a Beast which emerged from shadow, halted, and glared upward.

His will blazed forth in A'i'ach. Yonder was the monster which had his kind of bond to humans. If he had already gained a knife thereby, what might that being have gotten, what might it get, to wreak worse harm? If nothing else, killing it ought to shock its companions, make them think twice about their murderousness.

A'i'ach moved to battle. About him, the starwings happily danced and mated. ***

Jannika must search for an hour before she made her contact. An ouranid could not undertake to be at an exact spot at a given time. Hers had simply informed her, while she fastened the transmitter on him, that his group was currently in the neighborhood of Mount MacDonald. She flew there and cast about in ever-deepening darkness until her indicator shone green. Having established linkage, she rose to three kilometers and set the autopilot to make slow circles. From time to time, as her subject passed northeast, she moved the center of her path.

Otherwise she was engaged in trying to be her ouranid. It was impossible, of course, but from the effort she was learning what could never have come to her through spoken language. Answers to factual questions she would not have thought to ask. Folkways, beliefs, music, poetry, aerial ballet, which she could not have known for what they were, observing from outside. Lower down in her, dimmer, but more powerful—nothing she could write into a scientific report: a sense of delights, yearnings, wind, shiningness, perfumes, clouds, rain, immense distances, a sense of what it was to be a heaven-dweller. Not complete, no, a few wavery glimpses, hard to remember afterward; yet taking her out of herself into a new world agleam with wonder.

The thrill was redoubled tonight by A'i'ach's excitement. Her impressions of what he was experiencing had never been stronger or sharper. She floated on airstreams, life-scents and song possessed her, she was a drop in an ocean beneath Ruii the mighty, there was no home to hopelessly long for because everywhere was home.

The Swarm came at last upon a cloud of glitterbugs, and Jannika's cosmos went wild.

For a moment, half terrified, she started to switch off her helmet. Reason checked her hand. What was happening was just an extreme of what she had partaken in before. Ouranids seldom took much nourishment at a single time; when they did, it had an intoxicating effect. She had also felt their sexuality; A'i'ach's maleness was too unearthly to disturb her, as his dromid's femaleness had disturbed Hugh when she mated and later shed her hindquarters. Tonight the ouranids held high revel.

She surrendered to it, crescendo after crescendo, oh, if she only had a man here, but no, that would be different, would blur the sacred splendor, the Promise, the Promise!

Then the Beasts arrived. Horror erupted. Somewhere a strange voice screamed for the avenging of her shattered bliss.

—As she trotted along a bare ridge, Erakoum had thought, with a leap of her pulse, that she spied afar a faint blue ray of light in the air. She could not be certain, through the brilliance cast by Mardudek, but she altered her course in hopes. When she had scrambled a long while among stones and thorns, the glimmer disappeared. It must have been a trick of the night, perhaps moonglow on rising mists. That conclusion did nothing to ease her temper. Everything about the Flyers was unlucky!

Because of this, she was behind the rest of the pack. Her first news of quarry came through their yells. "*Hai-ay, hai-ay, hai-ay!*" echoed around, and she snarled in bafflement. Surely she would arrive too late for a kill. Nonetheless she bounded in that direction. If the Flyers did not get a good wind, she could overtake them and follow along from cover to cover, unseen. Maybe they would not go farther than she had strength for, before they chanced on a fresh upwelling of firemites and descended anew. Breath rasped in her gullet, the hillside struck at her feet with unseen rocks, but eagerness flung her on till she reached the place.

It was a glade, brightly lit though crisscrossed by shadows, cut in half by a small ravine. The firemites swirled about against the forest murk, like a glinting dustcloud. Several females crouched on the turf and ripped at the remnants of their prey. The rest had departed, to trail the escaped Flyers as Erakoum planned.

She stopped at the edge of trees to pant, looked up, and froze. The mass of Flyers was slowly and chaotically streaming west, but a few lingered to cast down their pitiful weapons. From the top of one, dim light beamed aloft. She had found what she sought.

"*Ee-hah!*" she screamed, sprang forward, shook her javelin. "Come, evilworker, come and be slain! By your blood shall you give to my next brood the life you reaved from my first!"

There was no surprise, there was fate, when the eerie shape spiraled about and drew nearer. More would be settled this night than which of them was to survive. She, Erakoum, had been seized by a Power, had become an instrument of the Prophet.

Crouched, she cast her spear. The effort surged through her muscles. She saw it fly straight as the damnation it carried—but her foe swerved, it missed him by a fingerbreadth, and then all at once he was coming directly at her.

They never did that! What sheened in his seaweed grip?

Erakoum grabbed after a new javelin off her back. Each knot in the lashing was supposed to give way at a jerk, but this jammed, she must tug again, and meanwhile the enemy loomed ever more big. She recognized what he held, a human-made knife, sharp as a fresh obsidian blade and more thin and strong. She retreated. Her spear was now loose. No room for a throw. She thrust.

With crazy glee, she saw the head strike. The Flyer rolled aside before it could pierce, but blood and gas together foamed darkly from a slash across his paleness.

He spurted forward, was inside her guard. The knife smote and smote. Erakoum felt the stabs, but not yet the pain. She dropped her shaft, batted her arms, snapped jaws together. Teeth closed in flesh. Through her mouth and down her throat poured a rush of strength.

Abruptly the ground was no more beneath her hind feet. She fell over, clawed with forefeet and hands for a hold, lost it, and toppled. When she hit the side of the ravine, she rolled down across cruel snags. She had an instant's glimpse of sky above, stars and firemites, the

Mardudek-lighted Flyer drifting by and bleeding. Then nothingness snatched her to itself.—

Folk at Port Kato asked what brought Jannika Rezek and Hugh Brocket home so early, so shaken. They evaded questions and hastened to their place. The door slammed behind them. A minute later, they blanked their windows.

For a time they stared at each other. The familiar room held no comfort. Illumination meant for human eyes was brass-harsh, air shut away from the forest was lifeless, faint noises from the settlement outside thickened the silence within.

He shook his head finally, blindly, and turned from her. "Erakoum gone," he mumbled. "How'm I ever going to understand that?"

"Are you sure?" she whispered.

"I . . . I felt her mind shut off . . . damn near like a blow to my own skull . . . but you were making such a fuss about your precious ouranid—"

"A'i'ach's *hurt!* His people know nothing of medicine. If you hadn't been raving till I decided I must talk you back with me before you crashed your flitter—"

Jannika broke off, swallowed hard, unclenched her fists, and became able to say: "Well, the harm is done and here we are. Shall we try to reason about it, try to find out what went wrong and how to stop another such horror, or not?"

"Yeah, of course." He went to the pantry. "You want a drink?" he called.

She hesitated. "Wine."

He fetched her a glassful. His right hand clutched a tumbler of straight whisky, which he began on at once. "I felt Erakoum die," he said.

Jannika took a chair. "Yes, and I felt A'i'ach take wounds that may well prove mortal. Sit down, will you?"

He did, heavily, opposite her. She sipped from her glass, he gulped from his. Newcomers to Medea always

said wine and distilled spirits there tasted more peculiar than the food. A poet had made that fact the takeoff
point for a chilling verse about isolation. When it was
sent to Earth as part of the news, the reply came after a
century that nobody could imagine what the colonists
saw in it.

Hugh hunched his shoulders. "Okay," he growled.
"We should compare notes before we start forgetting,
and maybe repeat tomorrow when we've had a chance
to think." He reached across to their recorder and
flicked it on. As he entered an identification phrase, his
tone stayed dull.

"That is best for us too," Jannika reminded him.
"Work, logical thought, those hold off the nightmares."

"Which this absolutely was—All right!" He regained
a little vigor. "Let's try to reconstruct what did happen.

"The ouranids were out after glitterbugs and the
dromids were out after ouranids. You and I witnessed
an encounter. Naturally, we'd hoped we wouldn't—I
suppose you prayed for that, hm?—but we knew there'd
be hostilities in a lot of places. What shocked the wits
out of us was when our personal natives got into a fight,
with us in rapport."

Jannika bit her lip. "Worse than that," she said.
"They were seeking it, those two. It was not a random
encounter, it was a duel." She raised her eyes. "You
never told Erakoum, any dromid, that we were linking
with an ouranid too, did you?"

"No, certainly not. Nor did you tell your ouranid
about my liaison. We both know better than to throw
that kind of variable into a program like this."

"And the rest of the station personnel have vocabula-
ries too limited, in either language. Very well. But I
can tell you that A'i'ach knew. I was not aware he did
until the fight began. Then it reached the forefront of
his mind, it shouted at me, not in words but not to be
mistaken about."

"Yeah, same thing for me with Erakoum, more or
less."

"Let's admit what we don't want to, my dear. We have not simply been receiving from our natives. We have been transmitting. Feedback."

He lifted a helpless fist. "What the devil might convey a return message?"

"If nothing else, the radio beam that locks us onto our subjects. Induced modulation. We know from the example of the glitterbug larvae—and no doubt other cases you and I never heard of—how shall we know everything about a whole world?—We know Medean organisms can be extremely radio-sensitive."

"M-m, yeah, the terrific speed of Medean animals, key molecules more labile than the corresponding compounds in us. . . . Hey, wait! Neither Erakoum nor A'i'ach had more than a smattering of English. Certainly no Czech, which you've told me you usually think in. Besides, look what an effort we had to make before we could tune them in at all, in spite of everything learned on the mainland. They'd no reason to do the same, no idea of scientific method. They surely assumed it was only a whim or a piece of magic or something that made us want them to carry those objects around."

Jannika shrugged. "Perhaps when we are in rapport, we think more in their languages than we ourselves realize. And both kinds of Medeans think faster than humans, observe, learn. Anyway, I do not say their contact with us was as good as our contact with them. If nothing else, radio has much less bandwidth. I think probably what they picked up from us was subliminal."

"I guess you're right," Hugh sighed. "We'll have to sic the electronicians and neurologists onto the problem, but I sure can't think of any better explanation than yours."

He leaned forward. The energy which now vibrated in his voice turned cold: "But let's try to see this thing in context, so we can maybe get a hint of what kind of information the natives have been receiving from us. Let's lay out once more why the Hansonian dromids

and ouranids are at war. Basically, the dromids are
dying off, and blame the ouranids. Could we, Port
Kato, be at fault?"

"Why, hardly," Jannika said in astonishment. "You
know what precautions we take."

Hugh smiled without mirth. "I'm thinking of psychological pollution."

"What? Impossible! Nowhere else on Medea—"

"Be quiet, will you?" he shouted. "I'm trying to bring
back to my mind what I got from my friend that your
friend killed."

She half rose, white-faced, sat down again, and waited.
The wine glass trembled in her fingers.

"You've always babbled about how kind and gentle
and esthetic the ouranids are," he said, at her rather
than to her. "You swoon over this beautiful new local
faith they've acquired—the windborne flight to Farside,
the death in dignity, the Nirvana, I forget what else. To
hell with the grubby dromids. Dromids don't do anything but make tools and fires, hunt, care for their
young, live in communities, create art and philosophy,
same as humans. What's interesting to you in that?

"Well, let me tell you what I've told you before,
dromids are believers too. If we could compare, I'd
give long odds their faiths are stronger and more meaningful than the ouranids'. They keep trying to make
sense of the world. Can't you sympathize the least bit?

"Okay, they have a tremendous respect for the fit-
ness of things. When something goes seriously wrong—
when a great crime or sin or shame happens—the whole
world hurts. If the wrong isn't set right, everything will
go bad. That's what they believe on Hansonia, and I
don't know but what they've got hold of a truth.

"The lordly ouranids never paid much attention to
the groundling dromids, but that was not symmetrical.
The ouranids are as conspicuous as Argo, Colchis, any
part of nature. In dromid eyes, they too have their
ordained place and cycle.

"All at once the ouranids change. They don't give

themselves back to the soil when they die, the way life is supposed to—no, they head west, over the ocean, toward that unknown place where the suns go down every evening. Can't you see how unnatural that might seem? As if a tree should walk or a corpse rise. And not an isolated incident; no, year after year after year.

"Psychosomatic abortion? How can I tell? What I can tell is that the dromids are shocked to the guts by this thing the ouranids are doing. No matter how ridiculous the thing is, it hurts them!"

She sprang to her feet. Her glass hit the floor. "Ridiculous?" she yelled. "That *Tao*, that vision? No, ridiculous, that's what your . . . your fuxes believe—except that it makes them attack innocent beings and, and eat them—I can't wait till those creatures are extinct!"

He had risen likewise. "You don't care about children dying, no, of course not," he answered. "What sense of motherhood have you got, for hell's sake? About like a balloon's. Drift free, scatter seed, forget it, it'll bud and break loose and the Swarm will adopt it, never mind anything except your pleasure."

"Why, you—Are you wishing you could be a mother?" she jeered.

His empty hand swung at her. She barely evaded the blow. Appalled, they stiffened where they stood.

He tried to speak, failed, and drank. After a full minute she said, quite low: "Hugh, our natives were getting messages from us. Not verbal. Unconscious. Through them—" she choked—"were you and I seeking to kill each other?"

He gaped until, in a single clumsy gesture, he set his own glass down and held out his arms to her. "Oh, no, oh, no," he stammered. She came to him.

Presently they went to bed. And then he could do nothing. The medicine cabinet held a remedy for that, but what followed might have happened between a couple of machines. At last she lay quietly crying and he went out to drink some more.

*   *   *

The wind wakened her. She lay for a time listening to it boom around the walls. Sleep drained out of her. She opened her eyes and looked at the clock. Its luminous dial said three hours had passed. She might as well get up. Maybe she could make Hugh feel better.

The main room was still lighted. He was asleep himself, sprawled in an armchair, a bottle beside it. How deep the lines were in his face.

How loud the wind was. Probably a storm front which the weather service had reported at sea had taken a quick, unexpected swing this way. Medean meteorology was not yet an exact science. Poor ouranids, their festival disrupted, they themselves blown about and scattered, even endangered. Normally they could ride out a gale, but a few might be carried to disaster, hit by lightning or dashed against a cliff or hopelessly entangled in a tree. The sick and injured would suffer most.

A'i'ach.

Jannika squeezed her lids together and struggled to recall how badly wounded he was. But everything had been too confused and terrible; Hugh had diverted her attention; before long she had flitted out of transmission range. Besides, A'i'ach himself could hardly have ascertained his own condition at once. It might not be grave. Or it might. He could be dead by now, or dying, or doomed to die if he didn't get help.

She was responsible—perhaps not guilty, by a moralistic definition, but responsible.

Resolution crystallized. If the weather didn't preclude, she would go search for him.

Alone? Yes. Hugh would protest, delay her, perhaps actually restrain her by force. She recorded a few words to him, wondered if they were overly impersonal, decided against composing something more affectionate. Yes, she wanted a reconciliation, and supposed he did, but she would not truckle. She redonned her field garb, added a jacket into whose pockets she stuffed some food bars, and departed.

The wind rushed bleak around her, *whoo-oo-oo*, a

torrent she must breast. Clouds scudded low and thick,
tinged red where Argo shone between them. The giant
planet seemed to fly among ragged veils. Dust whirled
in the compound, gritty on her skin. Nobody else was
outdoors.

At the hangar, she punched for the latest forecast. It
looked bad but not, she thought, frightening. (And if
she did crash, was that such an enormous loss, to herself or anyone else?) "I am going back to my study
area," she told the mechanic. When he attempted to
dissuade her, she pulled rank. She never liked that, but
from the Danubian ghosts she had learned how. "No
further discussion. Stand by to open the way and give
me assistance if required. That is an order."

The little craft shivered and drummed on the ground.
Takeoff took skill—with a foul moment when a gust
nearly upset her—but once aloft her vehicle flew stur-
dily. Risen above the cloud deck, she saw it heave like
a sea, Argo a mountain rearing out of it, stars and
companion moons flickery overhead. Northward bulked
a darkness more deep and high, the front. The weather
would really stiffen in the next few hours. If she wasn't
back soon, she'd better stay put till it cleared.

The flight was quick to the battleground. When the
inertial pilot had brought her there, she circled, put on
her helmet, activated the system. Her pulse fluttered
and her mouth had dried. "A'i'ach," she breathed, "be
alive, please be alive."

The green light went on. At least his transmitter
existed on the site. He? She must will herself toward
rapport.

Weakness, pain, a racket of soughing leaves, tossing
boughs—"A'i'ach, hang on, I'm coming down!"

A leap of gladness. Yes, he did perceive her.

Landing would be risky indeed. The aircraft had a
vertical capability, excellent radar and sonar, a computer and effectors to handle most of the work. However, the clear space below was not large, it was cleft in
twain, and while the surrounding forest was a fair wind-

break, there would be vile drafts and eddies. "God, into Your hands I give myself," she said, and wondered as often before how Hugh endured his atheism.

Nevertheless, if she waited she would lose courage. Down!

Her descent was wilder still than she had expected. First the clouds were a maelstrom, then she was through them but into a raving blast, then she saw treetops grab at her. The vehicle rolled, pitched, yawed. Had she been an utter fool? She didn't truly want to leave this life. . . .

She made it, and for minutes sat strengthless. When she stirred, she felt her entire body ache from tension. But A'i'ach's hurt was in her. Called by that need, she unharnessed and went forth.

The noise was immense in the black palisade of trees around her, their branches groaned, their crowns foamed; but down on the ground the air, though restless, was quieter, nearly warm. Unseen Argo reddened the clouds, which cast enough glow that she didn't need her flashlight. She found no trace of the slain ouranids. Well, they had no bones; the dromids must have eaten every scrap. What a ghastly superstition—Where was A'i'ach?

She found him after a search. He lay behind a spiny bush, in which he had woven his tendrils to secure himself. His body was deflated to the minimum, an empty sack; but his eyes gleamed, and he could speak, in the shrill, puffing language of his people, which she had come to know was melodious.

"May joy blow upon you. I never hoped for your advent. Welcome you are. Here it has been lonely." A shudder was in that last word. Ouranids could not long stand being parted from their Swarms. Some xenologists believed that with them consciousness was more collective than individual. Jannika rejected that idea, unless perhaps it applied to the different species found in parts of Nearside. A'i'ach had a soul of his own!

She knelt. "How are you?" She could not render his

sounds any better than he could hers, but he had learned to interpret.

"It is not overly ill with me, now that you are nigh. I lost blood and gas, but those wounds have closed. Weak, I settled in a tree until the Beasts left. Meanwhile the wind rose. I thought best not to ride it in my state. Yet I could not stay in the tree, I would have been blown away. So I valved out the rest of my gas and crept to this shelter."

The speech held far more than such a bare statement. The denotation was laconic and stoical, the connotations not. A'i'ach would need at least a day to regenerate sufficient hydrogen for ascent—how long depended on how much food he could reach in his crippled condition—unless a carnivore found him first, which was quite likely. Jannika imagined what a flood of suffering, dread, and bravery would have come over her had she been wearing her helmet.

She gathered the flaccid form into her arms. It weighed little. It felt warm and silky. He cooperated as well as he was able. Just the same, part of him dragged on the ground, which must have been painful.

She must be rougher still, hauling on folds of skin, when she brought him inside the aircraft. It had scant room to spare; he was practically bundled into the rear section. Rather than apologizing when he moaned, or saying anything in particular, she sang to him. He didn't know the ancient Terrestrial words, but he liked the tunes and realized what she meant by them.

She had equipped her vehicle for basic medical help to natives, and had given it on past occasions. A'i'ach's injuries were not deep, because most of him was scarcely more than a bag; however, the bag had been torn in several places and, though it was self-sealing, flight would reopen it unless it got reinforcement. Applying local anesthetics and antibiotics—that much had been learned about Medean biochemistry—she stitched the gashes.

"There, you can rest," she said when, cramped, sweat-soaked, and shaky, she was done. "Later I will give you an injection of gas and you can rise immediately if you choose. I think, though, we would both be wisest to wait out the gale."

A human would have groaned: "It is *tight* in here."

"Yes, I know what you mean, but—A'i'ach, let me put my helmet on." She pointed. "That will join our spirits as they were joined before. It may take your mind off your discomfort. And at this short range, given our new knowledge—" A thrill went through her. "What may we not find out?"

"Good," he agreed. "We may enjoy unique experiences." The concept of discovery for its own sake was foreign to him . . . but his search for pleasures went far beyond hedonism.

Eager despite her weariness, she moved into her seat and reached for the apparatus. The radio receiver, always open to the standard carrier band, chose that moment to buzz.

Argo in the east glowered at the nearing, lightning-shot wall of storm in the north. Below, the clouds already present roiled in reds and darknesses. Wind wailed. Hugh's aircraft lurched and bucked. Despite a heater, chill seeped through the canopy, as if brought by the light of stars and moons.

"Jan, are you there?" he called. "Are you all right?"

Her voice was a swordstroke of deliverance. "Hugh? Is that you, darling?"

"Yes, sure, who the hell else did you expect? I woke up, played your message, and—Are you all right?"

"Quite safe. But I don't dare take off in this weather. And you mustn't try to land, that would be too dangerous by now. You shouldn't stay, either. Darling, *rostomily*, that you came!"

"Judas priest, sweetheart, how could I not? Tell me what's happened."

She explained. At the end, he nodded a head which still ached a bit from liquor in spite of a nedolor tablet.

"Fine," he said. "You wait for calm air, pump up your friend, and come on home." An idea he had been nursing nudged him. "Uh, I wonder. Do you think he could go down into that gulch and recover Erakoum's unit? Those things are scarce, you know." He paused. "I suppose it'd be too much to ask him to throw a little soil over her."

Jannika's tone held pity. "I can do that."

"No, you can't. I got a clear impression from Erakoum as she was falling, before she cracked her skull apart or whatever she did. Nobody can climb down without a rope secured on top. It'd be impossible to return. Even with a rope, it'd be crazy dangerous. Her companions didn't attempt anything, did they?"

Reluctance: "I'll ask him. It may be asking a lot. Is the unit functional?"

"Hm, yes, I'd better check on that first. I'll report in a minute or three. Love you."

He did, he knew, no matter how often she enraged him. The idea that, somewhere in the abysses of his being, he might have wished her death, was not to be borne. He'd have followed her through a heavier tempest than this, merely to deny it.

Well, he could go home with a satisfied conscience and wait for her arrival, after which—What? The uncertainty made a hollowness in him.

His instrument flashed green. Okay, Erakoum's button was transmitting, therefore unharmed and worth salvaging. If only she herself—

He tensed. The breath rattled in his lungs. Did he *know* she was dead?

He lowered the helmet over his temples. His hands shook, giving him trouble in making the connections. He pressed the switch. He willed to perceive—

Pain twisted like white-hot wires, strength ebbed and ebbed, soft waves of nothingness flowed ever more often, but still Erakoum defied. The slit of sky that she could see, from where she lay unable to creep further,

was full of wind. . . . She shocked to complete awareness. Again she sensed Hugh's presence.

"Broken bones, feels like. Heavy blood loss. She'll
die in a few more hours. Unless you give her first aid,
Jan. Then she ought to last till we can fly her to Port
Kato for complete attention."

"Oh, I can do sewing and bandaging and splinting,
whatever, yes. And nedolor's an analgesic stimulant for
dromids too, isn't it? And simply a drink of water could
make the whole difference; she must be dehydrated.
But how to reach her?"

"Your ouranid can lift her up, after you've inflated
him."

"You can't be serious! A'i'ach's hurt, convalescent—
and Erakoum tried to kill him!"

"That was mutual, right?"

"Well—"

"Jan, I'm not going to abandon her. She's down in a
grave, who used to run free, and the touch of me she's
getting is more to her than I could have imagined. I'll
stay till she's rescued, or else I'll stay till she dies."

"No, Hugh, you mustn't. The storm."

"I'm not trying to blackmail you, dearest. In fact, I
won't blame your ouranid much if he refuses. But I
can't leave Erakoum. I just plain can't."

"I . . . I have learned something about you. . . . I
will try."

*** A'i'ach had not understood his Jannika. It was not
believable that helping a Beast could help bring peace.
That creature was what it was, a slaughterer. And yet,
yet, once there had been no trouble with the Beasts,
once they had been the animals which most interested
and entertained the People. He himself remembered
songs about their fleetness and their fires. In those lost
days they had been called the Flame Dancers.

What made him yield to her plea was unclear in his
spirit. She had probably saved his life, at hazard to her

own, and this was an overpowering new thought to him. He wanted greatly to maintain his union with her, which enriched his world, and therefore hesitated to deny a request that seemed as urgent as hers. Through the union, she helmeted, he believed he felt what she did when she said, with water running from her eyes, "I want to heal what *I* have done—" and that kind of feeling was transcendent, like the Shining Time, and was what finally decided him.

She assisted him from the thing-which-bore-her and payed out a tube. Through the latter he drank gas, a wind-rush of renewed life. His injuries twinged when his globe expanded, but he could ignore that.

He needed her anchoring weight to get across the ground to the ravine. Fingers and tendrils intertwined, they nevertheless came near being carried away. Had he let himself swell to full size, he could have lifted her. Air harried and hooted, snatched at him, wanted to cast him among thorns—how horrible the ground was!

How much worse to descend below it. He throbbed to an emotion he scarcely recognized. Had she been in rapport, she could have told him that the English word for it was "terror." A human or a dromid who felt it in that degree would have recoiled from the drop. A'i'ach made it a force blowing him onward, because this too raised him out of himself.

At the edge, she threw her arms around him as far as they would go, laid her mouth to his pelt, and said, "Good luck, dear A'i'ach, dear brave A'i'ach, good luck, God keep you." Those were the noises she made in her language. He did not recognize the gesture either.

A cylinder she had given him to hold threw a strong beam of light. He saw the jagged slope tumble downward underneath him, and thought that if he was cast against that, he was done for. Then his spirit would have a fearful journey, with no body to shelter it, before it reached Beyond—if it did, if it was not shredded and scattered first. Quickly, before the churning airs could take full hold of him, he jetted across the brink. He contracted. He sank.

The dread as gloom and walls closed in was like no other carouse in his life. At its core, he felt incandescently aware. Yes, the human had brought him into strange skies.

Through the dankness he caught an odor more sharp. He steered that way. His flash picked out the Beast, sprawled on sharp talus, gasping and glaring. He used jets and siphon to position himself out of reach and said in what English he had, "I haff ch'um say-aff ee-you." ***

—From the depths of her deathplace, Erakoum looked up at the Flyer. She could barely make him out, a big pale moon behind a glare of light. Amazement heaved her out of a drowse. Had her enemy pursued her down here in his ill-wishing?

Good! She would die in battle, not the torment which ripped her. "Come on and fight," she called hoarsely. If she could sink teeth in him, get a last lick of his blood— The memory of that taste was like sweet lightning. During the time afterward which refused to end, she had thought she would be dead already if she had not swallowed those drops.

Their wonder-working had faded out. She stirred, seeking a defensive posture. Agony speared through her, followed by night.

When she roused, the Flyer still waited. Amidst a roaring in her ears, she heard, over and over, "I haff ch'um say-aff ee-you."

Human language? This *was* the being that the humans favored as they did her. It had to be, though the ray from its head was hidden by the ray from its tendrils. *Could Hugh have been bound all the while to both?*

Erakoum strove to form syllables never meant for her mouth and throat. "Ha-watt-tt you ha-wannit? Gho, no bea haiar, gho."

The Flyer made a response. She could no more follow that than he appeared to have followed hers. He must have come down to make sure of her, or simply to mock her while she died. Erakoum scrabbled weakly after a spear. She couldn't throw one, but—

From the unknownness wherein dwelt the soul of Hugh, she suddenly knew: He wants to save you.

Impossible. But . . . but there the Flyer was. Half delirious, Erakoum could yet remember that Flyers were seldom that patient.

What else could befall but death? Nothing. She lay back on the rock shards. Let the Flyer be her doom or be her Mardudek. She had found the courage to surrender.

The shape hovered. Her hair sensed tiny gusts, and she thought dimly that this must be a difficult place for him too. Speech burst and skirled. He was trying to explain something, but she was too hurt and tired to listen. She folded her hands around her muzzle. Would he appreciate that gesture?

Maybe. Hesitant, he neared. She kept motionless. Even when his tendrils brushed her, she kept motionless.

They slipped across her body, got a purchase, tightened. Through the haze of pain, she saw him swelling. He meant to lift her—up to Hugh?

When he did, her knife wounds opened and she shrieked before she swooned.

Her next knowledge was of lying on turf under a hasty, red-lit sky. A human crouched above her, talking to a small box that replied in the voice of Hugh. Behind, the Flyer lay shrunken, clutching a bush. Storm brawled; the first stinging raindrops fell.

In the hidden way of hunters, she knew that she was dying. The human might staunch those cuts and stabs, but could not give back what was lost.

Memory—what she had heard tell, what she had briefly tasted herself—"Blood of the Flyer. It will save me. Blood of the Flyer, if he will give." She was not

sure whether she spoke or dreamed it. She sank back
into the darkness.

When she surfaced anew, the Flyer was beside her,
embracing her against the wind. The human was carefully using a knife on a tendril. The Flyer brought the
tendril in between Erakoum's fangs. As the rain's full
violence began, she drank.—

A double sunrise was always lovely.

Jannika had delayed telling Hugh her news. She
wanted to surprise him, preferably after his anxiety
about his dromid was past. Well, it was; Erakoum would
be hospitalized several days in Port Kato, which ought
to be an interesting experience for all concerned, but
she would get well. A'i'ach had already rejoined his
Swarm.

When Hugh wakened from the sleep of exhaustion
which followed his bedside vigil, Jannika proposed a
dawn picnic, and was touched at how fast he agreed.
They flitted to a place they knew on the sea cliffs,
spread out their food, and sat down to watch.

At first Argo, the stars, and a pair of moons were the
only lights. Slowly heaven brightened, the ocean shimmered silver beneath blue, Phrixus and Helle wheeled
by the great planet. Wild songs went trilling through
air drenched with an odor of roanflower, which is like
violets.

"I got the word from the Center," she declared while
she held his hand. "It's definite. The chemistry was
soon unraveled, given the extra clue we had from the
reviving effect of blood."

He turned about. "What?"

"Manganese deficiency," she said. "A trace element
in Medean biology, but vital, especially to dromids and
their reproduction—and evidently to something else in
ouranids, since they concentrate it to a high degree.
Hansonia turns out to be poorly supplied with it.
Ouranids, going west to die, were removing a significant percentage from the ecology. The answer is sim-

ple. We need not try to change the ouranid belief. Temporarily, we can have a manganese supplement made up and offer it to the dromids. In the long run, we can mine the ore where it's plentiful and scatter it as a dust across the island. Your friends will live, Hugh."

He was quiet for a time. Then—he could surprise her, this son of an outback miner—he said: "That's terrific. The engineering solution. But the bitterness won't go away overnight. We won't see any quick happy ending. Maybe not you and me, either." He seized her to him. "Damnation, though, let's try!"

Note: This story forms part of *Medea: Harlan's World*, Harlan Ellison ed., Phantasia Press (first edition), 1985.

DEATHWOMB

The courier slipped out of flightspace and paused for a navigational sight. It was still very far from the berserker sun, so far that that fierce blue-white A star was only the brightest of many. Others crowded heaven, unwinking brilliances, every hue from radio to gamma, save where the Milky Way foamed around blackness or a nearby dark nebula loomed like a thunderhead. The torpedo shape of the courier shimmered wanly amidst them.

Having gotten its bearings, it accelerated under normal drive. At first it was receding, but soon it had quenched its intrinsic velocity and thereafter built up sunward speed. The rate of that, uncompensated, would have spread flesh and bone in a film through any interior. But there were neither cabins nor passengers; the courier was essentially solid-state.

It began to broadcast, at high power and on several wavebands. The message was in standard English. *"Parley. Parley. Parley."* As haste mounted, frequencies changed to allow for Doppler shift, to make certain the message would be received. After all, the courier was unmistakable human work. Unless they had some reason not to, the berserkers would attack it. Such a move would be motivated less by fear of what a warhead might do to one of their proud battlecraft than what might happen to the asteroid mines and spaceborne factories they had established.

Motivation; fear; pride—nonsense words, when used about a set of computer-effector systems, unalive, belike unaware, programmed to burn life out of the universe.

But then, the courier was an automaton too, and nowhere nearly as complex or capable as the least berserker.

"*Parley. Parley. Parley.*"

In due course—time made no difference to a thing that had no consciousness, but the sun blazed now with a tiny disc—a warship came forth to meet it. That was a minor vessel, readily expendable, though formidable enough, a hundred-meter spheroid abristle with guns, missile launchers, energy projectors. Its mass, low compared to a planetkiller's, made it quite maneuverable. Nonetheless flight was long and calculation intricate before it matched the velocity which the courier by then had.

"*Cease acceleration,*" the berserker commanded.

The courier obeyed. The berserker did likewise. Globe and minute sliver, they flew inert on parallel courses, a thousand kilometers apart.

"*Explain your presence,*" was the next order. (Command! Obedience! More nonsense, when two robots were directly communicating.)

"*Word from certain humans,*" the courier replied. "*They know you have moved into this region of space.*"

Being a machine exchanging data with another machine, it did not add the obvious. No matter how vast astronomical distances are, an operation of that size could not stay hidden long, if it took place anywhere in that small portion of the galaxy where humans had settlements with high technology. Devices even simpler than the courier, patrolling over light-years, were sure to pick up the indications on their instruments, and report back to their masters. Of course, those were not necessarily all the humans in the stellar neighborhood. Nor did it follow that they could do much to prevent onslaughts out of the new base. Their own strength was thinly scattered, this far from the centers of their older civilizations. At best, they could marshal resources for the defense of some worlds—probably not all.

The berserker did not waste watts inquiring what the message was. It merely let the courier go on.

"Their analysis is that you will soon strike, while you continue to use the mineral and energy resources of the planetary system for repair and reproduction. If an overwhelming human force moves against you, you will withdraw; but that cannot happen in the immediate future, if ever. My dispatchers offer you information of value to your enterprise."

Logic circuits developed a question. *"Are your dispatchers goodlife?"*

"I am not programmed with the answer, but there is no indication in my memory banks that they wish active cooperation with you. It may be a matter of self-interest, the hope of making a bargain advantageous to them. I can only tell you that, if the terms are right, they will steer you to a target you would not otherwise know about: an entire world for you to sterilize."

Radio silence fell, except for the faint seething of the stars.

The berserker, though, required just a split second to make assessment. *"Others shall be contacted before you leave. We will arrange a rendezvous for proper discussion, and you will bring a record of the proceedings back to your humans. Within what parameters do they operate?"*

The Ilyan day stood at midmorning when Sally Jennison came home. The thaw and the usual storms that followed sunrise were past and heaven was clear, purplish-blue, save for a few clouds which glowed ruddy here and there. Eastward the great ember was climbing past Olga; shadows made sharp the larger craters upon the moon. Below, the Sawtooth Mountains rose dusky over the horizon, Snowcrown peak agleam as if on fire.

Elsewhere land rolled gently, so that the Highroad River flowed slow out of the west on its way to Lake Sapphire. The boat had left wilderness behind and was in the settled part of Geyserdale. Grainfields rippled tawny on either side; they had thus ripened, been harvested, been resown, ripened again with the haste that the brief Ilyan year brought about, several times since the expedition departed. A village of beehive-rounded houses was visible in the northern distance, and occasional natives working near the stream hailed Sally and her companion. They were not many, for she had yet to hear of any society on this planet where persons liked to crowd together. Timberlots were plentiful, high boles and russet foliage. Steam blew from encrusted areas where hot springs bubbled, and once she saw an upward spout of water.

Insectoids flitted on glittery wings. A windrider hovered aloft. River and breeze murmured to each other. Air had warmed as day advanced, and grown full of pungencies. An unseen coneycat was singing.

The peacefulness felt remote from Sally, unreal.

Abruptly it broke. She had hooked her transceiver into the electrical system of the boat's motor and inserted a tape for direct readout and continuous, repeated broadcast: *"Hello, University Station. Hello, anybody, anywhere. This is the Jennison party returning after we stopped hearing from you. I've called and called, and gotten no response. What's wrong? Reply, please reply."*

Sound from the set was a man's voice, harsh with tension, the English bearing a burred accent unfamiliar to her: "Wha's this? Who are ye? Where?"

She gasped, then got her balance back. Years in strangeness, sometimes in danger, had taught her how to meet surprise. Underneath, she felt a tide of relief—

she was not the only human left alive on Ilya!—but it carried an ice flow of anxiety. What had become of them, her friends, every one of the hundred-odd researchers and support personnel at the base and exploring around the planet?

She must wet her lips before she could answer. "Sally Jennison. I've been doing xenological work in the field, Farside, for the past twenty days or so." The man was perhaps not used to the slow rotation of Ilya. "Uh, that would be about six months, Terrestrial. When communication cut off—yes, of course I could send and receive that far away, we do have comsats in orbit, you know—I grew alarmed and started back."

"Where are ye?" he demanded. "Who's wi' ye?"

"I'm on the Highroad River, passing by Dancers' Town. About a hundred fifty klicks west of the station, it is. I've only one partner left, a native who lives near us. The rest of my expedition, all natives too, have disembarked along the way and gone to their own homes."

Anger flared. "Enough!" she exclaimed. "Jesus Christ! Suppose you tell me who *you* are and what's going on?"

"No time," he said. "Your people are safe. We'll ha' someone out in an aircar to pick ye up as fast as possible. Meanwhile, cease transmission. Immediately."

"What? Now you listen just a minute—"

"Dr. Jennison, the berserkers are coming. They may arrive at any minute, and they must no' detect any electronics, any trace o' man. Under martial law, I lay radio silence on ye. Turn your set off!"

The voice halted. Numbly, Sally reached for the switch of her unit. She slumped on her bench, stared, scarcely noticed that she was still at the rudder.

Rainbow-in-the-Mist stroked a four-fingered hand shyly over hers. In a short-sleeved shirt, she felt his plumage (not hair, not feathers, an intricate, beautiful, sensitive covering for his skin) tickle her arm. "Have you news at last, Lady-Who-Seeks?" he trilled, whistled, hummed.

"Not quite," she said in English. They could under-

stand if not pronounce each other's languages, though
the new intonation had baffled him. "Whoever it was
did claim my people are safe."

"That good makes any ill very slight." He meant it.

But your people are in mortal danger! she almost
cried out. *Your whole world is.*

She gazed at her friend of years as if she had never
before seen any of his kind—body somewhat like hers,
but standing only to her chin and more gracile; round
head, faun ears, short muzzle, quivering cat-whiskers,
enormous golden eyes; delicate gray sheen of plumage;
the belt, pouch, and bandolier that were his entire
garb, the steel knife he carried with such pride not
because it was a rare thing in his chalcolithic society but
because it was a present from her. . . . She had seen
images of planets the berserkers had slain, radioactive
rock, ashen winds, corrupted seas.

But this is insane! she thought suddenly. *They've
never heard of Ilya. They couldn't have, except by the
wildest chance, and if that happened, how could that
man have known?*

*And he wanted me to stop sending in case a berserker
detected it, but what about the flyer he's dispatching for
me? . . . Well, that may be a risk he feels he has to take,
to get me under cover in a hurry. A small vehicle is less
likely to be spotted optically within a short time-slot than
a radio 'cast is to be picked up electronically.*

*But what about our relay satellites? What about Uni-
versity Station itself, buildings, landing strip, playing
field, everything?*

*Why didn't anybody mention me to those . . . human
. . . invaders?*

Rainbow-in-the-Mist patted the yellow hair falling in
a pony tail past her neck. "You have great grief, I
sense," he breathed. "Can your wander-brother give
comfort in any way?"

"Oh, Rainie!" She hugged him to her and fought not
to weep. He was warm and smelled like spices in the
kitchen when she was a child on Earth.

A buzz from above drew her heed. She saw a tear-drop shape slant down from the eastern sky. It crossed the sun's disc, but a brief glance straight at a red dwarf star didn't dazzle her vision. She identified it as an aircar. The model was foreign to her. Well, her race had colonized a lot of planets over the centuries, and no planet is a uniform ball; it is a world. Ilya alone held mystery and marvel enough to fill the lifetimes of many discoverers—

The car landed on the left bank, where springturf made an amethystine mat. A man sprang out and beckoned to her. He was tall, rawboned, clad in a green uniform which sunlight here gave an ugly hue. His tunic was open at the throat and carelessly baggy at the beltline, around a sidearm, but his stance bespoke discipline.

She brought the boat to shore, stopped the motor, got out. Seen close, the man was craggy-featured and clean-shaven. Furrows in the weathered face and white streaks through the short dark hair suggested he was in his forties, Earth calendar. Comet insignia glittered on his shoulders and a sleeve patch displayed calipers athwart a circuit diagram.

In his turn, he gave her a raking glance. She was almost thirty, not much less in height than he, well-built, lithe from a career spent in the field. He gave her a soft salute. "Ian Dunbar, captain, engineer corps, Space Navy of Adam," he introduced himself. His accent was similar to that of the fellow who had happened to hear her call, but a trained ear could tell that it was not identical. Likely he hailed from a different continent . . . yes, she knew about Adam, since the planet was in this general region, but her information was scanty. . . . "Please get inside. We'll gi' your fere a ride too if he wishes."

"No, he'll bring the boat in," she objected.

"Dr. Jennison," Dunbar said, "yon's too large a craft to singlehand wi'out a motor, which we shall ha' to remove and bring back wi' us." He turned his head toward the car. "Cameron, Gordon, out and to work!" he shouted.

"Aye, sir." Two younger men in the same uniform, without officer's emblems, scrambled forth, bearing tools.

The hand of Rainbow-in-the-Mist stole into Sally's. "What is happening?" he asked fearfully. And yet he had met the charge of a spearhorn, armed with nothing but his knife, and distracted the giant till she could retrieve her rifle. He had been her second in command when she fared away to study natives as unknown to him as to her—most recently, when the quest took them to lands which never saw the moon that hung forever in his home sky and which he called Mother Spirit. . . .

"I don't know," she must admit. "There was talk of an, an enemy."

"What does that mean?" he wondered. Nowhere on Ilya had she heard of war or even murder.

"Dangerous beings, maddened beasts." The thought of nuclear missiles and energy beams striking this place was like a drink of acid.

"Hurry along!" Dunbar rapped.

Sally and her comrade squeezed into the rear seat beside him. The two noncoms followed, after stowing the motor and other stuff from the boat. They took the front, one of them the controls. The aircar lifted. In spite of everything, Rainbow-in-the-Mist caroled delight. He seldom got to fly.

Sally felt how Dunbar perforce pressed against her. She didn't want to be, but was, aware of his maleness. It had been long since she said goodbye to Peter Brozik and Fujiwara Ito. The first a planetologist, the second a molecular biologist, her lovers couldn't very well go xenologizing with her.

Apprehension stabbed. How were they? Where?

It turned to resentment. "Well, Captain Dunbar," she clipped, "now will you tell me what the hell is going on?"

The ghost of a smile flitted over his starkness. "That

is wha' I believe your folk would call a tall order, Dr. Jennison."

"Huh?" She was surprised.

"Ye're originally fro' North America on Earth, true?"

"Y-yes. But how do you know, when an hour ago you didn't know I existed?"

He shrugged. "Speech, gait, style. I've seen shows, read books, met travelers. Just because we Adamites are out near the edge o' human expansion, take us no' for rustics." The ghost sank back into its grave. The gaze he turned on her was bleak. "Maybe we were once, our forefathers, and glad to be, but the berserkers ended that. Wha' I would like to find out this day is why nobody told us about ye, Dr. Jennison. We'd ha' sent a car to fetch ye. Now I fear ye're trapped, in the same danger as us."

Sally checked her temper, pinched her lips, and made her blue stare challenge his gray before she said: "I can scarcely give you any ideas before I have some facts, can I? What's been happening? Who are you people, anyway? And what's become of mine?"

Dunbar sighed. "We've evacuated them. Aye, 'twas hasty and high-handed, no doubt, but we were under the lash oursel's. The first thing we removed was the comsats; that's why ye were no longer receiving or being heard, though 'twas but a short time before we imposed silence on every transmission. Meanwhile—"

The car started downward. Sally looked past Dunbar, out the window. She choked back a scream.

Lake Sapphire shone enormous below, surrounded by the rural tranquility she had known throughout her stay on Ilya. Eastern mountains, red sun-wheel, scarred and brilliant moon were untouched. But where the Highroad River emptied into the lake, where University Station had clustered, was a blackened waste, as if a noonday turf fire had spread over that ground and consumed the very buildings, or the berserkers had already commenced their work.

* * *

Space was steely with stars. None shone close in the loneliness here. What established this rendezvous point was triangulation on distant galaxies.

Emerging from flightspace, the berserker homed on a broadcast that Mary Montgomery's ship had been emitting while she waited. Instruments showed the vessel draw nigh and match intrinsics—lay to—a thousand kilometers off. Magnifying optics showed it as no bigger than hers, though a hedgehog of armament, dim shinings and deep shadows near the Milky Way.

Alone in the main control room, for her crew was minimal, she settled herself into a command chair and pressed the lightplate which would signal her readiness to talk. Around her, bulkheads stood dull-hued, needles quivered across dials, displays went serpentine, electronics beeped and muttered. The air from the ventilators smelled faintly of oil, something a bit wrong in the recyclers, no matter what. Her old bones ached, but no matter that, either.

The berserker's voice reached her. It was derived from the voices of human captives taken long ago, shrill, irregular, a sonic monster pieced together out of parts of the dead, terrifying to many. Montgomery sniffed at it, took a drag on her cheroot, and blew a smoke ring toward the speaker. *Childish bravado*, she thought. But why not? Who was to witness?

"Parley under truce, is this still agreed?" the berserker began.

Montgomery nodded before recollecting how pointless the gesture was. "Aye," she said. "We've somewhat to sell ye, we do."

"Who are you, where is that planet your courier bespoke, what is your asking price?"

Montgomery chuckled, though scant mirth was in her. "Easy, my ghoulie. Ye, your kind, ye've established yoursel's in these parts again, so as to kill more, no? Well, last time my home suffered grimly. We've better defenses this while, we can fight ye off, yet 'twould be at high cost. Suppose, instead, we direct ye to another inhabited world—not a human colony, for we're no traitors, understand—a world useless to us, but wi' life upon it for ye to scrub out, aye, e'en an intelligent species. They're primitives, helpless before ye. A single capital ship o' yours could make slag o' the planet in a day or two, at no risk whatsoe'er. In exchange for such an easy triumph, would ye leave us in peace?"

"Who are you?"

"Our world we call Adam."

The berserker searched its memory banks. "Yes," it said. "We struck it three hundred and fifty-seven Terrestrial years ago. Considerable damage was done, but before the mission could be completed, a task force of the Grand Fleet arrived and compelled us to retreat. We were only conducting a raid. We had no reinforcements to call upon."

"Aye. Since then, Adam has gained strength."

"And this time we have a base, a planetary system, raw materials to build an indefinite number of new units. Why should we not finish Adam off?"

Montgomery sighed. "Were ye human—were ye e'en alive, conscious, insultable, ye metal abomination— I'd ask ye to stop playing games wi' me. Well, but I suppose your computer does no' ha' the data. 'Tis been long since ye last came by. So hearken.

"In spite o' the wounds ye inflicted, Adam has a larger population now than then, much more industry, a small but formidable space navy, a civil defense that reaches through the whole system 'tis in. Ye could no' take us out before the marshalled human forces arrive to drive ye back fro' this sector. Howe'er, we'd liefest be spared the loss o' blood and treasure that standing ye off would entail. Therefore we offer our bargain—a world for a world."

Lack of life did not mean lack of shrewdness. "If the target you would betray is so soft," the berserker inquired, "why should we not afterward turn on you?"

Montgomery drew a little comfort from the bite of

smoke in her mouth, more from the family picture above the control console. Her husband was in it, and he had died, oh, Colin, Colin . . . but her sons and daughters stood strong beside their wives and husbands, amidst her grandchildren and his. She had volunteered for this mission because a human was needed —no computer that humans could build was flexible enough—and if negotiations broke down and the berserker opened fire, why, she was old and full of days.

"I told ye ye'd find us a hard nut to crack," she answered, "and this ye can verify by a scouting flit. Only pick up the stray radiations fro' orbital fortresses and ships on patrol. Afterward think wha' ground-based installations we must ha' likewise—whole rivers to cool energy projectors—Ah, but ye do no' really think, do ye?"

"Nevertheless, it might prove logical for us to attack you, especially if we have been able to accomplish part of our sterilizing objective without loss."

Montgomery made a death's-head grin at the image of the ship among the stars. "But see ye," she declared, "before we turn over yon hapless planet to ye, we'll send forth courier robots far and wide. They'll bear witness—our recordings, your electronic signature— witness to the treaty, that we gi' ye the information in return for immunity.

"Ye've struck bargains wi' humans erenow. Break one as important as this, and how much goodlife can ye hope to recruit in future?"

The machine did not ask any further questions such as she would have asked in its place. For instance, how would humans throughout space react to fellow humans, Adamites, who had sold out a living world in order that they themselves be spared a war? Subtleties like that were beyond a machine. Indeed, Montgomery confessed wearily to herself, they were beyond her, and every expert who had debated the issue. There might not be great revulsion, and what there was might not last long. Nonhuman intelligences were rare, scientifi-

cally valuable, but, well, nonhuman. Your first obligation was to your kindred, wasn't it?

And it was nonhumans that had built the first berserkers, untold ages ago, and programmed them to
destroy everything alive, as a weapon in a damned
forgotten war of their own. Wasn't it?

Silence hummed, pressed inward, filled her skull.
Then:

"This unit is equipped to make agreement on behalf
of our entire force," the berserker said. "Very well, in
principle. To begin, provide some description of the
planet you would give us."

The sun plodded toward noon while Olga waned.
The moon's night part was not invisible where it hung
halfway up heaven, east-southeast beyond the Sawtooths.
A tenuous atmosphere caught and sunlight on clouds,
reflected Ilyalight, made a shimmering alongside the
pocked daylit horn; the north polar cap reached thence
like a plume.

Sally was used to the sight, but all at once she wondered how alien it might be to Dunbar: a somber red
sun showing six and a half times as wide as Sol did on
Earth, taking more than a week to go from midday to
midday but less than a month from midsummer to
midsummer; a moon almost four times the breadth of
Luna in Terrestrial skies, more than twenty times the
brightness, that never rose or set save as you traveled
across Ilya—What was the sky of Adam like?

That hardly seemed relevant to the disaster around.
But she had been stunned by it, and the hours after she
landed had hailed more blows upon her. Descent to the
caverns the Adamites had dug while, above, they tore
University Station apart and sank the fragments beneath the lake—uniformed strangers swarming antlike
through those drab corridors, loud orders, footfalls, throb
of unseen machinery—a cubicle found for her to sleep
in, a place assigned at the officers' mess, but she had no
appetite—warm, stinking air, for there had been no

time to install anything but minimal life support, when the complex of workshops, command posts, barracks must be gnawed out of rock and reinforced till it could withstand a direct hit of a megaton—a fantastic job in so short a span, even granting powerful, sophisticated machines to do most of the labor—*Why, why, why?*

Andrew Scrymgeour, admiral in overall charge of operations, received her, though only for a brief interview. He had too many demands on him as was. Weariness had plowed his face; the finger that kept stroking the gray mustache was executing a nervous tic; he spoke in a monotone.

"Aye, we're sorry we missed ye. I set an inquiry afoot when I heard. As nigh as my aide can find out, 'twas because o' confusion. Such haste on our part, ye see, and meanwhile such anger among your folk, arguments, refusals that bade fair to become outright physical resistance, did we no' move fast and firmly. Other scientists were in the field besides ye, o' course, scattered o'er half this globe. We sought them out and brought them in, thinking they were all. We did no' stop to check your rosters, for who would wish anyone left abandoned? Somehow we simply were no' told about ye, Dr. Jennison. Doubtless everybody among your friends took for granted somebody else had gi'en that word, and was too furious to speak to us unless absolutely necessary. Moreo'er, we could no' lift the lot o' them off in a single ship, we required several, so on any one vessel 'tis being assumed ye must be aboard another."

Yes, Pete and Ito will be horror-smitten when they learn, Sally thought. *Worst will be the helplessness and the not knowing; worse for them than me, I suppose. (Oh, it isn't that we've exchanged vows or anything like that. We enjoy each other, minds more than bodies, actually. But it's made us close, affectionate. I've missed them very much, calm and grizzled Ito, Pete's vitality which a man half his age might envy—)*

"Where have you taken them?" she demanded.

Scrymgeour shrugged. "To Adam. Where else? They'll

be comfortably housed until arrangements can be made for sending them onto their homes, or where'er is appropriate. Maybe e'en back here, to take up their work again." He sighed. "But that requires clearing the berserkers fro' this sector o' space. Meanwhile, travel may prove so dangerous that our authorities will deem it best to keep your folk detained, for their own safety."

"For their silence, you mean!" she flared. "You have no right, no right whatsoever, to come in like this and wreck all we've built, halt all we've been doing. If Earth found out, it might be less ready to send naval units to help defend Adam."

Scrymgeour's bushy brows drew together. "I've no time to argue wi' ye, Dr. Jennison," he snapped. " 'Tis unfortunate for us as well as ye that ye were overlooked in the evacuation." He curbed his temper. "We'll do wha' we can. I'll see to it that an officer is assigned to ye as . . . liaison, explainer." Dour humor: "Also chaperon, for ye realize we've but a handful o' women on Olga now, and they too busied for aught o' an amorous nature. Not that our men would misbehave, I'm sure; but 'twill be as well to make plain for them to see that they're no' to let themsel's be distracted fro' their duty, e'en in their scant free times."

Sally tossed her head. "Don't worry, Admiral. I have no desire to fraternize. Am I permitted to take myself out of their presence?"

"Go topside, ye mean?" He pondered. "Aye, no harm in that, gi'en proper precautions. We do oursel's. Howe'er, ye shall always ha' an escort."

"Why? Don't you think I might conceivably know my way around just a tiny bit better than any of your gang?"

He nodded. "Aye, aye. But 'tis no' the point. Ye mustn't stray far. Ye must e'er be ready to hurry back on the first alarm, or take cover if the notice is too short. I want someone wi' ye to make sure o' that. 'Tis for your sake also. The berserker is coming."

"If I couldn't dive underground before the strike,"

she sneered, "what's the point of my ducking under a bush? The whole valley will go up in radioactive smoke."

"Ah, but there's a chance, extremely small but still a chance, that the berserker would spy ye fro' above." Scrymgeour bit off his words. "Pardon me. I've my job on hand. Return to your quarters and wait to hear fro' the officer detailed to ye."

That turned out to be Ian Dunbar. So it was that she found herself wondering what he thought of her sky.

"Ye see," he disclosed awkwardly—shyly?—"the part o' the task I'm in charge o', 'tis been completed, save for minor and routine tinkerings. I'll no' be much needed any more until action is nigh. Meanwhile, well, we owe ye somewhat. Apology, explanation, assistance in rebuilding when that becomes possible. I'll . . . take it on mysel' . . . to speak for that side o' us . . . if ye're willing."

She gave him a suspicious glance, but he wasn't being flirtatious. Quite likely he didn't know how to be. He stared straight ahead of him as they walked, gulped forth his words, knotted knobbly fists.

The temptation to be cruel to such vulnerability was irresistible, in this wasteland he had helped make. "You've given yourself plenty to do, then. Four universities in the Solar System pooled their resources, plus a large grant from the Karlsen Memorial Foundation, to establish a permanent research group here. And how do you propose to restore the working time we'll've lost, or repair the relationship with natives that we've painstakingly been developing?" She swept a hand to and fro. "You've already created your own memorial."

Cinders crunched underfoot. Grit was in the breeze. The settlement had been razed, bulldozed over, drenched in flammables, and set alight. Whatever remained unburnt had been cast in the lake. She must admit the resemblance to a natural area damaged by a natural fire was excellent.

Dunbar winced. "Please, Dr. Jennison. Please do no'

think o' us a barbarians. We came to wage war on the olden enemies o' all humankind, all life." After a pause, softly: "We respect science on Adam. I'd dreams mysel' as a lad, o' becoming a planetologist."

Despite her will, Sally's heart gave a small jump. That was what her father was. *Oh, Dad, Mother, how are you, at home on Earth? I should never have stayed away so long.*

—No. I will not let myself like this man.

"Don't change the subject," she said as sharply as she could manage. "Why have you come to Ilya? What crazy scheme have you hatched, anyway?"

"To meet the berserker when it arrives. Ye'd absolutely no defenses in this entire planetary system."

"None were needed."

They left the blackened section behind and trod on springturf, a living recoil beneath the feet, purple studded with tiny white flowers. Following the lakeshore, several meters inland, they started up a slope which ended in a bluff above the water. Now the wind was clean; its mildness smelled of soil and growth.

"The berserkers would never have dreamed life was here," Sally said. "It's so great a miracle."

"Berserkers do no' dream," Dunbar retorted sternly. "They compute, on the basis o' data. Ilya's been described in newscasts, aye, at least one full-length documentary show. Ye've been publishing your findings."

"The news sensation, what there was of it, died out ten or fifteen years ago, when no berserker was anywhere near this part of space—or near our inner civilizations either, of course. Besides, how would they pick up programs carried on cable or tight beam—between stars, in canisters? As for publication since the original discovery, I don't believe berserkers subscribe to our specialized scientific journals!"

"Well, they do know."

"How? And how can you be sure of it?"

"Our intelligence—I'm no' at liberty to discuss our methods. Nor is that my corps, ye remember."

"Why haven't they come already, then? We'd've been a sitting duck."

He blinked. "A wha'?"

She couldn't help smiling. His puzzlement made him too human, all of a sudden. "An Earth expression. North American, to be exact. I don't know what sort of waterfowl you have on Adam."

His haggardness returned. "Few, sin' the berserkers visited it."

After a moment, he offered a reply of sorts to her question. "We can no' tell when the raid will happen. We can but prepare for it as fast and as best we are able."

They surmounted the bluff and stopped to rest. A while they stood side by side, gazing out over the broad waters. He breathed no harder than she did. *He keeps in shape, like Dad*, she thought. The wind ruffled her hair and cooled away the slight sweat on her face, phantom caresses.

"I take it," she said at last, slowly, "you couldn't detach any large force from the defense of Adam itself. So what have you brought? What are your plans?"

"We've a few spacecraft hidden on both the planet and yon moon. Everything is electronically shielded. Heat radiation fro' the base will no' matter in this area, which had it already." Dunbar gestured ahead. "My task was mainly beneath the loch. We've installed certain ultra-high-powered weapons . . . camouflage and cooling alike—" He broke off. "Best I say no more."

She scowled at the upborne silt and shapeless trash which marred the purity of the wavelets. That defilement would surely mean nothing to a berserker—what did a robot know of the nature it was only intended to murder?—but to her, and Rainbow-in-the-Mist, and everybody else who had dwelt near these shores and loved them—

Her wits were beginning to straighten out, though her head still felt full of sand. "You're laying a trap," she said.

He nodded. "Aye, that's obvious." His laugh clanked. "The trick is to keep it fro' being obvious to the enemy, until too late."

"But . . . hold on . . . won't the disappearance of our works be a giveaway?"

"Make the foe suspicious, ye mean? Nay, that's the whole point. They know no' that Earth is aware o' this planet. 'Twas found just by chance, was it no', in the course o' an astrophysical survey? The general staff on Adam has decided that that chance could become an opportunity for us, to gi' them a blow in their metal bellies."

Dunbar glanced at her, at his watch, and back again. His tone gentled. "Lass—Dr. Jennison—'tis late by human clocks. Ye've had a rude shock, and I'm told ye've no' eaten, and ye do look fair done in. Let me take ye to some food and a good long sleep."

She realized it herself, weariness and weakness rising through her, breaking apart whatever alertness she had left. "I suppose you're right," she mumbled.

He took her elbow as they started down. "We need no' talked any further if ye'd liefer no'," he said, "but if ye would like a bit o' conversation, shall we make it about somewhat else than this wretched war?"

Mary Montgomery drew breath. "We discovered it by sheer accident," she told the berserker. "An astrophysical survey. Diffusion out o' yon nebula has minor but interesting effects on ambient stars—and on some more distant, as stellar light pressure and kinks in the galactic magnetic field carry matter off until it reaches a sun. An expedition went forth to study the phenomena closer. Among the samples it picked, more or less at random out o' far too many possibilities for a visit to each—among them was a red dwarf star, middle type M. They found it has a life-bearing planet."

An organic being should have registered surprise. The machine afloat in space said merely: "That is not believed possible. Given a low-temperature heat source, the range of orbits wherein water can be liquid is too narrow."

" 'Tis no' impossible, just exceedingly improbable, that a planet orbit a cool sun in the exact ellipse necessary."

"And it must have the proper mass, be neither a giant dominated by hydrogen nor an airless rock."

"Aye, that makes the situation unlikelier yet. Still, this world is o' Earth size and composition."

"Granted that, it must be so close to its primary that rotation becomes gravitationally locked, not even to two-thirds the period of revolution, but to an identity. One hemisphere always faces the sun, the other always faces away. Gas carried to the dark side will freeze out. Insufficient atmosphere and hydrosphere will remain fluid for chemical evolution to proceed to the biological stage."

Montgomery nodded her white head. Inwardly she wondered if the berserker carried that knowledge in its data banks or had computed it on the spot. Quite plausibly the latter. It had an enormous capability, the pseudo-brain within yonder hull. After all, it was empowered—no, wrong word—it was able to bargain on behalf of its entire fleet.

Hatred surged. She gripped her chair arms with gnarled fingers as if she were strangling the thing she confronted. *Nay,* she thought in the seething, *it does no' breathe. Launch a missile, then!* . . . *But none we ha' aboard could get past the defenses we know such a berserker has, and it would respond wi' much better armament than we carry. It could simply fire an energy beam, to slice our ship in twain like a guillotine blade going through a neck.*

Nay, no' that either, she thought, aware that the issue was altogether abstract. *'Tis o' destroyer class, no' big enough to hold the generator that could produce a beam strong enough. Dispersion across the distance between us—A dreadnaught could do so, o' course, though e'en its reach would be limited and the cut*

*would be messy. To slash a real scalpel o'er this range,
ye need power, coolant, and sheer physical size for the
focusing—aye, ground-based projectors, like those we've
built across Adam.*

*If a fight breaks out here, the berserker will swamp
our own screens and antimissiles. As for its response, it
need not e'en get a hit. A few kilotons o' explosion
nearby will serve full well to kill us by radiation.*

*But my mind is wandering. We're no' supposed to
provoke a battle. I ha' indeed grown old.*

She chose to prolong matters a little, not to tease the
enemy, which had no patience to lose (or else had
infinite patience), but to assert her life against its unlife.
"A philosopher o' ours has observed that the improbable must happen," she said. "If it ne'er did, 'twould be
the impossible."

The hesitation of the machine was barely sufficient
for her to notice. "We are not present to dispute definitions. How does this planet you speak of come to be
inhabited? Where is it? Be quick. We have too many
missions to undertake for the wasting of time."

Montgomery had long since won to resolution; but
the words would not die, they stirred anew. —*Then
one of the twelve, called Judas Iscariot, went unto the
chief priests, And said unto them, What will ye give
me, and I will deliver him unto you? And they covenanted with him for thirty pieces of silver.*

She heard her voice, fast and flat: "Besides being in
the right orbit, this Earth-sized planet has a Mars-sized
companion. Therefore they are locked to each other,
not to their sun. The period o' their spin is nine and a
quarter Terrestrial days, which serves to maintain atmospheric circulation. True, nights get cold, but no' too
cold, when winds blow aye across the terminator; and
during the long day, the oceans store mickle heat. The
interplay wi' a year that is about twenty-two Terrestrial
days long is interesting—but no' to ye, I'm sure. Ye are
just interested in the fact that this planet has brought
forth life for ye to destroy.

"Ye ha' no' the ships to spare for a search, if ye're to carry out any other operations before an armada from our inner civilizations comes out against ye. Red dwarf stars are by far the commonest kind, ye ken.

"Make the deal. Agree that, if this world is as I've described, ye'll stay your hand at Adam, whate'er ye may do elsewhere. Let the couriers disperse wi' the attestation o' this compact between us. After that I'll gi' ye the coordinates o' the star. Send a scout to verify—a small, expendable craft. Ye'll find I spoke truth.

"Thereafter, a single capital ship o' yours can write an end to yon life."

Sally Jennison woke after twelve hours, rested, hungry, and more clear-headed then felt good. The room lent her had barely space for a bunk and her piled-up baggage from the boat. Swearing, she wrestled forth a sweatsuit, got it on, and made her way to the gymnasium of which she had been told. Men crowded the narrow corridors but, while she felt the gaze of many, none seemed to jostle her purposely, nor did any offer greetings. *A sour, puritanical pack, the Adamites,* she thought. *Or am I letting my bitterness make my judgments for me?*

A workout in the women's section, followed by a shower and change into fresh garments, took some of the edge off her mood. By then it was near noon on the clock; the rotation of the newcomers' planet was not much different from Earth's. She proceeded to the officers' mess, benched herself at the long table, and ate ravenously. Not that the food was worthy of it; her field rations had been better.

A sandy-haired young woman on her right attempted friendliness. "Ye're the stranded scientist, no? My sympathies. I'm Kate Fraser, medical corps." Reluctantly, Sally shook hands. "Ye're a . . . xenologist, am I right? Maybe, if ye've naught else to do, ye'd consider assisting in sickbay. Ye must know first aid, at least, and we're shorthanded. 'Twill be worse if we take casualties, come the action."

"That's no' to speak o' here, Lieutenant Fraser," warned a skinny redheaded man sitting opposite. "Besides, I do no' believe she'd fit into a naval organization." He cleared his throat. "Wi' due respect, Dr. Jennison. See ye, every hale adult on Adam is a reservist in the armed forces until old age. Thus we're better coordinated in our units than any co-opted civilian could possibly be." Pridefully: "The berserkers will no' get nigh enough again to Adam to bombard it."

Anguish and anger kindled anew in Sally. "Why did you want to interfere on Ilya, then?"

"Forward strategy," said Fraser. The redhead frowned at her and made a shushing motion.

It went unseen by a very young officer whose plumpness, unusual in this assemblage, suggested a well-to-do home. " 'Tis no' sufficient to throw back the damned berserkers," he declared. "They'll still be aprowl. Travel and outlying industries will still be endangered, insurance rates stay excruciating."

Sally knew little about Adam, but a memory stirred in her. After the last assault impoverished them and their planet, many of the people went into new endeavors requiring less in the way of natural resources then the original agriculture-based society had done. A stiff work ethic and, yes, a general respect for learning gave advantages that increased through the generations. Adamite shipping and banking interests were of some importance nowadays, in their stellar sector. *Prim race of moneygrubbers*, she thought.

"The basic problem to cope wi'," the boy went on, "is that the berserkers are von Neumann machines—"

"That will do, Ensign Stewart!" interrupted the redhead. "Report to my office at fifteen hundred hours."

Scarlet and white went across the youthful cheeks. Sally guessed Stewart was in for a severe reprimand.

"Sorry, Dr. Jennison," said the redhead. His tone was not quite level. "Military security. Ah, my name is Craig, Commander Robert Craig."

"Are you afraid I'll run off and spill your secrets to the enemy?" Sally jeered.

He bit his lip. "Surely no'. But wha' ye do no' know, the berserkers can no' torture out o' ye. They could, understand. They've robots among them o' the right size, shape, mobility—like soulless caricatures o' humans."

"What about you?"

"The men, and such officers as ha' no need to know, simply follow orders. The key officers are sworn to ne'er be taken alive." Craig's glance dropped to his sidearm. Stewart seemed to regain pride.

"Can we no' talk more cheerful?" asked Fraser.

The effort failed. Conversation sputtered out.

Ian Dunbar's place had been too far up the table for him to speak with Sally. He intercepted her at the messhall door. "Good day," he said in his odd fashion, half harsh, half diffident. "Ha' ye any plans for the next several hours?"

She glared at the angular countenance. "Have you a library? I've nothing to read. Our books, our tapes— the station's, my own, like all our personal property— are gone."

He winced. "Aye, o' course, we've ample culture along in the data banks, text, video, music. I'll show ye to the screening room if ye wish. But—um-m, I thought ye might liefer ha' some private speech, now that ye're rested. Ye could ask me whate'er ye like, and within the limits o' security I'd try to gi' honest answers."

Is this a leadup to a pass at me? she wondered. *—No, I don't suppose so. Not that it matters a lot. I'm certain I could curb him. But I suspect he curbs himself tighter than that.* "Very well. Where?"

"My room is the only place. That is, we could go topside again, but there are things ye should perhaps see and—Naturally, the door will stand open."

A smile flitted of itself across Sally's lips.

Accompanying him through the passageways, she asked why men and machines continued busy. He explained that, while the basic installations were complete, plenty more could be done in whatever time remained, especially toward hardening the site. Let her remember that the berserker would come equipped to incinerate a world.

She almost exclaimed: *You're not doing a thing to protect the Ilyano!* but blocked the impulse. Later, maybe. First she needed to learn a great deal, and that required coolness: for her refreshed brain realized how little sense everything made, of what she had heard thus far.

"You told me you're an engineer, Captain Dunbar," she angled instead. "What specialty?"

"Heavy, high-energy devices, for the most part," he replied. "In civilian life I've been on projects throughout scores o' light-years. My employers are . . . contractors supplying technical talent, ye might say. 'Tis one o' the items Adam has for export."

"How interesting. Could you tell me something I've been wondering about? I heard a reference to it when I didn't have a chance to inquire what it meant or go look it up."

His mouth creased with the pleasure of any normal man consulted by an attractive woman. "Aye, if I know mysel'."

"What's a von Neumann machine?"

He broke stride. "Eh? Where'd ye hear that?"

"I don't think it's among your secrets," she said blandly. "I could doubtless find it in the base's reference library, which you just invited me to use."

"Ah—well—" He recovered and went onward, moving and talking fast. " 'Tis no' a specific machine, but a general concept, going back to the earliest days o' cybernetics. John von Neumann proposed it; he was among the pioneers. Basically, 'tis a machine which does something, but also fro' time to time makes more like itsel', including copies o' the instructions for its main task."

"I see. Like the berserkers."

"Nay!" he denied, more emphatically than needful. "A warship does no' manufacture other warships."

"True. However, the system as a whole—the entire berserker complex, which includes units for mining, refining, production—yes, it functions as a von Neumann machine, doesn't it? With the basic program, which it copies, being the program for eradicating life. Additionally, the program modifies itself in the light of experience. It learns; or it evolves."

"Aye," he conceded, his unwillingness plain upon him, "ye can use that metaphor if ye insist."

For a moment, she wished she hadn't asked. What had it gained her? A figure of speech, scarcely anything else. And what a chilling image it was. Not alone the fact of berserker auxiliaries ripping minerals out of planets and asteroids, digesting them to fineness, turning them into new machines which carried the same code as the old, the same drive to kill. No, what made her shiver was the sudden thought of the whole hollow universe as a womb engendering the agents of death, which later came back and impregnated their mother anew.

Dunbar's words brought deliverance. His mood had lightened, unless for some reason he wanted to divert her from her idea. "Ye're a sharp one indeed," he said almost cordially. "I look forward to better acquaintance. . . . Here we are. Welcome."

Officers' quarters were individual chambers, four meters square. That sufficed for a bed, desk, shelves, dresser, closet, a couple of chairs, floor space for pacing if you grew excited or simply needed to ease tension. The desk held a computer terminal, eidophone, writing equipment, papers; the occupant must often work as well as sleep on the spot.

Sally looked around, curious. Fluorescent lighting fell chill on plastered walls and issue carpeting. Personal items were on hand, though—pictures, a few souvenir objects, a pipe rack and ashtaker, a tea set and hotplate, a small tool kit, a half-finished model of a sailing ship on ancient Earth. "Sit ye down," Dunbar urged. "Can I brew us a pot? I've ooloong, jasmine, green, lapsang soochong, as ye prefer."

She accepted, chose, granted him permission to smoke.

"And why not shut the door, Captain?" she proposed. "It's so noisy outside. I'm sure you're trustworthy."

"Thank ye." Did an actual blush pass beneath that leathery tan? He busied himself.

The largest picture was a landscape, valley walled by heights, lake agleam in the foreground. It did not otherwise resemble Geyserdale. Ground cover was sparse Terrestrial grass and heather. Cedars sheltered a low house from winds that had twisted them into troll shapes. A glassy-bottomed crater marred a mountainside; stone had run molten thence, before congealing into lumps and jumbles. Clouds brooded rain over the ridges. Above them, daylight picked out the pale crescents of two moons.

"Is that scene from Adam?" she inquired.

"Aye," he said. "Loch Aytoun, where I was born and raised."

"It seems to have . . . suffered."

He nodded. "A berserker warhead struck Ben Creran. The area was slow to recover, and has ne'er been fertile again as 'twas formerly." He sighed. "Though 'twas lucky compared to many. We've deserts fused solid like yon pit. Other places, air turned momentarily to plasma and soil vaporized down to bedrock. And yet other places — but let's no' discuss that, pray."

She studied his lean form. "So your family isn't rich," she deduced.

"Och, nay." He barked a laugh. "The financiers and shipping barons are no' as common among us as folklore has it. My parents were landholders, on land that yielded little. They wrung a wee bit extra out o' the waters." Proudly: "But they were bound and determined their children would ha' it better."

"How did you yourself achieve that?"

"Scholarships through engineering school. Later, well-paid jobs, especially beyond our own planetary system."

You'd have to have considerable talent to do that, she thought. Her gaze wandered to another picture near the desk: a teen-age boy and girl. "Are those youngsters yours?"

"Aye." His tone roughened. "My wife and I were divorced. She took custody. 'Twas best, I being seldom home. That was the root reason why Ellen left. I see them whene'er I can."

"You couldn't have taken a sedentary position?" she asked low.

"I do no' seem to be the type. I mentioned to ye before that I wanted to be a planetologist, but saw no openings."

"Like my father," she blurted.

"He is a planetologist?"

"Yes. Professor at a college in western Oregon, if that means anything to you. He doesn't do much field work any more, but it used to take him away for long stretches. Mother endured his absences, however."

"A remarkable lady."

"She loves him." *Of course she does. It was ever worth the wait, when Dad at last returned.*

"Tea's ready," Dunbar said, as if relieved to escape personal matters. He served it, sat down facing her with shank crossed over knee, filled and ignited his pipe.

The brew was hot and comforting on her palate. "Good," she praised. "Earth-grown, I'd judge. Expensive, this far out. You must be a connoisseur."

He grinned. It made his visage briefly endearing. *"Faute de mieux.* I'd liefer ha' offered ye wine or ale, but we're perforce austere. I daresay ye noticed the Spartan sauce on our food. Well, as that fine old racist Chesterton wrote,

" 'Tea, although an Oriental,
Is a gentleman at least — ' "

Startled, she splashed some of hers into the saucer. "Why, you sound like my father now!"

"I do?" He seemed honestly surprised.

"A scholar."

Again he grinned. "Och, nay. 'Tis but that on lengthy voyages and in lonely encampments, a fellow must needs read."

A chance to probe him. "Have you developed any particular interests?"

"Well, I like the nineteenth-century English-language writers, and history's a bit o' a hobby for me, especially medieval European—" He leaned forward. "But enough about me. Let's talk about ye. What do ye enjoy?"

"As a matter of fact," she admitted, "I share your literary taste. And I play tennis, sketch, make noises on a flute, am a pretty good cook, play hardnose poker and slapdash chess."

"Let's get up a game," he suggested happily. "Chess, that is. I'm more the cautious sort. We should be well matched."

Damn, but he does have charm when he cares to use it! she thought.

She tried putting down any further notions. The men who attracted her had always been older ones, with intelligence, who led active lives. (A touch of father fixation, presumably, but what the hell.) Dunbar, though —she would not, repeat not, call him "Ian" in her mind—he was—

Was what? The opposition? The outright enemy?

How to lure the truth out of him? *Well, Dad used to say, "When all else fails, try frankness."*

She set her teacup on the shelf beside her chair: a hint, perhaps too subtle, that she was declining continued hospitality. "That might be fun, Captain," she declared, "*after* you've set me at ease about several things."

For an instant he looked dashed, before firmness and —resignation?—deepened the lines in his countenance. "Aye," he murmured, " 'twas clear ye'd raise the same questions your colleagues did. And belike more, sin' ye've a keen wit and are not being rushed as they were."

"Also, I have a special concern," Sally told him. "Not that the rest don't share it, but it was bound to affect me harder than most of them. You see, my study hasn't been the structure of the planet or the chemistry of life on it or anything like that. It's been the natives themselves. I deal directly with them, in several cases intimately. They—certain individuals—they've become my friends, as dear to me as any human."

Dunbar nodded. "And today ye see them threatened wi' extermination, like rats," he said, his tone gentler than she would have expected. "Well, that's why we came, to protect them."

Sally stiffened. "Captain, I know a fair amount about the berserkers. Anybody must, who doesn't want to live in a dream universe. If a planet is undefended, and you assure me they suppose Ilya is, then a single major vessel of theirs can reduce it in a couple of days. Therefore, they'll not likely bother to send more than that."

Dunbar puffed hard on his pipe. Blue clouds streamed past his visage and out the ventilator. She caught a tart whiff. "Aye, we've based our plans on the expectation."

"You seem to have planted your most potent weapons, ground-based, here. The berserker will scarcely happen to show first above this horizon. No, it'll assume orbit and start bombardment above some random location — sending a line of devastation across Ilya, from pole to pole, till it's swung into your range."

"That's what our spacecraft are mainly for, Dr. Jennison. They're insufficient to destroy it, but they'll draw its attention. Chasing them, it'll come into our sights."

"You're risking countless lives on that hope."

"Wha' else ha' we? I told ye, wi'out this operation, the planet is foredoomed anyhow."

"And you came in pure, disinterested altruism," she challenged, "for the sake of nonhuman primitives whom none of you had ever even met?"

He grinned afresh, but wolfishly now. "No, no. Grant us, we'd ha' been sorry at such a cosmic tragedy. Howe'er, from our selfish viewpoint, there'll be one berserker the less, o' their most formidable kind."

She frowned, drummed fingernails on shelf, finally brought her glance clashing against his, and said: "That doesn't make sense, you know. Considering how many units their fleet must have, your effort is out of all proportion to any possible payoff."

"Nay, wait, lass, ye're no' versed in the science o' war."

"I doubt any such science exists!" she spat. "And I'd like to know how *you* know the enemy knows about Ilya. And—"

A siren wailed. A voice roared from loudspeakers, beat through the door, assailed her eardrums. *"Attention, attention! Hear this! Red alert! Berserker scout detected! Battle stations! Full concealment action!"*

"Judas in hell!" ripped from Dunbar. He sprang out of his chair, crouched over his computer terminal, punched frantically for video input. Woop-woop-woop screamed the siren.

Sally surged to her feet. She looked over Dunbar's shoulder No radar, of course, she realized, nothing like that, which the intruder might notice; instruments in use were passive, optics, neutrino detectors, forcefield meters—

They did not spy the vessel from Lake Sapphire. The coincidence would have been enormous if it had passed above. However, from devices planted elsewhere the information, scrambled to simulate ordinary radio noise, went to the fortress. His screen showed a burnished spindle hurtling through the upper air. It passed beyond sight.

He sagged back. She saw sweat darken his shirt beneath the arms. She felt her own. "The scout," he whispered. " 'Tis verified—"

"Bandit has left atmosphere and is accelerating outward," chanted the loudspeaker. *"Reduce to yellow alert. Stand by."*

Silence rang.

Slowly, Dunbar straightened and turned to Sally. His voice rasped. "We'll ha' action soon."

"What did it want?" she asked, as if through a rope around her neck.

"Why, to make sure Ilya remains unguarded."

"Oh . . . Captain, excuse me, this has been a shock, I must go rest a while."

Sally whirled from him and stumbled out into the hallway. "No, don't come along, I'll be all right," she croaked. She didn't look behind her to see what expression might be on his face. He didn't seem entirely real. Nothing did.

The knowledge grew and grew inside her, as if she were bearing a death in her womb. *Why should the berserkers send a scout? The original chance discovery and whatever investigation followed, those should have been plenty. In fact, why didn't they strike Ilya at once, weeks ago?*

Because they didn't know, until just lately. But the Adamites say they did. And the Adamites were expecting that spyship.

Then it must be the Adamites who betrayed us to the enemy. Are they goodlife? Do they have some kind of treaty with the berserkers? If not, what is their aim?

What can I do? I am alone, delivered into their hands. Must I sit and watch the slaughter go on?

Even as she groped her way, an answer began to come.

A few food bars were left in her baggage. She stuffed them into pockets of her coverall. Ilyan biochemistry was too unlike Terrestrial for a human to eat anything native to the planet. By the same token, she was immune to every Ilyan disease. Water would be no problem—unless it got contaminated by radioactive fallout.

Return to Dunbar's room, she thought desperately. *If he's still there. If not, find him. Persuade him . . . But how? I'm not experienced in seduction or, or anything like that . . . Somehow, I've got to talk him into covering for me.*

He saved her the trouble. A knock on her door caused her to open it. He stood outside, concern on his countenance and in his stance and voice. "Forgi' me, I'd no' pester ye, but ye acted so distressed—Can I do aught to help?"

The knowledge of her power, slight though it was, came aglow in Sally like a draught of wine. Abruptly she was calm, the Zen relaxation upon her which Ito had tried to teach, and totally determined. Win or lose, she would play her hand.

"Don't you have duties, Captain?" she asked, since that was a predictable question.

"No' at once. The berserker scout is definitely headed out o' this system. 'Twill take fifty or sixty hours at least for it to report back and for a major ship to get here. Belike the time will be longer." He hesitated, stared at the floor, clamped his fists. "Aye, they'll soon require me for final inspections, tests, drills, briefings. But no' immediately. Meanwhile, is there any comfort I can offer ye?"

She pounced. "Let me go topside," she said mutedly.

"Wha'?" He was astonished.

I'm not used to playing the pathetic little girl, she thought. *I'll doubtless do it badly. Well, chances are he won't know the difference.* "It may be my last walk around this countryside I love. Oh, please, Captain Dunbar—Ian—please!"

He stood silent for several heartbeats. But he was a decisive man. "Aye, why no'? I'm sorry—surely ye'd liefer be alone—my orders are that I must accompany ye."

She gave him a sunburst smile. "I understand. And I don't mind at all. Thank you, thank you."

"Let's begone, if ye wish." Willy-nilly, she found that his gladness touched her.

Save for the pulse of machines, the corridors had quieted. Men were closing down their construction jobs and preparing for combat. As she passed a chapel, Sally heard untrained singers:

"— Lord God o' warrior Joshua,

Unleash thy lightnings now!"

She wondered if the hymn spoke to Dunbar or if he had left the Kirk and become an agnostic like her.

What did that matter?

A ladder took them past a guard station where the sentries saluted him, and up onto desolation. A breeze off the lake cooled noontide heat. Clouds blew in ruddy-bright rags. Olga was a thin arc, with streamers of dust storm across the dark part. Sally pointed herself at a stand of trees some distance beyond this blackened section, and walked fast.

"I take it ye want as much time as possible amidst yon life," Dunbar ventured.

She nodded. "Of course. How long will it remain?"

"Ye're too pessimistic, lass—pardon me—Dr. Jennison. We'll smite the berserker, ne'er fear."

"How can you be sure? It'll be the biggest, most heavily armed, most elaborately computer-brained type they've got. I've seen pictures, read descriptions. It'll not only have a monstrous offensive arsenal, it'll bristle with defenses, forcefields, antimissiles, interceptor beam projectors. Can your few destroyers, or whatever they are, can they hope to prevail against it, let alone keep it from laying—oh—enormous territories waste?"

"I told ye, their main purpose is to lure it to where our ground-based armament can take o'er."

"That seems a crazy gamble. It'll be a moving target, hundreds of kilometers aloft."

"We've no' just abundant energy to apply, we've knowledge o' where to. The layout o' such a ship is well understood, fro' study o' wrecks retrieved after engagements in the past."

Sally bit her lip. "You're assuming the thing is . . . stupid. That it'll sit passive in synchronous orbit, after failing to suspect a trap. Berserkers have outsmarted humans before now."

Dunbar's tone roughened. "Aye, granted. Our computer technology is not yet quite on a par wi' that o' the ancient Frankensteins who first designed them. The monsters do no' behave foreseeably, e'en in statistical fashion, the way less advanced systems do. They learn from experience; they innovate. That's wha's made them mortal dangers. Could we build something comparable—"

"No!" said ingrained fear. "We could never trust it not to turn on us."

"M-m-m . . . common belief. . . . Be that as it may, we do lack critical information. Nobody has studied a modern, updated berserker computer, save for fragments o' the hardware. Software, nil. Wha' few times a capture looked imminent, the thing destroyed itsel'." Dunbar's chuckle was harsh. "No' that the weapons employed usually leave much to sweep up."

"And nevertheless you think you can trick one of their top-rated units?"

"They're no' omnipotent, Dr. Jennison. They too are bound by the laws o' physics and the logical requirements o' tactics. Humans ha' more than once defeated them. This will be another occasion."

Ash gave way to turf. "Maybe, maybe," the woman said. "But that's not enough for me. The berserker will fight back. It will employ its most powerful weapons. You've hardened your base, but what have you done to protect the neighborhood? Nothing."

He wilted. "We could no'," he answered in misery. "We know naught about the natives."

"My colleagues do. They'd have undertaken to make arrangements with them."

"Rightly or wrongly, our orders were to clear your team out o' the way immediately and completely, out fro' underfoot, so we could get on wi' our task," Dunbar said shakily. "I hate the thought o' losing lives, but wha' we do is necessary to save the whole native species."

The shaw was close. The man's sidearm sat within centimeters of Sally's hand. She felt no excitement, only a vivid sense of everything around her, as she snatched it from its holster and sprang back.

"Oh no!" she cried. "Stop where you are!"

"Wha's this?" He jerked to a halt, appalled. "Ha' ye gone schizo?"

"Not a move," she said across the meters of living sod. The pistol never wavered in her grip. "At the least suspicion, I'll shoot, and believe me, I'm a damn good shot."

He rallied, mustered composure, said in a flat voice: "Wha' are ye thinking o'? I can scarce believe ye're goodlife."

"No, I'm not," she flung back. "Are you?"

"Hoy? How could ye imagine—"

"Easily. Your story about the berserkers chancing upon Ilya doesn't hang together. The sole explanation for everything I've witnessed is that *you* informed them, you Adamites, you called them in. Dare you deny?"

He swallowed, ran tongue over lips, bowed his head. "We've a trap to spring," he mumbled.

"For a single trophy, you'd set a world at stake? You're as evil as your enemy."

"Sally, Sally, I can no' tell ye—"

"Don't try. I haven't the time to spill, anyway. I'm going to do what you'd never have let me, lead the natives hereabouts to safety . . . if any safety is to be found, after what you've caused. Go back! This instant! I'll kill anyone who tries to follow me."

For a long while he looked at her. The wind soughed in the darkling trees.

"Ye would," he whispered finally. "Ye might ha' asked leave o' the admiral, though."

"Would he have granted it, that fanatic?"

"I can no' tell. Maybe no'."

"It wasn't a risk I could take."

"Fro' your standpoint, true. Ye're a brave and determined person."

"Go!" She aimed the pistol between his eyes and gave the trigger a light pressure.

He nodded. "Farewell," he sighed, and trudged off. She watched him for a minute before she disappeared into the woods.

The deathmoon slipped out of flightspace and accelerated ponderously toward the red sun. Starshine glimmered off the kilometers-wide spheroid that was its hull. The weak light ahead cast shadows past gun tur-

rets, missile tubes, ray projectors, like the shadows of
crags and craters on a dead planet.

A radar beam brought word of the double world. The
berserker calculated orbits and adjusted its vectors accordingly. Otherwise nothing registered on its receivers
but endless cosmic rustlings.

The solar disc waxed, dark spots upon bloody glow.
The target globe and companion glimmered as crescents. The berserker was slowing down now, to put
itself in a path around the one which was alive.

It passed the other one. Abruptly, detectors thrilled.
Engines had awakened, spacecraft were scrambling from
both planets—human vessels.

The berserker tracked them. They numbered half a
dozen, and were puny, well-nigh insignificant. Not quite;
any could launch a warhead that would leave the berserker a cloud of molten gobbets. However, even at-
tacking together they could not saturate its defenses. It
would annihilate their missiles in midcourse, absorb
their energy beams, and smash them out of existence,
did they choose to fight.

Should it? Within the central computer of the berserker, a logic tree grew and spread. The humans might
be present by chance (probability low). If not, they had
some scheme, of which the revelation by the Montgomery unit had been a part (probability high). Ought the
berserker to withdraw? That might well be the intent of
the humans; they often bluffed. The assumption that
they were strong in this system would affect strategy, as
by causing underestimation of their capabilities elsewhere.

The berserker could retreat, to return in an armada
invincible against anything the humans might have here.
But this would mean postponing attacks elsewhere. It
would buy the enemy time he much needed, to bring
help from distant sectors. Whole worlds might never
get attended to.

Information was necessary. The berserker computed
that its optimum course was to proceed. At worst, a

single capital unit would perish. It considered dispatching a courier back to base with this message, calculated that the humans would detect and destroy the device before it could enter flightspace, and refrained. Its own failure to report in would warn the others, if that happened.

The berserker moved onward—majestically, a human would have said—under its great imperative, to kill.

First, if possible, it should dispose of the opposing spacecraft. They were widely dispersed, but generally maneuvering near the target mass. Computation, decision: Move their way, seek engagement, meanwhile establish orbit, commence sterilization, lash back at any surviving human vessel which dared try to distract the berserker from its mission.

It swung inward. The little ships did likewise, converging on a volume of space above the terminator. The berserker followed. A destroyer accelerated audaciously forth. The berserker shifted vectors to shorten the range. This brought it near the fringes of atmosphere, at less than orbital speed. Its track curved gradually downward. But the parameters were in its data banks, its drive was already at work to bring it up again, it was simply using gravitation as an aid.

Lightning lanced out of the night below.

Electronically fast, the ship's fire control center reacted. Even as sensors recorded the slash of energy through metal, and went blank before that fury, a missile sprang.

There was only time for the one. Then the berserker tumbled around itself, sliced across. Stars danced about, incandescent drops that had been armor, before they cooled and went black. Radar-guided, light-fast, the beam carved again, and again. Cut free of every connection, the central computer drifted in its housing amidst the pieces, blind, deaf, dumb, helpless.

The human vessels spurted to salvage the fragments before those could become meteors.

*   *   *

A newly gibbous Olga gleamed red-cold over Snow-crown. Mountains beyond were jagged ramparts under constellations Earth had never seen. In a hollow of the foothills, campfires cast flickery gleams off eyes and eyes, as three hundred or more Ilyans huddled close. They said little, in that enormous silence.

Sally Jennison crouched likewise. She, the alien, her skin bare beneath its garb, needed the most help against gathering chill. Her friends, the leaders of the exodus, squatted to right and left. She could almost feel their questioning.

Rainbow-in-the-Mist uttered it: "How long must we abide, Lady-Who-Seeks? The food we have brought grows scant. The younglings and the old suffer. But well you know this."

"I do," Sally replied. Breath smoked ghost-white from her lips. Hunger made her light-headed; her own rations had given out many hours ago, as she took the Geyserdale folk eastward to shelter. "Better hardship than death."

Feather-softly, he touched her hand. "Yours is the worst case," he fluted. "We would not lose you whom we love. When can everybody turn back?"

"When the danger is past—"

Behind those ridges that barred view of the west, heaven sundered. A sheet of blue-white radiance momentarily shrouded stars and moon. Trees and shadows were as if etched. Ilyans shrieked, flung arms over faces, clutched infants to their bodies. Sally herself stumbled bedazzled.

"Hold fast!" she yelled. "Rainie, tell them to stay brave! We're all alive!"

The ground sent a shudder through her bones. She heard rocks bounce down slopes. The rags of brilliance began to clear from her vision.

She went about among the Ilyans with her lieutenants, helping, reassuring. They had not panicked, that was not in their nature, and although they were more vulnerable to actinic light than she was, it didn't seem that anybody's sight had been permanently damaged; intervening air had blotted up the worst. She wept in her relief.

After minutes the sound arrived, a roar whose echoes cannonaded from hill to hill for what seemed like a long while. But there had been no second hell-flash. Whatever had happened, had happened.

"Is the danger past?" asked Rainbow-in-the-Mist when stillness had returned.

"I . . . think so," Sally answered.

"What next shall we do?"

"Wait here. You can hold out till—oh, dawn. Though if things go well, it should end sooner. My fellow creatures ought to arrive in their vehicles and ferry you back before then."

"Home?"

She disliked admitting: "No, I fear not. Your homes are smashed and burnt, as you yourselves would have been if we'd not fled. It'll be a year or two"—brief Ilyan years—"till you can rebuild. First we'll distribute you among your kindred in the unharmed hinterlands.

"But I must go tell the humans. Best I start off at once."

"*We* will," Rainbow-in-the-Mist said. "I've better night vision, and can find things to eat along the way, and . . . would not let you fare alone, Lady-Who-Saved-Us."

She accepted his offer. He would have insisted. Besides, he was right. Without a partner, she might not survive the trek.

Unless, to be sure, the men of Adam came looking for her in their aircars, wearing their light-amplifier goggles.

They did.

"We're unco busy," Admiral Scrymgeour had snapped. "No time for official briefing, debriefing, any such nonsense. Later, later, just to satisfy the bureaucrats. In the interim, Dr. Jennison, now that ye've gotten some sleep and nourishment, I detail Captain Dunbar to explain and discuss. He deserves a rest himsel'." Did he wink an eye?

She had inquired if they might leave the clamor and closeness underground, to talk in peace (if peace was possible between them) Dunbar had agreed. Residual radioactivity wasn't dangerous topside unless exposure was unreasonably prolonged. Warmly clad, they sought the bluff above Lake Sapphire.

Olga stood nearly full, a rosiness on which few scars showed, only dark emblazonings and streamers of brightness that were high-floating clouds. A frost ring surrounded it, and stars. Through windless cold, it cast a nearly perfect glade over the water. Beyond, mountains reared hoar, Snowcrown a faintly tinged white. Ice creaked underfoot, almost the single sound. It covered scorched turf, leveled homesteads, trees shattered to kindling, with a glittery blanket. Come sunrise, growth would begin again.

Dunbar spoke softly, as though unwilling to violate the hush: "Ye've naught to fear fro' us, ye realize. True, belike ye'd no' ha' been released on your errand o' mercy if ye'd applied. Overcaution, same as when ye appeared in your boat. Howe'er, ye did break free, and saved those many lives. Our consciences are eternally in your debt."

"What about yourself?" she wondered. "You failed in your duty."

He smiled like a boy. "Och, they're glad I did. And in any case, no' to be modest, I carried out my real duty wi' full success. That's wha' matters. The episode wi' ye will simply not get into the record."

She nodded in troubled wise. "You demolished the berserker, yes."

"Wrong!" he exulted. "We did no'. 'Twas the whole point. We captured it."

Her pulse stumbled. She stared at him.

He grew earnest. "We could no' tell ye, or your colleagues, in advance. The attempt might ha' been a failure. If so, we'd want to try afresh elsewhere—

different ruse, o' course, but same basic objective. Meanwhile, we could no' ha' risked word about that intention getting out and forewarning the enemy, could we?"

"But now—?" she breathed.

He faced her. Beneath his shadowing hood, eyes shone forth. "Now," he said, "we can make amends to ye, to Ilya. We'll mount guard o'er this world, at least until a gathered alliance can assume the task. No' that I await another attack. When they ne'er hear fro' the ship they sent, the berserkers will likeliest become leery. They've much else they want to do, after all, before they're forced out o' the entire sector."

Compassion touched her. "Including an assault on Adam?"

"Maybe. If so, they'll no' succeed. They may well no' e'en try. The fact that we fooled them should gi' them pause. Be that as it may, we've strength to spare— including our weapons on the ground, and more that we can install roundabout this planet—strength to spare for Ilya." His lips tightened. "We did do its folk a wrong—perforce; in a righteous cause; nonetheless a wrong. We pay our debts, Dr. Jennison."

"But what *was* your cause?" she asked in bewilderment.

"Why, I told ye. To capture intact a first-line berserker unit. No' the actual ship, though study o' the pieces will prove rewarding, but its brain, the principal computer, hardware and software both, before it could destroy itself.

"To that end, we lured a single craft here, where we'd assembled a ray projector. Our weapon has the gigawatts o' power, the lake for cooling, the sheer physical dimensions for precision, that it could dissect a berserker across two or three thousand kilometers."

Her gloved hands caught his. Fingers closed together. "Oh, wonderful!" Her admiration retreated. "Yes, I can see how the data will be very helpful; but can they make that big a difference?"

"They can change everything," he replied.

After a moment, during which breath smoked between them, he said slowly: "Ye inquired about von Neumann machines. Ye were correct; that is wha' the berserker fleet is, taken as a whole. A self-reproducing system whose basic program is to seek out and kill all that's alive.

"Well, wha' if we humans created another von Neumann machine, a system whose basic program is to seek out and kill *berserkers?*"

Her response was unthinking, automatic: "I've read something about that. It was tried, early in the war, and didn't work. The berserkers soon learned how to cope with those machines, and wiped them out."

"Aye," he agreed. "The ancient Builders built too well. Our race could no' make computers to match theirs, in scope, flexibility, adaptability, capacity for evolution. We must needs develop living organization, dedication, skill, humans an integral part o' the control loop. And 'tis no' served us badly. We've saved oursel's, most o' the time.

"But . . . there is no end to the war, either. They've the cosmos to draw on for the means o' building more like themsel's."

Sally remembered her image of a womb, and shivered.

"On the basis o' what we're going to learn," she heard Dunbar say, "let us make machines which will be likewise, but whose prey is berserkers."

"Dare we?" she replied. A crack rang loud through midnight as frost split a fallen tree apart. "Might they turn on us also, at last?"

She thought she saw stoicism on his face. "Aye, the old fear. Maybe, on that account alone, humankind will unite to forbid our undertaking.

"Or maybe we'll do it, and 'twill prove no single answer by itsel'. Then at least our hunter machines will bring attrition on the enemy, take pressure off us, help us deliver the final hammerblow.

"And if no' e'en that comes to pass, why, we've still gained information beyond price. Once we've examined our . . . prisoner, we'll understand today's berserkers far better. We'll become able to fight them the more readily."

It blazed from him: "Is that no' worth the risk and cost to Ilya, Sally?"

At once he was abashed. "Forgi' me," he said, while his hands withdrew from hers. "Dr. Jennison."

She regarded him by the icy brilliance. The thought came to her that perhaps robots that hounded robots were nothing to fear. Perhaps dread lay in the fact that a war which went on and on must, ultimately, bring forth men who were as terrible as their enemies.

She didn't know. She wouldn't live long enough to know. She and he were merely two humans, by themselves in a huge and wintry night.

She took a step forward, renewed their handclasp, and said, "We can argue about it later, Ian. But let's be friends."

Note: This story forms part of *Berserker Base,* Fred Saberhagen ed., Tor Books, 1985. The concept of the berserkers is Fred Saberhagen's and is here used with his permission.

MURPHY'S
HALL

This is a lie, but I wish so much it were not.

Pain struck through like lightning. For an instant that went on and on, there was nothing but the fire which hollowed him out and the body's animal terror. Then as he whirled downward he knew:

> Oh, no! Must I   Only a month,
> leave them already? a month.
> *Weltall, verweile doch, du bist so schön.*

The monstrous thunders and whistles became a tone, like a bell struck once which would not stop singing. It filled the jagged darkness, it drowned all else, until it began to die out, or to vanish into the endless, century after century, and meanwhile the night deepened and softened, until he had peace.

But he opened himself again and was in a place long and high. With his not-eyes he saw that five hundred and forty doors gave onto black immensities wherein dwelt clouds of light. Some of the clouds were bringing suns to birth. Others, greater and more distant, were made of suns already created, and turned in majestic

Catherine's wheels. The nearest stars cast out streamers of flame, lances of radiance; and they were diamond, amethyst, emerald, topaz, ruby; and around them swung glints which he knew with his not-brain were planets. His not-ears heard the thin violence of cosmic-ray sleet, the rumble of solar storms, the slow patient multiplex pulses of gravitational tides. His not-flesh shared the warmth, the blood-beat, the megayears of marvelous life on uncountable worlds.

Seven stood waiting. He rose. "But you—" he stammered without a voice.

"Welcome," Ed greeted him. "Don't be surprised. You were always one of us."

They talked quietly, until at last Gus reminded them that even here they were not masters of time. Eternity, yes, but not time. "Best we move on," he suggested.

"Uh-huh," Roger said. "Especially after Murphy took this much trouble on our account."

"He does not appear to be a bad fellow," Vladimir said.

"I am not certain," Robert answered. "Nor am I certain that we ever will find out. But come, friends. The hour is near."

Eight, they departed the hall and hastened down the star paths. Often the newcomer was tempted to look more closely at something he glimpsed. But he recalled that, while the universe was inexhaustible of wonders, it would have only the single moment to which he was being guided.

They stood after a while on a great ashen plain. The outlook was as eerily beautiful as he had hoped—no, more, when Earth, a blue serenity swirled white with weather, shone overhead: Earth, whence had come the shape that now climbed down a ladder of fire.

Yuri took Konstantin by the hand in the Russian way. "Thank you," he said through tears.

But Konstantin bowed in turn, very deeply, to Willy.

And they stood in the long Lunar shadows, under the high Lunar heaven, and saw the awkward thing come to rest and heard: "Houston, Tranquillity Base here. The Eagle has landed."

Stars are small and dim on Earth. Oh, I guess they're pretty bright still on a winter mountaintop. I remember when I was little, we'd saved till we had the admission fees and went to Grand Canyon Reserve and camped out. Never saw that many stars. And it was like you could see up and up between them—like, you know, you could *feel* how they weren't the same distance off, and the spaces between were more huge than you could imagine. Earth and its people were just lost, just a speck of nothing among those cold sharp stars. Dad said they weren't too different from what you saw in space, except for being a lot fewer. The air was chilly too, and had a kind of pureness, and a sweet smell from the pines around. Way off I heard a coyote yip. The sound had plenty of room to travel in.

But I'm back where people live. The smog's not bad on this rooftop lookout, though I wish I didn't have to breathe what's gone through a couple million pairs of lungs before it reaches me. Thick and greasy. The city noise isn't too bad either, the usual growling and screeching, a jet-blast or a burst of gunfire. And since the power shortage brought on the brownout, you can generally see stars after dark, sort of.

My main wish is that we lived in the southern hemisphere, where you can see Alpha Centauri.

Dad, what are you doing tonight in Murphy's Hall?

A joke. I know. Murphy's Law: "Anything that can go wrong, will." Only I think it's a true joke. I mean, I've read every book and watched every tape I could lay hands on, the history, how the discoverers went out, farther and farther, lifetime after lifetime. I used to tell myself stories about the parts that nobody lived to put into a book.

The crater wall had fangs. They stood sharp and grayish white in the cruel sunlight, against the shadow which brimmed the bowl. And they grew and grew. Tumbling while it fell, the spacecraft had none of the restfulness of zero weight. Forces caught nauseatingly at gullet and gut. An unidentified loose object clattered behind the pilot chairs. The ventilators had stopped their whickering and the two men breathed stench. No matter. This wasn't an Apollo 13 mishap. They wouldn't have time to smother in their own exhalations.

Jack Bredon croaked into the transmitter: "Hello, Mission Control . . . Lunar Relay Satellite . . . anybody. Do you read us? Is the radio out too? Or just our receiver? God damn it, can't we even say goodbye to our wives?"

"Tell 'em quick," Sam Washburn ordered. "Maybe they'll hear."

Jack dabbed futilely at the sweat that broke from his face and danced in glittering droplets before him. "Listen," he said. "This is Moseley Expedition One. Our motors stopped functioning simultaneously, about two minutes after we commenced deceleration. The trouble must be in the fuel feed integrator. I suspect a magnetic surge, possibly due to a short circuit in the power supply. The meters registered a surge before we lost thrust. Get that system redesigned! Tell our wives and kids we love them."

He stopped. The teeth of the crater filled the entire forward window. Sam's teeth filled his countenance, a stretched-out grin. "How do you like that?" he said. "And me the only black astronaut."

They struck.

When they opened themselves again, in the hall, and knew where they were, he said, "Wonder if he'll let us go out exploring."

Murphy's Halt? Is that the real name?

Dad used to shout, "Murphy take it!" when he blew his temper. The rest is in a few of the old tapes, fiction plays about spacemen, back when people liked to watch that kind of story. They'd say when a man had died,

"He's drinking in Murphy's Hall." Or he's dancing or
sleeping or frying or freezing or whatever it was. But
did they really say "Hall"? The tapes are old. Nobody's
been interested to copy them off on fresh plastic, not
for a hundred years, I guess, maybe two hundred. The
holographs are blurred and streaky, the sounds are
mushed and full of random buzzes. Murphy's Law has
sure been working on those tapes.

I wish I'd asked Dad what the astronauts said and
believed, way back when they were conquering the
planets. Or pretended to believe, I should say. Of
course they never thought there was a Murphy who
kept a place where the spacefolk went that he'd called
to him. But they might have kidded around about it.
Only was the idea, for sure, about a hall? Or was that
only the way I heard? I wish I'd asked Dad. But he
wasn't home often, those last years, what with helping
build and test his ship. And when he did come, I could
see how he mainly wanted to be with Mother. And
when he and I were together, well, that was always too
exciting for me to remember those yarns I'd tell myself
before I slept, after he was gone again.

Murphy's Haul?

By the time Moshe Silverman had finished writing
his report, the temperature in the dome was about
seventy, and rising fast enough that it should reach a
hundred inside another Earth day. Of course, waters
wouldn't then boil at once; extra energy is needed for
vaporization. But the staff would no longer be able to
cool some down to drinking temperature by the crude
evaporation apparatus they had rigged. They'd dehy-
drate fast. Moshe sat naked in a running river of sweat.

At least he had electric light. The fuel cells, insufficient to operate the air conditioning system, would at
least keep Sofia from dying in the dark.

His head ached and his ears buzzed. Occasional diz-
ziness seized him. He gagged on the warm fluid he
must continually drink. *And no more salt*, he thought.

Maybe that will kill us before the heat does, the simmering, still, stifling heat. His bones felt heavy, though Venus has in fact a somewhat lesser pull than Earth; his muscles sagged and he smelled the reek of his own disintegration.

Forcing himself to concentrate, he checked what he had written, a dry factual account of the breakdown of the reactor. The next expedition would read what this thick, poisonous inferno of an atmosphere did to graphite in combination with free neutrons; and the engineers could work out proper precautions.

In sudden fury, Moshe seized his brush and scrawled at the bottom of the metal sheet: "Don't give up! Don't let this hellhole whip you! We have too much to learn here."

A touch on his shoulder brought him jerkily around and onto his feet. Sofia Chiappellone had entered the office. Even now, with physical desire roasted out of him and she wetly agleam, puffy-faced, sunken-eyed, hair plastered lank to drooping head, he found her lovely.

"Aren't you through, darling?" Her tone was dull but her hand sought his. "We're better off in the main room. Mohandas' punkah arrangement does help."

"Yes, I'm coming."

"Kiss me first. Share the salt on me."

Afterward she looked over his report. "Do you believe they will try any further?" she asked. "Materials so scarce and expensive since the war—"

"If they don't," he answered, "I have a feeling—oh, crazy, I know, but why should we not be crazy?—I think if they don't, more than our bones will stay here. Our souls will, waiting for the ships that never come."

She actually shivered, and urged him toward their comrades.

Maybe I should go back inside. Mother might need me. She cries a lot, still. Crying, all alone in our little apartment. But maybe she'd rather not have me around.

What can a gawky, pimply-faced fourteen-year-old boy
do?

What can he do when he grows up?

O Dad, big brave Dad, I want to follow you. Even to
Murphy's . . . Hold?

Director Saburo Murakami had stood behind the table in the commons and met their eyes, pair by pair.
For a while silence had pressed inward. The bright
colors and amateurish figures in the mural that Georgios
Efthimakis had painted for pleasure—beings that never
were, nymphs and fauns and centaurs frolicking beneath an unsmoky sky, beside a bright river, among
grasses and laurel trees and daisies of an Earth that no
longer was—became suddenly grotesque, infinitely alien.
He heard his heart knocking. Twice he must swallow
before he had enough moisture in his mouth to move
his wooden tongue.

But when he began his speech, the words came forth
steadily, if a trifle flat and cold. That was no surprise.
He had lain awake the whole night rehearsing them.

"Yousouf Yacoub reports that he has definitely succeeded in checking the pseudovirus. This is not a cure;
such must await laboratory research. Our algae will
remain scant and sickly until the next supply ship brings
us a new stock. I will radio Cosmocontrol, explaining
the need. They will have ample time on Earth to prepare. You remember the ship is scheduled to leave
at . . . at a date to bring it here in about nine months.
Meanwhile we are guaranteed a rate of oxygen renewal
sufficient to keep us alive, though weak, if we do not
exert ourselves. Have I stated the matter correctly,
Yousouf?"

The Arab nodded. His own Spanish had taken on a
denser accent, and a tic played puppet master with his
right eye. "Will you not request a special ship?" he
demanded.

"No," Saburo told them. "You are aware how expensive anything but an optimum Hohmann orbit is. That

alone would wipe out the profit from this station—
permanently, I fear, because of financing costs. Likewise would our idleness for nine months."

He leaned forward, supporting his weight easily on
fingertips in the low Martian gravity. "That is what I
wish to discuss today," he said. "Interest rates represent competition for money. Money represents human
labor and natural resources. This is true regardless of
socioeconomic arrangements. You know how desperately short they are of both labor and resources on
Earth. Yes, many billions of hands—but because of
massive poverty, too few educated brains. Think back
to what a political struggle the Foundation had before
this base could be established.

"We know what we are here for. To explore. To
learn. To make man's first permanent home outside
Earth and Luna. In the end, in the persons of our
great-grandchildren, to give Mars air men can breathe,
water they can drink, green fields and forests where
their souls will have room to grow." He gestured at the
mural, though it seemed more than ever jeering. "We
can't expect starvelings on Earth, or those who speak
for them, to believe this is good. Not when each ship
bears away metal and fuel and engineering skill that
might have gone to keep *their* children alive a while
longer. We justify our continued presence here solely
by mining the fissionables. The energy this gives back
to the tottering economy, over and above what we take
out, is the profit."

He drew a breath of stale, metallic-smelling air. An-
oxia made his head whirl. Somehow he stayed erect and
continued:

"I believe we, in this tiny solitary settlement, are the
last hope for man remaining in space. If we are main-
tained until we have become fully self-supporting, Syrtis
Harbor will be the seedbed of the future. If not—"

He had planned more of an exhortation before reaching the climax, but his lungs were too starved, his pulse
too fluttery. He gripped the table edge and said through

flying rags of darkness: "There will be oxygen for half of us to keep on after a fashion. By suspending their other projects and working exclusively in the mines, they can produce enough uranium and thorium that the books at least show no net economic loss. The sacrifice will . . . will be . . . of propaganda value. I call for male volunteers, or we can cast lots, or—Naturally, I myself am the first."

—That had been yesterday.

Saburo was among those who elected to go alone, rather than in a group. He didn't care for hymns about human solidarity; his dream was that someday those who bore some of his and Alice's chromosomes would not need solidarity. It was perhaps well she had already died in a cinderslip. The scene with their children had been as much as he could endure.

He crossed Weinbaum Ridge but stopped when the domecluster was out of sight. He must not make the searchers come too far. If nothing else, a quick dust storm might cover his tracks, and he might never be found. Someone could make good use of his airsuit. Almost as good use as the algae tanks could of his body.

For a time, then, he stood looking. The mountainside ran in dark scars and fantastically carved pinnacles, down to the softly red-gold-ocher-black-dappled plain. A crater on the near horizon rose out of its own blue shadow like a challenge to the ruddy sky. In this thin air—he could just hear the wind's ghostly whistle—Mars gave to his gaze every aspect of itself, diamond sharp, a beauty strong, subtle, and abstract as a torii gate before a rock garden. When he glanced away from the shrunken but dazzling-bright sun, he could see stars.

He felt at peace, almost happy. Perhaps the cause was simply that now, after weeks, he had a full ration of oxygen.

I oughtn't to waste it, though, he thought. He was pleased by the steadiness of his fingers when he closed the valve.

Then he was surprised that his unbelieving self bowed over both hands to the Lodestar and said, "*Namu Amida Butsu.*"

He opened his faceplate.

That is a gentle death. You are unconscious within thirty seconds.

—He opened himself and did not know where he was. An enormous room whose doorways framed a night heaven riotous with suns, galaxies, the green mysterious shimmer of nebulae? Or a still more huge ship, outward bound so fast that it was as if the Milky Way foamed along the bow and swirled aft in a wake of silver and planets?

Others were here, gathered about a high seat at the far end of where-he-was, vague in the twilight cast by sheer distance. Saburo rose and moved in their direction. Maybe, maybe Alice was among them.

But was he right to leave Mother that much alone?

I remember her when we got the news. On a Wednesday, when I was free, and I'd been out by the dump playing ball. I may as well admit to myself, I don't like some of the guys. But you have to take whoever the school staggering throws up for you. Or do you want to run around by yourself (remember, no, don't remember what the Hurricane Gang did to Danny) or stay always by yourself in the patrolled areas? So Jake-Jake does throw his weight around, so he does set the dues too high, his drill and leadership sure paid off when the Weasels jumped us last year. They won't try that again—we killed three, count 'em, three!—and I sort of think no other bunch will either.

She used to be real pretty, Mother did. I've seen pictures. She'd gotten kind of scrawny, worrying about Dad, I guess, and about how to get along after that last pay cut they screwed the spacefolk with. But when I came in and saw her sitting, not on the sofa but on the carpet, the dingy gray carpet, crying—She hung onto that sofa the way she'd hung on Dad.

But why did she have to be so angry at him too? I mean, what happened wasn't his fault.

"Fifty billion munits!" she screamed when we'd got trying to talk about the thing. "That's a hundred, two hundred billion meals for hungry children! But what did they spend it on? Killing twelve men!"

"Aw, now, wait," I was saying, "Dad explained that. The resources involved, uh, aren't identical," when she slapped me and yelled:

"You'd like to go the same way, wouldn't you? Thank God, it almost makes his death worthwhile that you won't!"

I shouldn't have got mad. I shouldn't have said, "Y-y-you want me to become . . . a desk pilot, a food engineer, a doctor . . . something nice and safe and in demand . . . and keep you the way you wanted he should keep you?"

I better stop beating this rail. My fist'll be no good if I don't. Oh, someday I'll find how to make up those words to her.

I'd better not go in just yet.

But the trouble *wasn't* Dad's fault. If things had worked out right, why, we'd be headed for Alpha Centauri in a couple of years. Her and him and me— The planets yonderward, sure, they're the real treasure. But the ship itself! I remember Jake-Jake telling me I'd been dead of boredom inside six months. "Bored aboard, haw, haw, haw!" He really is a lardbrain. A good leader, I guess, but a lardbrain at heart—hey, once Mother would have laughed to hear me say that— How could you get tired of Dad's ship? A million books and tapes, a hundred of the brightest and most alive people who ever walked a deck—

Why, the trip would be like the revels in Elf Hill that Mother used to read me about when I was small, those old, old stories, the flutes and fiddles, bright clothes, food, drink, dancing, girls sweet in the moonlight. . . .

Murphy's Hill?

*　　*　　*

From Ganymede, Jupiter shows fifteen times as broad as Luna seen from Earth; and however far away the sun, the king planet reflects so brilliantly that it casts more than fifty times the radiance that the brightest night of man's home will ever know.

"*Here* is man's home," Catalina Sanchez murmured.

Arne Jensen cast her a look which lingered. She was fair to see in the goldenness streaming through the conservatory's clear walls. He ventured to put an arm about her waist. She sighed and leaned against him. They were scantily clad—the colony favored brief though colorful indoor garments—and he felt the warmth and silkiness of her. Among the manifold perfumes of blossoms (on plants everywhere to right and left and behind, extravagantly tall stalks and big flowers of every possible hue and some you would swear were impossible, dreamlike catenaries of vines and labyrinths of creepers) he caught her summery odor.

The sun was down and Jupiter close to full. While the terraforming project was going rapidly ahead, as yet the moon had too little air to blur vision. Tawny shone that shield, emblazoned with slowly moving cloud bands that were green, blue, orange, umber and with the jewel-like Red Spot. To know that a single one of the storms raging there could swallow Earth whole added majesty to beauty and serenity; to know that, without the magnetohydronamic satellites men had orbited around this globe, its surface would be drowned in lethal radiation, added triumph. A few stars had the brilliance to pierce the luminousness, down by the rugged horizon. The gold poured soft across crags, cliffs, craters, glaciers, and the machinery of the conquest.

Outside lay a great quietness, but here music lilted from the ballroom. Folk had reason to celebrate. The newest electrolysis plant had gone into operation and was releasing oxygen at a rate 15 percent above estimate. However, low-weight or no, you got tired dancing—since Ganymedean steps took advantage, soaring and bounding aloft—mirth bubbled like champagne

and the girl you admired said yes, she was in a mood
for Jupiter watching—

"I hope you're right," Arne said. "Less on our
account—we have a good, happy life, fascinating work,
the best of company—than on our children's." He
squeezed a trifle harder.

She didn't object. "How can we fail?" she answered.
"We've become better than self-sufficient. We produce
a surplus, to trade to Earth, Luna, Mars, or plow
directly back into development. The growth is expo-
nential." She smiled. "You must think I'm awfully
professorish. Still, really, what can go wrong?"

"I don't know," he said. "War, overpopulation, envi-
ronmental degradation—"

"Don't be a gloomy," Catalina chided him. The lam-
bent light struck rainbows from the tiara of native crystal that she wore in her hair. "People can learn. They
needn't make the same mistakes forever. We'll build
paradise here. A strange sort of paradise, yes, where
trees soar into a sky full of Jupiter, and waterfalls tumble slowly, slowly down into deep-blue lakes, and birds
fly like tiny bright-colored bullets, and deer cross the
meadows in ten-meter leaps . . . but paradise."

"Not perfect," he said. "Nothing is."

"No, and we wouldn't wish that," she agreed. "We
want some discontent left to keep minds active, keep
them hankering for the stars." She chuckled. "I'm sure
history will find ways to make them believe things
could be better elsewhere. Or nature will—Oh!"

Her eyes widened. A hand went to her mouth. And
then, frantically, she was kissing him, and he her, and
they were clasping and feeling each other while the
waltz melody sparkled and the flowers breathed and
Jupiter's glory cataracted over them uncaring whether
they existed.

He tasted tears on her mouth. "Let's go dancing,"
she begged. "Let's dance till we drop."

"Surely," he promised, and led her back to the
ballroom.

It would help them once more forget the giant mete-
oroid, among the many which the planet sucked in from
the Belt, that had plowed into grim and marginal Outpost Ganymede precisely half a decade before the Martian colony was discontinued.

Well, I guess people don't learn. They breed, and
fight, and devour, and pollute, till:

Mother: "We can't afford it."

Dad: "We can't not afford it."

Mother: "Those children—like goblins, like ghosts,
from starvation. If Tad were one of them, and somebody said never mind him, we have to build an interstellar ship . . . I wonder how you would react."

Dad: "I don't know. But I do know this is our last
chance. We'll be operating on a broken shoestring as is,
compared to what we need to do the thing right. If they
hadn't made that breakthrough at Lunar Hydromagnet-
ics Lab, when the government was on the point of
closing it down—Anyway, darling, that's why I'll have
to put in plenty of time aboard myself, while the ship is
built and tested. My entire gang will be on triple duty."

Mother: "Suppose you succeed. Suppose you do get
your precious spacecraft that can travel almost as fast as
light. Do you imagine for an instant it can—an armada
can ease life an atom's worth for mankind?"

Dad: "Well, several score atoms' worth. Starting with
you and Tad and me."

Mother: "I'd feel a monster, safe and comfortable en
route to a new world while behind me they huddled in
poverty by the billions."

Dad: "My first duty is to you two. However, let's
leave that aside. Let's think about man as a whole.
What is he? A beast that is born, grubs around, copu-
lates, quarrels, and dies. Uh-huh. But sometimes something more in addition. He does breed his occasional
Jesus, Leonardo, Bach, Jefferson, Einstein, Armstrong,
Olveida—whoever you think best justifies our being
here—doesn't he? Well, when you huddle people to-

gether like rats, they soon behave like rats. What then of the spirit? I tell you, if we don't make a fresh start, a bare handful of us but free folk whose descendants may in the end come back and teach—if we don't, why, who cares whether the two-legged animal goes on for another million years or becomes extinct in a hundred? Humanness will be dead."

Me: "And gosh, Mother, the fun!"

Mother: "You don't understand, dear."

Dad: "Quiet. The man-child speaks. He understands better than you."

Quarrel: till I run from them crying. Well, eight or nine years old. That night, was that the first night I started telling myself stories about Murphy's Hall?

It *is* Murphy's Hall. I say that's the right place for Dad to be.

When Hoo Fong, chief engineer, brought the news to the captain's cabin, the captain sat still for minutes. The ship thrummed around them; they felt it faintly, a song in their bones. And the light fell from the overhead, into a spacious and gracious room, furnishings, books, a stunning photograph of the Andromeda galaxy, an animation of Mary and Tad: and weight was steady underfoot, a full gee of acceleration, one light-year per year per year, though this would become more in shipboard time as you started to harvest the rewards of relativity . . . a mere two decades to the center of this galaxy, three to the neighbor whose portrait you adored . . . How hard to grasp that you were dead!

"But the ramscoop is obviously functional," said the captain, hearing his pedantic phrasing.

Hoo Fong shrugged. "It will not be, after the radiation has affected electronic parts. We have no prospect of decelerating and returning home at low velocity before both we and the ship have taken a destructive dose."

Interstellar hydrogen, an atom or so in a cubic centimeter, raw vacuum to Earthdwellers at the bottom of

their ocean of gas and smoke and stench and carcino-
gens. To spacefolk, fuel, reaction mass, a way to the
stars, once you're up to the modest pace at which you
meet enough of those atoms per second. However, your
force screens must protect you from them, else they
strike the hull and spit gamma rays like a witch's curse.

"We've hardly reached one-fourth c," the captain
protested. "Unmanned probes had no trouble at better
than 99 percent."

"Evidently the system is inadequate for the larger
mass of this ship," the engineer answered. "We should
have made its first complete test flight unmanned too."

"You know we didn't have funds to develop the robots for that."

"We can send our data back. The next expedition—"

"I doubt there'll be any. Yes, yes, we'll beam the
word home. And then, I suppose, keep going. Four
weeks, did you say, till the radiation sickness gets bad?
The problem is not how to tell Earth, but how to tell
the rest of the men."

Afterward, alone with the pictures of Andromeda,
Mary, and Tad, the captain thought: *I've lost more than*
the years ahead, I've lost the year behind, that we
might have had together.

What shall I say to you? That I tried and failed and
am sorry? But am I? At this hour I don't want to lie,
most especially not to you three.

Did I do right?

Yes.

No.

O God, oh, shit, how can I tell? The Moon is rising
above the soot-clouds. I might make it that far. Com-
missioner Wenig was talking about how we should maintain the last Lunar base another few years, till industry
can find a substitute for those giant molecules they
make there. But wasn't the Premier of United Africa
saying those industries ought to be forbidden, they're

too wasteful, and any country that keeps them going is an enemy of the human race?

Gunfire rattles in the streets. Some female voice somewhere is screaming.

I've got to get Mother out of here. That's the last thing I can do for Dad.

After ten years of studying to be a food engineer or a doctor, I'll probably feel too tired to care about the Moon. After another ten years of being a desk pilot and getting fat, I'll probably be outraged at any proposal to spend my tax money—

—except maybe for defense. In Siberia they're preaching that strange new missionary religion. And the President of Europe has said that if necessary, his government will denounce the ban on nuclear weapons.

The ship passed among the stars bearing a crew of dead bones. After a hundred billion years it crossed the Edge—not the edge of space or time, which does not exist, but the Edge—and came to harbor at Murphy's Hall.

And the dust which the cosmic rays had made began to stir, and gathered itself back into bones; and from the radiation-corroded skeleton of the ship crept atoms which formed into flesh; and the captain and his men awoke. They opened themselves and looked upon the suns that went blazing and streaming overhead.

"We're home," said the captain.

Proud at the head of his men, he strode uphill from the dock, toward the hall of the five hundred and forty doors. Comets flitted past him, novae exploded in dreadful glory, planets turned and querned, the clinker of a once living world drifted by, new life screamed its outrage at being born.

The roofs of the house lifted like mountains against night and the light-clouds. The ends of rafters jutted beyond the eaves, carved into dragon heads. Through the doorway toward which the captain led his crew, eight hundred men could have marched abreast. But a single form waited to greet them; and beyond him was darkness.

When the captain saw who that was, he bowed very deeply.

The other took his hand. "We have been waiting," he said.

The captain's heart sprang. "Mary too?"

"Yes, of course. Everyone."

Me. And you. And you. And you in the future, if you exist. In the end, Murphy's Law gets us all. But we, my friends, must go to him the hard way. Our luck didn't run out. Instead, the decision that could be made was made. It was decided for us that our race—among the trillions which must be out there wondering what lies beyond their skies—is not supposed to have either discipline or dreams. No, our job is to make everybody nice and safe and equal, and if this happens to be impossible, then nothing else matters.

If I went to that place—and I'm glad that this is a lie—I'd keep remembering what we might have done and seen and known and been and loved.

Murphy's Hell.

COMMENTARY

Perhaps the story you have just read has shocked you, coming as it does after others that are generally optimistic. If so, I'm glad. It's supposed to.

Some of these tales have not been exactly cheerful. However, until this latest, they have all presupposed that humankind will survive and, more than that, as William Faulkner said, prevail. We will suffer our individual sorrows and shared troubles, but we will keep going, and on the whole it will be toward greatness. Over and far above the growth of knowledge and power will be the growth of the spirit.

One would like to believe that.

Liking is not enough. Belief is not. More civilizations are down in dust than are alive. More kinds of creatures are. The universe did not come into existence in order to bring forth Western man, or Homo sapiens, or life on Earth. It does not continue in order to maintain them. Survival is up to us.

There have been cries of crisis and divinings of doom as far back as written records go, and doubtless further still. Most have been exaggerated, or outright frauds. Most of those we hear today are. Some, though, have been true. Some today are.

Often, probably oftenest, the disastrous mistakes have occurred well before the catastrophes. The consequences have worked subtly and pervasively until it was too late, the society was too far gone. Thus, the Hellenic world never developed a polity appropriate to its scope, and things went from bad to worse until the brute simplicity of the Roman universal state came as a relief, for a while. Once brilliantly inventive, China slowly strangled itself with its own bureaucracy; stagnation and ultimate disintegration appear to have become inevitable after an imperial decree in the Ming dynasty banned maritime enterprise. The fifteenth-century conciliar movement in Western Europe failed to reform the Church, with consequences including Protestantism, the wars of religion, and the rise of absolute monarchy. The United States of America—but this is not supposed to be a partisan document.

Let me simply declare that among all the dire warnings we hear these days, two or three do concern things that could destroy us. To give up our endeavor in space would be one of the quiet and all-devouring mistakes.

"Limits to growth" is an utterly pernicious doctrine. Along with much else, it embodies cruel racism, in that it would condemn most of humanity to perpetual want. "Appropriate technology" is a slogan by which a few demagogues, some of whom must know better and are therefore consciously lying, rouse hordes of ignoramuses who can't be bothered to learn a little elementary science. Nevertheless we *are* using up this planet at a rate which has become terrifying. There *are* right and wrong ways to provide for our needs, and turning Earth into a single slurb is not among the right ones.

Look up. Space begins about fifty miles above your head. Yonder are all the materials, energy, elbow room, and wonderful discoveries to make that our species can ever require. Whether or not we reach the stars (and we can eventually, with or without Einsteinian speed limits laid on us, if we really want to) the Solar System holds more than enough.

It is my considered opinion that, without access to space, without opening space for people to use, industrial civilization does not have much longer to live. At best, our near-future descendants will revert to the norm of history, which Alfred Duggan described as "peasants ruled by brigands;" and it won't matter if the brigands retain a certain amount of high tech. At worst, our species will go the way of the dinosaurs—who enjoyed a far lengthier day and left the globe in far better shape.

Oh, conceivably, something in between could be achieved, new technologies employing low energy and lean resources. It's highly improbable, but it is conceivable and I've even speculated about it in fiction. Of course, first the vast majority of us, four or five billion living individuals, must die in various ghastly ways.

"Murphy's Hall" is a parable about our failure in space. It is unrealistic in assuming that we will get so far as to send off a starship before the night falls over us. Yet history does tell of magnificent efforts that in the end came to naught.

Will it set the American space program in their number? For too long, now, that endeavor has been fumbling and faltering. The Soviets proceed methodically, and perhaps on that account tomorrow belongs to them. Or perhaps not; this, and the more recent entrants, seem fragile baskets in which to lay our hopes. Should Americans not once again carry their share, and so earn a say in what shall happen?

You can help, you who read these words, help more then you may realize. Uphold the dream. Speak to your friends. Write to your legislators, your newspaper, the White House. Offer to arrange displays in your local schools and public library. Join an advocacy organization. What you can do is limited only by what you truly wish to do—just like human achievement in the starry universe.

Meanwhile, I'd like to close this book on the same note. The following, final story goes back to optimism, to the assumption that we will make the wise choices. Indeed, it's quite lighthearted. However, that which it springs from, that which it implies, is altogether serious.

HORSE TRADER

B.C. 250: *The aeolipile of Heron spun in the temple at Alexandria, hissing softly to itself and blowing jets of steam into the fire-lit dimness. It was only for display, an embryonic turbine which would develop no further because nobody saw any practical use for it. Elsewhere in the universe, on a planet not altogether unlike Earth, propeller-driven ships plied the sea around one continent. It had not occurred to their builders that anything but muscle power could turn the shafts.*

A.D. 1495: *Leonardo da Vinci regarded his airplane model wistfully and laid it aside. It could have flown had an adequate power plant been available. He did not know that on a world whose sun was to him a star they used efficient internal-combustion engines, and that for several reasons — among them the fact that aerial life had never evolved there — they did not think of giving themselves wings.*

A.D. 1942: *The Allied nations were searching with an intensity approaching desperation for a means of detecting the enemy submarines whose wolf packs harried their convoys and threatened to snap the thin Atlantic lifeline. Ultrasonics looked promising, but that was a little-known field in which researchers must start from*

*the very bottom. In the same galactic neighborhood,
the people of Sumanor on the planet they called Urish
could have told the humans everything about ultrasonics. It would have been a fair exchange, for on Urish
they had never heard of submarines.*

A.D.2275: The rangy blond man with the somewhat
improbable name of Auchinleck Welcome stepped off
the sidewalk and strode across the springy warmth of
the floor to the doorway. Suitably dignified flame-letters
danced above it to spell out

BUREAU OF INTERCULTURAL EXCHANGE
Technical Division

Some irreverent soul had painted a horse on the door
and Welcome, who scorned stuffiness, was pleased that
that been allowed to remain. After all, this new outfit of
his was known across the width of the Solar System,
and beyond, as the Horse Traders.

The door retracted for him and he passed through
the outer office, nodding to the attendants of the computer terminals and other apparatus. "Waltzing Matilda" whistled softly from his lips. A live receptionist
guarded the inner suite, token of the eminence he had
gained. She smiled when he waved. Continuing, he
entered the sanctum of his primary assistant, Kirsten
Ernenek, and stopped.

"Good mornwatch," he greeted. Despite all his years
in space, a hint of Australia lingered in his voice. "How's
life?"

"Fine for me," the Greenlander answered. "Busy
today for you."

"Who's first?"

She glanced at the memory display on her desk. "The
duck from Epsilon Indi. Robotics, you know. Have you
met him yet?"

"No, too busy. He'll have been going through the
usual preparatory stuff anyhow." Welcome sighed. "When

will Health get it through their heads that humans don't catch extraterrestrial diseases?"

"Always the first time. And then the diplomats and so on had their own routines for him and his team."

"I know, I know." Welcome suppressed impatience. Ernenek couldn't be sure what she needed to tell him, when he'd scarcely been a month on the job. Her years of service would have gotten the directorship for her when it fell suddenly vacant, did policy not require someone with extrasolar field experience as well as a broad scientific-technological background. Newly home from an engineering project on Alpha Centauri A III, where the intricacies of local native civilization laid as many demands on him as nature did, Welcome had found himself under the barrage of an offer that improved with every day he hesitated. He might not be ideal, but the state of the bureau varied between somnolent and frantic, and one of the frantic times was upon it.

He took forth a battered corncob pipe and began loading it. The eagerness with which he had awakened came back to him. Thus far he'd been trying to learn the ropes. The practical side of that included details of bargains which had, essentially, been made before his arrival—interesting, but not challenging. Meanwhile the backlog of new work piled up. Today he was to start on it. "Robotics," he said. "Do the Indians, uh, Epsilonians really have something new to show us?"

"Maybe." Ernenek giggled. "At least he's cute." Glancing again at the memory: "And then you'll be opening negotiations with 61 Cygni A, Tau Ceti, and 70 Ophiuchi B."—the usual metonymy for representatives of individual societies, or equivalents of societies, on worlds as variegated as ever Earth had been. "And be nice to the Centaurian."

"Eh?" The beings among whom Welcome had earlier been laboring possessed no information the Horse Traders might want. They got a helping hand in exchange for allowing human xenologists to study their culture, which showed that they were in fact businesscreatures as shrewd as any who came here.

"Alpha Centauri B II," Ernenek explained.

Welcome almost dropped his pipe. "Hoy, wait a minute! Nobody on that planet had gotten beyond the early Iron Age."

"True. Nevertheless, the clan of Brogu on the continent of Almerik persuaded our authorities to give passage to one Helmung. He wants spaceships and atomic energy in exchange for witchcraft."

"Oh, no."

"Headquarters wants you to humor him, if you can within reason. It seems the scientists have discovered his particular folk have some unique ability, possibly due a mutation, and hope to study it. I'll fill you in as necessary, but our information is very scanty." Ernenek grinned. "Good luck, boss."

Welcome shrugged and proceeded into his own office. The bounciness of his stride had a cheering effect on him. He had not been on Luna long enough to take its gravity for granted.

This new Centaurian could scarcely prove as bad as the betentacled monster whose antics had caused the previous director to take abrupt and early retirement. That one was from a folk on Eta Cassipeiae A II, who appeared to have reached an early stage of the scientific revolution and might have gotten useful insights. It had flown into a berserk fury when the director repeatedly declined to recommend trading the null-null drive for a system of astrology which, taking galactic drift into account, was guaranteed infallible.

Yet from another "nation" on that same planet had come a set of fermentation-like processes whose microorganisms and techniques, suitably modified, brought about a minor revolution in certain branches of molecular engineering on Earth. The possessors had been happy to exchange it for a knowledge of electron microscopy and gas chromatography.

The briefings Welcome had gotten suggested that the

envoys from Cygni, Ceti, and Ophiuchi, possibly also
Indi, might be carrying information of comparable importance. Might be. They were all playing close to their
chests, of course. His duty was to find out for certain,
work out a mutually satisfactory swap for whatever looked
worthwhile, and pass his recommendations upstairs.
They would probably be accepted, after politicians and
bureaucrats had made the inevitable unnecessary changes.

Too bad everything was happening at once. Communication between different species was difficult enough
under the easiest of conditions. But occasional pile-ups
were inevitable when you tried to arrange things across
interstellar distances, and this one was the reason Welcome had gotten his new position.

Awe touched him. More than four years had passed
in the outside universe—however short the interval was
for those aboard the spaceship—while he and his family
returned from the very nearest star to Sol. No material
treasure was worth such hauling. But knowledge was;
and, given the null-null drive which permitted speeds
close to that of light, it was far better to transport bodily
the possessors of that knowledge than to wait decades
between laser-borne question and answer. The cost was
bearable, considering that you sometimes gained a capability your race might otherwise not dream of. As the
only spacefarers in regions explored thus far, humans
naturally came to operate the only cultural clearing-
house. The monopoly on astronautics would presently
be ending; already two other races had the data and
were building the capability. Earth might or might not
continue to control the profitable information mart. Welcome supposed he hoped it would.

He sat down at his desk. The chair molded itself to
his angular contours with a sensuousness that reminded
him of how long he had been leading a bachelor's
existence. His gaze roved the office. It was large, taste-
fully decorated in the Neoflamboyant style. A broad
viewport gave on the magnificent Lunar desolation. A
glare on the highest peaks shouldering above the hori-

zon bespoke dawn on its way. As yet, though, Earth dominated heaven. His look lingered on its blue and white. His wife and children were there, with her mother in Sydney, while he devoted every waking hour to mastering this job. He hoped they wouldn't have to wait much longer.

Had he been wise to accept? Working for a private contractor had many advantages over working directly for the government. Everything had happened in such a rush, the spokesman for the bureau had been so insistent and Welcome still half dazed by the transition to Earth after his years in alienness.

He shoved his doubts aside and ran quickly through his mind what he had been told about the delegation from Epsilon Indi.

They appeared to be intrinsically amiable, nicer than humans. At least, every culture the explorers encountered on the inhabited second planet had been anxious to please them, and they had returned quite excited about the cybernetics of the most advanced society. So now a group of Epsilonians had arrived to dicker. (The name was inconsistent with common usage, but damn it, "Indians" *was* too confusing.) Welcome expected to get some rather low-pressure salesmanship. After all, besides being unaggressive, the ducks couldn't be sure how much their hosts already knew.

Still, there were bound to be surprises. No two races were alike, and most went through a range of internal differences fully equal to that between, say, Irishman and Bushman or Baptist and Buddhist. The bulk of the bureau's work amounted to ongoing interaction with those that had established technological-commercial relationships in the past. Newcomers were fairly rare and wholly unpredictable. That was why the Horse Traders were allowed to operate as informally as they did, and nevertheless used up department heads faster than any other branch of the government.

Ernenek's voice from the intercom jarred him out of his reverie: "The envoy Rappapa of Kwillitch to see you, Freeman Welcome." He heard confused noises in the background and, he believed, half-stifled laughter in her tones.

"Send him in, please."

The man rose as the door retracted. Considering how motley were notions of courtesy, he did best to stick by his own.

"HUP-two-three-four! HUP-two-three-four! HUP-two-three-four!"

Welcome caught his breath. A platoon of dolls was coming in.

No, robots, shiny humanoid robots about twelve centimeters tall. They goosestepped in perfect formation, accompanied by four tanks and half a dozen helicopters built to scale. Behind them, shrilly quacking his commands, waddled the Epsilonian. In a vague way he resembled an ostrich, a hundred and twenty centimeters high, blue-feathered and crested. Instead of wings, he had skinny four-fingered arms, which carried a large box studded with controls. His head was big, round, and popeyed, with a flexible spatulate bill of bright orange hue.

"HUP-two-three-four! Com-pan-ee—HALT! Ri-i-ght—FACE! Prese-ent—ARMS!"

The toy soldiers obeyed and snapped to attention. The tanks stopped likewise. The helicopters buzzed to their stations, one just above Welcome.

"How do you do, how do you do, noble sir?" The Epsilonian bowed, touching the floor with his beak. Though his English was fluent, his vocal organs made a gabble of it that Welcome would have needed long practice to understand. The transponder hung at his throat like a locket converted this to standard speech, to which the sounds he himself uttered lent a quality suggestive of, well, a duck. "I trust that you in splendid health find yourself?"

"Yes, thank you," said Welcome faintly. "Excuse me while I pick up my jaw."

"If I your excellency's noble jaw have caused to fall, it is to be of the most apologetic," said the Epsilonian.

"Never mind," replied Welcome. "Please sit down, Freeman Rappapa. If you wish to," he added in haste, unable to remember whether this species ever did.

"If you will it of indifference find, I will stand in the luminous presence of your excellency," said Rappapa. "Among my greetings-to-you-conveying people, only nesting females sit."

"I — uh, do you smoke?" Several races enjoyed tobacco, and didn't suffer effects requiring counteractants. At the same time, they couldn't get proper nourishment from Terrestrial food, and it was poisonous to some. . . . Welcome extended a box of cigars.

"You are to be superlatively thanked," said Rappapa, accepting one. "*Whichuwaki!*" A helicopter descended and shot out a flame to light it for him.

Welcome seated himself. "I take it those are robots."

"Of a most humble sort, for demonstration purposes alone," said Rappapa. "They are powered by microwaves from this box, as your excellency undoubtedly perceives. The brain circuits are also herein contained. Each machine had its individual brain, controlling the external body, or any number of brains can be conjoined to form a unit of correspondingly greater capabilities."

Welcome forced impassivity on himself. Inwardly, his heart leaped. If the Epsilonians had carried miniaturization that far, what else could they do?

"May I add that they can act at individual discretion, within the limits of the basic directives?" added Rappapa eagerly. "Possibly toys for your delightful children or household servants for their important parents?"

"Our homes these days are already rather fully automated," Welcome said.

"Of a most suredly! These, I repeat, are illustrative only. It has insignificantly occurred to us that your splendid spaceships could be supplied with brains of this general type, eliminating the need for crews."

"M-m, yes, we've had something of the kind in mind

ourselves, since we began to get an idea of your cybernetics."

"It is for a strangeness that you, who so daringly bridge the stars, have not long since surpassed us in this humble endeavor."

"Well, it's not so odd, really." Welcome rekindled his pipe. "Countless factors go to determine what directions technology takes in any given society, and at what speeds. The general background of knowledge and tradition, current needs and demands, individual abilities, organization, economics—sheer accident too, I suppose. Of course, there's bound to be a certain unity. You can't operate spacecraft without pretty sophisticated computers, for instance. However, the society may emphasize some lines of development at the expense of others. In fact, that always seems to happen.

"And then planetary conditions differ so much, not to speak of the intelligent species that have evolved under them. Environment gives its special suggestions and opportunities for certain kinds of discoveries. Innate psychological bents come into play.

"So within the tiny volume of the galaxy that we've visited to date, my race has gone furthest in developing transportation and energy sources. Your people stayed on their planet till mine arrived, but went in heavily for robotics and related matters. On 70 Ophiuchi A II they're super-biologists, their genetic engineers make ours look neolothic, but they never even considered nuclear power plants. Et cetera, et cetera. It would be strange, wouldn't it, if one species excelled in everything?"

"I am blinded by the clarity of your explanation," said Rappapa. "Sir, dare I hope that you will find our little skill worthy of consideration?"

"Indeed you may," said Welcome. "Is there anything in particular you would like to have from us, or do you first want to look over the, uh, catalogue?"

"Your incredible process of baryonic electromotive

force generation would prostrate us of Kwillitch with joy."

The human rubbed his chin, That was certainly a reasonable enough asking price. Indeed, his conscience hurt him a bit.

"I think that can be arranged," he answered blandly. "You realize this is going to be a long and complicated business, even before formal negotiations can start. Those will be on a higher level than mine. This department is concerned with preliminary studies."

"My team stand aquiver, clutching the material they have brought along until they can display it for the contemplation by their august human counterparts."

"M-m, let's be frank, Freeman Rappapa. Neither side wants to give anything away, except perhaps a small free sample. What the teams will be studying are presentations, generalized, but at the same time specific enough that they'll learn what it is they are being offered. Precise details, proprietary information, tricks of the trade, all that will come afterward, when the exchange contract has been drawn up."

The Epsilonian nodded till his crest rippled. "We have taken anguishing pains preparing for these discussions."

"I'm sure you have. Just the same, the work will go slowly, and up many a blind alley." Much of Welcome's indoctrination had been devoted to this. "Simply adapting basic speed-learning techniques to each other's mentalities will take a while. Then, most likely, explanations will often have to backtrack. For instance, our side will have to make sure your side knows enough about magnetronics before it can explain much about baryonics to you." He paused. "Excuse me, please, when I tell you things you must have heard or thought of over and over. I'm new in this post, you know. But the simple fact that I'm not sure precisely what you are aware of—that illustrates the problems ahead, doesn't it? Essentially, the first task of our teams will be to develop courses of study for each other."

"That is a scheme of the slyest magnanimity," burbled Rappapa.

Welcome blinked, wondered how innocent the little being actually was, and decided to let it pass. "Excellent." He slouched back in his chair and went on to everyday matters. How did the Epsilonians like the quarters, the food, the entertainment, everything that had been prepared for their arrival? Were they enjoying themselves in what leisure time they had? What would they especially like to see and do? Doubtless they wished to take tours of Earth. They should inform their hosts of anything that would make their stay in the Solar System pleasant.

And disarm them, make them more receptive to our proposals. Well, why not? We don't plan to cheat them, but when something as important as this is involved, naïveté would be criminal.

Rappapa quacked lengthy praises. His party had already been escorted around the dome, met the other extraterrestrials currently there, been lavishly feted.

Welcome nodded. There was not, because there could not be, any rule against the different delegations having contact and perhaps driving their own bargains independently of Earth.

In point of fact, such a deal was going on. The Tau Cetian knowledge of nucleonics had turned out to be inferior to the human, but the representative of 61 Cygni A V—who had come alone—was willing to trade some high-pressure chemistry for it.

Welcome didn't care very much. For one thing, both parties would need the facilities here, and he intended politely but firmly to require a quid pro quo for that. Moreover, if events made it seem a desirable course, he could get the Cygnian chemistry in exchange for something else than had originally been proposed. Or perhaps he could get it from Tau Ceti. Once somebody had acquired a technology, he/she/it/they had the right to resell it. At least, that might as well be enshrined in the law, since a prohibition would be unenforceable.

The Horse Traders must needs operate among all parties and play both ends against the middle.

"On a lower plane than your excellency, I think—"

The buzz of the intercom cut through Rappapa's eloquence. Welcome pressed Accept and heard Kirsten Ernenek cry half hysterically, "No, you can't go in there, he's busy—Boss, look out!"

A thunderous crash sounded on the door. Rappapa squawked and made a Lunar-gravity leap to get behind his platoon. The door withdrew and Thevorakz of Dzuga, Dominator from Tau Ceti III, stalked in, waving his arms and roaring.

He was a centauroid, with quadrupedal gray body and lashing feline-like tail. The upper torso, swathed in a black robe and cowl, reached as high as a tall man's and resembled it appproximately. A bristling white walrus mustache beneath a flat nose concealed the lack of a chin. A forest of brow overhung ruby eyes that glared as if to set the office afire. His ears twitched and his hoofs stamped.

"You!" His bass bellow required no transponder to be understandable by Welcome. That was just as well, for it would have overwhelmed the rendition. "You low, thiefing monthter! You thcum! You dominated! I do not like you!"

Welcome got up, grateful for the expanse of desk in front of him. He tried hard to keep his own voice level. "What's the matter, Dominator Thevorakz?"

"I thpit my cud on you! I foul your floor! I go home to Dzuga and come back with an army!"

In the doorway, Ernenek squeaked and sprang aside for the envoy from 61 Cygni A V. The gleaming two-meter sphere rolled grandly in on its wheels and laid a mechanical hand on Thevorakz's rump. The viewer swiveled toward Welcome. It looked uncomfortably like a gun.

Inside, breathing hydrogen at a pressure of several hundred bars, the being known to humans as George —individuals not having names on its world—said with a coldness that somehow registered in the flat artificial voice: "My impetuous associate outpaced me, but I bring the same complaint."

Welcome gulped. It had been a long, difficult, and expensive proposition to contact the natives of New Uranus and get one of them to make the trip. In their environment, they had learned things about the chemistry of ultra-dense materials that Earth industries very much wanted to know. In exchange they desired sufficient information about nucleonics and solid-state electronics that they could design apparatus to work under conditions at home. It looked as if they were going to get the first from Tau Ceti. If Welcome let the deal for the second collapse too—

He decided that a show of indignation was his best bet. "May I ask the meaning of this intrusion? Freelady Ernenek surely told you both that I was in conference with the team chief from Epsilon Indi."

"That *amorakz!*" shouted the Cetian. "Throw him out!"

"Help," wailed Rappapa. His robots formed a hollow square around him.

"We will have calm," George commanded. "I believe you, Freeman Welcome, know perfectly well why we are here."

"No, I don't," the man said.

"You do tho!" roared Thevorakz.

"I will describe the situation," George said. "The Tau Cetian group and I made a bargain quite rapidly and easily. Both sides possessed the basic theories beforehand. What was desired, to expedite applications on our respective planets, was specifics, especially constants: for example, the neutron capture cross sections of various isotopes. Therefore, yesterday we made our first exchange. In return for what Dominator Thevorakz gave me, he received a data disc containing many tables of high-pressure chemical data, such as physical properties and equilibrium constants. This he put in his strongbox. Now he has returned to his room after his morning meal in the refectory reserved for his delegation, and found the box open and the disc missing. Diligent search failed to discover it. He reported the loss to me and we determined to question you."

"You don't think we — No!" gasped Ernenek.

"I'm sorry to hear about this," Welcome said, forcing steadiness upon himself. "I'll get an investigation started at once."

"By you!" bawled Thevorakz. "And you are the mithbegotten dominated who thtole it!"

Welcome returned to indignation mode. "Sir, you are insulting not only my integrity, but that of Earth. You violate the sacred obligation of guest to host. I demand an immediate apology." He stalked from behind the desk.

"I will help our excellency," quacked Rappapa. "Company forward! On the double! Hup-hup-hup-hup-hup!" The robots swung into goosestepping formation at Welcome's heels.

Thevorakz gave way a little. "If I am mithtaken, I will pay you an apology," he mumbled. "But the dithc had better be found, and you had better proof you did not take it."

Welcome turned to George, hoping for some sanity, however bleak. "Do you imagine we'd stoop to theft?" he asked.

"I reserve my opinion pending additional information," replied the chill voice. "It would be to your economic advantage to steal these data, and buy something else that we Cygnians know. You would obtain two technological advances in exchange for one. However, the possibility exists that some other of the parties is responsible. Everyone has heard about the bargain."

Welcome lashed out: "Maybe the Tau Cetians did it themselves, to embarrass us into giving them more than we otherwise would. Or you could have done it, George."

He turned and paced back and forth, the robots scampering to avoid his feet. "Mind you, I make no accusations," he went on. "I said what I just said only in order to show you how that sort of thing gets us nowhere. I'll call the dome police at once. Meanwhile, please return to your quarters. I'll notify you as soon as anything turns up."

George rolled ponderously out in reverse. Thevorakz snorted and tramped after it. Rappapa signalled his mechanical followers to form up in a corner.

Welcome realized that he was trembling. "A pretty mess!" he groaned. "A wonderful start to my new job, eh?"

"I am with humble firmness assured that your excellency will soon penetrate the depths of all dastardliness," said Rappapa.

"Um, yes, thanks." Welcome glanced sharply at the Epsilonian. *At least, I suppose I mean thanks.* "Sorry for your sake too, your having your business interrupted. But if you don't mind, I'm going to be rather busy for the next while—"

"Of course. I shall not obtrude." Rappapa lifted his voice. "Compan-ee, ten-SHUN! Right—FACE! Forward —MARCH! Hup-two-three-four, hup-two-three-four—" His infantry and armor trailed him out, his air force whickered above his crest and tail feathers.

Ernenek leaned against the wall and stared at Welcome. "Now what?" she breathed.

"Get me M'Gamba," he told her, and returned to his desk.

When the police chief's dark face was on the comscreen, Welcome gave him a slightly censored account of events. M'Gamba scowled. "A bad business," he said.

"Redundant statement of the month, that," Welcome replied. "If that disc isn't recovered, and fast, it could mean the crippling, maybe the destruction, of this entire operation."

"Oh, now. After you've coped with a few more crises, you'll see less doom ahead of you."

"Yes, I am a new chum," Welcome snapped, "but I have studied the history, and I got my appointment because I've had practical experience with nonhumans. Not only with the natives where I last was; we had technical people from three different planets, and my company had dealt with more than that in the past. See here. We are all mutually alien, and in profound as well as obvious ways. Our being limited to light speed communications hasn't expedited a deeper understanding, you know. So we're apt to see nonhuman personalities as caricatures, because the nuances escape us. That makes for less respect and more suspicion than the truth probably warrants. Now doesn't it stand to reason that *they* have a similarly limited perception of *us*? It's all too easy to think the worst of somebody you can't empathize with in depth. If we lose a reputation that's shaky at best, the whole enterprise could sputter out to naught. Or somebody else could take the business away from us."

M'Gamba grimaced. "Such as the Tau Cetians? God forbid. Do you think they faked the burglary to discredit us?"

"I'm tempted to think so. But don't you see, that's exactly the sort of reaction I'm afraid of, if we're on the receiving end."

"Be that as it may," the chief said, "I know what you will receive if this isn't resolved quickly."

"The sack. Yes." Welcome hoped his wince didn't show. His former employer would probably take him back, but a disgraced man would not get any of the challenging assignments that led onward and upward through the corporate ranks. His dream was to make a good record with the Horse Traders and then after some years, when he had licked the major problems and the work was getting too routine for his taste, return to private industry. The offers would then be kingly.

M'Gamba smiled. "I did not mean to sound unsympathetic," he said. "My department stands to lose by this also. Very well, we will get to work here, and I'll call you as soon as I have anything." He switched off.

That registered at Ernenek's desk, and she entered. "You have a pile of memorandums and such waiting," she reminded him. "Shall I help you go through them?" Seeing his haggardness, she exclaimed impulsively, "Oh, Auch, I am sorry. What rotten luck for you."

"For everybody everywhere," he sighed. "Yes, thanks, I do want to keep busy and I do need you to guide me through the maze."

She lowered her stocky frame to a chair opposite his and activated her side of the infotrieve on the desk. "What do you mean, everybody everywhere?" she asked.

The personal touch, the first-name friendliness, the concern in her broad countenance were comforting. "Maybe I'm not being philosophical, Kirsten, only maundering," he said. "But something great is in embryo among the stars, a whole new thing, a . . . a civilization of civilizations. These technical exchanges are just a beginning. I think in the long run what will really matter are the subtler things, arts, faiths, emotions, inspirations, insights, the growth of the spirit. But it's so frail, the embryo. This wretched business could poison it." He flushed. "Never mind me. I'm a plain engineer. Ought to stick to what I know a little about, right? Let's get cracking."

The first police report reached him in less than two hours. He sat frowning as he fitted it into the general background.

The suites for visitors were all on the fourth sublevel below the dome. Each was equipped to maintain, as nearly as possible, conditions that the occupants would find congenial—although at present George alone could not go freely about in the Terrestrial areas. The vagaries of communication and transport over different intersteller distances, as well as the dissimiliar paces of developments on the various planets, had brought it about that delegates were simultaneously on hand from five suns—Epsilon Indi, Tau Ceti, 61 Cygni A, 70 Ophiuchi B, and (*God help us*, Welcome thought) Alpha Centauri B. They had been on Luna for periods ranging from ten to thirty days, and had mingled freely in shared curiosity; the sublevel where they lived included a gymnasium, a games and television room, and a chamber for quieter sociability.

Yesterday evening Moira Petersen, administrative chief of the dome, had given a reception for the guests. Welcome regretted now that he had begged off in order to get a proper night's rest before commencing his duties in earnest. Every nonhuman had attended. The Tau Cetians had told the police officers that they got back late to their quarters and went directly to bed— well, to their stalls. Not until after breakfast did Thevorakz notice that they had been burgled.

Whoever did it was confoundedly clever. There was a computer-controlled electronic lock on the outer door of each suite, programmed to recognize individuals as well as to open for a key bearing a time-varied code on the molecular level. At the first sign of anything untoward, the lock was supposed to alert the nearest police patrol. Nothing of the kind had happened. Once inside, the thief found a strongbox magnetically anchored and shut with an archaic but well-designed mechanical lock. He (?) had sliced it apart with an energy torch, taken the disc, and walked (?) out, securing the suite entrance again before proceeding elsewhere.

Welcome puffed unhappily on his pipe, though his palate was starting to feel mummified. Nobody on Earth knew how to fool a computer lock.

To be sure, Thevorakz himself, or one of his associates, might have faked the evidence.

"The torch could be from any of the workshops on the third sublevel," said M'Gamba over the screen. "They're open all the time, you know, for the use of anyone who has to build a model or whatever. No stockroom clerks or guards or anything; some of our visitors would consider that an insult. They can request advice or assistance if they wish. The thief need only have taken the torch when nobody was present, and returned it afterward. But how did he pass that door?"

"How many keys to it?" Welcome inquired.

"Each of the Cetians has one, and each insists his has never left his person. Then Petersen's office and mine keep one apiece in case of emergency."

"That puts Earth in a poor light, doesn't it?"

"Well, if anybody but a Cetian tried to get in, the computer would have to be satisfied that the errand was legitimate. Likeliest it would have Thevorakz paged and consult him. Oh, the place was secure against anything I can think of. Though I can't think how to convince the aliens beyond any doubt they consider reasonable."

"Was anyone absent for any length of time during the party?"

"We're still working on that. Individuals wandered around from common room to common room, and maybe elsewhere, as the whim struck them. Alcohol and every alien kind of mind-befuddler were freely available. That creature in the tank may well be the only guest who wasn't at least mildly intoxicated by 2200 hours or so."

"How goes the search for the disc?"

"We're checking every available square centimeter in the dome, without much hope. We've requested permission to go through the delegates' apartments, but so far none except the Epsilonians have waived privacy and invited us to do so."

"Let's see if we can persuade the rest." Welcome smiled sourly. "Good hunting, Chief."

"Enjoy your lunch," M'Gamba gibed amiably and blanked screen.

Welcome realized that he didn't want any.

A few minutes later, Moira Petersen called him. "What have you to say?" she demanded.

"I expect you've heard everything," he sighed. "No, I have no ideas."

She compressed her lips. "Then I suggest you acquire some. Count yourself lucky that I must go to

Earth today. I expect to find this mess resolved when I return. That will be in four days."

Welcome bridled. She wasn't his superior. . . . Well, not exactly. But she could make his task impossible for him. On the other hand, she could be helpful if she chose. Had she been hinting? "It would make all the difference, not to have general headquarters breathing down our necks here," he ventured.

Her sleek gray head nodded. "Or the politicians, the news media, the special interests—yes." Her lips quirked the least bit upward. "As a matter of fact, I wasn't scheduled to leave till tomorrow. I'm supposed to speak at a conference and—No matter. I think I can cover this up for you while I am there." She grew stiff again. "But no longer. And in all honesty, Freeman Welcome, if the scandal breaks, I will see you and Chief M'Gamba sacrificed before I am."

"Understood," he grunted.

"If I succeed, you'll have four days," she said brightly. "That's assuming nothing else goes wrong and you resolve the problem with no public sensation. Well, it has been nice talking with you, but I have to run now."

"Give everybody my regards," Welcome muttered.

Left to himself, he exercised the more picturesque parts of his vocabulary. The intercom cut him short: "The envoy Orazuni of Inyahuna, planet 70 Ophiuchi B I, to see you, Freeman Welcome."

The man blinked. "Oh, yes. He did have an appointment, didn't he? Send him in, please." He composed himself as much as possible and rose when the being entered.

Orazuni looked rather like a medieval concept of a demon. His slim body sloped forward on clawed feet, counterbalanced by the long, thick tail. The six-fingered hands were also clawed, and the pointed ears of almost winglike size. However, the head, though bald, was like an abstract sculpture of a handsome human's, high in the cheekbones, curved in the nose, sharp in the chin, and the large golden eyes were beautiful by any

standard. He wore a green tunic and scarlet cloak, and
carried a portfolio under one arm.

"Good day, Freeman Welcome," he said, bowing.
He had no need of a transponder; his English was
perfect Harvard. "I trust you are in good health and
spirits?"

*My health won't stand much more of this, and wouldn't
I love a glass of spirits?* "As much as I trust you are,
sir," Welcome replied. The jab was merely to relieve
his frustration a tiny bit. He had met the Ophiuchian
earlier, and enjoyed talking with him, although it was
clear that this was a sharp bargainer.

"Thank you." Orazuni sat down on the tripod of legs
and tail and declined the proferred cigar. "I have heard
of an unfortunate incident."

"I was afraid you would have. Can you suggest
anything?"

Orazuni shrugged. "One prefers not to become involved in such matters," he said delicately. "My group
has decided to show good faith by permitting a search
of our quarters. I shall so notify the police."

"Thank you. The more cooperation we get, the sooner
we'll clear this up." *Assuming we can.* Welcome con-
structed a smile. "Will you be as easy to deal with in
line of business?"

"One has one's own people to think of first, does one
not?" Orazuni opened his portfolio and took out a sheet
of paper covered with an intricate diagram. "In the
preliminary discussions on my planet, your representatives proposed that each side present the other, uncon-
ditionally, with a specific example of the kind of
technological advance that its special knowledge can
bring about. That was reasonable."

Welcome nodded. It was standard procedure, though
not every extraterrestrial negotiator agreed to it.

Orazuni smiled, revealing pointed teeth. The fact
that he could nevertheless sound like a man showed
how different his vocal organs actually were. "It did
confront us with a pretty problem," he continued. "Our

biological technology appears to be well in advance of yours, but it was developed for our biochemistry, which is not identical with the Terrestrial. How, then, could we make it of more than academic interest to you? Fortunately, the variations are not extreme. Our respective proteins incorporate several of the same amino acids, for example. Pardon me for rehearsing what you already know. I do it in order to help make clear the real point. Given information about your type of life, our scientists were enabled to deduce correlative principles by which techniques applicable to our type can be modified to use on yours."

A thrill passed up Welcome's backbone and stirred the hair on his scalp. He had studied the reports of the explorers. Doubtless humans wouldn't want to make Earth's biosphere over into a single organism, totally integrated and at the service of the intelligent species, as the Inyahunans had done on their world. But such a capability had equally revolutionary uses—for instance, making easy the conversion of barren globes into blossoming paradises for colonists—

"To prove that we possess this kind of knowledge, here is a specimen development for your medical profession to investigate." Orazuni waved the paper. "Naturally, what I hold here is simply an illustration, for emphasis. The full account fills a data disc. It includes instructions for synthesis and outlines tests by which safety and efficacy can quickly be demonstrated."

"Some kind of medicine?" Welcome wondered. "We've pretty well eliminated disease on our own, you know. What's left is practically always curable."

"I would not be tactless or unkind," Orazuni purred. "But are we mistaken in our impression that recreational drugs significantly harm a substantial percentage of your population?"

Welcome grimaced. "They do. I suppose it's a price we pay for high-tech civilization and a great deal of individual liberty."

"You need pay it no longer, my friend. I know you

have treatments to break addiction, the physiological dependence on a substance. I also know they are distressing and expensive, and give no guarantee that the sufferer will not return to his habit. Here, in the form of a pseudovirus, is a preventive. One injection, and the person is safe for a lifetime. He cannot become addicted to anything; the process is blocked."

Welcome whistled. "Tremendous!" Perhaps not an undiluted blessing. The use of hard drugs might increase. But if everybody could take them or leave them alone, he dared hope most people would choose the latter.

Orazuni laid the paper on the desk. By itself it was useless, of course, except as a come-on. "And what have you to show us?" he inquired blandly.

Haggling already at the free sample stage, are we? "Why, well, you understand I haven't had a chance to familiarize myself with enough details. But, uh, as I recall, you don't have the magnetronic tube, and it ought to be quite useful in the sort of nanotechnology you do. I can send for a disc immediately, and arrange for demonstrations and instructions to commence in, oh, twenty or thirty hours."

"That is acceptable," said Orazuni. "We can take it for granted that both offerings will prove satisfactory, can we not? Thus we can begin discussing the terms of the real exchange immediately."

Welcome leaned back. "Isn't that going a bit fast?"

Orazuni ignored the murmur. "Seventeen light-years and a fraction lie between our suns," he declared. "Sending small packets of knowledge to and fro would consume lifetimes, even given longevity such as you too have learned how to bestow on yourselves. Let us make a total transfer in a single operation. Everything we know for everything you know."

Welcome sat bolt upright. "What?" he exclaimed. "Now wait a bloody minute!"

Orazuni raised his hairless brows and waited.

"I mean—look here," Welcome said. "It isn't fair.

We'd be glad to give you baryonics, industrial catalysis, neutrino modulation, and—and if I recommend it strongly, the government might even agree to the null-null drive. But you're going too far. Your culture can't use all our information." *Unless to sell it to somebody else. Undersell us, maybe?*

"We'd need to maintain large technical missions on each other's planets for a long time," he went on. "For us, at any rate, it'd be hard to find that many top-rank people who'd agree to go, at fantastic salaries. And shipping the equipment they'd need would tie up practically our whole space fleet for the duration of the voyage. And as for what you taught us, I don't believe we could learn it, assimilate it, put it to use, in less time than if we received it piecemeal." *Nor could we find out how much of it, if any, was fake, until too late. Impolite to say that. Please don't force me to, Orazuni.*

"But biological science is holistic in a way that physical science is not," the Ophiuchian argued. "We cannot give you ours in any meaningful sense without giving you the entire basis of it. Do you wish to ruin us, Freeman? What will our poor race have left to trade for further information from you?"

"The new developments that the knowledge we do give you will suggest and make possible," Welcome replied. "I suspect, for example, that our quantum theory of crystallography will let you increase the complexity of your genetic syntheses by an order of magnitude." He put elbows on desk, bridged his fingers, and peered across them in the most Machiavellian style he could achieve. "Remember, we're not biological ignoramuses on Earth. We could duplicate everything you have done, given time. Simply the knowledge that such things are possible is half the battle."

Orazuni shrugged and smiled. "As for that, we could send students to Earth to learn your physics and engineering."

"They could read a lot, sure," Welcome said. "That wouldn't be much use without instructors who've had practical experience. Your people wouldn't know what to look for or where to start."

He left the rest unspoken, though it was abundantly plain. Now that the civilizations had gotten the idea of Horse Trading, they weren't going to be particularly hospitable to unsponsored learners from outside. It wasn't a question of censorship. When there was no material trade to speak of between the stars, how could a visitor pay for his stay and his education? He *must* be financed by his hosts. And how could he get such a scholarship without his folk having been equally forthcoming?

"Your point is well taken," Orazuni admitted. "Allow me to observe that the situation is symmetrical. We can repeat developments you have made. It does seem a pity to have such duplication of effort. On the other hand, you may be right about a limiting rate at which knowledge can efficiently be transferred. Let us explore these ideas a little."

They dickered for a while in gentlemanly fashion. From time to time Orazuni dipped into his portfolio— he never let it go, and the rumor was that he slept with it—to show another tempting scrap. For his part, Welcome dwelt on the value of high-strength alloys and gaseous superconductors. He wished he knew more about the Inyahunan culture. Humans had found the people polite but reserved: "secretive" might not be too strong a word.

Yet the discussion soon went smoothly. The Ophiuchian dropped his extravagant asking price down toward a set of technologies that looked acceptable. When at length they adjourned, the two beings were not far from agreement.

"I think we can come to terms in another session or two," Welcome said. Thank God, something had gone right, this miserable mornwatch! "Naturally, that'll be only in principle. You may be empowered to sign a treaty, but I am not. Besides, everybody concerned will have a vast amount of study and detail work to do, before the political wrangling commences. But I imagine that within about a year there'll be a mutually satisfactory contract."

"I shall confer with my colleagues," Orazuni told him, "and I expect they will approve. In addition, they must choose a successor for me. I wish to go home."

Welcome was astonished. "What? You haven't been here any longer than—uh—"

"The *Messenger* leaves for 70 Ophiuchi next week, I believe."

Welcome nodded. When a world was as interesting as the one yonder, the scientific and cultural foundations financed what amounted to a shuttle service. "But don't you want to do some real sightseeing first?"

"Thank you, my species is not given to tourism. My wives and I will find adult grandchildren when we return. More importantly, the Organic Council prefers to question a person who was here, rather than examine no more than a recorded report. They can then begin the better to prepare for the future."

That didn't sound very logical. When transit time was so long, what difference did another year or two make? Well, doubtless the emotional drives of Ophiuchians were not identical with those of Earthlings; and he, Welcome, was supposed to extend his guests every possible courtesy. "All right, I can arrange passage for you, though it is short notice. Probably you and I should meet with the new head of your delegation before you go. Let me get a bit acquainted, eh?"

Orazuni stood up. Welcome did too. "A last matter, if you will pardon my touching again on a painful subject," Orazuni said. "I am curious. About that theft last night—how was it committed?"

"That's an excellent question," Welcome replied, grim once more. "You know about computer locks."

"Of course." Orazuni stroked his narrow chin and gently waved his ears. "If the crime was not committed by the Cetians themselves—or, forgive me, by a human—then the guilty party presumably has a knowledge of electronics advanced beyond Earth's."

"I'd say so."

"Cybernetics?" breathed Orazuni. He bowed. "Well, I will not occupy more of your time. Good day, Freeman Welcome."

He left, ever so graciously waving his tail.

The human wandered over to the viewport and stood blindly staring out. Earth's bright half-disc had shrunk further as daylight crept up the Lunar mountains. *Small, complicated circuits,* he thought. *Epsilon Indi? Damn, I don't want to believe that. Rappapa's such a pleasant little chap. But you never know, do you?*

M'Gamba called him up again in late midwatch, just when he had decided to pop out and get a sandwich after all. "We found the disc," he said.

"You did?" For an instant, Welcome's heart bounded. Then the joy sagged. "You did."

"Lying in a corner of Shop Number Seven," M'Gamba said with an equal lack of enthusiasm. "We gave it back to the Cetians, but they didn't exactly beslobber us with gratitude."

Welcome shrugged. "I should think not. Seven's the computer shop, right? Obviously the thief ran off a copy for himself when nobody else was there and left the original. A microcopy, I'll be bound; the 61 Cygnians can't cram data into anything like as small a compass as our equipment can. Now all we need do is find an item two or three centimeters in diameter, two or three millimeters thick."

"And whoever has it has acquired a whole new technology for nothing. I imagine George is furious too, though what I can't imagine is how we can tell for certain."

"Never mind. We still have to find the burglar. Have you been through the suites?"

"All but the Cetians' and George's. The Cetians

wouldn't hear of it, and we've no way to search rooms set for New Uranus conditions. No, we've found nothing."

Welcome gnawed his lip a moment, took a deep breath, and blurted his suspicions of Epsilon Indi.

The police captain nodded. "That's crossed my mind," he said. "I wasn't sure it was compatible with their psychology, but you know them better—at least, you've studied what is known about them—so if you think so—"

Welcome sighed. "I took Rappapa for a dinkum cobber. But we've got to follow the trail wherever it leads. Go through their suite again on some pretext. Try to use detectors on them individually unbeknownst to them. Or whatever occurs to you."

"All jets," said M'Gamba glumly, and clicked off.

The intercom buzzed. "The envoy Helmung dur Brogu-Almerik, planet Alpha Centauri B II, wishes to see you, Freeman Welcome," said Ernenek. Her tone was less than sprightly.

"All right, send him in," groaned the man. "It's that kind of day."

The door seemed less to retract than retreat. A giant stamped in, two and a half meters tall, more than wide enough to match. The butt of his spear thumped on the floor, his chain mail jingled, his sword rattled on its toggle. In appearance he was fairly humanoid, if you overlooked such details as proportions of features, blue skin, or antennae above the beady eyes. A black mane bristled around a battered face tattooed in lightning-bolt stripes of red and yellow. "Waw!" he hailed.

"How do you do, Freeman Helmung," Welcome said most softly. The Centaurian's head was so far above his.

"Quiet, I will speak!" The volume hurt the human's ears, though the tone was actually a musical counter-tenor and Helmung formed English words without artificial help.

"Just as you wish." Welcome extended his cigar box. While at the other Alpha Centaurian sun, he had naturally gotten curious about the neighboring race and read what he could find. Their biochemistry was remarkably similar to his. Still, he half hoped tobacco would make Helmung gag.

The colossus grabbed a handful, popped them into his mouth, and chewed noisily. "Not bad," he grunted, swallowed, spat a great gob on the floor, and sat down. Since no chair would hold him, he picked the desktop. "I am Helmung dur Brogu-Almerik. Look on me and be afraid." That was likeliest a ritual greeting, for he added in friendlier wise, "You may call me Skull Smasher."

"Ah, yes, to be sure." Welcome decided to stay on his feet. "I trust you've been enjoying your stay with us?"

"Not enough fights. No females. Yours too small anyway. That Orazuni, he is good sort and gives me much booze. You can *hialamar* the rest." Welcome did not inquire what it was to *hialamar* and suspected he would not care to know. "I am great sorcerer. I have much *vingutyr*."

"You have much everything," Welcome agreed in haste.

"*Vingutyr* is—is what I have much of. That is why I am great sorcerer." A thunderous belch. "I show you how you wish your enemies dead. You show me how make ships-that-fly and weapons-that-bang. We go sack many worlds."

"Well, now, um, we have very few witches on Earth these days," Welcome demurred.

"Ha! I knew you was backward." Helmung jumped up. "Look, dance of death, begins this way." He pranced around, waving his spear and chanting.

"Isn't there something about sticking pins into a doll?" asked the man weakly.

Helmung halted. "Obsolete. Brogu is modern peoples. My father, top witch in Almerik, study from Earthmen. Learn scientific method. He go on to figure laws of witchcraft." Helmung tucked the spear under his arm and ticked off points on his fingers. "Law of

like-makes-like. Law of touch." Welcome realized that
he must be his folk's equivalent of an intellectual. "Law
of part for whole. Law of—"

"I say," Welcome nerved himself to interrupt, "hold
on, will you? There's a good fellow. Excuse me half a
tick."

His desk being available to him, he said into the
intercom: "Flash me a précis, will you, Kirsten?" She
had anticipated his need. Words unrolled immediately
upon his comscreen. Luckily, he was a speed reader.

Confound it this barbarian must have something *worth
the time of a division chief. Ah, yes*— A paragraph
referred to a limited degree of telekinesis observed in
this clan and no other. The parapsychologists were anxious to study it under controlled conditions. Sensing an
opportunity, the clan lords had required that first one
of them be taken to that mart of the arts which they had
heard mentioned.

*Why couldn't the explorers keep their ruddy mouths
shut? Can this bloke toss boulders around by pure will
power? Br-r-r.*

He turned back to his visitor. "I understand," he said
cautiously, "that you can move things without touching
them."

To his surprise, Helmung didn't boast. "Little things.
Not heavy. Earthmen showed us game called dice.
Powerfullest wish-mover we got, he won much trea-
sure. But he had be much powerful."

"I see." Welcome suppressed an impulse to mop his
brow.

He knew virtually nothing about parapsychology, but
nobody was well-informed. Abilities of that kind were
so rare, feeble, and sporadic in humans that scientific
research had never gotten far with them. In a vague
fashion, he recalled that current theory attributed the
phenomena to a linkage between the neural and the
local quantum fields, whatever that meant. It did imply
that the energies involved were minute.

"Would you care to show me?" he asked. "I'm fascinated."

"Is little thing," Helmung snorted. "Why not I magic somebody dead for you?"

"Maybe later." Welcome crossed to a cabinet and opened it. Therein rested a modest array of laboratory equipment. His predecessor had once had occasion to wish she could perform certain tests immediately, on the spot, instead of going down to the shops. Against the possibility of another such moment, she had had this installed.

Welcome brought an oscilloscospe back to his desk, plugged it in, and generated a steady sine wave on its screen. "Can you change that wiggly shape there?" he asked. Electrons ought to be readily moveable.

"Easy," said Helmung. "I heard about atoms. Orazuni told me more."

"Yes, as a biologist, I daresay he's specially interested in you himself. Go ahead, if you please."

Helmung squeezed his face in concentration. The effect was hideous. Welcome saw the trace on his instrument jerk widly, slither about, and form a pornographic drawing. "Uh, beautiful, beautiful," he mumbled and turned it off.

Helmung rubbed his palms together. "Now how you build ships-that-fly?" he demanded.

"I don't think that's quite appropriate—"

The Centaurian's mane erected. The arm that wasn't holding the spear shot forward. A hand like an asteroid miner's grapnel closed on Welcome's blouse and lifted the man off his feet. "Brogu witchcraft not good enough for you, ha?" howled forth.

"Guk!" Welcome sprattled helpless. "L-l-let me go, or—" He wasn't sure what.

Helmung obliged while declaring, "I am patient man, but you show me how build ships before I get mad, okay?"

Welcome collected his shaken wits. "Look here. my dear fellow," he said fast. "I'd like to, you know, but

I'm not the boss. Besides, I'm not a, a shipwright. Also, I'm afraid you won't find any takers anywhere. They still cling to the dolls-and-pins theory on Earth. Antiquated, reactionary, yes, but there you are. And building a spacecraft isn't like building a war galley. You'd need tools you don't have and wouldn't know how to use. Why don't you go to the social room, relax, have a drink, think this business over? We could show you lots of other things that really would help your people. Alloys, for example. Wouldn't it be fine if your farmers had unbreakable plowshares?"

Mollified if not instantly convinced, Helmung stared out the viewport and said thoughtfully, "Might be. They beat them into swords."

They won't be able to, which is bloody well what I have in mind. "Oh, and ways to make liquor," Welcome proposed. "You've tried our gin and whisky, haven't you? What say?"

He winked, and Helmung guffawed, and presently the interview ended in good fellowship and a floor bespattered with cigar juice. When the huge mail-clad form had slouched out, Welcome made a dash for the cabinet. Behind the apparatus he kept a three-starred bottle of his own.

He touched the intercom. "Put your desk on automatic and come back in, Kirsten, if you will," he said. "I want to pick your brains. And I've a notion that by now you too will appreciate a drink."

Two hours later, they were fairly sure that they had identified the species of the thief.

They had spent the time in hard-thinking discussion and in close study of all material on the four possible planets that seemed relevant. Four planets; Helmung they could eliminate immediately, and it made no sense that a human would steal the information when any attempt to profit by it would scream his guilt aloud.

None of the delegates could have known in advance that a theft would be possible and made preparations for it. He (?) must have seen the opportunity and seized it, more or less on impulse, using whatever instruments were available to him. This argued for his having the technology for the job, whether or not anything like a computer lock existed on his home world.

That in turn ruled out the 70 Ophiuchians. They understood the principles; else they could never have accomplished what they did in their chosen biological fields, especially on the molecular level. However, to derange the lock—fool it—take command of it—required a method of electronic control more sophisticated than anything humankind had yet developed. (And that wasn't for lack of trying on the part of certain persons such as industrial spies.) Moreover, the operation had been carried out with a smoothness, a skill, bespeaking long experience with complex systems of that type.

61 Cygni? You couldn't be sure what George did or did not have at its disposal, but the fact that it had come there in quest of electronic and magnetronic technology showed that the crime was beyond its capabilities. Besides, why should it steal back the disc it had just traded away? If the object had not been recovered, the Cetians would have been entitled to another one. As for some far-fetched attempt to discredit Earth, there was no evidence that New Uranus had any interest in setting itself up as a rival.

Nor did it make sense that the Cetians themselves had faked the crime. They might cherish daydreams about someday taking the business away from humankind, but that would have to be a project carefully designed and carried out over a period of a century or more. The Dominators didn't have the subtlety or the patience necessary. Probably no civilization did; conspiracies operating across light-years didn't seem too practical. Anyway, Thevorakz and his merry band had had no expectation of the possibility that something of this sort could be done.

By elimination, Epsilon Indi.

Reluctantly, Welcome called M'Gamba. "I don't want

to pester you," he said, "but I do have a rather strong lead. First, though, what can you tell me?"

"We're working along," said the police chief. "Except for Freelady Petersen and her assistant—they've left the Moon—we've now questioned every human in the dome who was anywhere near the scene of the crime, on duty or off. We used the encephalotron to bring out total recall. Nobody stood on his or her rights and refused, which welds down the fact that this was not the work of any of our people. By feeding all their accounts into the computer for comparison and analysis, we've established that every member of the Ophiuchian and Epsilonian delegations was in sight of somebody or other until the party ended and the Cetians went to their quarters. We do have blank spots as far as the others are concerned."

"Epsilonians—" Welcome frowned. "Have your agents checked on them as I urged?"

"Well, they've managed to pass in detector range of three. By detector I mean an instrument set to resonate when it comes close to a coded disc. You know those pouches the ducks generally wear around their necks, to carry things in? One of them—Srnapopoi, her name is—does have a microdisc. But it can't be the copy of the stolen one, can it?"

"Can't it?" Welcome grinned without humor. "Look, Chief, a circuit technology as advanced as theirs should be able to take over a computer lock."

"I tell you, they were under observation all evening."

"But were their robots?"

M'Gamba snapped his fingers. "Why didn't I think of that?"

"Oh, you had plenty else to do, and then, the robots appear to be such ridiculous little toys, what? Ernenek and I have been reviewing explorers' reports from that planet. Most machinery there is small but incredibly able."

"A delicate matter. The delegates don't quite have diplomatic status, if only because formal diplomatic relations were never established, but they have the next thing to it. We can't go making arrests on bare suspicion."

"Oh, come now," Welcome snapped. "If your agents can't find a way to lift a pouch off a duck, you'd better go Earthside and recruit a few pickpockets for your force."

M'Gamba rattled a laugh. "Lieutenant Yamaguchi gives magic shows. His hobby. I'll put him directly on it. Stand by."

Welcome stared for a while at the empty screen before he hailed Ernenek, who had returned to her own desk. "I think you'd better have Rappapa come here," he said.

"Oh, Auch, must we?" He heard the pity.

"I think so. Psychological impact, assuming the payoff is what we expect. Have him paged and say I'd like a conference."

Welcome stuffed his pipe. His look went out to the long shadows and abrupt dazzle of Lunar dawn. The savagery of the scene matched his mood. Once this confrontation was done, he'd cancel everything else for the day and seek his bottle in earnest.

Rappapa bustled in, accompanied by no more than a helicopter. "Twice in one arbitrary diurnal period?" he quacked. "I am flatteningly flattered by such hyperattention on the part of your busy-with-vast-problems self."

"I need your help," the human dragged out of his throat. "Care for a cigar?"

"Gratitude erupts from me. If there is any way of even the most micrometric that I can be of assistance—"

Welcome drew harshly on his pipe. "It's this business of the theft," he said. "If we don't resolve it, it'll undermine the foundation of trust that this whole enterprise rests on. Shrewd bargaining is one thing, lawlessness another. At the same time, the burglar is a representative of an entire civilization. Arrest could touch off an unholy row."

"Anyone who would ponder the violation of your excellency's lavish hospitality deserves dedignification," said Rappapa furiously.

"It's not that simple, I'm afraid," Welcome plodded on. "When word takes years or decades to travel back and forth, how do you make yourself clear about something as emotional as this? I can imagine the sense of injury festering, antihuman sentiment growing, unforeseeable long-range consequences. Don't you think, Freeman Rappapa, it would be best for the thief's own people too, if he gave up his loot voluntarily? We'd forgive him, and this whole nasty business need never go beyond our circle."

"First the much-to-be-struggled-with question of ascertaining the pilferish person arises," said Rappapa. "Does your excellency the assistance of my abject self in solving the mystery desire?"

So he's going to stall. "If the thief freely confesses, I'll understand that he acted from the highest motives of planetarism," Welcome pledged desperately. "I would not discriminate against him in any way."

Rappapa waved his cigar like a baton. "Behold the magnanimity of the great-minded!"

"If we have to track him down ourselves, though, word will get out to our authorities. They may well feel that they must be stern."

"They should be. Your excellency burrows to the very fundament of justice."

The com unit buzzed. *Here goes,* thought Welcome. He switched it on. M'Gamba looked bleakly out at him.

"Well?"

"It worked," said the captain. "Yamaguchi found the suspect in a shop preparing a model, distracted her attention, and slipped the minidisc out. He rushed it to the lab, and it's the Cygnian material, all right. What should we do now?"

"Sit tight. I'll call you back." Welcome clicked off and turned to Rappapa. "Did you hear?" he said. "We've found the thief and recovered the loot."

"I gather, I gather." The Epsilonian jittered about, crest aflutter. "Who was it?" he quacked. "Who is the low, vile, not-to-be-mentioned-without-expectoration wretch?"

Welcome's words dropped like stones, "Her name is Srnapopoi. *As nearly as I can pronounce it.*

Rappapa stopped dead. "Srna—"

"Yes."

"B-but—*tonnaquo whichu krx killuwi*—it is not of the possible!" Rappapa wailed. He began violently quivering. "Believe me, excellent excellency, we are p-p-pure as transistor grade silicon."

"Any member of your party should be able to figure out how to take over a computer lock and put your robots onto the job," Welcome said wearily. "And Srnapopoi was carrying the stolen data."

"A copy! A second copy, m-made by the c-c-criminal to divert suspicion. It would be easy to slip such a small thing . . . into her pouch . . . when she had put it aside for a moment. By mere chance is it hers. I avow this!"

Welcome rose, walked around his desk, laid a hand on the bobbing head. "Don't take it so hard," he said gently. "I'm sure Srnapopoi acted on her own initiative. We can leave the disposal of her case to you."

"But she could not have done it!" Rappapa cried. "The robots can only *my* orders obey!"

Welcome stepped back, appalled. He had offered an out, and the duck hadn't taken it.

Yet . . . would anyone cool enough to seize the opportunity and pull the job blow his jets like this when accused? Or, for that matter, hide the swag so clumsily? Of course, these were nonhumans . . .

Rappapa broke into quite humanlike tears. "We are besmirched and have lost your confidence," he sobbed. "You consider me a not-fit-to-wipe-the-feet-on egg-eater. What will my nestmates say?"

"Now, now—"

"They will say, *'Twiutiuk poipoi tu spung Rappapa.' "

Helplessly, Welcome ruffled his hair. "All right, all right. If you didn't do it, who did?"

The Epsilonian rubbed his bulging eyes. "It is necessary to protect the Kwillitchian self by the true monster finding," he said with a hint of his former perkiness. "Will you give me out of your polychromatic mercy a chance?"

"Certainly. Because if you're not guilty, then we've still got to discover who is." Welcome sat down on a corner of the desk. Inwardly, he moaned. To start over again, just when he thought he was finished—but damn it, you could not flat-out call a delegate a liar when there was the remotest chance he wasn't. "Let us assume you did not do it. That leaves two possibilities, the Cygnian and the Cetians themselves."

"Would you from the scintillant heights of intellect descend to explain the omission of 70 Ophiuchi and Alpha Centauri?"

"Well, the Centaurian is obvious. He may not be as stupid as he acts, but he's positively too ignorant. As for Ophiuchi, Orazuni and his people were never out of sight of a human during the time the burglary must have happened—if it did happen." Fairness compelled Welcome to add, "Neither were you Epsilonians. But you had your robots."

"Could not Orazuni have hidden-away robots?"

"No. The humans on your planet who arranged for you to go, and those aboard the spaceship, knew everything you had in your baggage, didn't they? We don't risk allowing anything in that might cause a serious accident. No Ophiuchian could have nobbled a key, and besides, a key alone is not sufficient to make a computer lock admit you. Conceivably Orazuni's group brought along some kind of bacteria or whatever that can take over the circuits. But in fact this is impossible, because they don't know that much electronics. They came here mainly to learn more."

Rappapa uttered a soft quack. "That leaves only some

elaborate and implausible-on-the-face-of-it plot by the Cetians or the Cygnian."

"I don't see how it can have been George. It commands less electronics than the Ophiuchians. With that dense hydrogen atmosphere on New Uranus, they never developed even a vacuum tube. As for the Cetians—"

"No, wait!" Rappapa shrilled. He stared before him till his eyes seemed in danger of falling out. "Robot," he said low. "Or . . . agent . . . duly instructed and sent to perform foul deed while the weaver of the plot sits at intricate ease in public view."

Welcome's own eyes widened.

"*Killuweetchungu!*" squawked Rappapa. "Let us begone!"

"Wait, wait," urged Welcome, while sudden apprehension jolted through him. "Let's think this out."

"We have no time to think! The honor of Kwillitch languishes. Come!"

Rappapa bounded off. The door got out of his way barely soon enough. Welcome cursed and charged after him. If that impulsive featherhead accused an innocent being—

Kirsten Ernenek saw a hundred and twenty centimeters of squawking Epsilonian, followed by a hundred and ninety centimeters of cursing human, followed by eighteen centimeters of valiantly laboring helicopter, shoot through her office. She sprang up and raced after them. The receptionist saw the parade go by and, excited, joined it. A computer technician saw them pounding past and took out after the receptionist.

Rappapa's legs churned. He screeched and whistled his way down the ramp to the fourth sublevel. Thevorakz emerged from his quarters to see what the fuss was about, in time for Rappapa to unbalance him by darting between his legs, Welcome to bowl him over, and Ernenek, the receptionist, and the technician to trample across him. As he rose, howling his fury, the helicopter collided with his head. He snarled and galloped after the rest.

George came rolling in the opposite direction. "Where lurks the Centaurian?" Rappapa clacked.

The Cygnian pointed. "In the social room," it said.

Rappapa vaulted the metal shell. Welcome and Ernenek made Lunar-gravity leaps over it. The others drew up short, until Thevorakz soared in a running broad jump above the entire traffic jam. Then they came in his wake. George stared after them, shrugged its mechanical shoulders, and trundled impertubably on its own way.

The social room was nearly deserted. In one corner, an Epsilonian with nothing better to do screened a murder mystery. Helmung's enormous form stood draped over the bar, clutching a bottle. Orazuni tail-sat close by and chatted with him.

"There they are!" yammered Rappapa. "There abide the excessively diabolical thieves!"

"Shut up, you bloody fool—" Welcome tripped on a chair and went flat on the floor. Ernenek halted, stood above him, and made hand signals to divert the others before they dashed across him. They milled about.

Welcome crawled back to his feet. Rappapa had grabbed Helmung by the baldric and was quacking at him. "What is this, small tasty-looking fat one?" fluted the barbarian. "And why?"

Rappapa remembered to speak English, which the transponder made intelligible. "We want to know how much Orazuni paid you to be his tool!"

"My, my," the Ophiuchian murmured. His devilishly handsome features registered amusement and tolerance. "Our colleague is a trifle overwrought, is he not, Freeman Welcome?"

Thevorakz brushed assorted beings aside and clumped to the bar. "I demand an apology!" he thundered. "I did not come twelve light-yearth to be walked on!"

"Let me go," said Helmung, and batted Rappapa loose.

"Compan-ee—HELP!" crowed the Epsilonian.

"I must say this is a most undignified scene," declared Orazuni.

"Will you apologize to me," raged Thevorakz, "or mutht I thtomp you flat?"

"I go my place," said Helmung. "Leave me alone." He shouldered his way through the crowd.

"Stop, thief!" yelled Rappapa. His robots marched in the door. "I refer to the Centaurian," he told them.

"Now, see here, this farce has gone on quite long enough," Orazuni said exasperatedly to Welcome.

"Stop him too!" cried Rappapa. "He the information has!"

"I also demand an apology," stated Orazuni. "You may deliver it to me in my quarters."

He started to go. Thevorakz reached out and grabbed a handful of his cloak. "Maybe you better thtay a while too," the Cetian rumbled.

Helmung noticed the robots deploying before him. "I see little men!" he gasped. He waved his arms and chanted an incantation.

A detachment of robots swarmed up some ornamental drapes, took them down, and set about hobbling him with them. Helmung's hands dropped. Abruptly he looked crushed. "My witchcraft not works here," he mumbled. "I want go home."

Welcome decided he had better assume leadership. He was supposed to. What Rappapa had in mind was now clear to him. "Helmung," he asked in his quietest voice, "did you open the door to the Cetian apartments for Orazuni?"

The Centaurian donned self-righteousness. "I promise him I not tell anybody," he said. "You torture me, you do anything, I not tell how I did."

Orazuni trilled a laugh. "No matter," he said. "Here is the extra copy." He fished in his portfolio, extracted a minidisc, and tossed it to Welcome. "And now, my friends, if you will excuse me, this has been a somewhat strenuous day and I would like to retire."

*   *   *

"It should have been obvious, I suppose," said Welcome to M'Gamba and Ernenek when the three of them met in his office. "That attempt to get the Epsilonians blamed couldn't have thrown us off for long. But Orazuni didn't need much time. I daresay that briefcase of his includes a circuit to baffle detectors. All he needed was to have us baying down his false trail till he'd embarked for home. We did know, however, that he'd been cultivating Helmung's acquaintance ever since he learned about the telekinesis. Probably his interest was scientific at first, but it soon occurred to him that if Helmung could control electron streams with such precision that he can draw pictures on an oscilloscope, he could surely take control of a computer lock. He could practice on the Ophiuchians' door. The Cygnian chemistry would be a fine thing to have, especially if it came free of charge."

"Did Orazuni hope to get more out of it than that?" asked M'Gamba.

"Indirectly. I've been talking with him, and he was quite frank, downright cheerful. He stood to make an enormous personal profit at home. But also, on his planet, they do entertain notions of someday taking our dominant position away from us. This affair would not only have given them a nice piece of knowledge to sell elsewhere, besides what they gained legitimately, but have made the first crack in the basis of our operations. Well, Orazuni is leaving next week, empty-handed."

"What about the rest of the Ophiuchians?"

Welcome smiled lopsidely. "We keep a sharp eye while we deal with them. What else? We need their technology. Officially nothing has happened. When rumors get out, as they're bound to, we'll tell the news johnnies there was a minor mixup due to difficulties of cross-cultural communication."

"I wonder what Orazuni bribed Helmung with," Ernenek said.

Welcome blushed. He had archaic ideas about gentlemanly conduct in the presence of a lady. "Well, ah, I did inquire, and—Oh, you'd find out regardless. Orazuni promised to concoct an infallible love potion, a hormone mixture tailored to Centaurians. As part of my bargain with him—we're both anxious to keep the peace—the Ophiuchians will deliver the goods. Already Helmung's faunching to go home and try it. That should put his clan in a happy and cooperative mood, and we'll have him off our necks."

"We'd better start thinking about precautions," M'Gamba warned. "Maybe the Ophiuchians can do the same thing for humans."

Welcome blushed deeper and looked toward the viewport. The sun was well aloft, Earth had dwindled and paled in his eyes, but the moonscape bore a new kind of harsh beauty. "What a day this has been," he breathed. "Kirsten, d'you suppose we can look forward to some nice dull routine for a while?"

"A short while," Ernenek replied. "We've received a lasercast from the *Courier*. She's entering the Solar System with a delegation from Beta Hydri. They bring a knowledge of amphitronics."

"What in the universe is that?"

"It's a name the expedition scientists coined. They admit they don't know either."

POUL ANDERSON

Poul Anderson is one of the most honored authors of our time. He has won seven Hugo Awards, three Nebula Awards, and the Gandalf Award for Achievement in Fantasy, among others. His most popular series include the Polesotechnic League/Terran Empire tales and the Time Patrol series. Here are fine books by Poul Anderson available through Baen Books:

THE GAME OF EMPIRE
A *new* novel in Anderson's Polesotechnic League/Terran Empire series! Diana Crowfeather, daughter of Dominic Flandry, proves well capable of following in his adventurous footsteps.

FIRE TIME
Once every thousand years the Deathstar orbits close enough to burn the surface of the planet Ishtar. This is known as the Fire Time, and it is then that the barbarians flee the scorched lands, bringing havoc to the civilized South.

AFTER DOOMSDAY
Earth has been destroyed, and the handful of surviving humans must discover which of three alien races is guilty before it's too late.

THE BROKEN SWORD
It is a time when Christos is new to the land, and the Elder Gods and the Elven Folk still hold sway. In 11th-century Scandinavia Christianity is beginning to replace the old religion, but the Old Gods still have power, and men are still oppressed by the folk of the Faerie. "Pure gold!"—Anthony Boucher.

THE DEVIL'S GAME
Seven people gather on a remote island, each competing for a share in a tax-free fortune. The "contest" is ostensibly sponsored by an eccentric billionaire—but the rich man is in league with an alien masquerading as a demon . . . or is it the other way around?

THE ENEMY STARS

Includes for the first time the sequel to "The Enemy Stars": "The Ways of Love." Fast-paced adventure science fiction from a master.

SEVEN CONQUESTS

Seven brilliant tales examine the many ways human beings—most dangerous and violent of all species—react under the stress of conflict and high technology.

STRANGERS FROM EARTH

Classic Anderson: A stranded alien spends his life masquerading as a human, hoping to contact his own world. He succeeds, but the result is a bigger problem than before . . . What if our reality is a fiction? Nothing more than a book written by a very powerful Author? Two philosophers stumble on the truth and try to puzzle out the Ending . . .

You can order all of Poul Anderson's books listed above with this order form. Check your choices below and send the combined cover price/s to: Baen Books, Dept. BA, 260 Fifth Avenue, New York, New York 10001.*

THE GAME OF EMPIRE • 55959-1 • 288 pp. • $3.50   _____
FIRE TIME • 55900-1 • 288 pp. • $2.95   _____
AFTER DOOMSDAY • 65591-4 • 224 pp. • $2.95   _____
THE BROKEN SWORD • 65382-2 • 256 pp. • $2.95   _____
THE DEVIL'S GAME • 55995-8 • 256 pp. • $2.95   _____
THE ENEMY STARS • 65339-3 • 224 pp. • $2.95   _____
SEVEN CONQUESTS • 55914-1 • 288 pp. • $2.95   _____
STRANGERS FROM EARTH • 65627-9 • 224 pp. • $2.95   _____

THE KING OF YS
POUL AND KAREN
ANDERSON

THE KING OF YS—
THE GREATEST
EPIC FANTASY
OF THIS DECADE!

by Poul and Karen Anderson

As many authors that have brought new life and meaning to Camelot and her King, so have Poul and Karen Anderson brought to life a city of legend on the coast of Brittany . . . Ys.

THE ROMAN SOLDIER BECAME A KING, AND HUSBAND TO THE NINE

In *Roma Mater*, the Roman centurion Gratillonius became King of Ys, city of legend—and husband to its nine magical Queens.

A PRIEST-KING AT WAR WITH HIS GODS

In *Gallicenae*, Gratillonius consolidates his power in the name and service of Rome the Mother, and his war worsens with the senile Gods of Ys, that once blessed city.

HE MUST MARRY HIS DAUGHTER—
OR WATCH AS HIS KINGDOM
IS DESTROYED

In *Dahut* the final demands of the gods were made clear: that Gratillonius wed his own daughter . . . and as a result of his defying that divine ultimatum, the consequent destruction of Ys itself.

THE STUNNING CLIMAX

In *The Dog and the Wolf*, the once and future king strives first to save the remnant of the Ysans from utter destruction—then use them to save civilization itself, as the light that once was Rome flickers out, and barbarian night descends upon the world. In the progress, Gratillonius, once a Roman centurion and King of Ys, will become King Grallon of Brittany, and give rise to a legend that will ring down the corridors of time!

Available only through Baen Books, but you can order this four-volume KING OF YS series with this order form. Check your choices below and send the combined cover price/s to: Baen Books, Dept. BA, 260 Fifth Avenue, New York, New York 10001.

ROMA MATER • 65602-3 • 480 pp. • $3.95 _____
GALLICENAE • 65342-3 • 384 pp. • $3.95 _____
DAHUT • 65371-7 • 416 pp. • $3.95 _____
THE DOG AND THE WOLF • 65391-1 •
544 pp. • $4.50 _____

THE MANY WORLDS OF
MELISSA SCOTT

*Winner of the John W. Campbell Award
for Best New Writer, 1986*

THE KINDLY ONES: "An ambitious novel of the world Orestes. This large, inhabited moon is governed by five Kinships whose society operates on a code of honor so strict that transgressors are declared legally 'dead' and are prevented from having any contact with the 'living.' . . . Scott is a writer to watch."—*Publishers Weekly*. A Main Selection of the Science Fiction Book Club.

65351-2 • 384 pp. • $2.95

The "Silence Leigh" Trilogy
FIVE-TWELFTHS OF HEAVEN (Book I): "Melissa Scott postulates a universe where technology interferes with magic. . . . The whole plot is one of space ships, space wars, and alien planets—not a unicorn or a dragon to be seen anywhere. Scott's space drive and description of space piloting alone would mark her as an expert in the melding of the [SF and fantasy] genres; this is the stuff of which 'sense of wonder' is made."—*Locus*

55952-4 • 352 pp. • $2.95

SILENCE IN SOLITUDE (Book II): "[Scott is] a voice you should seek out and read at every opportunity." —*OtherRealms*.   65699-7 • 324 pp. • $2.95

THE EMPRESS OF EARTH (Book III):
65364-4 • 352 pp. • $3.50

A CHOICE OF DESTINIES: "Melissa Scott [is] one of science fiction's most talented newcomers. . . . The greatest delight of all is finding out how she managed to write a historical novel that could legitimately have spaceships on the cover . . . a marvelous gift for any fan."—*Baltimore Sun*   65563-9 • 320 pp. • $2.95

THE GAME BEYOND: "An exciting interstellar empire novel with a great deal of political intrigue and colorful interplanetary travel."—*Locus*
55918-4 • 352 pp. • $2.95

To order any of these Melissa Scott titles, please check the box/es below and send combined cover price/s to:

Baen Books
Dept. BA
260 Fifth Ave.
NY, NY 10001

Name _____

Address _____

City _____ State _____ Zip __

THE KINDLY ONES ☐   FIVE-TWELFTHS OF HEAVEN ☐
A CHOICE OF DESTINIES ☐   SILENCE IN SOLITUDE ☐
THE GAME BEYOND ☐   THE EMPRESS OF EARTH ☐

BAEN BOOKS

Have You Missed?

DRAKE, DAVID
At Any Price
Hammer's Slammers are back—and Baen Books has them!
Now the 23rd-century armored division faces its deadliest
enemies ever: aliens who *teleport* into combat.
55978-8 $3.50

DRAKE, DAVID
Hammer's Slammers
A special *expanded* edition of the book that began the
legend of Colonel Alois Hammer. Now the toughest, mean-
est mercs who ever killed for a dollar or wrecked a world
for pay have come home—to Baen Books—and they've
brought a secret weapon: "The Tank Lords," a brand-new
short novel, included in this special Baen edition of *Hammer's Slammers*.
65632-5 $3.50

DRAKE, DAVID
Lacey and His Friends
In Jed Lacey's time the United States computers scan
every citizen, every hour of the day. When crime is detected, it's Lacey's turn. There are a few things worse than
having him come after you, but they're not survivable
either. But things aren't really that bad—not for Lacey and
his friends. By the author of *Hammer's Slammers* and *At
Any Price*.
65593-0 $3.50

**CARD, ORSON SCOTT; DRAKE, DAVID;
& BUJOLD, LOIS MCMASTER**
(edited by Elizabeth Mitchell)
Free Lancers (Alien Stars, Vol. IV)
Three short novels about mercenary soldiers—never be-
fore in print! Card's hero leads a ragtag group of scientific
refugees to sanctuary in Utah; Drake contributes a new
"Hammer's Slammers" story; Bujold tells a new tale of
Miles Vorkosigan, hero of *The Warrior's Apprentice*.
65352-0 $2.95

DRAKE, DAVID
Birds of Prey

The time: 262 A.D. The place: Imperial Rome. There had never been a greater empire, but now it is dying. Everywhere its armies are in retreat, and what had been civilization seethes with riots and bizarre cults. Against the imminent fall of the Long Night stands Aulus Perennius, an Imperial secret agent as tough and ruthless as the age in which he lives. But he stands alone—until a traveller from Earth's far future recruits him for a mission so strange it cannot be disclosed.

55912-5 (trade paper) $7.95
55909-5 (hardcover) $14.95

DRAKE, DAVID
Ranks of Bronze

Disguised alien traders bought captured Roman soldiers on the slave market because they needed troops who could win battles without high-tech weaponry. The leigionaires provided victories, smashing barbarian armies with the swords, javelins, and discipline that had won a world. But the worlds on which they now fought were strange ones, and the spoils of victory did not include freedom. If the legionaires went home, it would be through the use of the beam weapons and force screens of their ruthless alien owners. It's been 2000 years—and now they want to go home.   65568-X $3.50

DRAKE, DAVID, & WAGNER, KARL EDWARD
Killer

Vonones and Lycon capture wild animals to sell for bloodsport in ancient Rome. A vicious animal sold to them by a trader turns out to be more than they bargained for—it is the sole survivor of the crash of an alien spacecraft. Possessed of intelligence nearly human, it has two goals in life: to breed and to kill.

55931-1 $2.95

David Drake

"Drake has distinguished himself as the master of the mercenary sf novel."—Rave Reviews

To receive books by one of BAEN BOOKS most popular authors send in the order form below.

AT ANY PRICE, 55978-8, $3.50 . . . . ☐

HAMMER'S SLAMMERS, 65632-5, $3.50 . . . . . . ☐

LACEY AND HIS FRIENDS, 65593-0, $3.50 . . . ☐

FREE LANCERS, (ALIEN STARS #4),
    65352-0, $2.95 . . . . ☐

BIRDS OF PREY, hardcover, 55912-5, $7.95 . . . ☐

BIRDS OF PREY, trade paper, 55909-5, $14.95 . . ☐

RANKS OF BRONZE, 65568-X, $3.50 . . . . ☐

KILLER, 55931-1, $2.95 . . . . ☐

Please send me the books checked above. I have enclosed a check or money order for the combined cover price made out to: BAEN BOOKS, 260 Fifth Avenue, New York N.Y. 10001.